DOC SPEARS   JASON ANSPACH   NICK COLE

EXIGENCY

DARK OPERATOR   **BOOK 4**

GALAXY'S EDGE

Edited by Lauren Moore
Published by Galaxy's Edge Press

Cover Art: Tommaso Renieri
Cover Design: Ryan Bubion
Formatting: Kevin G. Summers

Website: www.GalaxysEdge.us
Facebook: facebook.com/atgalaxysedge
Newsletter (get a free short story): www.InTheLegion.com

KILL TEAM 3 DARK OPS

PVC PATCH

No one was supposed to know his name. His exploits too remarkable, his victories too numerous, dark operator Kel Turner is a victim of his own success.

The powerful who control the Republic fear Kel and what he represents: a threat to their hegemony. And if they can't control him, they'll destroy him.

At a deadly crossroads, Kel is made to choose between love and duty. But his foes are ignorant that he has a third choice.

Win.

By empty hand, blaster, or wits alone, Kel is the master of all the tools of lethal combat. He will use them all to succeed. Not even his own death matters, because for a legionnaire, the only failure is the failure to do what's right.

All legionnaires know their lives are less important than their honor. A legionnaire's life is short. The Legion is eternal.

01

"What choice do I have? We either let them board or they vent us into space with a thousand holes in our hull!" Jim Yomiuri pleaded.

Kel had never seen the man this distressed. He'd been with the *Callie*'s captain in other tense situations, though only one of those had involved the threat of violence to the ship and its crew—the man's entire family. Kel had intervened in that situation to bring about a speedy resolution. He intended to do so again.Kel stood with the captain and his first officer, Eric, on the command deck. The Macrobian xebec had moved to a kilometer off the nose of the *Callie's Dream*, so close that Kel could make out the warship's sharp profile without enhancement. The ship pattern was common for a corsair in this part of the edge. It had most likely been built in the shipyards of D'uladheen or Synar and taken as a prize by the Macrobian pirates generations before. Human generations, at least. The average Macrobian lived for a half a millennium.Xebec were fast, responsive ships that carried small cargos, making them ideal for short jumps to nearby systems. What the hull design lacked in cargo space, it made up for in its ability to make rapid orbital descents and equally rapid turnarounds on the ground. When Macrobia was an active trading partner with the Wuhen and Golnara, ships like these had formed virtual trails in space from their constant travel to the sister systems. The introduction of the Bhat root had changed all that.

To other races, the root had no discernible effect. It was a bitter plant with no nutritional value. To the Macrobians, it held mild hallucinogenic and mood elevating properties that energized the user at the cost of aggression and paranoia as one of its side effects. Its introduction to the culture had likely hastened its civil war.

"Once they're on board, I'm sure we can come to an understanding." Even as the captain spoke these words, his eyes—wide with terror—accentuated how ludicrous the wishful plan sounded when spoken aloud.

Jim Yomiuri wasn't fooling anyone, least of all himself.

"We'll just give them what they want," Eric said. "The relief supplies will still get to the surface and—"

"Once they board us, they won't stop at seizing the cargo," Kel interrupted coldly. He scanned the surface of the xebec. A single ion cannon sat on the superstructure above its bow. While he couldn't see any other cannon turrets on the raider, he didn't doubt that there was hidden gunnery in the form of electron guns, useful for frying communication dishes at close range. The weapons could also scramble the neurons of any spacers working outside the ship. Close-range ship's weapons ideal for deterring counterattacks without causing catastrophic damage to a prize, Kel reckoned.

Kel had seen panic before. Men's minds flailing like gasping fish drying on duracrete, reality overwhelming their coping abilities, unable to comprehend the futility of their efforts. Kel thought Jim and Eric's delusions were odd. Pilots were trained to handle emergencies. If the *Callie* had experienced a thruster freeze on descent, he had no doubt the captain would be the picture of competence, calmly working the problem to save his ship without a trace of indecision, a lifetime of training and preparation making the course of action instinctive. He saw none of that fitness now.

"If the pirates believe they can pilot the *Callie*, they'll likely kill all the flight crew," Kel continued. "If they can't pilot her, they'll force you to do it for them. If you resist, they'll murder your family in front of you one at a time until you cooperate. If they don't want the ship, they'll take the cargo, some hostages for ransom, then scuttle. Any captive they can't ransom or sell as a slave, they'll simply kill. If we're lucky." Kel made sure his friend the captain was listening. "There's no scenario where they take the cargo and let you and your family go free with your ship intact. Abandon that hope right now, Jim."

Jim looked to Eric for support. His first officer and brother-in-law's mouth opened, but issued no words. Kel didn't have time to explain further, but he had no doubt in his mind that he'd just spoken the plain truth to these men.

The House of Reason invested trillions over decades in developing Macrobia with hopes of bringing it into the fold of the Republic. There'd been a planetary government, and a stable one at that. The longevity of the average Macrobian meant steady claws usually guided them. During the Savage Wars, the Republic used the planet as an arms depot and stationed troops there. After hundreds of years of waxing and waning human presence, it had not been until the last decade that the Republic Ex-Planetary diplomats pushed reforms on the planet. What was initially one senator's pet project became a target of the galactic media, and with it the impetus to bring the glory of the Republic to the Macrobians.

The politicians and diplomats helped institute a democratic republic with a federal parliament that had largely replaced the ancient tribal form of rule. Linking the upheaval of their traditional political system to monetary aid and other incentives had given the House of Reason another world they could now call part of the coalition of civilized worlds.

Kel tried to avoid the conceit of hindsight. The history of the Republic often demonstrated that changes imposed rather than generated by the culture itself—like the Macrobians' representative government—didn't last. The concept of individual rights had never existed among the aliens. And why should it?

Kel didn't judge alien races as he would humans. Rightly or wrongly, he was only interested in how nuances of any particular culture would affect the accomplishment of his current mission. Alien minds and alien cultures were just that—alien. Trying to make them resemble those of a human Republic world never made sense to him. It was nothing more than building an attractive house of sticks over an invisible fault line.

Whether the appearance of Bhat was a coinciding free radical or the causative factor of the societal meltdown on Macrobia, its arrival at a time of other social change combined to make for a detrimental situation in this arm of the galaxy. The tribal civil war broke out soon after the drug's introduction. The planet dissolved into sects ruled by the once customary tribal and religious laws in a manner that made the pre-Republic Macrobian era seem placid and tame by comparison. What objections the meddling Liberinthine elite had once held for the traditional culture and history of Macrobia no longer mattered. Easier to pretend it never existed and that their interference was too late rather than causative. Abandoned by the Republic, Macrobia was proscribed as hostile and ungovernable. The big tremors appeared and shook the house into splinters, just like hidden cracks beneath any structure always will. Eventually. Inevitably. And with deadly results.

The pile of collapsed beams that was the current state of affairs on Macrobia was undoubtedly multifactorial, academically interesting, and completely incidental to solving the problem Kel now faced. The planet was a failed state, filled with rival tribes that produced nothing but pirates. Only desperate or unscrupulous merchants— or the naïve—made port call there. The *Callie* wasn't crewed by desperate merchants. Nor were they unscrupulous. Kel had thought they should be beyond naivete. He was wrong.

"No chance to run before we try to jump?" Kel asked, knowing the answer before he'd asked the question.

"The *Callie*'s not built for speed off the starting line," Eric said, confirming Kel's fears. "Spinning up the jump drive will take minutes. They'll detect the field in time to react."

The xebec continued to close on them. It had been several minutes since the last communication from the pirates. Now, a tight-beam transmission penetrated the viewer.

"Lassst chance-ah, voor-la," the gray-scaled face hissed in Standard.

When shots from the ion cannon first passed their prow, Kel dashed to his quarters to don his armor. He had not needed it in the three weeks he'd been aboard the *Callie*. There'd been no uncertainty on his part to travel with his full kit. Lieutenant Kelkavan Turner had options most legionnaires did not. Whether on orders from Dark

Ops or as he was now—on leave—he had no requirement to travel unarmed or unequipped. It was an unspoken mandate as well as their commander's policy that dark operators be available for action at all times, ready to act of their own accord.

Throwing his hands up in surrender, the captain said, "Please, we don't want any trouble. We carry food and medicines to aid your planet. We are stationary and our jump drive is shut down. We will give you whatever you want. As the captain, I promise full cooperation of my crew."

The pale lizard's thick tail flicked back and forth behind its head. "We approach, voor-la. Receive us-sss well if you de-sssire mercy."

The transmission ended.

When it had been sprung on them that the *Callie* would be traveling to the Macrobian system, Kel started rehearsing for worst-case scenarios. His gut told him that a fight was coming. Preparing for violent encounters was his specialty. Kel had spent time skimming the mass of material available to him on the holonet, looking for the essential knowledge that might give him an edge. What he had gleaned from a brief review of the system had satisfied his need to ready himself, but also quashed the well of shame he knew he would feel later if he failed to do so. He was ready for whatever may come. Being unprepared was a sin, an abomination, something hateful to his being. Readiness was more than just habit. And the mind had to be ready as much as the body. Young legionnaires who thought a charged blaster was all they needed didn't live to be old leejes.

He'd not dealt with this specific species before but noted that their anatomy was not unlike that of most other reptasaurians. They were all incredibly tough and resilient to damage as well as uncommonly strong. But the Macrobians' thick hides allowed them to survive vacuum without suits. Their low metabolic rate meant they could function without oxygen for extended periods, and the nictitating membranes that covered their eyes afforded them protection from the harsh temperatures of space.

Just as important as the physical characteristics of the potential threat were the cultural. The Macrobian world held an indecipherable mixture of racial and tribal customs. What was once a culture capable of interspecies cooperation and trade had been replaced with one characterized by xenophobia and criminal predation. Macrobia's recent history was rife with instances of lawlessness and savagery. While there were tribes that still carried out peaceful relations with the rest of the galaxy, it was not the norm. The Bhat drug released whatever proclivity for such behavior that had lain dormant.

One report Kel pondered delved into a social discourse on the value of piracy to the planet. That the Macrobian language translated the concept of the pirate as "space savior" was telling. Kel was uninterested in the supposed egalitarian motivation of the corsairs. He was only interested in their actions. Captured crews became hostages. Spacers not part of a corporate fleet willing to pay a ransom ended up subjects for ritual torture and consumption.

The word "voor-la" translated simply to "heathen." Depending on context, an alternative translation was "fodder." As in, nourishment. Kel knew all he needed to know about his potential adversary. Physically indomitable. Culturally xenophobic. Psychologically brutal.

And not choosy about food sources.

Kel had strongly recommended against taking this contract in the first place. The Yomiuris had become wealthy over the last several years as merchant spacers, in part due to Kel's aid. When he first met them, they were struggling to survive as interstellar traders. Now, they were at the top of the industry. As he'd gotten reacquainted with the family over the last few weeks, he tried to be nonjudgmental about some of the new attitudes the family displayed.

"The Macrobians are victims," Caroline Yomiuri had opined to the gathering in the galley. "Their society has undergone a great upheaval, not in small part due to the Republic's constant meddling in local affairs."

Many of the family nodded as they sat together to discuss the potential contract. Kel was still struggling to remember the names of a dozen of the adults now crewing with the *Callie*. Since he'd last been with the family, there had been several turnovers of crew rotating through service for the ship's long voyages away from their home world. Next door in the wardroom, the children entertained themselves as the adults conferred.

Kel had nodded as well. "I don't disagree. But that's irrelevant. Do you really want to take the risk of traveling there? The place is a dumpster fire."

Jim had frowned at that. "That's not their fault. I think the risk is minimal. No one lands on Macrobia because of the piracy threat. Eric and I got to talk to one of the local pilots who makes a run there on a weekly basis. They jump into the system and wait for a tight beam from their receiving freighter to let them know it's safe before proceeding into high orbit to do the cargo exchange. It's of no benefit to the local merchants to lose off-world traders to the pirates. They pay protection to the local tribes to avoid just that kind of complication."

Eric then joined in. "It's not unusual for us to replenish another vessel underway or to offload cargo in micro-G. Some of the smaller systems don't have spacefields rated to handle the *Callie*'s mass. We're good at ship-to-ship transfers. Besides, the goods we'll transport include medicine and food. Just because there are some tribes that are barbaric doesn't mean the whole planet should suffer. If people like us don't try to do the right thing, who will?"

"We're also not doing it without recompense," Caroline, the ship's purser, continued. "Galactic Hugs is offering a very fair compensation given the potential risk."

Kel was vaguely familiar with the private charity. Its advertisements invariably centered around holo montages of various beleaguered edge races, and always ended with the call for donations to help relieve their sufferings. He'd seen much suffering in the galaxy. He was not immune to its reality. Kel believed in doing the right thing, always. How that was defined, however, was up to interpretation. To him, protecting the weak was the right thing. The Yomiuris were the weak.

"We've been extremely fortunate. Blessed," Caroline said. "If we can do some good in the galaxy, how can we turn our backs? If everyone tried to do some good, the galaxy would be a better place."

Kel knew he'd lost the argument before it had begun. The family had made up their minds. Still, a vote was taken. The adult crew members raised their hands in the affirmative. Everyone, save Tara.

"All those opposed?" the captain said, and his daughter's hand flew up.

Kel didn't get a vote. He was not a member of the crew. He watched as Tara's sole opposition brought frowns from those around her.

She stood. "The potential risk outweighs any benefits. We aren't the only crew available to run humanitarian goods to the Macrobians. They could come to Wuhen and get the cargo themselves, if it's so important. They are not planet-locked. They choose to use their hold-space to run drugs instead of carrying humanitarian relief supplies to their own people."

Shortly before the family meeting, Kel had sat with Tara in the small wardroom, sipping kaff as she asked Kel's opinions on the matter. She'd more than ably made the case against for the both of them. Kel smiled, proud of her, thinking about their quiet talk that morning. As they sat, he'd sneaked his hand under the table to hold hers. Auntie Meiko, the ship's cook, saw their concealed display and winked at Tara.

At least one person in the family approves, Kel thought. *But will anyone else?*

"Noted," their captain, Tara's father, concluded. "Let's get underway."

As the gathering broke up, Tara moved to where Kel stood before departing for her duty station.

"Where will you be?" she asked in a whisper.

Kel smiled. "I'll go help Ochio with the loading. I'm still a provisional spacer," he said, referring to his temporary assignment as a deckhand while on the *Callie*. Her brother was now a deck officer and, along with her Uncle Tan, was in charge of cargo operations on the ship. "But after we're underway, I'm going to be in my quarters preparing for our rendezvous over Macrobia. We should be there by the next shift."

"I don't mean to be disloyal to my family, but I think they're wrong," she replied with sadness. "We have been fortunate, but I don't see how any desire to pay back our good fortune to the universe offsets the risks here."

Kel took a moment to look into her eyes. They were clear and perfect. He wanted to lose himself in their reflection. "You're the best of the crew with a blaster. Stop by my quarters. I have an extra one for you. It's much higher power than the ones in your arms locker."

He paused, wanting to tell her that everything was going to be fine, but he couldn't lie to her. "Make sure you pick it up, okay?"

The memories chased Kel as he raced to reappear on the command deck. Jim and Eric looked to him, their shock at seeing him in his armor evident. Kel's carbine clung to his chest by the magic of the mag-sling. Most of what they knew about him was from their relatively short time together when Kel had changed the course of their fortunes.

On that particular mission, Kel was under official cover. Most often he used the cloak of an industrial security consultant. It gave people the perception that he must have a military background to allow such work, and satisfied most curiosities about his manner and bearing. With the Yomiuris, they'd first known him under a cover name posing as an economic diplomat. His profession had become evident when he rescued them from a potentially violent situation. Jim once voiced his suspicions about Kel's military background, which Kel answered with silence. It was never brought up again.

Kel liked that the family appreciated him for who he was, not from any status he carried for being an elite legionnaire. He wanted to keep it that way.

They didn't know who I am. Not really. Now I have to show them.

"Kel. I guess this is the perfect time for you to say, 'I told you so,'" Jim said, a tremor in his voice. "What do we do?"

"Distribute blasters and secure the bridge. Give the order for everyone to suit up and to lock down in quarters."

"Kel, what are *you* going to do?" Eric asked to his back.

He paused without turning back, trying to think of the right words. Nothing came to him. Words didn't matter now. They were past that. The swish of the door closing behind him cut off his friend's weak plea to be careful. Red filled his vision. *You don't want me to be careful. You want me to save you. Careful won't do that.* Now a smile came to him; he had his permission to be who he was. And he had an unspoken answer for Eric.

I'm going to kill them all. Or die trying.

02

Kel trotted to the main airlock and reviewed his options. He'd begun working through contingencies the moment the family had taken their vote. Even before. If he thought about it, there probably wasn't a time when he didn't prepare himself to take charge. To use violence. To dominate any situation. For him, it was as natural as drawing breath.

The *Callie* had no armaments. She was a cargo vessel, not a war machine. He briefly entertained the idea of ambushing the pirate's skiff as it approached the airlock. He could disable or destroy the vessel from the hull of the *Callie* with his K-17. It would not be difficult. However, the pirate xebec would most certainly retaliate by immediately firing on them.

Getting away via jump drive would take minutes to create a field for FTL. The *Callie* wasn't a smuggler's freighter dangerously engineered to disappear at a moment's notice. If the lizards detected their power spike building for a jump, they would never escape. While the pirates were certainly barbarous, it would be a mistake to underestimate their abilities as spacers. They had a history of success in capturing or destroying vessels as large as the *Callie*. Kel's research revealed a paucity of information about the actual tactics used by the pirates in their prize-taking activities, knowledge that would have been useful to him now.

I could really use some more time, Kel told himself, a moment of doubt undermining him. *I don't think I can pull this off alone.* To his frustration, he couldn't come up with a better option. *Help isn't coming.* He dismissed his negativity. *It's all on me. And look on the bright side. If I pull it off, it'll make for a great story at the Century Club.*

He moved down the corridor from the crew and command section and ducked through the hatchway to the small waist deck. It was a vital intersection, the kind he looked for when boarding a vessel. The inner doors of the main lock stood on the hull side, the hatchway to the cargo hold across from him. Vac suit lockers lined the inner bulkhead. He sealed the hatch behind him and coded it to lock, then placed a weld at several spots as insurance. The small act would give the Yomiuris more time to mount a defense against the boarders in case he failed.

He opened the cargo bay hatch. Beyond stood the mountains of crates and containers secured to the floor of the cavernous hold. He turned back to the airlock and opened the inner doors. Stepping into the lock, he scanned for points to conceal the stunners as he took them off his chest. *Oh, how I wished I'd taken some mimetic anti-personnel mines along!* Kel remembered looking at the M3s as he'd loaded his grav container back in the team room. *Last time I'll ever feel guilty about my instinct for overkill!*

When packing out of the team room for his vacation, he'd grabbed the attitude control jet package for his armor, thinking that while on the ship there might be the opportunity for him to do EVA. At the time, he was envisioning some kind of repair mission that would let him use his ship seizure skills to impress the Yomiuris, not combat. He put a smear of breacher glue on the stunners and armed them, then set one in each of the chamber's upper corners. That would have to do. He took a nano-drone and tossed it on the header as he exited and sealed the inner doors behind him.

"Flight deck, what's the ETA on the skiff?" he asked.

A panicked report came from Jim. "They're mating now!"

Kel ran into the cargo bay and found his spot. A pyramid of containers revealed a shelf on the second tier just wide enough for him to stand on. He scaled the crates and leaned forward around the corner to expose his K-17, aiming into the corridor in front of the personnel lock. That would be his first kill zone.

"Where's the xebec? What's the distance?" he asked as he brought up the feed from his drone. The outer lock doors were still closed.

"Five hundred meters. They're right on top of us!" Eric replied.

Good. To fire the ion cannon from such a close distance would risk damaging their own ship from secondary explosions. They wouldn't do that—if they were rational. Kel was unsure about whether or not they were. He doubted it. Still, it allowed himself to hope that the ion cannon was out of play. "Captain. Turn off the grav decking in the cargo bay and the main lock."

"Done."

Kel's boots automatically gripped the surface of the crate as the artificial gravity shut down. Given their ability to survive in space without them, the pirates would most likely not be wearing vac suits or have maglock boots. He would have a tremendous advantage over them in a micro-G enviro.

Kel thought carefully before he spoke the last words he intended to for a while. "Things are going to happen quickly. Watch your internal feed of the bay. I'll give you instructions as I go. I'll tell you what to do and when. If I don't make it, fight until the last. Don't quit. If they get past me and get a foothold on the ship, it's better to risk a jump and the xebec firing at you than to let the family be taken alive. Kill any of them I fail to eliminate. If you make it out of system, you won't have to worry about a re-boarding by the pirates."

The captain gasped. "Kel—"

He closed the channel.

The exterior lock opened and Kel watched the reptilian pirates pass themselves hand over hand along the rail and into the compartment. Six giant beasts crowded into the lock before the outer doors sealed again. They all had enviro helmets and carried blasters. Only one alien wore grav boots. *I peg him as the senior man.* The rest moved with ease, floating around the chamber. Kel kept one eye on the drone feed as he watched the green flashing cursor in his bucket. As the inner doors opened, Kel looked at the link and activated the stunners.

The lock filled with purple arcs of electrical energy. Kel directed his attention from the feed in his left eye back to the deck in front of the lock. The pirate nearest the exit fell out of the lock, stunned, and forward into the corridor. Kel shot him in the chest and the head. The creature's body twisted and convulsed as it floated farther out into the waist deck, and away toward the sealed doors leading to the crew section.

Kel grasped the edge of the crate and pulled himself forward with one arm, cradling his carbine in the other. He drew his knees toward his chest and pushed off the face of the crates, propelling himself through the cargo bay doors and into the corridor. While still floating, he rotated his body toward the lock's opening and fired rapidly, filling the space with dispersed blaster fire.

Bodies writhed in the lock as he floated past. The stunners and his blaster fire gave the desired effect. One of the pirates' blasters discharged ineffectively into the chamber but away from Kel.

Still floating, Kel looked up in anticipation of hitting the sealed crew compartment hatch headfirst. As he tried to pivot before using his armor's thrusters to arrest his forward motion, he was struck in midair. An impact at his back spun him in a wild rotation and he bounced off the doors and up toward the ceiling. His boots activated as they flung toward a surface. He went from flailing loosely to a sudden stop, facing upside down and with his back to the compartment, temporarily blind.As both of his feet found purchase, he turned just as a wide gray tail filled his visor, knocking his head backward. He bit his own tongue, instantly regretting not having his teeth clenched. The bleeding reptasaurian convulsed violently in midair. Half its head was missing, yet its knife-wielding hands flailed, unconsciously stabbing in every direction, its tail lashing out randomly. Kel brought his carbine up and shot the monster. Each impact sent the beast in a new vector around the corridor. As it floated in front of the cargo bay, he aimed a shot center mass to drive it away from him and through the hatch.

Kel spit blood from his mouth down into the bucket. Some of the blood floated into his vision. "Captain. Turn on the grav decking," is what he meant to say. What came out was, "Capdain, durn om de grab de becking." He pushed off the ceiling and turned in midair to land on his feet, now oriented with the rest of the ship. The pull of gravity returned, and the blood dropped out of his vision.

The lock held a mass of writhing reptasaurs on the deck. One raised his weapon toward Kel as he fired another series of pulses into the lizard, followed by deliberate shots into the rest of the scaly beasts. He couldn't use a full-power particle charge on his K-17 without the very real risk of damaging the ship. *Thank Oba they weren't immune to the stunners!* Placing four of the powerful devices in the lock had increased their effectiveness greatly. Without them, he would have been fighting the pirates one-against-six. He looked down at the bodies stacked on each other, still squirming and twitching. He would have taken out his monomolecular blade and severed each of their spines near the base of the neck if he had the time. He didn't. The chrono in his bucket counted four minutes since the raiders had first boarded.

Kel clicked his teeth, very much aware of the pain in his mouth, and paused to look at the screen he had preset, slaving the exterior view from the port side of the *Callie*. This was the first look he'd gotten of it since the fighting started. While he could pull up every image supplied by the ship's internal and external viewers, he couldn't pay attention to them. It took several team members to manage such information while in a combat engagement. For the thousandth time in the last few hours, he wished the rest of Kill Team Three were with him.

The pirate skiff was docked to the *Callie*'s port lock by a universal ring and held steady just a few meters off the hull. Kel made his decision. He dragged a twitching body out of the threshold to join the others and closed the inner lock. "Captain, I've eliminated the threats on the *Callie*; now I'm moving to the skiff." His tongue was working better now. "I need you to make a slow thruster rotation to keep the xebec on our starboard side. I don't want them to have a direct visual of the skiff. Make it slow, like we're drifting, and hold it. How copy?"

"I saw! There's one on the deck in the cargo bay. He's not moving! What's next?"

"Make that attitude adjustment I asked for and stand by," Kel said sharply. He didn't have time to give the man a blow-by-blow of what he hoped to accomplish in the next few minutes. He raised his weapon toward the outer door as the lock cycled open. He moved laterally with its motion to see into the short tunnel that was the docking ring. The outer lock of the skiff was open! Kel activated the *Callie*'s lock to close behind him as he passed through and took the few steps to stand in front of the skiff's inner lock.

The craft was only ten meters long. There could not be many lizards on the other side, but there should be at least a pilot, someone to control the craft while the crew raided their prize. Kel closed the outer lock and waited for the chamber to cycle as the inner door automatically opened. He tossed a stunner forward and into what he hoped would be the pilot compartment and counted to three, the purple arcs filling the tubular space ahead.

He drove through, following his weapon, but there was no one aboard. The pirates had trusted the docking ring to keep the skiff mated to the *Callie*. Perhaps they had left the outer lock of their own boat open to allow the immediate return of their pilot after gaining a foothold on the huge cargo ship. Whatever the reason, it didn't matter now. Kel was grateful for the lucky break.

After a quick search, he found and activated the docking ring release. When the indicator showed retraction, he moved forward to the open pilot station. The skiff had been a prize captured from a human victim; the back of the seat had been roughly sliced out to accommodate the large lizards who operated it. He located the life support and atmosphere controls and vented the compartment. He then returned to the lock and found the manual controls that allowed him to open both sets of doors. Crafts like these were used as tenders and platforms for exterior hull repairs. The need to have a vented crew compartment was common.

Kel stepped out of the lock and pushed off to land onto the *Callie*'s hull. His minor mass would impart little momentum back to the skiff, which would stay in position relative to the larger ship. Captain Yomiuri had done exactly as Kel had asked. The starfield above the *Callie* was frozen in place. Kel looked at the chronometer. Seven minutes had passed. Whatever comms the pirate boarding party and the xebec maintained, they wouldn't indefinitely suspend their curiosity while being out of contact with their corsairs.

He activated his armor's mimetic camouflage. As he tramped forward, the arm of his armor turned gray like the ship beneath him. It would be difficult for the Macrobian crew to identify Kel against the hull if he were stationary. If they saw him from the right angle moving against the darker background of space, they could spot him. Though the program was good, the armor couldn't perfectly predict from which direction it would be viewed.

Kel didn't plan to remain on top of the *Callie* for long. Assaulting across a ship's hull was more of a controlled plod than a run. He moved one leg at a time, waiting the micro-second for his boot's grip to solidify before lifting the next one. He noted that another three minutes had passed since his last time check. He crouched to pull himself over the top of the port side to settle onto the dorsal hull and begin his run again.

The xebec was rising up and over the *Callie* to get eyes on the port side. The game was up and they were coming! It was now or never. Kel made a judgment about the vector, placed his carbine across his chest, and pushed off toward the approaching ship. His visor gave him the range and he picked a spot on the ship, letting his attitude jets make corrections as the distance closed. It wasn't far. The pirates had moved within docking range in anticipation of their boarding party successfully seizing the cargo ship.

The pirate ship's hull rushed into his vision as he brought his knees to his chest and tucked forward at the last moment, reversing his body's orientation along its flight vector as his jets automatically assisted and gave a quick burst. He landed softly amidships on the hull. It was a maneuver he'd performed hundreds of times and could do without conscious thought and on demand.

The xebec was nowhere near the mass of the *Callie*. It took him no time to reorient to his new location and turn to the bow. The cannon turret lay ahead, its short, wide barrel pointing at the *Callie*. He reached behind him as he trotted and pulled the package from its position on the small of his back.

At least the guilt about my overkill instinct didn't extend to all the items in my team room cage, he chuckled. *Overkill is always underrated.*

03

Kel didn't know where the xebec's command deck was, but thought it most likely lay forward. Before him sat the faceted turret, perched on the superstructure of a gunner's pod. An external sensor array lay on one side of the short tower, a directional communication dish on the other. These were good clues that reinforced his guess. The command deck couldn't be far away. The ship likely would not have more than two decks given its relatively small size.

When he reached the base of the hull projection, Kel looked up. The junction of the turret and the top of the superstructure formed a small ledge. Seams and ninety-degree angles were always helpful to locate when the purpose was destruction.

Perfect place for a breaching charge.

He climbed the few meters up the hull with one hand, pushing off his toes to reach the spot. The turret sat motionless the entire time. Kel placed the charge and used the link on his wrist to program it. The menu in his bucket registered the inputs.

-Narrow dispersion

-100% effect

The charge could be set to vary the shape and area of the cutting effect. It was capable of making neat holes in durasteel hulls pretty as a patio door and wide enough for two legionnaires, all the way down to a wickedly narrow—

but deep—boring cut. This would vent any compartments beneath it, leaving jagged edges that were all but impossible to seal without expensive internal shielding technology. Not something a ship like this would have.

Kel hoped to disable the cannon and cut deeply into the ship with the charge at full power. He reversed his course and looked about the hull for a place to seek cover. All he saw of the dorsal hull was flat and bare. He loped back to the port side and over, reorienting toward the bow to where he could see the *Callie* in front of him at a right angle.

Satisfied he was clear of the blast, Kel brought up an audio link to the *Callie*'s command deck. "Captain. Get ready to power up and jump out of here."

He listened to Jim's hurried banter with his co-pilot as the red breaching charge indicator flashed in his bucket's visor.

"We're ready to spin up the drive. But what about you, Kel?" the captain asked. "We can't leave you."

"I'll make my own way. Go. You won't have long."

Kel activated the charge. The explosion's vibration traveled through the hull and into his armor. He knelt to peer over the edge of the dorsal hull before vaulting over, wanting to avoid any large objects that might be ejected in his direction. The turret hurtled away. A jet of atmosphere bled from the rent and turned to ice, more detritus following at high velocities from within the depths of the ship. Jackpot.

As his feet locked onto the dorsal hull, Kel raced to what was left of the superstructure. Light flooded out of a large hole in its side, a gaping tear leading down into the ship. The charge had left a meter-wide breach beneath the tower. He brought the K-17 up and chose a path that looked like it would lead deepest into the ship. Making sure both feet were locked on the deck, he launched his grenade, stepped back momentarily to allow it to finish its explosive discharge, then went headfirst into the breach.

He pulled himself down, grasping the snakes of conduits and tangled wires revealed by the blast to reach the deck. Righting himself, Kel felt his boots take hold on the thick grated floor. For the moment, the grav decking was disrupted. But there was no guarantee things would remain that way, particularly given the pirates' ability to stay alive even when facing decompression.

Kel was out of stunners. He grabbed another grenade off his chest and loaded it into the port beneath the launcher before moving to the next jagged hole in the deck that had been breached, leading straight down to the next level. Looking down through the crater, he saw half a reptilian body floating across the compartment. He had ten more grenades. He aimed into the hole, angling up toward the edge of his vision and what he pictured was the lengthwise orientation of the compartment, and fired. Before he could step back, spall from the explosion flew out, bouncing harmlessly off his armor. *Too close*, he thought. Not even Dark Ops armor was a perfect hedge against having to take risks in these tight spaces. Frag of your own creation could kill you just as efficiently as an enemy blaster.

Now there were choices to make. He could drop down another deck or try the hatch to his front. Fighting from top down was always preferred but Kel didn't know where he was going, only that he had to take control of the ship.

Stay on top, then.

Kel activated the hatch before him and stepped back. He soon saw debris floating through the darkness across the portal. The other side of the hatch was vented of atmosphere as well, then. More damage done deep within the forward part of the ship.

"*Callie*, if you are receiving me, respond."

Silence.

They must have successfully jumped the ship. Kel relaxed slightly. With the Yomiuris gone, some of the time constraints on his actions eased. He moved to one side of the hatch, then the other, seeing as much of what he could in either direction before committing. Clearing any space by yourself was a plan of failure. Doing so on a ship full of murderous lizards was suicide.

The corridor was dark, and Kel's bucket effortlessly made the scene bright as daylight to him. He activated one of the programs contained in his forearm link and controlled by the HUD in his bucket. Seizing denied spacecraft was a common mission requirement for Dark Ops, and the tech that supported it was good. He moved down the corridor, another hatch at its end his goal. Along the way were two other hatches leading starboard and port, respectively. He paused at each, using the compartment integrity sensors to probe the other side of the bulkhead. Through the closed hatches, the program read the compartments as both vented and unpowered. Nothing above ambient temperature showed. Satisfied no one was likely to pop out behind him, he moved to the final hatch at the end of the passage. It would be the logical location for either the command deck or ship's operations center.

The other side of the sealed hatch was under pressure and powered. Fuzzy blobs of warm but cooler-than-human shapes were bunched closely on the other side. Dark Ops had developed many tactics, techniques, and procedures for clearing and seizing ships. The intrusive programs contained in their links allowed the operator to spoof or override virtually any ship's system. Commercial shipping rarely had encrypted or protected code controlling a ship's internal functions. Kel had the ability to vent compartments, unlock sealed hatches, and turn off sections of power within a ship at will. If a DO operator went rogue with such tech, he could be quite a successful pirate himself. Instead, the capability was developed to allow the operator a range of options when storming a vessel.

Kel's plan was one of his preferred. With no hostages or friendlies on the ship, he didn't have to use restraint. He'd been on the receiving end of the assault he was about to make, having acted as OPFOR on just such a training evolution more than a few times. He knew from experience how effective and disorienting the method could be. When the pressurized atmosphere disappeared like the flash of a shooting star, anyone not in a vac suit would feel like their brains melted. Ears burst. Sinuses bled. Bowels evacuated.

His link confirmed communication with the ship's systems and that the intrusive program now dominated the weak computer. He stood beside the hatch, as deep into the corner as he could get, and made sure he had total contact with his grav boots and the deck. He scrolled through the action options menu and confirmed his selection.

"Surprise, losers," he said inside his bucket. *Suck vacuum, lizards.*

The hatch opened with a strain and atmosphere exploded out of the compartment. He turned into the now fully open hatch and was greeted with the sight of a Macrobian filling his line of vision above the K-17. He hammered the trigger three times in rapid succession, holding the holo-dot on the center of the beast's chest, and continued his movement to the far side of the hatchway before rushing in to find the rest of the cold blobs his sensor told him were there.

Two more disoriented Macrobians were rising from duty station stools when Kel fired two quick bursts into the chest of the lizard on his left then drove his carbine toward the other monster's chest, firing another two bursts in the same rapid rhythm. Without pause he drifted his sight up to the cranial vault of the right-hand target, its open mouth and flicking tongue registering surprise as its chest erupted, and fired a single blast into its head. Kel snapped his eyes back to the first lizard's head and did the same. The two bodies ceased moving by their own power and floated dead in the gravity-free bridge.

That never happens off the range, Kel thought. He'd practiced a box drill virtually every day of his life. He'd never had the opportunity to use the technique in real combat. *Bigg would be proud.*

Kel shook his head at the realization that his first thoughts after the encounter involved picturing his team sergeant and mentor in all things.

The Macrobians weren't in enviro helmets. A piece of skull bounced off a bulkhead and floated closer. Bluish blood leaked from the earhole. Clear, thick mucus mixed with the blood in a cloud of sticky droplets. As tough as the reptasaurians were, the sudden pressure differential had to have been brutal. Killing them had been merciful, as well as necessary.

Sensors showed the room clear. Kel was free to enter.

Normally, the operator would have tossed a stunner into the compartment before entering. Kel had none left.

He could take one of the grenades for his carbine and swipe it down to low yield before tossing it by hand, but that might deny his hopes of preserving the functionality of the pilot station. So long as the ship were sound, he could make the short jump to Wuhen and safety. At worst, he could make it to the planet surface below.

First things first, he thought as he took a breath and pushed into the chamber.

A tail struck him squarely in the visor, snapping his head back and knocking him stumbling backward into the corridor.

The kelhorned sensor didn't light on anyone in the corner!

His carbine came up and he fired blindly, still seeing spots in his vision. A large shape loomed in the compartment. Kel fired his grenade launcher.

Kel felt the overpressure through his armor. His breath was shoved out of his lungs as he hit the wall and a warning in his visor indicated an armor breach. He struggled to regain lucidness, leaning against the corridor bulkhead for a moment.

Not again! Gotta look out for those krellin' tails.

Gas streamed from his left leg and slowly reduced to nothing as his bucket told him the auto-seal function was active. Now his leg burned. It wasn't bad, but he knew he'd taken some kind of penetrating injury. He leaned against a bulkhead and looked into the compartment, then down the corridor behind him to see if any other pirates were moving to join the fight against the intruder.

Got to move.

When he stood, his leg ached deeply. The nano-gel in the inner layer of his armor would be moving to cover whatever size wound it was and would soon excrete a local anesthetic to numb the spot. He put it out of his mind as he moved into the compartment, weapon up, prepared for any resistance on the other side. He collapsed the entire compartment from where he stood just inside the hatch and relaxed.

Well, that got the job done.

A large lizard with the remnants of an enviro helmet lay at his feet, still as a stone and satisfyingly perforated with enough holes to make a colander envious.

Kel looked around the compartment. It was obviously the command deck. It was obviously destroyed. Sparks spewed from smoldering consoles, fighting the vacuum to extinguish them by reigniting every few seconds before extinguishing again. There would be no resurrecting command functions of the ship from here. He headed back down the corridor.

How many pirates would there be on this ship? he wondered. He did some quick calculations. He'd killed six aboard the *Callie*, the four on the command deck, and passed another body on his way here. There could be another dozen or more on the ship to take charge of the prize cargo and another dozen elsewhere operating the ship's systems. He made a decision.

Kel moved down the corridor, bypassing the two hatches he'd already probed, and came to a companionway leading down to the next deck. Some of the ship's functions remained intact; lights bloomed from below. He grabbed the railing on either side, stepped into the space of the open deck hatch, and gave a gentle pull to propel himself to the floor.

He landed on his good leg and came to a gentle stop as his boots reconnected. His calf was quite numb now. He tested his weight gingerly before moving toward the source of the lights. The corridor turned sharply left, and he pushed into the space with his weapon forward. Another bare corridor, with a sealed hatch at the end, and in Standard a placard read, "Main Engineering." Along the left inboard bulkhead was another hatch. He scanned it. There was power in the compartment and it was under atmosphere. Cool blobs told him what he needed to know. He took a grenade and swiped it to the lowest discharge setting, replaced it on his chest where he could easily reach it, and took a breath.

Kel commanded the compartment to decompress violently. After allowing it to vent, he slid right to scan through the threshold. Three Macrobians lay splayed and unmoving on the deck, blue-tinged blood seeping from their earholes. Kel shoulder-checked each corner as he moved in, then commanded the hatch to seal behind him and reestablish life support. He menaced the prostrated forms with his weapon as the nearest one lifted its huge head to look up at him.

As atmosphere pressurized the compartment, the reptasaurians' thickly muscled bodies eased. Kel keyed the external comm of his bucket. He'd already set his translator program to the most common language of the Macrobians.

"Who's in charge here?" he said, the strange sibilant language filling the space.

The lizard looking up at him pointed to his ear and made a motion with its head. He understood. The thing was deaf. He boosted the output of his speaker and asked again.

"WHO'S IN CHARGE HERE?"

The creature replied in passable Standard, "You are."

"You're karkin' right I am."

Kel wasn't adept reading the body language of the Macrobians, so whether it was wishful thinking on his part or true acquiescence on the part of the lizard named Shaakan, the ship's engineer, was just a guess. The alien certainly *seemed* to cower as he promised cooperation.

Shaakan eyed the grenade in Kel's hand, his thick tail limp and his claws held against his chest. "Yesss. Yesss. No fight. No fight. You Sissskandar. You in charge."

In a mix of pidgin Standard and his own language, Shaakan assured Kel there were many hatchlings at home he was responsible for, that the crew would cooperate, and that the safe return to the surface of Macrobia was their common goal.

"Mak-ssshong, mak-ssshong Khaychang. Stupid. Stupid," he said, referring to their leader whom Kel had dispatched on the command deck with his grenade. His translator now picked up as the engineer spoke strictly in its own language. "Khaychang was rash and headstrong, always. But when successful, brought much wealth to our clan. Had we known that a *crusader* was among your crew, we would never have attempted such a feat."

Kel still held the grenade in his left hand. He explained by translator that if he were assaulted and dropped the grenade, it would burst in a wide radius and kill everyone else on board by breaching the hull.

And, if it detonated near the exterior hull, Kel thought, *that might even be true.*

"Legionnaire. Legionnaire," one of his assistants said clearly, its tongue flicking at Kel as it performed a stationary dance, rhythmically swaying from side to side as it spoke.

"You know what a legionnaire is?" Kel asked the Macrobian who'd spoken from behind the engineer, Shaakan. The lizard was smaller in stature than Shaakan but appeared much older.

"Death. Legionnaire bring death. Always."

"It's good to hear you've been taught how we stack the tiles." Kel could not have agreed more with its assessment.

"We do not understand," Shaakan said.

"Just know that I will kill us all if you try anything mak-ssshong," Kel repeated, trying his best at Macrobian. "I know legionnaires who'd make belts out of all of you."

The lizards stood in the center of the engineering section. As a group, they sunk their necks into their shoulders and swayed as they hummed together in what Kel took for submission.

"No one will attempt rebellion. We pledge submission to your authority," Shaakan said in his own language. "It is our way. When honorable defeat is met, we exalt the victor. If we must be your slaves, we will bear the burden for our clan."

"I won't be making slaves of you. When we hit the surface, you're free to return to your homes. I have other plans."

Necks arched, the pale lizards looked at each other. Kel wasn't sure, but he thought he had perhaps made a positive step in cementing what he hoped would be a beneficial but short working relationship.

"Truly?" Shaakan asked. "We do not become property of your clan?"

"Truly. You get us to the planet safely and help me get to a consulate, and you'll never see me or anyone from my clan again." Tongues rapidly flicked the air. "But no Bhat. I see anyone chewing that stuff and getting the crazy idea they can overpower me, and..." He held up the grenade to finish his thought.

"No. No," Shaakan said. "We are spacers and engineers. We do not consume the Bhat as the warriors do. Any fool knows that way lies madness. Ships that lift with crews polluted with Bhat never return. Madness."

More tongues flicked the air in agreement.

"Well, all right then, shipmates. Let's get to work."

Kel found a workstation console and eased onto the stool, relieved that he was off his left leg for a moment. Shaakan apprised him of the situation and asked permission to act. The crew would need to dog any hatches that could still hold atmosphere. They also had to cut loose the damaged superstructure to prevent it from coming free on atmospheric entry and crashing back into the ship. Finally, Shaakan explained that while he was no pilot, he was sure he could program the auxiliary flight control system and get them safely landed.

"There are no sister clans with ships in space from which we could request aid. Any other clans that hear our request would fall on us as prey. We are on our own."

"It's a sound plan, engineer. Please make it so."

Shaakan seemed to bolster up when Kel addressed him by his professional title. The Macrobian bobbed his head, then turned to direct his spacers to action.

Kel projected a holo from his link in front of him. Reading large amounts of material in the visor HUD strained the eyes. No matter how close the projection came to achieving a focal plane near infinity, reading many lines of material in the bucket was draining. It also reduced awareness of everything outside the bucket. Kel thought he had the crew's cooperation, but his threat of violence had to remain real. Situational awareness was the first step.

He wanted to locate a neutral if not friendly port for landing. The Republic no longer maintained a diplomatic post on the world. When it had, the population center of Kanchatka had also held most of the consulates and diplomatic missions from around the galaxy. A year-old holo from the Spiral News Network was saved in the file. A report from the city discussed the poor representation of foreign missions as worlds called diplomats home from the dangerous planet. Of those remaining, the Ootari consulate was the only one that Kel recognized as having semi-decent relations with the Republic.

The Ootari were one of many insectoid races in the galaxy. He'd had no personal dealings with them, but from general knowledge knew they were poised to become Republic members. By reputation they were bellicose and cliquish, traits commonly encountered among hive-type races. They seemed the most likely candidates to render him aid.

He turned to see Shaakan at his side, staring at the images as well. "Kanchatka. It is the center of the old council. Times were much better then."

Kel was curious. "When did things get so bad on your world, Shaakan?" He was learning more about the body language of the reptasaurians as he interacted with them. If he had to guess, the gurgling noise Shaakan made before answering was an emotional preamble.

"Life is hard across my world. Always. I am not so young, though, that I cannot remember the time before. Before the voor-la cared to come to our world."

Shaakan saw Kel tilt his head in response to the word, "heathen."

"I mean no disrespect. You are a mighty warrior. Not all who come to Macrobia show honor. I can remember when no off-worlders came to our world. We traveled the star-ways and kept our home secret to prevent just such contamination. We should have stayed on the ground."

Kel listened with rapt attention as the Macrobian told him about the history of their planet, how they explored the near systems, discovered Wuhen and Golnara, and developed trade with them. He talked about learning the spacer's trade from his family. "My clan was one of the first to travel the stars. At the age of fitness, I was allowed to join my clan in space. I come from a long line of engineers—those who run the ships, not pilot them. When I reached the age of responsibility, I was allowed to ascend and learned to tend the jump engines and the FTL drive. It has been my life's work. Now, since the chaos, I no longer tend the engines in hyperspace. We hang in the system for days at a time under repulsor drive, waiting for the few ships that still come, waiting to capture them. It is... not the true way."

"How did your people come to develop jump drive?" Kel asked. "Did you receive the technology from another race? Or did the Macrobians develop their own?"

The lizard canted his head. "What causes you to ask this? Do you think our people are incapable of such!"

The creature's sense of pride was challenged.

"No, engineer," Kel said truthfully. "I'm only curious. There are many stories on many worlds regarding how

FTL was discovered. There are those like my own people who claim to have discovered the technology on their own. There are those who claim it was given to them by ancient races. I wondered if you had similar tales in your culture."

Shaakan inflated the sac underneath his jaw, a bright red amidst the pale scales of his skin, then it receded. He did this several times. Was he laughing? "That is most entertaining. Yes, warrior. Yes. There are old woman's tales of just such things. How amusing. No. Who invented the drive has been lost to history, but that it has existed for many *chatckas* is factual."

The translator did not have an equivalent for the period of time the word represented.

The engineer continued. "I know these engines like the face of she who hatched me. There is nothing about them that I cannot recognize, no matter how divine I consider them to be. If an alien race brought us the technology, it is as familiar to me as my own claws."

Kel found himself impressed with the engineer. "Shaakan, I must make planetfall in Kanchatka. It is where I can make contact with my own people."

The lizard seemed to consider this, and made the gurgling noise again. "It is where the voor-la remain. My clan nest is far from there, warrior."

Kel nodded. "We may have respect for each other, engineer, but I doubt your clan would protect a voor-la like me."

The red sac expanded again. "You are correct, warrior. There would be difficulties. I could not promise you safety. And I would not want you to wreak destruction upon those dear to me."

"Then Kanchatka it is, engineer."

The lizard paused. "It was not always such, as I said. You are a human from the Republic, yes?"

Kel had not removed his bucket to show himself to the Macrobians. "That is correct, engineer."

"My clan welcomed the first visitors from the Republic. My brood mother was a member of the clan council. I remember meeting your kind for the first time. We knew how to treat visitors with respect then. Now, so many of the old ways are gone. This younger generation..."

He did not finish his thought.

Kel tried to process what the engineer had told him. If he understood him correctly, he had been present when the first Republic diplomatic mission had visited Macrobia, at least three hundred years before.

"Shaakan, how old are you?"

"I am still young for my people, yes. Do you doubt my ability?"

Sket, Kel thought. He had stepped on the lizard's pride again. "No, of course not."

"I promise you, I have reached the age of responsibility. I am the ship's engineer."

Now Kel laughed. "I don't doubt your ability. I know you are a competent engineer. If you were present when the first Republic visitors negotiated the treaty to allow us to stage on your world during the Savage Wars, you must be over three hundred years old."

"I have over forty stolaree. I am older than many, but not as old as some. I have not yet reached the age of wisdom. When I do, I will take my place on the clan council and leave the stars. I cannot say I will miss them, living as we do now."

Kel felt sympathy for the engineer. "Engineer, please inform me when we are ready for reentry."

The lizard bobbed his head several times and turned to his spacers.

Kel set his mind to figuring out the Macrobian time equivalents. He pulled up one of the files on his link and found a reference. A stolaree was about a dozen standard years. That meant that the engineer was almost five hundred years old.

He continued to read as he tried to remember the term Shaakan had used when describing the period of time over which his culture had used FTL. The Standard transliterations of the words for the Macrobian time references scrolled by. *Praalmar*? *Shalkanda*? *Chatckas*! That was it.

Oba, that's over 1500 years! Shaakan said his people had used FTL for "many" of the time periods. How many was that? Three? That was almost 5000 years...

Kel would turn twenty-eight Standard years old next month. If he lived that long.

04

The grav decking and inertial compensators were turned off to divert as much available power to the structural integrity field as possible. Everyone on board needed to keep the ship from breaking up during reentry.

Though he was no spacer, Kel understood and agreed with the engineer's reasoning. In securing the xebec, he had done a lot of damage to the craft. Now he hoped not to die as a result of his successful one-legionnaire assault.

They'd maneuvered under repulsor drive to orbit over Macrobia while emergency repairs were carried out. The engineer gave Kel a rundown of what they had accomplished.

"I wish to offer assurances, warrior, but I cannot. As much as is in my power to do, I have done. If voor-la have gods you pray to, ask for their help, as I have of the Great-Mother in her nest."

Kel looked around the deck of the engineering section at the many lizards curled into tight balls, tucked into small padded recesses along the bulkheads. Shaakan sat upright strapped into a backless chair, his tail wrapped around the pedestal. Kel sat next to him strapped onto the other stool, his grav boots holding him in place as he had no tail to assist his stability. He had powered down the grenade and returned it to his chest pouch.

"I have faith in you, engineer. I wish we had met under different circumstances."

Shaakan's neck sac expanded again. "You are a curiosity to me, warrior. Yes, I too wish we had met differently. No matter. You will go to your nest and I to mine." The engineer spoke into the ship's comm. "Commencing descent." His claws tapped the console in front of him as Kel watched the viewer. There wasn't much else he could do but watch and wait. "The flight computer is controlling our landing. I have some ability to control the ship if we become unstable. It depends on our outer hull. You wisely did not damage our drives with your attack, but if our hull comes apart because our field cannot be maintained, no amount of power will matter."

Kel hoped the shipyard that had built the xebec had a good rating for space worthiness.

The pull of gravity returned as their freefall around the planet halted and they began their descent through the atmosphere.

"The truth is that no pilot can affect the ship he pilots during an unpowered reentry," Shaakan stated. "I have been engineer to great pilots and captains. Khaychang was strong, but he was neither great nor a pilot. The flight computer did all of his flying." The ship shook violently and the heat of reentry engulfed them in flames. "Only the foolish pilot believes he brings the ship to safety at these times. It is the engineer that provides the ship safe return."

Kel felt the repulsor drive kick in and the craft started to slow as it entered the upper atmosphere.

"The greatest strain on the craft is past," Shaakan said, sounding relieved. "We are under power and intact. Your voor-la gods give you thick scales of luck, warrior."

"It was your skill, engineer." Kel unbuckled and stood. The lizards crawled out of their gravity pods and moved to stations around the section, some leaving through the main hatch to tend the landing sponsons. "*Kanchatka*, engineer. Find us the landing field, and you and your clan mates are free."

Kel rested his hand on his pistol. He was not so relieved to be alive to now assume that his safety was secured.

Shaakan's gaze flicked down to Kel's hand. "As I have promised, we approach now."

Below them sprawled a large city, an isthmus dividing a mountain range on one side from the desert on the other.

"It has been a lengthy time since I made port there. I can be of some service to aid you on your way. My crew will need to make further repairs before we lift again for home. I must also bargain for the taxes the port master will try to collect from us. Do not be alarmed when my crew arms themselves on landing. It will be for our protection from the warlord who claims the port, whoever that may now be."

Kel wanted to believe the engineer but could not relax his guard. "Thank you, engineer. If you can assist me to find the consulates of the voor-la, I will be grateful."

The lizard bobbed its head. "As my captor, you could threaten me as your prisoner. Instead, you continue to act with respect. There is a saying, 'In defeat, defiant. In victory, humble.' I do not think many in the galaxy know this anymore. We have lost our way."

"Engineer, as many worlds as I have traveled to, as many races as I have known, there are few who do. But they do exist. I have met them."

Kel thought about the many alien races he'd worked with. The number of times he'd heard similar words only served to convince him that among warriors, there were some universal truths. He'd often found himself feeling more in common with soldiers from an alien world than he had with civilians from his own. But always, he was reminded that there were much deeper differences between humanity and other species that were beyond reasoning. He had no fantasies about "going native" with the Ruhar or the Disciplined of Qulingat't, or even the Macrobians, as fascinating as he found them to be.

"Secure for landing," Shaakan said throughout the ship's comms.

Kel noticed that there had been no communication with a ground controller as the engineer piloted the ship across the desert to the spacefield at the city's edge. A large, empty freighter sat at an unnatural angle in the sand, surrounded by the smaller rusted and equally derelict hulls of a dozen other ships that littered the edge of the duracrete. There were few craft on the landing pads, one a xebec similar to their own, and several other medium cargo vessels.

Near the largest building at the access road entrance was a golden luxury yacht with a spherical multifaceted bow that reminded Kel of an insectoid eye. Could that belong to the Ootari? A long, red-fringed canopy attached to the ship shaded a path to the forward crew ramp. Besides the luxury yacht, nothing down there suggested an offworld presence.

There was no movement apparent on the field during their descent. They landed without incident, and Kel felt the last surge of the repulsor drive engines before they shut down and the decking vibrations ceased.

Shaakan unbuckled and stood. "The sooner I can get you on your way, the sooner we can lift. If we can depart before too long, we may evade attention. Let us hurry."

Kel followed the lizard out of the compartment and back through the forward section to reach a crew hatch on the external hull. Shaakan undogged the hatch and let a short ramp deploy before he marched ahead of the legionnaire and off the ship.

The sun was bright, the sky cloudless. The main lock opened as lizards disembarked and busied themselves making the ship ready to lift again, checking the landing gear and tightening loose bolts with autospanners. As they walked toward the open hanger nearest the golden yacht, Kel looked back at the xebec. If you were to look at the rear section, it appeared none the worse for wear. Forward of where the superstructure once sat was the disaster Kel had worked so hard to create, large sections of the hull were missing. Visible through the gaps in the port side plating, a lone stringer ran fore and aft. The intact stringer was probably the miracle that allowed them to survive reentry.

Shaakan saw him surveying the damage. "We will make a sub-orbital return home. Our craft will not enter space again without extensive work. Come, let us find you escort."

Kel turned to follow his guide across the field and into the hanger. Prostrated lizards lay curled up on duracrete shaded beneath the hanger roof. The workers had not been disturbed by their landing and were not alerted by their footfalls now. A small runabout sat in the center of the hanger with as many Macrobians in states of recumbency on and under the shuttle vehicle. A lone lizard stepped out of a small office to see who had entered, glanced at Kel, and quickly darted back inside.

The engineer strode after the retreating lizard, speaking loud and fast in a way Kel's translator could not follow.

A narrow head poked out of the door, tongue flicking the air. Kel followed behind Shaakan as the engineer continued in the new language of gurgles and clicks, not the soft Macrobian hisses he was accustomed to hearing. The figure stepped cautiously out of the office to stand before the larger, older lizard addressing it. Kel remained a few steps back, watching and listening as Shaakan gestured toward his human companion. The engineer turned back to Kel.

"Where do you wish to go? This one says he can take you."

Kel looked out at the apron and pointed. "I need to go where the owner of that ship resides. Does it belong to the Ootari diplomatic delegation?"

Shaakan translated and by the amount of verbiage used, Kel judged the maintenance worker gave a long and detailed answer. "He says it belongs to the insect voor-la and that they have a compound in the city. This one is not old or wise, but I believe he speaks of the diplomatic mission you seek."

"Any humans in Kanchatka?" Kel queried, waiting for Shaakan to repeat the translation process with the local. The response came quickly.

"He says there may be, but he has seen them only rarely. The insects he sees regularly. They come to the spacefield at least weekly to take the yacht."

Kel considered his options. "Tell him I want him to take me to the Ootari compound. He'll do that and I can trust him not to take me somewhere I don't want to go? Like to friends of his who will try to kidnap me for ransom? Better warn him that I wouldn't take kindly to that and that he'd be the first to die."

Shaakan bobbed his head. "I have already explained my predicament and that you are a great warrior and have warned him that we are all in great peril if we do not cooperate. I have offered to pay him on your behalf from our ship's stores for his trouble. He is satisfied. You can trust that he will do as I have asked."

"Then that's all I can ask of you, engineer. I release you and your crew to return to your home." Shaakan hesitated to move, as if waiting for Kel to say more. When the lizard said nothing, Kel continued. "What will you do when you return home?"

Shaakan swayed from side to side as he had seen the lizards do when they seemed to be in distress. "I will repair the ship. When I'm done, I will step aside and let another become engineer. This is my clan's last ship. Our best warriors are gone. If we lose this ship, our clan will be destitute and will have no means to survive. I have no desire to be on another raid that fails. Best to seek another way for my hatchlings to eat."

Kel felt sympathy for the engineer, but there was little he could do. He had spared their lives after attacking his surrogate family's vessel. He doubted the Yomiuris would have gotten as good a deal from the corsairs had they been successful in seizing the *Callie*.

"I'm glad we met, Shaakan. Take my advice; follow your instinct to find another way to earn for your hatchlings. Piracy won't let you live to the age of wisdom."

The ride into the city was tense. The open repulsor sled gave Kel no way to conceal himself as they drifted through the busy conglomerations of multi-storied adobe and thatch-roofed buildings. They wove through curving streets that opened into large plazas where Macrobians on foot dodged vehicles weaving through the masses. Kel saw lizards mounted on large smooth-skinned quadrupeds with long snouts and tails, rope bridles filling thin-lipped mouths that bore no teeth. He imagined the immense beasts would still be capable of inflicting great damage, toothless or not.

It soon became apparent to Kel that he did not seem to draw any attention from the locals as he rode through the city. Realizing this, he relaxed but kept his head on a swivel, anticipating trouble at any moment. His driver spoke to him occasionally in the same indecipherable language he had heard Shaakan use. Kel's bucket provided no translation so he remained silent. Finally, Kel tried the Macrobian language he had used to communicate so well with the engineer. "How much farther?"

The driver startled as it looked at Kel, swerving into a group of mounted lizards traveling in the opposite undivided lane. One of the massive animals reared and its rider flew off as Kel's driver regained control and righted their path.

"You speak high-tongue! You me fool. You not stupid-stupid."

Kel wasn't in the mood for a conversation. "How much farther?"

The lizard's tongue flicked rapidly several times before answering. "Soon now."

Kel grunted in the way he had heard Shaakan do. The driver took the hint that he wasn't inviting a discussion, returning his attention to the road. They moved out of the low part of the city toward the foothills where the streets' layout became less chaotic and more grid-like. Kel recognized the foreign influences in the architecture, though much of it had been long since abandoned or destroyed, whether from the civil war or from the kind of neglect he was used to seeing in alien cities once the foreign visitors left.

The driver gestured toward a group of buildings in a walled compound and made the proclamation, "Rich bugs," as he pulled up to the duracrete curb. A pair of Macrobians flanked a solid gate halfway down the wall, each wearing a gold sash and carrying blaster rifles of a type he didn't recognize. The lizards would be contract security for the consulate.

This must be the place.

Kel hopped out and before he could address the driver, the sled zipped away. He took a look around before he approached the guard station. There was no traffic on the street, no pedestrians on the walks. The surrounding buildings appeared neglected and empty. The neighborhood had every telltale sign that it had been the embassy row of the city, now all but empty save the Ootari compound. Kel did not want to provoke an armed confrontation with the consulate guards, but had no other means for approach. He slung his carbine across his back to appear less threatening and began walking, ready to spread arms wide to show lack of hostile intent.

He should be under observation by now. Security within the compound would be alerting the guard station of his approach. He was going over his options for establishing contact with the consular officer. He decided it was best to explain to the guards that he was a human member of the Republic requesting aid from the Ootari consulate, and see if that got him a meeting with at least a low-level staffer. Then he could explain his situation.

Kel ran over a speech a few times in his head as he walked down the wall. The two lizard guards had no choice but to step out and confront him, when a black luxury repulsor sedan pulled up alongside and rocked to a halt. Kel's hand went to his pistol as the passenger door slid back to reveal a human in a white synth-silk suit and dark glasses.

"Kel Turner, I presume? I know some people who are worried about you."

Kel rode in the back with Mister Robert Taylore, his Macrobian bodyguard in one of the rearward facing seats, eyeing him suspiciously as they rode. Kel's carbine rested between his legs, his bucket on the seat beside him, a stream of cold air blasting down the neck of his armor, and a fruit juice pouch sweating cold beads in his hand. Taylore, undoubtedly a cover name, had not identified himself as such but was almost certainly a case officer from Republic Intelligence.

Taylore held his own pouch, wiping the chilly perspiration off onto his white suit pants, the drops rolling off, leaving the suit pristine. "I tried to get you at the spacefield, but you were too quick for us. I caught up to the crew of the corsair you hijacked—I want to hear the whole story eventually—and after convincing them that I was actually trying to help you, they directed me to your destination. The senior lizard told me that if I meant you harm, to turn back and save my own life," the man said with a laugh.

"You must've made quite an impression. I saw their ship. It's amazing it held together."

Kel laughed to himself. Shaakan was still showing appreciation for his respectful treatment even after their parting. The lizard had an almost human sense of honor.

"The Yomiuris and the Galactic Hugs staff were burning up the hypercomm pipeline from the embassy in Wuhen to the Ootari consulate," Taylore said. "I'm sure I don't have to tell you what a persistent bunch of ninnies those folks are. I've negotiated three ransoms in the last year for crews carrying aid shipments to Macrobia for them. Nonsense." The man took a long pull off his drink before continuing.

"Anyway, the Ootari consular officer called me. I thought that we were most likely looking at another ransom situation with you as the hostage and was preparing the message for all stations. Then my sources at the spacefield called to tell me there was a legionnaire on the ground. I put two and two together and made a dash to see what the situation was."

So, my presence didn't go wholly unnoticed despite the lack of reception, Kel thought. Just because his arrival hadn't generated an obvious response didn't mean it had escaped the attention of the informants on Taylore's payroll. Kel admired that.

Taylore examined Kel for a few moments before speaking again. "I got the first part of the story—the Galactic Hugs' contract ship getting waylaid and escaping back to Wuhen—but how did you get involved? I haven't had the time to get word to my people on Wuhen and ask who you are. Who are you?"

Now Kel felt a sense of amusement. For the first time he could remember, he was the one in the position holding all the critical information when dealing with RI. He took a long pull from his own drink, savoring the feeling of the man's anticipation building. As much fun as it would be to shut the man out, he did need his help. "Get me headed to Wuhen and I'll gladly tell you the whole tale."

Taylore was a professional. Kel told him the story but left out key elements, such as the fact that he was on leave and that he was an operator in Dark Ops. The man most likely knew that's where he was from but had the courtesy not to make Kel deny it. He gave the intelligence officer a true and detailed accounting of his actions seizing the xebec. Despite himself, the man showed awe and amazement as Kel gave him a blow-by-blow account, his eyes widening in surprise at all the best parts of Kel's story.

"I'm not primarily interested in the Macrobian pirates at this time," Kel lied. He'd continue to evade the man's curiosity about what had brought him to this region. One way to do that was by distraction. Let Taylore answer some questions. "I did get some insights into their culture during our association. The Macrobian spacers were interesting. Likeable, even. Did Bhat cause all this?" Kel gestured out the window at an open landfill overflowing with mountains of garbage, indicating they were nearing the spaceport.

Taylore nodded. "I've been here two years. I was a witness to the dissolution of their society. Yes, the Bhat drove much of it, but it was only *one* of the warlords' tools. When the move to a franchised system of electing representatives came, a lot of the younger Macrobians found a way to catapult ahead of the traditional means to take the reins of leadership. They figured out representative democracy pretty quickly."

Kel was taking a liking to the man.

"When the first clan region successfully elected a factotum who had not reached the age of wisdom, many others soon followed. When enough of the federal parliament was filled with young lizards trying to bring home more bread and circuses, it didn't take long for tribes that felt they'd scored less from the public coffers to go to war with tribes that had done better. The Bhat just seemed to fuel some of those jealousies, and soon, it was all-out war.

"The central government collapsed soon after. Once the economy dried up and the only source of income was crime against off-worlders, it was the last nail in the coffin. The Republic washed their hands of the place and their isolation took hold."

Kel nodded. It was a succinct explanation of the events the man had witnessed, and uncommonly honest. "What's going to happen to them?" he asked.

The man shrugged. "There doesn't seem to be an easy way back to normalcy for them. Did you know they're probably the longest-lived race in the galaxy? The Republic spent years studying the local biology, trying to discover the basis for their longevity. When troops were stationed here, a large contingent of research scientists collocated with them—for at least fifty years before the Savage Wars died down in this arm of the galaxy. As near as I can figure, Paxaas here," he said, nodding to the Macrobian bodyguard, "is over three hundred years old and is still considered a young adult among his clan. Amazing, isn't it?"

Kel saw they were headed onto the duracrete road leading back to the spaceport. "We headed to the field again?"

"I'm the wizard who grants wishes. You're going back to Wuhen on the first thing warping space, and it turns out that's the Ootari diplomatic yacht. When you were sighted, I started the ball rolling. The Ootari are anxious to see you off the planet as soon as possible. As the only diplomatic mission still here, they get put in the middle of most of these hostage situations. They make it a point of pride to demonstrate their superior negotiating abilities dealing with the pirate clans, even if I end up being the Republic's bagman most of the time. Wrapping up your visit on Macrobia and returning you to the fold of the Republic ASAP just puts the Ootari up another notch in status within the Republic, at least in their own multifaceted eyes. The Ootari had a flight planned to Wuhen today, anyway. Getting you on board was their offer."

Kel knew the Ootari were to be made full members of the Republic. It seemed reasonable they would want to use the odd circumstances to render aid, hoping to speed their acceptance.

As they floated onto the field, Kel noticed the xebec was gone. He'd half hoped to introduce Shaakan to the intelligence officer. Perhaps there was a useful connection there? Kel didn't even know what clan or region the engineer was from. It wouldn't happen.

The golden yacht stood in the same place, but now a luxury repulsor sled was parked by the nearby canopy. Two huge Ootari warriors stood in the canopy's shade, just outside the yacht. The guards' antennae twitched in their direction as Taylore's sedan pulled up, their sharp claws clutching blaster rifles.

"Come on, they're waiting for you," Taylore said as the bodyguard opened the door of the sedan and stood aside. "I'll make the introductions."

Kel put his bucket on, collected his carbine and let it snap to his chest as he stepped out. The large insectoids tensed, and Kel moved the weapon to his back as he stepped to follow behind Taylore to the canopy.

"Greetings," Taylore addressed the two Ootari, "I have the Republic dignitary traveling with you to Wuhen at the invitation of the consul general."

One insectoid stepped forward and pointed a claw at Kel. "He must surrender his weapons."

Kel wanted to tell them where they could stick their request to surrender his weapons but deescalated on his own. He had expected as much. The Ootari were assisting him. It was most unlikely that they would use the opportunity to harm him. "Do you have a secure locker for arms, or are you going to be handling my weapons? Because I'm carrying items that could be dangerous if tampered with by someone ignorant of their controls, though I'm sure you're both quite capable."

"That won't be necessary," a voice said from the top of the ramp in the somewhat tinny but not unpleasant voice formed by insectoid mouthparts. "Let our guest proceed. We have nothing to fear from a protector of the Republic such as a legionnaire." The Ootari standing in the entry deck gestured him up, its shimmering vest reflecting a rainbow of colors. It was the hallmark of importance only a clotheshorse or a diplomat would wear on such an impoverished world. "Mister Taylore, that was especially quick work. I trust your report to your own mission will reflect the nature of our joint participation in resolving this matter so efficiently."

This had to be the consul general himself.

"Indeed, sir," the RI officer said as the Ootari guard relaxed slightly and returned to his post. "May I present Mister Kel Turner, our, uh, special representative. Mister

Turner, this is Consul General Padlo Ranmark of the Ootari Embassy."

"Actually, it's Lieutenant Turner, but I'd be pleased if you would call me Kel," he said, looking up the ramp at the garishly adorned Ootari.

"Excellent! Imagine my good fortune to be on a first-name basis with a hero of the Legion. You must call me Padlo. As you no doubt know, our own language is quite incomprehensible to human ears, so we assume names easier for the human mouth to pronounce, but it is very much a familiar one used by my friends. I'm sure by the end of our journey we will be at least that. Come aboard, Kel. I should warn you, though, that there will be a fare for this berth. I am expecting payment in the form of a full re-vealing of the events that brought you to make planetfall on Macrobia. Spare me no details! Come."

Kel turned to the RI man before ascending. "Thanks for the lift. Can you get word to Wuhen that I'm on my way? The embassy military liaison and your people are probably going to expect a full debrief, and I'd rather get it out of the way as soon as possible so I can return to my previous mission."

Which was enjoying some downtime with my friends, he said to himself.

"I'm on it, Lieutenant. And, if I failed to say so, that was an amazing piece of work, even for a legionnaire."

Kel grunted and smiled as he extended his hand to Taylore. "Take care of yourself, Robert. I hope your next posting is a little less hectic."

"I'm always careful with my wishes. The way the galaxy is and doing what we do, this may be as good as it gets."

05

Kel followed one of the guards up the ramp, the other at Kel's back. As they entered the boarding deck, the consul general gestured into the cabin.

"I'm certain we can make you comfortable, Kel," he said. "As with many craft, this one was built with the human form in mind, but quite easily accommodates my species. My aide will show you to one of the staterooms. I insist you take your time to refresh yourself and then join me in the main lounge."

"This way, sir," an Ootari with a dark metallic green carapace said. Kel knew the Ootari colorations helped differentiate the sexes, and her significantly protuberant abdomen suggested she was female. Perhaps she was gravid? They passed through the main lounge on their way to the staterooms. The yacht's interior was as ostentatiously apportioned as the exterior gold finish would have led him to believe. Thick-cushioned furniture with ornately carved features and bright woven coverings lined the space. Works of art—painted, not holo—covered the bulkheads.

Kel thanked his guide and was soon left alone in the stateroom. The fresher had a sonic shower, and Kel didn't hesitate to shed his weapons and armor and step in. When he was done, he put his dirty silks in the shower and let them get a treatment before donning them again. He looked in the mirror. *I don't feel as tired as I look*, he thought, noting the fatigue in his face. He couldn't remember when he'd last eaten. He found his way back to the main lounge where the consul general awaited him.

"Please have a seat. The captain informs me we'll be lifting soon. You must be thirsty, yes? We have human rations for you once we're underway. They may not be gourmet, but I doubt they'll be the worst meal you've ever consumed. Am I correct in my assumption? That a legionnaire has been through greater discomforts?"

Kel was feeling at ease, though not ready to be disarmed by the courtesy he was being shown. "I'm grateful for your hospitality, Consul General Ranmark..."

"Please, it's Padlo. Any courtesy we can extend to you is a pleasure, I assure you."

This was his first personal experience with the Ootari. They had a reputation for being pugnacious. Maybe that was just the warrior caste. They also held a reputation for diplomacy. They lived in hive communities, which was assumed to be the soil from which their reputation for excellence in achieving cooperation had sprung. He also knew that the Ootari had a history of forcibly colonizing weaker worlds and displacing native species when it suited them.

"Please, Kel," the diplomat continued, "I am truly curious about how you came to be here. You have my full attention if you'll tell me your tale while our meals are prepared."

Kel had been thinking about the request—really, the warning—that his benefactor had given him by letting him know that he was expecting a full accounting of his actions against the corsairs. He knew that the consul general was likely a member of his government's intelligence service and would make a report of whatever they discussed. Anything Kel spoke of regarding his recent exploits could reveal Dark Ops' capabilities and techniques.

He chose an evasive tack. Clamming up wouldn't work. But acting the part of a friendly moron, one urbane politician to another, just might do. "I wouldn't dream of being so discourteous as to deny your request, Padlo." If the Ootari's strategy was to put Kel at a disadvantage by an abundant display of geniality, Kel would respond by being obsequious. "Of course, my talents don't include self-aggrandizement, so you'll have to take that into consideration during my description of the events."

I can be just as bombastic as this character, he decided.

His host's antennae twitched and chirped in what Kel guessed passed for a laugh. "Oh, I believe it would be more work to diminish your role in the incident. Please, I'm all tympanum," he said as he tilted his thorax at Kel with an auditory receptor prominently aimed at him.

"Well, it was really dumb luck. When the pirate vessel had us heaved-to, it seemed as though we were going to be in serious trouble." Kel continued to speak in non-concrete terms, providing no firm detail about his actions, making the events sound as though things had transpired naturally, and that the pirates' defeat was a result of their own ineptitude rather than by his intervention.

"I returned with the pirates to their ship to attempt a negotiation, and while engaged in a complex arbitration, their engineer appeared to say that their drive was going hypercritical. The plasma induction coils were apparently severely misaligned and in need of maintenance. No sooner had that been made more apparent than by the explosion.

"It was a coincidently advantageous situation, and one that I took advantage of when I contacted the *Callie's Dream* and told them to jump."

The diplomat turned its antennae down, pointing toward Kel. "So, you didn't storm the ship?"

Kel faked a self-deprecating laugh. "While that would make for a more dramatic story, the truth is, no."

"You make your part in it sound quite incidental, Kel."

Kel knew he had to spin a more interesting tale to achieve some plausibility with the Ootari. "Oh, I'll admit to some rough play on my part to gain the cooperation of the crew. They were miffed when they realized that the *Callie* had jumped during their moment of crisis. I had to kill the chief pirate and several of his heavies before they began to see things my way. Actually," he said quite truthfully, "the technical crew was very benign and even professional. They were motivated to return to the surface and saw the logic of my request."

Ranmark's antennae twitched for a moment in contemplation. "Well, I guess it's lucky that they allowed you to board their vessel armed, then?"

Was the Ootari taunting him with a potential flaw in his story?

"No. They had disarmed me." He did not finish his sentence.

Let him come up with mental scenarios to fit what I just told him.

The Ootari's antennae shot straight up. "You overcame the crew... while unarmed?"

Kel let the question hang in the air for a moment, then said, "I wasn't unarmed for long." He was tired of the evasive conversation and before his host could ask another question, decided to counterattack with his best tool: unbalancing his opponent by misdirection and distraction. "It really isn't that interesting a story. I would like to ask a favor of you, though, Padlo. The political upheaval on Macrobia is a fascinating case study to an amateur student of galactic politics like myself. I'm curious as to why the Ootari are the last major government to maintain a diplomatic posting on Macrobia."

Ranmark responded without hesitation. "My government is committed to diplomatic intercourse throughout the galaxy. If we can be of some use in returning Macrobia to peace, it is our duty to make the attempt."

Kel was anticipating the canned response.

"Very noble, truly," he said, raising the pouch of hydration fluid in a toast to the diplomat. His gesture was well received as the Ootari made a chitter and raised his own pouch in return.

"Thank you, Kel. Oh, our food has arrived." The shimmering green carapace of the assistant appeared from behind Kel carrying two trays. Kel leaned back to make way for the server to place the tray on the small table between him and his host.

"I'm sorry we don't have better fare to offer, but I hope it is to your liking."

Kel recognized the textured mass of calories in the dish in front of him as one of the reconstituted nutritional composites that were basic crew rations. Many of the smaller ships couldn't store large quantities of fresh food in stasis, and the rations were the mainstay of most if not all of the meals when underway. If he had to guess from its slightly green hue, it was probably "Nutritional Blend Number Three."

He didn't have to concoct a lie about the food in front of him. "I assure you, this meal is as welcome as any gourmet feast I've ever been invited to. Thank you." Kel prided himself on being able to ignore hunger for extended periods of time. After the past eighteen hours he'd experienced, his body was ready to eat. The rush of combat kept him fueled for hours, but even a highly conditioned and trained legionnaire had limits.

Kel waited for his host to start. A plate stacked with different shapes of plant material in different colors and fiber weaves sat in front of him. As Padlo lowered his jaw to the stacked leaves, Kel picked up his own utensil and dove into the food. His hand had a slight tremor as he moved a spoonful into his mouth, the hole in his stomach now painfully evident. Padlo remained focused on his own meal, giving Kel time to reequip himself both physically and mentally. He was still engaged in polite hostilities with the diplomat, and Kel was ready to attack.

"Of course, I've read about the Ootari experience on Markash Seven."

Ranmark's head raised from his plate and he stopped chewing.

Target lock acquired, Kel thought.

"I suppose, depending on how one defines peace, it could be considered a peaceful resolution."

Markash Seven was an edge world not particularly close to the Ootari sphere of influence. It was inhabited by a race of marsupial-like furbearers with a decent level of galactic-tech that allowed them travel and trade with neighboring worlds. The race had been ruled by a hereditary monarchy. A popular uprising against the ruling class developed a decade ago, accompanied by an insurgent movement and mass civil unrest. The Ootari were positioned to assist the Markash monarchy and in the absence of a Republic presence, the world soon became a client state of the Ootari.

Ample evidence suggested that the Ootari had assisted the Markash Seven monarchy in instituting a brutal campaign against its citizens with death camps and mass murder a cornerstone of the counterinsurgency effort. Now Markash was no longer a sovereign world but a virtual puppet of the Ootari. Though not a member of the Republic, the Markash were allowed representation in the Republic Senate, though not a voting member. Any conflict or issue that had the Ootari at its center could be guaranteed to have vocal advocates on the Senate floor from Markash.

Markash Seven had a wealth of natural resources and was in closest proximity to a dead star that held a ready source of naturally occurring neutronium, a powerfully dense material with potentially endless applications, including weaponry. RI deduced that the Ootari had both fomented and supported as well as ultimately quashed the uprising. All in all, it was an example of a fairly masterful play by the Ootari to insinuate and maintain control over a valuable but weaker world. Kel had studied the situation in his Operations and Intelligence course three years before and continued to follow developments, as he did on many worlds, anticipating the call to operate there.

"That's hardly similar to our presence on Macrobia!" Padlo blurted out. Kel had caught him off guard. Kel didn't allow him time to regain his balance.

"Or, Ashkadashi. It's a fascinating case study from the perspective that the extermination of the ethnic minority on the southern continent accompanied the expansion of the Ootari colony there."

The diplomat gasped. "That is neither a fair nor unbiased representation of events."

Kel half-listened as he continued his meal while Ranmark gave a lengthy discourse on events on both planets. He nodded and smiled where appropriate and feigned enlightenment frequently, wondering if his theatrical facial expressions were correctly interpreted by his host.

No matter, Kel thought. *I've got him on the run. He's explaining and rationalizing rather than probing me. Mission accomplished.* He'd been right that the diplomat's pride and level of education would mandate Padlo's detailed response, distracting him away from Kel's actions on the pirate xebec.

After an hour of one-sided conversation, Kel surrendered, hands raised. "I must say, I think I've had a rather myopic view of these events. I'm truly grateful for your perspective. It has given me quite a lot to consider. You know, it's so easy to be xeno-centric in this galaxy, despite its great diversity. To make the acquaintance of a being of your experience and insight has been a wonderful and unexpected conclusion to my detour." Kel made a show of checking his chrono. "Would you think me terribly rude to beg your pardon? It's been some time since I've slept, and I don't think I can carry on."

Without waiting for permission, he stood.

"Of course, Lieutenant." The diplomat returned to a formal address but remained seated. "I understand. Please rest well, and we'll inform you on arrival to the orbit of Wuhen."

Kel bowed and turned to depart. He noticed that one of the large Ootari guards had been seated in a small alcove behind Kel the entire time. He was not surprised. He entered his cabin and began assessing. His armor lay seemingly undisturbed, as did his weapons, but he could tell they'd been touched. He suspected that someone had tried to examine them but wasn't too concerned. Any attempt at intrusion into the systems would've been shut down without his bio-signature.

He donned his armor, pulled down the small cot from the wall, and propped himself against the bulkhead facing the cabin door with his carbine across his lap. He'd slapped a small proximity sensor on the door and activated it. The sensor would send him an annoying tone in his bucket if there was movement outside the cabin door. He wasn't expecting an assault while a guest of the Ootari, but it never hurt to be professionally paranoid. He had a special someone he'd like to see again. Hopefully soon.

Kel hadn't lied about his exhaustion. He was spent. He closed his eyes and, before he knew it, began a light, dreamless sleep.

As Kel stepped down from the golden yacht onto the sunny duracrete, he saw two well-dressed humans waiting at the bottom of the ramp. Embassy personnel, most likely. A limousine sat near, where two more large Ootari guards stood to receive the consul general who descended in front of Kel. He tightened the sling of his carbine, now strapped to his back, and followed.

The Ootari entered the vehicle and closed the door. A moment later the window went down. Ranmark addressed the humans from his seat. "I have your wayward son to return to you, friends. I hope our assistance is yet further proof of the Ootari affection toward the Republic of which we are members."

The middle-aged woman gave a tight-lipped smile. "We are most grateful, Consul General, and I look forward to sharing the news of our joint cooperation with the ambassador."

The Ootari glanced at Kel. "Lieutenant." He dismissed the legionnaire with a bow and his limousine floated away.

"What, no limo for me?" Kel asked. He was feeling rather high-spirited after his nap.

The woman sighed. "No, Lieutenant. Not today. I'm Kaarla D'lanadan, the senior consular officer. I'll be assisting you while on Wuhen. This is..."

Her companion stuck out his hand. "I'm Major Rylee Scott, Republic Army Intelligence Agency. I have some folks waiting for us at the embassy ready to ask you some questions."

Good. Kel was ready to get his after-action report done. Apparently, Robert Taylore had gotten a hyper-comm message off to Wuhen, which at the close distance between the worlds would have easily beaten their jump time.

"I'm ready. Let's go." Kel walked with the two off the duracrete toward the nearest building. He looked around at the parked craft, straining to see the *Callie*. She was a massive ship, but the surrounding hangars blocked his view.

"Looking for something?" the woman asked as they neared the pedestrian portal into the nearest building.

"Yes, I have some friends..."

The major stood aside at the automated door as a rush of bodies spilled through. Kel found himself suddenly in

Tara's arms, surrounded by the rest of the Yomiuri clan. He returned her hug as best he could without crushing her and quickly removed his bucket and clipped it to his waist before returning the hugs of the rest of the family.

"Oh, thank Oba! You have no idea how worried we were," Jim exclaimed.

Kel laughed as he tried to pull in everybody in the family in one embrace and assure them all that he was fine.

In fact, I've never felt better!

"They told us we couldn't talk about anything and made us sign some agreement," Tara said in his ear. Kel looked over at the major, who had been close enough to hear, and was nodding.

"Everyone on the *Callie*'s crew had to put a bio-signature to the Republic Espionage Act," the man confirmed. "Let's talk once we're on our way," he said, trying to usher the crowd back through the doors and into the shade of the building. "Lieutenant Turner will go back with you as soon as he can. Right now, he has some work to do."

Kel heard the dissent start.

"Auntie Meiko has a big meal prepared," Ochio Yomiuri complained. "We can't disappoint her!"

There was a general rumble of similar protests.

The major looked to Kel to intervene.

"Family," he said, addressing them all that way for the first time. "I promise I'll be with you as soon as I can. This is actually pretty important. The sooner I finish with them, the sooner we can be on our way again." Everyone looked disappointed, especially Tara. "What berth is the *Callie* in? They'll bring me straight to you. Promise."

Ms. D'lanadan spoke. "That's correct. I'll personally make sure the lieutenant is returned to you as soon as possible. You have my word," she said, trying to assuage the gathering.

"*Lieutenant*?" Tara asked him, eyebrows raised.

Cat's out of the bag, now!

Kel shrugged. "If you've signed the Espionage Act, I suppose we can talk about it later."

Tara shook her head as if tasting something sour and then chuckled. "Okay, then. I guess I'll have time to think of some questions." She stood on her tiptoes and planted a kiss on his cheek. Kel blushed. It was the first time she had shown affection to him publicly. He looked sheepishly behind Tara to her mother, Caroline, to see her grin back at him.

"If you need us, just bounce us," Jim Yomiuri said as he pulled Tara away. "We'll come get you anytime."

Kel followed the two embassy officials through another side door and into a garage where a speeder awaited. Kel got into the back, the pax door closed, and they floated off. He felt a little disoriented and giddy from the attention, like some kind of holo-celeb.

The consular officer clucked. "That's quite a family you have there. I've spent the day with them. They created a virtual riot getting into the embassy to report your disappearance. They were yelling for Republic Intelligence and carrying on about secret missions and a one-man killing machine saving them from pirates."

"Oh, boy." Kel winced. While he couldn't think of a different series of actions he could've taken, the attention he'd drawn to himself was an unwanted byproduct of the situation. "I'll take care of it," he tried to assure them. "I've never seen Auntie Meiko upset, though. I hope she understands why I'm late to dinner."

"The incident is contained and there's been no media attention, so it's no matter to the embassy," D'lanadan assured him. "I don't know about to your people, though. And by that I *don't* mean your family."

Kel dismissed her suggestion with a shrug. He thought about what Bigg, Braley, and even the colonel would say when they heard.

"It's what's expected of me."

It turned out that "as quick as possible" meant two days. After several hours of initial debrief in a secure room by Major Scott and another officer—a colonel from Army Intelligence—several Ex-Planetary diplomatic officers, and a representative from Republic Intelligence introduced to him only as "Mister Smith," he was dismissed with a summons to return in the morning. True to her word, Ms. D'lanadan had a driver deliver Kel to the *Callie* just as the sun was setting.

Kel apologized to Auntie Meiko for being late only to receive a tearful smile and a hug. The whole family sat with him in the main galley as he ate, the children taking turns sitting on Kel's lap. Later in the family's quarters, they sat and sipped kaff together as Kel tried to answer their questions. Jim and Caroline, their children Ochio and Tara, and the first officer Caroline's brother Eric, sat gathered in a circle, no one exactly sure how to begin.

"How much can you talk about yourself, Kel?" Caroline was the first to ask. "We don't want to get you in trouble, but we can't help but be curious. Does that make sense?"

A bobble of heads all around reminded Kel of puppy tails wagging in a pet shop window.

"I do understand, and what you're saying is very reasonable, given what you've seen of me lately," Kel admitted.

"Kel, we watched from the bridge," Eric said. "We saw everything, from how you fought those lizards to how you jumped to their ship and then destroyed it. We saw the ship explode as we jumped."

"What we saw was nothing short of incredible," said Jim. "It was like... some kind of holo-drama." He paused. "How was all that even possible?"

Kel knew he needed to explain.

"When you first met me, I was on a mission and working under an assumed name."

"Yes, we all understood that part. And it wasn't important to us then, and it's not important to us now," Tara interjected. "We know *who* you are. That's all that counts."

"You're a legionnaire, aren't you?" Jim blurted out. "The armor. I've seen it on news holos and in documentaries. But it's different. More, I don't know, deadly-looking."

Kel nodded his head. "Yes. I'm a legionnaire."

"But there's more to it than that, isn't there?" Ochio asked.

Kel nodded. "I'm in a special branch of the Legion that does... special things."

Tara looked concerned. "Are you always by yourself?"

This made Kel laugh.

"No. I work with a team of some very good people, so, no, I'm not *always* alone." He imagined introducing Poul and Sims to the Yomiuris. Poul would be playing acrobatic games with the children, and Sims would have Auntie Meiko laughing as he insisted on helping her in the galley.

They'd fit right in and have the family caring about them in no time, too. "But many of my missions I am by myself."

"Are you on a mission now?" Jim asked.

"No," Kel answered emphatically. "My only mission was to see you all and to... to reconnect." He suddenly had a hard time expressing his feelings. He knew he loved the Yomiuris, but it was not something he was able to say out loud.

"Kel," Caroline asked. "When you came to us, you were very upset. I asked you then if everything was all right. You've seemed very happy these last few weeks. I'll ask you again. Is everything all right?"

Now Kel smiled. He'd had an emotional reunion with the family and knew he'd appeared a bit brittle at first. It hadn't taken him long to accept the fact his last few operations had stressed him, and he been in denial about the toll it had taken. He'd seen it in others. Never in himself. He was realizing that he was not as hard as the armor he wore.

"I'm great, Caroline. I feel the best I can ever remember feeling. My command decided that I needed some time off, and the only people in the galaxy I wanted to be with were you."

Everyone smiled.

"Since we first met, there've been some tough times. But now, I feel more upbeat about things than ever." Kel had to admit that he'd been resistant to the idea of being forcibly put on leave. Now, he knew it was a wise move. He'd needed this break. He hoped the rest of the team was faring as well as he was.

"But then, this happens," Tara said. "You got put right back into combat. That wasn't very fair of us to do that to you." She had anger in her voice and glowered at her parents. They sat silent and shrunken, studying the ground.

"Hey, none of that!" Kel said. Everyone's eyes shot to him. "Sometimes, things just happen. Even the most aware and prepared person can be a victim. No one leads a blameless life."

Kel truly believed that to be the case. He sometimes perseverated about his own mistakes, even though he knew it was an unhealthy habit.

The captain let it out a huge breath. "Well, I can assure you that we've had a lot of discussions about this incident and the decisions that led up to it." Jim looked at Kel. "As the head of this family as well as also being the captain of the *Callie*, I've already apologized to everyone for my poor judgment in this incident, and I'm apologizing to you, Kel. Once again you put yourself in harm's way to save us from—"

"There's no need." Kel stood and moved to shake Jim's hand. The captain stood and took Kel's hand. "On a team, we always forgive each other. We're there to guard each other's backs. The team's like a family. There's no need to say more. It's only important that we learn from our errors and try to do better next time."

Kel was pulled into a warm family hug. Everyone in the Yomiuri family constantly showed signs of affection for each other. Especially between the parents and the kids, but also between the adults. They hugged each other as a greeting in the morning and whenever parting. He grew up with lots of hugs from his mom, but wasn't necessarily accustomed to such frequent signs of affection between adults. Now he found he liked it.

Tara moved closest to Kel and put both arms around him. "I like it when you say we're your family."

Seated again, Eric visited everyone's cup with more kaff from an ornately curved sapphire crystal pot. Little touches of beauty like that made the *Callie* more than just a ship, but a home for the family.

"So, you're a lieutenant?" Ochio asked.

Kel grinned. "Yup. That's actually a new development. I just got promoted before I went on leave. I'm not even used to the idea yet. Of course, in my job, the title doesn't really change anything about what I do. In most branches of the military, even the Legion, an LT is a junior leader, responsible for leading forty or fifty troops. I'm rarely ever responsible for anyone but myself."

"Well, you didn't get to be an officer without doing something pretty distinguishing. I know that much," Eric said, clearly baiting him for more of an explanation.

Kel shrugged. "Oh, it wasn't any one thing. I took the promotion at my commander's recommendation. A way to help my unit. It's a kind of a small organization, and they need people of higher ranks who are already familiar with the way we do things. Getting promoted from within is not that uncommon." At least, that's how he felt about it. Kel wanted to change the subject. "What's next?"

Everyone looked to Jim.

"Once they're through with you, we'll lift. I have a couple of potential contracts in the works and should know something by tomorrow. Will the officials be done with you by then?"

Kel sighed. "If I can finish my written report and go through their last round of questions, I'm pretty sure I can finish by tomorrow." He checked his chrono. "They want me back in the morning. If I can finish up tonight, maybe I can speed things along and be done with them early." He knew that was wishful thinking.

"I have a question for you, though," Kel said. "Do you think it's possible that I could get enough experience to test for my Spacer's Certificate while I'm with the *Callie*?"

Ochio was the first to respond. "Heck yes! Dad, Kel's been standing assistant watch with us since he's been on board and is picking up everything about the job. There's no reason he couldn't smash the exam with a little more experience and some study."

"Very true," Eric said. "In another month, I'd be confident that you'll have enough hours and knowledge to earn a rating."

Kel smiled. "I'd like to be able to stand a full watch and pitch in a little more around here."

Caroline laughed. "Sweetheart, I don't think anyone would ever accuse you of not pulling your weight on the *Callie*."

06

"I'm losing my grip," Kel said, panicking. He feared disappointing his dad more than he feared the jagged rocks below. The crashing waves were near deafening where they'd started the climb. His dad dropped Kel off at the inlet with the gear then anchored and swam to the rocky ledge, their empty boat gracefully riding the swells in the center of the cove to await their return. It would be a difficult swim back after the return climb down. But that was later. Now, halfway up the cliff face, the crashes were still loud enough to drown out any words not shouted.

"You're doing fine. Don't crowd the wall," his dad yelled back from the narrow ledge where he belayed Kel. "Trust your equipment." His dad didn't let him use autoascenders. It was all pitons and ropes. Cramping fingers and toes. Scraped and bleeding elbows and knees.

"Remember, son. You have to trust yourself. You're stronger than you know."

Kel was daydreaming when he should be focusing on his work. He stared at the words floating over the small desk in his stateroom.

If he concentrated, he could finish the rest of the report in an hour and be done with the damn thing. It was an abbreviated recounting of the same things they already had on holo of today's interviews. And he had no obligation to go into operational or technical details about how he achieved his outcomes. After a brief preamble on the situation, he filled his report with some of the same bullet points he had used when discussing his actions with the debriefers.

- *Neutralized Macrobian boarding party with small arms.*
- *Disabled offensive weapons.*
- *Gained access to hostile vessel in micro gravity.*
- *Seized ship and neutralized opposing force command element.*

He gave a more detailed intelligence summary of what he'd learned from the Macrobians, their intentions, as well as some of the anthropologic details he'd picked up talking with the engineer, Shakaan. He did the same regarding his interaction with the Ootari diplomat and his attempt to interrogate him.

It would suffice. He closed his link.

He again heard the waves on the cliffs. Smelled the salt in the air. His dad's reserved smile for him when they finished their swim back to the boat.

What brought that to mind? he wondered, still a little lost in the memory. It was a deep recollection. One he hadn't thought about in a very long time. It had been an important day. There'd been many days since then when he'd had to trust himself, but he supposed that was the day he'd first learned when doubt entered, it needed to be quelled.

He stared at the dark ceiling and tried to shut off his brain. His mind was active with thoughts of his next challenge: learning to be a spacer. He loved everything about charting routes through space, like he once did with his dad in their small boat. Of course, it wouldn't be anything near as basic, and he knew he wouldn't be learning those secrets just yet. Still, if he could stand a watch, it would make him feel better about his time on the ship. He wanted to be more than a passenger. It was important to him to be seen as competent, not only in his own eyes, but in those of the Yomiuris.

He drifted off thinking about the boy he once was. The one with the shaky arms.

It wasn't long before Kel was back in the secure room deep within the embassy with the same group of officials he had been questioned by the day before. He came in civilian dress and carried only his pistol, which he'd surrendered to the Marine security guard on entry. Though only the ambassador could order him disarmed on Republic property, Kel didn't feel like making the effort to protest, and went along with the security protocol to make things easy.

After a brief review of the events by Major Scott, to which Kel asserted agreement as they were presented, very few questions came up. Everyone looked at their pads, skimming the report Kel had bounced them.

Consular officer D'lanadan looked up. "I think we're done here. I briefed the department heads and the ambassador's chief of staff. There is one small thing, though. Could you please encourage your friends to distance themselves from the Galactic Hugs organization?"

Kel smiled. "I believe they've already come to that realization without needing to be asked."

She smiled back. "Thank goodness for small favors. While the Ex-Planetary Service and the Republic have a very neutral stance on nongovernmental aid organizations, the ambassador has a particularly negative view of some of their activities on Macrobia. They've endangered a lot of people and may even be working against our policies to isolate and punish Macrobia for their wantonly unlawful acts."

"Besides which," the quiet colonel added, "they're idiots."

Everyone laughed. Everyone except for the man at the other end of the table. Mr. Smith, wearing a dark, featureless suit. He stared at Kell and said, "What I want to know is where do you get the authority to act in the manner you did?"

Kel took a breath and forced himself to remain calm. "Excuse me?"

"You heard me. Under whose authority did you think that you could carry out a warlike act without express orders?"

What a grossly ridiculous question. The Republic Intelligence officer had to know the score. Kel couldn't figure out what the man's angle was. Was he trying to get Kel to admit to something? Kel was eager to spell it out for him.

"My actions are within Republic law covering the right to self-defense, specifically those regarding criminal acts in neutral space and specifically piracy by non-state actors. Whether acting as an agent of the Republic or as a private citizen, those rights are maintained."

Last night Kel had refreshed himself on the law governing his use of force to resolve the situation. He'd received lengthy training in the legal basis for his special authority as a Dark Ops member, but it was always best to be able to shut down questions of legality by knowing the law better than your accusers.

"Regardless, my mandate as a member of Silver covers my authority to act in this particular situation, and more. But you already know that." Silver was the cover name for Dark Ops, used when the unit had to be discussed confidentially. The unit was never referred to as Dark Ops when talking to outsiders. Except in special circumstances like this, it was never referred to at all. "You've already been contacted by the people who've confirmed my identity and what my mandate covers. Even so, none of that is necessary to justify my actions."

Kel looked at the man dispassionately. "Are we through?"

He had the sour-faced man dead to rights. The RI officer already knew he had no authority over Kel.

Major Scott received a nod from the colonel and smiled at Kel. "Lieutenant, I think that will be all for today. We may have some more questions later."

Kel stood. He was not about to tell the people in the room that he had no intention of being on Wuhen tomorrow. He did not need to ask their permission to leave and had been more than accommodating. He knew he would receive the full support of his command if any further questions about his actions were raised.

"A final word," Smith said from his seat as Kel turned to leave. "The Legion doesn't make policy. You don't get to run around the galaxy acting like knights."

The man's attitude was exasperating. It would have been easier to simply walk away, but Kel let himself be goaded into a reply.

"No. We don't make policy. But we do follow orders. I have a duty to act, even when sometimes I would prefer not to. And were it you kidnapped by Macrobian pirates, you'd find me there to pull you out. Even if I didn't want to."

Callie's hold was nearly full. They'd already offloaded the cargo previously intended for Macrobia and parked it in a warehouse on the south end of the spacefield where the charity organization could renew their effort to get the goods delivered to the beleaguered reptasaurs. When a Galactic Hugs representative attempted to reclaim the delivery fee, Caroline had shut him down.

"The *Callie* is indemnified against the loss of the cargo or the failure to make delivery due to acts of piracy. The act of piracy and the fact that we were boarded while on contract to you—following the course and rendezvous instructions stipulated by the contract—further indemnifies us from responsibility for the cargo.

"That we are returning the cargo to you is actually a good faith act not stipulated by the contract. We could have dumped the load in orbit. But reclaim our fee? You specifically declined cargo insurance and signed an R-verified bill of lading agreeing to our rules tariff. You don't have a leg to stand on. Try it. We have a keen legal representative who would take a great deal of pleasure in exposing your fecklessness before the Spacers Union."

Kel hadn't been there to witness the exchange but heard her retelling of it over lunch in the wardroom. He gladly broke his self-imposed midday fast when he saw that Auntie Meiko was making tall sandwiches stacked with some kind of thinly sliced animal protein topped with thicker cuts of a local cheese. It was his way of celebrating after recovering his pistol and escaping the embassy complex, knowing that he was seeing it for the last time.

"The guy was a worm," the *Callie*'s engineer Yoshi Yomiuri said. "He tried to guilt us into returning the fee as a charitable donation. Caroline was having none of it."

She shook her head. "Just when I think I've met every kind of fool you could meet anywhere in the spiral arms, I meet one worse than I ever imagined. Trying to turn our business's success into a reason to feel guilty, then to try to exploit that further, after we almost lost everything... well, it really lets me see those people for the self-serving asses that they are. I don't know how I could have been so foolish."

Uncle Yoshi put his hand over Caroline's. "It wasn't just you, kid. We all let those hacks guilt us into feeling like it was our obligation to risk our ship for the good of downtrodden species everywhere. Would they have dropped that ploy of theirs if we'd successfully completed that contract? After we were done with the Macrobian pirates, who would it have been next—bloodthirsty zhee or Savage cannibals? Galactic Hugs, indeed. Next time I see one of their ads, it's going to be all I can do to keep from smashing the emitter."

"Lesson learned," Kel added. "But there will be other opportunities to do good things. There always are."

Yoshi shook his head at Kel. "How does a kid like you get to be so wise? Do they teach you that in secret-spy camp or something?"

Caroline punched Yoshi in the shoulder.

"Hey, just kidding, all right?" the older man said sheepishly.

Kel laughed. "It's all right. I can take it." He dug into the last of his sandwich and picked up one of the pickled vegetables. It was slightly sour, but somehow complemented the sandwich perfectly.

"You like daikon?" Yoshi asked. "Have you ever had it before?"

"I do like it," Kel agreed. "My mom made food a little blander. She was from Muerian's World. I grew up eating a lot of seafood on Pthalo, but I've developed a taste for all kinds of cuisine." He was also aware he hadn't worked out in several days. That would change immediately.

"Pthalo, huh?" Yoshi asked. "Never been there, but I've heard it's quite the paradise."

"*We* weren't rich, I can assure you of that," Kel quickly said. "My dad worked as a mechanic repairing vehicles for a commercial service fleet. We weren't galactic trillionaires."

Yoshi chuckled. "They couldn't afford bots on Pthalo?"

Kel wiped his mouth. "There's a sense of luxury that's derived from doing the opposite. Why use a bot when you can afford actual humanoids to do the tasks?"

"So, more of the enigma that is Kel is revealed," Caroline kidded him. "Well, Meiko picked up some local stores, and I'm sure we're in for some treats for our trip out. Speaking of, I have work to do." She smiled at Kel and took her plate into the galley next door, leaving him alone with Yoshi. After a moment, Yoshi broke the silence. The older man was never particularly verbose around Kel but was always warm and friendly.

"Kel, the senior crew and I have been discussing your education as a spacer."

Kel perked up. "That's great. Is there a plan?"

The engineer nodded. "Tan and Ochio agree that you understand the basics of hold and cargo operations."

Kel had been trained in palletizing and loading from his earliest days in the Legion. As a jumpmaster, he had rigged many loads for space travel as well as for the more difficult task of dropping loads from craft into atmospheric and sub-orbital descent. What occurred in the hold of a huge cargo vessel like the *Callie* simply occurred on a much larger scale than what he was accustomed to.

"Learning how operations work on a ship like the *Callie* is a little different from how a Navy spacer might learn things. Whereas someone like yourself could certainly learn to be a flight deck officer without mastering any of the more basic tasks like what a deckhand or spacer needs to know, it's not how we do things on this ship.

"And while it's maybe more than what you would need to know to pass the first level of Spacer qualifications, there are a lot of tasks that you need to be competent in to be qualified to stand watch on the *Callie*. As opposed to the navy or a big commercial liner, which hires a lot of ex-Navy types, a crewmember on a ship like ours has to be multi-rated and trained. We're a small family crew. Everyone needs to be competent in as many specialties as possible."

Kel had assumed that must be the case. A navy ship the size of the *Callie* would easily have a crew two or three times as large as the Yomiuris' to perform its same functions.

"You already possess enough experience and knowledge so that with a little study, you could easily pass the Spacer exam for a third-class ticket to ride as a deckhand on a freighter. Your knowledge of EVA easily surpasses my own, and I've been a first-class engineer for more than thirty years. But that's not a skill you'll need for any of your Spacer quals.

"The first set of Spacer qualification exams test knowledge of safety procedures and shipboard operations. You clearly are a master of micro-gravity and vacuum operations, so there's going to be little we need to teach you about that. Operations like disaster response, you may not need much training in, either."

Kel nodded. Fire suppression, fixing hull breaches, isolating vented compartments or making them atmosphere worthy again, were all skills he possessed. He could create all those conditions and fix them. It was one of the advantages of studying how to destroy things; first you studied how things were built and what their weaknesses were. Then you learned the fun stuff—making things go boom.

"But to stand an independent watch on our ship, you're going to need to understand the systems and controls that operate the ship. The goal is not to turn you into an engineer or flight deck officer just yet, but you have to be conversant in the mechanisms of the ship. When you stand watch in engineering or on the command deck, everyone's lives are in your hands."

Kel understood perfectly. He felt excitement as he contemplated the number of new things he would be learning, things he'd always been curious about. It was a great opportunity.

"So, you're going to be spending the next two weeks with me in engineering during main shift, then taking an assistant watch every night with a rated crew member. You're going to be busy, young spacer, too busy studying to be playing kissy-face with my nephew's daughter."

Kel felt himself flush and opened his mouth to protest his innocence.

Yoshi laughed at his discomfort. "There, there, it's all right," he said. "You may not believe it, but I was young once, too. I know what raging hormones can do." He rose and grabbed his plate. "Come on, let's say bye to Meiko and get to work."

Kel stood and picked his dishes up off the table, unsure what to say.

Yoshi grimaced and leaned in to whisper, "Between us, it's not you I'm worried about."

"There are two main watch stations," Yoshi said as they walked to engineering. "One on the command deck and one in engineering. *When* we have an officer of the deck on watch in those two locations depends on the ship's status."

They left the habitation section that was the forward part of the ship, bypassing the waist deck section and descending by the central companionway to the bottom deck, and took the circuitous route aft toward engineering.

"When we're in jump space, there's no need to have someone in engineering full-time every shift. We're either FTL in jump space, or we're not."

"Yoshi, can you really be stuck in jump space?" It was one of the "what if" kind of things young legionnaires talked about when underway.

"What do you think? You've been to the ends of the galaxy in the Legion, right? You done some mission that says so?"

"I've never heard of it happening," Kel admitted. "But, you see it in holos and hear it from old spacers."

Yoshi grinned. "Theoretically? Maybe. Did it ever happen in the history of FTL development so many centuries ago? Who really knows? Like you said, it's the stuff of ho-los. If the drive failed, we'd simply dump into real space. Like I said, you're either FTL in jump space, or you're not. The jump drive can't fail from a criticality that would keep you in jump space. If it does fails, you just leave folded space wherever you are. Of course, you're not moving along a linear path, so where you come out might be far-ther away from your destination than where you started."

Kel had always wondered about the basis for that fear. He remembered a holo drama about spacers trapped in the void of jump space after their drive malfunctioned, slowly going mad before murdering each other. His own research had led him to believe it was fanciful non-sense—a fun scenario to ponder, but not a realistic fear. There was no substitute for getting to talk to a real expert like Yoshi, though. He had a feeling he was going to get an opportunity to ask a lot of curiosity-satisfying questions in the next two weeks.

"So, when we're in FTL space, watch is conducted from just the command deck. Environmental systems as well as engineering and navigation can all be monitored from there. When we are in-system stuck on hold in orbit and under repulsor drive, someone needs to be in engi-neering at all times."

On the lowest deck, Yoshi paused outside of the en-gineering hatch. "We generally aren't in an orbit for long, or if we are, we take a geostationary position until it's our turn to get into a descent corridor. I tend to stay in en-gineering full-time during those cycles. If we lose pow-er or have any issue, that's when having a human pres-ence monitoring our engines would make a difference. Sitting in a holding station awaiting a berth in one of the major hubs like Orion Station, it's also not critical to have someone in engineering full-time. The amount of power needed for the engines to maintain a stationary position in space doesn't require much monitoring.

"But there's still a person standing watch in engineering to assist me if needed. And if I do need a break, someone trained is there monitoring all systems."

Kel assumed that's why his and Meiko's quarters were nearest the central companionway, giving the engineer the shortest path to his engines in an emergency, and said as much.

"Nah. Our quarters are the roomiest, that's why." Yoshi put his hands on his midsection. "You may not have noticed, but I like my wife's cooking and get plenty of it! A little extra living room is necessary."

They both laughed. Kel dismissed Yoshi's self-deprecation. The man everyone called Uncle could not be considered fat in any way and he, like Kel, rarely ate lunch. At one time, all the adults on the *Callie* eschewed three full meals a day as a way of cutting costs on their slim margins. It was still a habit with some, but was no longer a necessity because of their budget.

Kel followed Yoshi through the hatch to see the teenaged Cam Yomiuri, Tan and Aggie's son, at one of the workstations, a datapad open next to him as he compared readings from the monitors in front of him to the pad. He looked over his shoulder as they entered.

"Hi, Uncle! Hi, Kel. Uncle Yoshi?" the young man said. "I've been running a test on the coils per the checklist. They're all showing alignment to within measurable limitations, less than a hundred-thousandth variation, but number three still seems to be the only one not *exactly* in synch with the rest."

Yoshi moved over to the console and reviewed the young man's findings. "Right you are, Cam. It's a good observation. But more than being aware that the measurement exists, you have to give it some significance. Did you compare the measurements to the log?"

The young man nodded. "Sure did. Before we spun up for our last liftoff, that variance wasn't there."

Now Yoshi smiled. "Very good. Did you compare it to the pre-lift check before that?"

"No, sir."

"Take a look. What's it showing?"

Cam swiped across his pad and when he found what he wanted, froze to read the data. "Hmm. It's almost exactly like what I recorded now, but in the positive instead of the negative direction, and for two of the coils beside number three." He frowned.

"The answer, my young engineer" Yoshi said, holding a professorial finger in the air, "was contained in your previous statement, 'within measurable limitations.' At such small harmonic frequencies, measurements to within greater than a hundred-thousandth are not significant. That so many of the coils are *exactly* the same frequency with each other is more of a statistical coincidence than it is a measure of the excellent condition of our engines. Don't get me wrong; I'm happy to see such perfect alignment. But I can tell you that any engineer seeing such close alignment beyond the limit of measurement would be ecstatic and would brag about his mastery of jump coil alignment. While it's great to notice such things, know what's significant and what's minutiae."

"Isn't it a ship engineer's job to worry about the minutiae?" Cam asked earnestly.

Yoshi laughed. "Yes. And what you're here to learn is *which* minutiae are actually important. Now run along and help your folks with the rest of the loading so we can lift. Hey!" The young man turned back. "You're not too big to give me a hug, spacer."

Cam moved back to let Yoshi give him a bear hug, then rub his hair before sending him off. "Thanks for spelling me so I could eat. Go do the same before reporting to the cargo hold."

"Of course, Uncle." Cam waved at Kel before he took off through the open hatch.

"He's got a real interest in engineering," Yoshi said, admiration in his eyes. "It'll be hard to not lose him to the Navy or to one of the engineering academies in a few years. If he does, maybe he'll eventually find his way back to the family business. That's the thing about being young. Endless possibilities."

Kel stayed in engineering during the lift and until the *Callie* slipped into FTL, watching Yoshi and listening in rapt attention as he described the processes during breaks between communication with Jim on the command deck. It was the same kind of teaching method Kel used, explaining what he did, paid attention to, ignored, anticipated.

Once well underway, Yoshi took out a datapad and bounced a document to Kel. "Start reading. *Kazamov's* is the Rosetta Stone of space engineering. A lot of the math may be too much for you. Don't worry about it. It does a great job of giving the big picture, then the principles behind it, and then the math behind them. Don't get bogged down in the nuts and bolts.

"You'll spend each main shift with me here, then another four-hour shift pulling a training watch with another member of the crew. As I said, we don't usually run an engineering watch under jump drive, but it's to get you familiarized with procedures."

Kel opened the document in front of him and started scanning. Each chapter started with a summary in plain Standard. Then a large section followed with detailed descriptions peppered with a lot of technical terms unfamiliar to him. Finally, each chapter concluded with pages and pages of squiggly characters, letters, and numbers that he knew were complex mathematics but might as well have been an alien language to him. For the first time in a long time, he felt overwhelmed. He looked up to see Yoshi smiling at his perplexity.

"Put that down and let's go." Yoshi picked up a toolbox. "Now that the lift drive is off, you can help with some regular maintenance tasks. Plenty of time for reading in your bunk."

Kel stowed the pad and followed the engineer into an access tunnel.

"Welcome to the big time, kid."

Kel only saw Tara during morning and evening meals, and again when she made short visits to engineering to check on him.

"Dad told me I couldn't be a watch supervisor for you," she told him on his first training watch. "He's afraid I'm going to be a distraction from your learning. I told him that's nonsense, but he insisted. He is the captain, after all. Even if he's my dad."

"It's okay, Tara. To tell you the truth, I'm so in over my head right now, I feel like I'm drowning. How much of this am I supposed to understand?" he said, showing her the section he was reading on cold plasma ignitors.

"Well, everything you can retain will come in handy at some point, but no one can understand it all in a week, or even a year. We all grow up with this as part of our basic education. It's the stuff of dinner conversation and even some of our family games. I promise you most of this will not even be on your Spacer exams. You won't get grilled on this stuff until you get into the engineer's mate qualifications."

Kel sighed with relief. "Tara, I have to tell you. I only had a basic education before I joined the Legion. Virtually everything I know is because I learned it in the Legion. Some of this math is gibberish to me. Actually, all of it is gibberish to me."

"I could stop by after your shift and go over some of it with you."

Her Uncle Tan was at the main engineering console and swiveled in his chair to face her. "Git now, young lady. My apprentice spacer has duties to perform. Scram."

Tara frowned and stuck her tongue out at him. "I'm going. I'll see you later then, Kel." When her uncle turned his back, Tara blew him a kiss before leaving. Kel grinned at her. After she left, Tan swiveled back to face him.

"You're snared, buddy. Trust me. I've spent my whole life around Yomiuri women. If you want away from my niece, you're going to have to pull another stunt like jumping ship to do it."

Every day, Kel got up before first shift and went to the cargo deck for physical training, then fit in smaller exercises wherever he could throughout his busy schedule. After finishing his watch, he returned to his bunk to study until he couldn't stay awake, then started the whole process the next day.

Some evenings after his four-hour training watch, he would be invited to Jim and Caroline's family quarters or to one of the other family cabins for some socializing. He never stayed long, begging off that he had to study. One morning he walked into the wardroom for kaff and a quick bite, still aching from his workout, when he overheard Eric and Yoshi having a conversation.

"He's really taking this seriously. I guess I shouldn't be surprised," he heard Yoshi say.

"Do you think he'll be ready for the third-class Spacer exam in a few weeks?" Eric asked.

"Heck, I wouldn't be surprised if he could sit for his first-class exam now. We could get him his first-class ride once he gets enough hours logged."

Kel held back. He wasn't above feeling pride at the compliment. He'd started to feel more like one of the crew and actually useful, instead of just a passenger taking up air on the ship.

Someday soon I'm going to have to stop playing and go back home, he realized. He wasn't sure how he felt about that. He still had almost two more months with the Yomiuris. For now, that was enough.

"We'll drop out of FTL this shift," Yoshi told Kel. "That's when the real work will start."

Kel sat with Uncle Yoshi looking at the main console. Uncle pointed at an astronav display. "We'll be stuck waiting for a berth. Kaylan is a pretty busy place. Could be a day or more. Hope you got plenty of sleep last night because you're on engineering duty with me until we land."

The insertion from FTL was smooth. Yoshi showed Kel what stations and monitors had to be attended and made everything seem simple and logical. He'd started to comprehend a lot of the operations necessary to monitor the different drives and what was normal during different phases of operation, and even the basis of the physics behind it all. This was technology he'd taken for granted his whole life. Now that he understood how it worked, it was a new world to him.

They had the ship's comm running in the background, listening to communications between the command deck and the ground controller. Kel was about to ask a question when Yoshi raised a hand. Kel heard it too. There was a long delay between Jim's outgoing transmission and the response from the spaceport controller. When the ground controller responded, it was obvious there was a problem.

"*Callie*, we're having trouble receiving your transmission. Please say again."

"Yoshi, are you hearing this?" the captain asked over the direct comm to engineering. "I'm going to go to the back-up transmitter and try again."

"Yes, Captain, I hear it. Try that and let's see what we get."

They listened as Jim gave instructions to Eric to try the smaller back-up array, and soon were conversing easily with the controller below. Yoshi frowned. "That's unusual." He keyed the comm. "Tan, can you come to engineering to spell me? I must check on something on the command deck. We're having trouble with our point-to-point comms."

"On my way," Tan responded.

"Stay here with Tan. Once he gets here, I'm going up to the flight deck to do some basic diagnostics. Eric's got his hands full co-piloting the ship just now." Soon Tan showed up and Yoshi dashed off with a datapad and toolbox in hand. Kel monitored his console as he'd been taught, and in no time the engineer reappeared.

"It's not a problem with the transmitter, it's almost certainly a problem with the dish. Not a big deal, because we've got good comms using the back-up dish. It's just smaller and not as capable. We can get it repaired on the ground, but it'll be expensive."

"Why's that?" Kel asked.

Yoshi explained that the solution for most any of those systems was to replace them wholesale as one unit. It was the fastest solution but also an expensive one. "Usually systems like that have something relatively minor wrong with one of the modular components, but to get it diagnosed and fixed takes a lot longer. We can't lift again until the main P-to-P dish is functional. It's a basic requirement."

Kel nodded.

"Also, those units are sealed in an inert atmosphere or in vacuum to prevent oxidation of the components.

We could try to troubleshoot it ourselves while in space, but I have a feeling it will be a problem too difficult to fix. Trying to do very fine work in EVA is difficult, especially if you don't have manipulators delicate enough to tackle such a task."

Kel frowned. "How long could something like that take for the techs to repair it groundside?"

"Hmm. Could be a week or more. It's happened to us before, and the fees for a rush job are astronomical. They always want to take the parts up to an orbital repair station and do the work there. That's a lot of time and money to get done quickly. Better to just suck it up and let them replace the whole thing. We may even get some value on our old dish."

Kel shrugged. "In my line of work, my gear supports me doing some pretty delicate activity in micro-G. What would it take for us to try?"

Yoshi raised his eyebrows. "Let's talk to the captain."

07

The edges of Kel's vision were losing their sharpness. He knew the signs of shallow water blackout, and this was the start of the pattern they'd warned about. He felt the fire in his lungs, the burn commanding him to breathe, but kept at it. The panels had to be done in sequence for a perfect score. Done out of sequence but otherwise correctly the hatch would still open, but he would lose points. Kel started again with the panel on the left, removing and checking the color code on the chips, then reinserting them one at a time before he went to the next panel. The only problem was that now he'd become confused as to the correct order. It was growing harder to concentrate.

Phase two had started with the pool. It simulated a lot of what it took to work in vacuum, and if Kel did this correctly, he'd move on with the rest of the class to the orbital next week and do it for real. By the end of phase one, they'd lost more than half of the class. It was the phase that separated those who thought they wanted to be legionnaires from those who would rather die than fail. Phase two was the beginning of learning the real skills a Legion warrior needed to be deadly. After this week, armor would be issued. Every day he felt closer to his goal.

Relieved, the hatch slid open as he turned the manual release, Kel's biceps cramping as he fought the lever into its cradle. He swam through, the light of the surface water beckoning him with the reward of a breath. The pain *was gone and he felt numb everywhere, just a faint tingle telling him he was alive. His vision grew darker, like the dimmer was being lowered on the sun itself. Hypoxia. He'd spent too long under on the same breath. Soon he would drown. He stayed calm and kicked to the surface, his lips breaking the water surface before the rest of him. He made it to the side of the pool where the instructor sat with a datalink in his hand.*

"Satisfactory, Candidate 117. Exit the pool." The man in the khaki trunks and the black seamball cap was tan and muscular. The instructor's command seemed clear. Kel understood. But the water felt good and he could breathe again.

Maybe in another minute...

Kel grinned stupidly but didn't move as he took in more breaths.

"Exit the pool, Candidate."

Kel's vision faded again just before his head went under.

"Kopersky, get him."

When Kel came to, someone had placed an oxygen hood on him. He sputtered and removed the hood to drain the last of the water he coughed out. He pushed away restraining hands. "I'm fine. Fit to fight, sir."

The instructor looked down at him and grinned. "Stand up. Look at me. What's the square root of 144?"

Kel snapped to parade rest. "Twelve, sir."

"You back with us, Candidate?"

"Yes, sir."

The instructor laughed. "You know what happened, Candidate?"

"Yes, sir. Hypoxia. Shallow water blackout."

"That's right. Walk with me."

Kel followed the instructor to the shade of the covered area and resumed his parade rest.

"Stand easy, Candidate 117."

Kel dreaded what would come next. He was about to be dismissed from Phase Two. He'd failed. His heart froze as if he'd swallowed an iceberg in one gulp. He kept his head up, waiting for the order to go back to the barracks and pack his gear with the other washouts of the day.

"Don't look so glum, 117. I'm not going to fail you."

His heart beat again.

"Do you know why that happened to you? You had a passing run. The sequence wasn't perfect, but it was an acceptable run. The hatch would've opened. At most, I'd have docked you five points. Do you know why you did that?"

"Yes, sir. I wanted the higher score."

"How'd that work out for you, Candidate?"

"Not so well, sir."

The instructor laughed. "We won't tolerate someone who panics. Or quits. You did neither. I'm not telling you it's bad to shoot for perfection, but there's a lesson in this I hope you'll keep with you. Know when it's time to move on, got me?"

The captain considered their proposal. The *Callie* would be in a holding orbit for at least eighteen hours waiting her turn to land. It was more than enough time to at least evaluate the problem in situ while they waited.

"If you're confident you can do it safely, we've got nothing to lose," Jim said, at last giving his approval.

Kel stood with Yoshi in one of the smaller locks on the starboard side forward of engineering. The lock was barely large enough to accommodate the two men and the small tool trunk with its tethered spanners and sockets secured around the rectangular surface. Yoshi snapped a line from the mobile trunk to his waist and began the sequence to exit, first turning off the grav decking so that they could check their boot function, then checking their environmental systems before cycling the compartment to vacuum.

Kel checked the readouts on Yoshi's vac suit and gave him the "Okay" hand signal, then showed Yoshi the readout from the link on his forearm showing the pressure readout and oxygen saturation in his own armor to complete the buddy-check. Yoshi returned the hand signal to Kel.

"That's a pretty slick getup, Kel," Yoshi said in admiration of Kel's armor. Kel was much taller than Yoshi and much broader, but in his armor, he dwarfed the man.

"It comes in handy," he agreed. He'd put the EVA booster rig over his armor but doubted he'd need it. They'd be taking a leisurely walk on the hull to where the main dish array sat on the dorsal forward hull and not spending any time out of contact with the *Callie*'s exterior. *You only regret the gear you don't bring*, was his motto. For the same reason, he wore his pistol, but did leave his carbine locked in his cabin.

"Expecting trouble?" Yoshi asked as he gestured to the blaster at his side.

"Yoshi, I don't go to the fresher unarmed," Kel said, only partially in jest.

"Hmm. Good thing for us. Okay, let's get to work."

It was a simple maneuver to ascend to the top of the hull and make their way forward to the superstructure that held many of the ship's external systems and sensors. Kel thought an ion cannon would mount easily to this spot on the hull. He made a mental note to research the law that governed such things. He'd seen armed merchant vessels many times and had some pretty good ideas about how to acquire just the right gun for the *Callie*'s defense.

As they neared the array, Kel looked out at the vastness of the galaxy. Kaylan's bright albedo edging the night terminator was barely visible from their geosynchronous position over the planet.

Yoshi was plodding ahead, looking down at the deck. The tool trunk floated along just behind him. Kel knew that his mentor couldn't be straining in the microgravity environment, and thought he knew what the issue was.

"Do you have the need to do much EVA on the *Callie*, Yoshi?"

Kel heard the engineer's somewhat labored breathing through his comms.

"Nope. Almost never. Mostly because it's rarely necessary, but as much because, well, I'm more of an enclosed spaces kind of guy. I don't really like heights."

Kel had seen Uncle Yoshi working in very confined spaces with no indication of claustrophobia. The man's head-down attitude as they walked was his way of ignoring the perspective of their position relative to the planet far below.

Kel admired Yoshi for it. To have a task that caused you anxiety and discomfort, but forging ahead and doing it anyway—because it was necessary—took real courage.

"Here we go," Yoshi said as they reached the domed pod that sat among the many other similar protrusions along the top of the ship. Yoshi gave the tool trunk a gentle pull. It floated toward him until he could position it next to him and activate its grav-plate to lock it to the hull. He knelt as he examined the access panel. "This will take us a while. Are you familiar with cold-welding?"

Kel assured him he was.

"The accesses are designed to resist that kind of process. Sometimes, though, despite the nonmetallic gaskets and nonoxidizing grease, it doesn't prevent molecular joining. Makes it damn difficult to get a panel off. Let's try."

Yoshi's breathing eased as he worked. To Yoshi the Engineer, the only thing in his world now was the problem in front of him. That he crouched on a ship floating thousands of kilometers above a planet no longer caused him anxiety.

The bolts were of a different composition than the housing to prevent seizing, and Yoshi backed out each bolt with an autospanner. These were all captured to the panel, so there was no chance of one floating away. The engineer placed the spanner head over the last bolt and activated the device, only to have it spin out of his hand and float away until the tether connecting it to the tool trunk snapped it back.

"It's always the last one," Yoshi said with a grunt, annoyed at the seized bolt. "I'm going to have to show it that I'm not taking no for an answer."

Yoshi headed for the trunk and mumbled curses.

"Mind if I give it a try?" Kel said as Yoshi reached for a long-handled wrench. "It's usually the first one for me. Maybe we'll cancel one another out."

"What's your plan, big fella? We don't want to shear that head."

"A little heat and some muscle can do wonders. I actually deal with this problem once in a while."

Kel explained that the attractive force of his armor's boots was much stronger than that of the commercial vac suit Yoshi wore. "I can give it a little more gentle encouragement with the wrench than you can. Failing that, a little directed heat may loosen it up. Worst case, I'll cut the head off. I can do it without damaging the panel, and if it's just the one, there shouldn't be a problem for the unit to remain sealed for at least one reentry."

Yoshi gave a grunt. "I like it. Okay, show me."

Kel set up on the bolt and let the wrench automatically fit itself to the head. He looked at the grav-boot scale and visually swiped it to maximum grip, and applied his weight to the wrench. Nothing. He let the wrench float out of the way and grabbed his plasma torch. He played with the external controls, ignited it, and bent forward over the bolt, focusing the flame to the bolt head. Yoshi stood at his side by the panel, watching intently but remaining quiet.

Kel knew that the engineer was showing a lot of trust in him. *Of course, I think I've earned the right to a little trust*, he thought. *Still, I better not screw it up.*

From experience Kel knew there would only be a short moment between warming the head enough to transfer heat down the bolt, to overheating and damaging it. He extinguished the small cutter and returned it to his armor. Glowing briefly, the bolt head soon returned it to its normally frosted appearance. He tugged the wrench to him and effortlessly snatched it from midair and tried again. The bolt started to spin. He changed to an autospanner and finished.

"That's how we do it!" Yoshi exclaimed. Together they tugged the panel away, the actuating arms then taking over and lifting the panel up and holding it in place. "Kel, you're not a trained spacer. Where did you learn to do this? In the Legion? I thought the Legion was all about shoot 'em up stuff."

Kel chuckled. "You're not wrong about that."

Yoshi was like many people who assumed things about the military. But it took a lot of skills to make the wheel turn.

"This is straight Navy engineer stuff, kid," Yoshi said, begging more of an explanation.

Kel nodded. "True. In my particular line of work, being able to access denied places is a necessity. We call it 'preparing for a fail-safe breach.' If I have to get into a building or a ship—portal or no portal—I make it happen. Sometimes it's necessary to do it without destroying things. Other times... not so much."

Behind his visor, Yoshi's bushy, gray eyebrows were raised as high as they could go. "Makes sense to me. Okay, let's start checking the component modules. Maybe I can show you something you don't already know."

"More like show me another thing I don't know," Kel said. He'd learned a lot from the man in a short amount of time.

After another hour of checking the individual modules, Yoshi found the culprit unit. He ran a diagnostic on each of the stacked rectangular modules, the next to the last one failing to show a green indicator after challenged. "Well, it wasn't the last one, but almost. Should've started at the bottom." He pulled the unit out and set it on the small shelf next to the modules and clamped it in place.

"Here's where it gets tricky. We don't have another unit to swap out for this one. I need to see why it doesn't check out." He reached into the tool trunk's center console, pulled out an old-fashioned loupe visor that attached to the vac helmet, then settled in front of the console. He used pliers to turn locking tabs on the housing, or tried to, but the tool kept slipping out of his hands. Yoshi cursed underneath his breath.

"Uncle Yoshi," Kel said, trying a persuasive approach. "Can I try? My gauntlets allow me fine control, much better than your protective gloves, and I have digital magnification in my bucket. I can see in much greater detail than your lenses, I bet. If you tell me what to do, it might be easier."

Yoshi looked at his own hands in the thick vac gloves. They were made to protect the wearer from puncture, not for fine work that required a light touch. "We have a manipulator, but I tell you, it's a lot harder to use than you'd think. I don't practice with it much, so I didn't even haul it out. Okay. Switch."

They changed positions and Kel moved in front of the small shelf. He turned the white light on from his bucket, greatly illuminating their work area, and followed Yoshi's directions as he removed the outer housing and stowed it. Yoshi peered into the box from Kel's side, trying to find a focal length that would let him evaluate the interior maze of parts under his loupes.

"There." Yoshi gestured with a pair of angled, long-nosed pliers. "Not surprising. Cheap parts and shoddy manufacturing."

Kel increased the magnification of his bucket and saw what Yoshi pointed out to him. There was a two-centimeter gap in a coated wire, the ends showing evidence that there had been thermal damage.

Yoshi clucked his tongue. "There was a surge or just a failure over time where there was a flaw in the wire. These small diameter gold wires are still about the best electrical conductor for low voltages. The stuff never oxidizes, but dang it, like anything, if it's manufactured out of spec or with flaws, this is what you get."

"Can we fix it?" Kel asked. It seemed like a simple task. "I've never tried soldering in micro-G."

"Hah!" Yoshi exclaimed. "Got you! Just when I thought this old bullitar was ready to be turned out to farm, there's still stuff I can teach a smart kid like you. Tell me, what do you actually know about cold welding?"

Kel told him. When placing breaching charges or mines against a ship's hull in space, it wasn't necessary to use any type of adhesive to secure the device in place. In vacuum, similar metals could bond together just by contact. Most hulls were composed of impervisteel, and frequently coated or painted. By vaporizing a spot on a hull with a plasma torch to remove any coating, just holding the similarly composed impervisteel casing of the charge to that bare spot bonded it molecularly, as surely as if it had been welded in place.

"That's a good use of the principle," Yoshi agreed. "Nothing so fancy required here, though." He carefully dug around in the trunk and produced a spool containing many different diameters of gold wire. "You're going to do the work, kid. Time to shine."

The gap was too wide to simply rejoin the wires. They would have to be bridged. Yoshi explained how Kel would use the set of micro-instruments to cut a new section of wire, crimp the ends to create more surface area for contact with the wire to be gapped, join them with some delicate pressure to cold weld, then seal the wire with some insulating foam. "It would all be simple to do on a bench back in engineering, but I think you can pull it off up here. It'll save a lot of time."

Yoshi watched, making only the rare comment while Kel worked. It took a couple of attempts to get a piece the correct size in place while holding the ends together with a pair of fine forceps to set the bond. Finally, Kel tugged the wires across each new weld, testing their hold. Solid. He took the fine tip applicator for the insulating foam and let it ooze out over the wire as he encouraged it to spread out with a gentle stroking motion. After a minute, he stepped back. "Take a look and see what you think."

"Looks good," Yoshi said. "Now for the acid test. Get the cover on and let's run a check." That done, Yoshi bent over and repeated the test. The green indicator appeared. "And Bob's your uncle. Or, Yoshi, in this case." He clicked over to the ship's channel. "Command deck, run a test on the main dish array. Should be operational."

Eric's voice responded. "Rog. Wait one, Yosh." In a minute, the answer came back to them. "Solid signal. Just sent a test bounce to the surface and got back a strong return. I think you did it."

They buttoned up the pod, torqued the bolts, inventoried their tools, and made their way back to the small engineering lock. As the inner doors opened, Yoshi removed his helmet. "Let's beat feet to engineering. We'll be getting ready to go dirtside soon."

Kel checked his chrono. They had been on the hull for five hours.

Yoshi placed a hand on Kel's shoulder. "Not that you need to hear it from me, but good job. Needless to say, you pass your engineering familiarization."

The praise meant a lot to Kel, and he let Yoshi know. "Thanks, Uncle Yoshi. It's a great feeling to be of use on the ship."

Yoshi smiled a moment before feigning a dour expression. "Now, after we pick up new cargo, I'll be turning you over to Jim and Eric for bridge familiarization. You're doing well, but don't get cocky. You've got a lot to learn yet." Then he broke back into his toothy grin. "You don't really need any more time in the dungeon with me. Something tells me you may already be up to snuff on a few of the tasks up there, too."

They were only on Kaylan for a day before they were back in jump space and headed for a new destination. After the process of unloading one cargo and taking on another, there had been little time for him and Tara to spend together. He was now in a bridge jump seat, looking over the shoulders of Jim and Eric as they worked, having just inserted into FTL.

"Stable and on course, Captain," Eric said.

"Confirmed. Well, then..." Jim said as he looked over his shoulder from the right-hand seat. "Let's talk about our upcoming time together." He pushed back in his bucket couch as Jim stayed in his co-pilot's seat.

"Of course, the goal isn't to get you up to speed to serve as a flight deck officer just yet," Jim said, "as fun as it is. There are a lot of things more important to our safety than piloting the ship, believe it or not."

Kel remembered what Shakaan had said about engineers being the ones truly responsible for a ship's safe return planetside.

"Yoshi's checked you out on all engineering systems including environmental, so being able to monitor those functions from the flight deck won't be unfamiliar. Did you get a chance to read the stuff I sent you?"

The captain had bounced Kel three packets of material, which he'd already skimmed. The largest of them, *Conduct of Flight Operations*, was also the most interesting. It went into great detail about bridge operations. Another was *Admiralty and Astral Law*, and the last, *Galactic Shipping Law Handbook*.

"Careful," Eric said without turning away from his console. "He's probably got them memorized. Let's not let him play family trivia night with us until we've had a chance to brush up."

Kel grinned. Tara had told him about the games they played to teach the children about spacefaring topics ranging from engineering to legal matters. "I only skimmed the legal texts. They're a little tough for me. The flight operations book is interesting, though."

Jim nodded. "And even there, it's not so much the flight material, but the emergency and communications protocols I want you to focus on. Procedures for deep-space and point-to-point communications are vital. If you were the only person on the ship capable of calling for help, knowing how to do so is critical."

Kel had to admit that though he could manage many communications tasks simultaneously through his bucket—especially with L-comm—he was a little handicapped because it made the process so easy. He could talk to his teammates, guide a Navy Raptor for close air support, interrupt and break into wave-propagated communications of a terrestrial force—you name it—and do so virtually at will so long as he was in range. He'd need to re-familiarize himself with standard comms to be able operate the ship's systems correctly.

"Most of the astro-maritime law is stuff a spacer picks up by being exposed to different situations and seeing how they're handled. You're in a descent corridor and a Wobanki racer cuts you off. How do you challenge him and how does the law support your action? What are our legal responsibilities to a ship in distress, beyond just the moral ones? What authority does the captain of a ship have when underway and not under the legal framework of a planetary or system-wide government? How about when in jump space where neither physical location nor temporal assignment exists? What legal constraints govern then?"

It all made sense to Kel. At least, that there was a lot to it. He knew none of the answers to the captain's hypotheticals, but would be looking up the law that governed those situations.

"So, you'll spend every main shift here with us," ," Jim explained. "Then you'll be pulling a full shift with a watch officer, rotating each night between second and third shift."

Eric looked over his shoulder toward Kel. "Still want to be a spacer?"

A week later, Kel sat with the two men as he listened to them discussing the approach to Paladon Two. The planet was a high-gravity world, and the two pilots needed to calculate whether landing was feasible. The *Callie* was a massive ship, laden or not, and no matter her propulsion systems, the task of bringing a huge freighter like theirs down to any planetary surface was always difficult and fraught with potential dangers.

Kel had known many Paladonians in the Legion. As a group, you could spot them easily by their squat bodies, massive limbs, and muscled abdomens of an endomorph somatotype. He'd never known one of his comrades from the heavy world to return home after his hitch. After five or six years off-world, it was too hard to reacclimate to the gravity and too pleasant living on a lower-G world. Acquired physical characteristics were not genetically transmitted. When a Paladonian had children on a 1-G world, no matter how many generations of their progenitors had spawned from the 1.4 G-world, their offspring attained the more random height and body type of most any human. Many was the time he'd jealously admired the sheer strength of the thickly muscled folks he met from the heavy world. Supposedly, Kel had some Paladonian ancestors on his father's side. He was curious to see the world firsthand.

But before they could get there, the pilots had to decide whether the *Callie* could tolerate the strain to land or whether the receiver would have to retrieve the cargo piecemeal in orbit? The shipper was unconcerned and their contract allowed for both possibilities. Kel listened intently as the two men conversed, reviewing their analysis.

Jim turned to include Kel in the discussion. "We knew when we took the contract that the final calculations might only give us the option of unloading in orbit. We took about a seventy-percent load to give us a better safety margin if, after our calcs, we thought we could land it."

Eric continued. "See, safety is the biggest concern, but partly economics. We're getting an excellent commission for the tonnage, even though we're not full, but the time we'd spend in orbit unloading would eat into a lot of that."

"By the numbers, we have more than enough of a safety margin to land it. But without a contract waiting for us on the ground ready for another destination, rather than shop for the perfect load for our hold, we'll cut and run deadhead to save any strain on the old girl lifting off."

Eric chimed back in. "The strain on the hull integrity field and the repulsors will be way higher lifting than when landing her."

It all made sense to Kel when they explained it in those terms, which he knew were dumbed down for his consumption.

"I suppose you have to abandon any freefall trajectory pretty early in the calculations, huh?" Kel asked.

Jim's eyebrows raised in surprise. "Yes. That's right. There's almost no freefall reentry in the approach we've programmed for landing on Paladon; it's all repulsor matched to keep strain to a minimum. How do you know about that?"

"I was looking over your shoulder while you reviewed your reentry plan. I'm not a pilot, but I have programs that help me with the same orbital mechanics. I'm a jumpmaster, so I'm responsible for calculating release points for the different orbital mechanics for geostationary repulsor-driven vehicles or from freefall orbital. Here..." Kel brought up his own datapad and showed Jim one of his programs, scrolling through the inputs and then showing him a sample computation from his last training jump.

"Uh, jumpmaster?" Eric asked. "As in, 'to jump,' like, from space onto a planet?"

Kel nodded. The act of orbital freefall insertion wasn't in itself classified, just some of the equipment and specific methods. He thought it might give the pilots some sense of where he was coming from experientially. Of course, his weaponizing the same method to drop a huge rock on a planet was not something he was going to discuss.

Jim shook his head. "You've lived an interesting life, Kel. Is there anything else you'd like to tell us about yourself? Magical abilities? Telepathy? Levitation? Has the Legion taught you psychokinesis?"

The two pilots chuckled. Kel felt a little self-conscious and it must have showed.

"Sorry, Kel," the captain apologized. "We're a pretty boring lot. You're the most interesting person we've ever had in the family."

Family! Kel's heart skipped a beat and warmth spread across his chest.

"But don't get too overconfident because we're so impressed by you. I won't let you fly the *Callie*. Yet."

One day on Paladon was enough for the crew. The host facility did most of the minor labor associated with running the offloading process. Though the robots did the actual work, they still needed to be supervised. The stevedores were apparently quite accustomed to unloading arriving freighters on behalf of the ship's own crew, and they worked happily and diligently, proud of their imperviousness to the gravity as they watched the off-worlders strain to simply stand and converse with the Paladonian workers. Even Tam and Ochio, so protective of the *Callie* that they never let someone outside the family operate the internal gantry cranes, gladly stood out of the way when a squat, hugely muscled man in orange coveralls offered to operate the control pad.

The children were all sent to their bunks to rest while Kel worked with the adults to supervise the operations until one-by-one, they too had to start taking shifts as the strain on their bodies became taxing. Kel stayed in the cargo hold the entire time, tired, but enjoying the strain. He worked out frequently under high-G back at the gym on Corsical. At the end of nine hours though, he too was feeling a deep ache in his skeleton and was relieved to see the last container being floated down off the port ramp. Tara and he would be passing out ligament regen tabs and placing stimulators on aching backs and necks once they were again in space.

Kel moved to Tam's office to comm the captain. "Sir, we're clear of all cargo. I'm ready to secure the ship on your order." Kel had been the last member of the crew left in the hold.

"Roger," Jim replied. "You can start sealing her. Tam and Ochio will be down directly to help. Caroline's gotten confirmation of delivery, so we should be able to lift as soon as ground control gives us a departure corridor. Yoshi, as soon as we're buttoned up, can you power us up so the grav decking can give us a little relief, at least in the habitation decks? For the kids?"

Yoshi answered. "Heck, I'll reverse polarity until we're floating, Captain."

08

Tailgate jumps from a Talon were a blast. The days of being delivered like a bomb out of the belly of a Goshawk from a hundred meters above a planet—crammed against other jumpers in full armor and gear, rewarded with only a few seconds of freefall followed by the briefest of parachute descents to be deposited on the ground like a bag of wet duracrete—were a distant memory for him. Though it was just team training and not a combat jump, there was still the anxiety. Standing at the edge of the ramp, the curvature of the horizon confirmed the surreal nature of what they did. Free fall was as close to flight as a human could get. It was only natural for birds.

It was his first freefall with his new kill team. Bigg jumpmastered, unimpressed with Kel's long jump log. "Nice of you to volunteer, eager boy. Prove to me you're not a paper tiger. Then we'll see about you running the show later, okay, new guy?"

Tem had laughed the loudest at Bigg's shutting him down.

"You haven't gotten any less aggressive, I see. Good to know, Turner."

He missed Tem.

The jump went smoothly. The adrenaline rush of cutting through the atmosphere headfirst at the speed of sound made him feel alive. The trouble came later.

If the anxiety hadn't hit him in orbit, why was it coming on here and now?

He climbed the tower without effort. The N-22 and pack tight on his back, he trotted up flight after flight of open grate stairs. The wind was high today and made the tower sway despite the open design. He reached the top where a pegged ladder without handrails or safety cage led through an open trap door to the top deck. He had maybe three minutes to get set, ready to deliver the shot that would initiate the assault.

He was a hundred meters above the ground. The platform was narrow, just wide enough for him to fit prone with his rifle. There were no railings. Nothing to prevent him from taking an accidental plunge off the edge to a certain death. The bot took an erratic course around the front room of the shoothouse, every so often taking a step to the front window to pantomime the movement of a human head snapping left and right in frenzied lookout, then quickly disappearing out of sight. He would only have moment to anticipate the hostage taker's appearance and make the shot.

"Sniper set."

"Assault, set." Captain Yost said. "I release control to you, sniper."

"I have control," Kel replied, taking deep breaths as he waited. The bot appeared and Kel broke the shot. He sent another as the sight settled, only noticing the neat hole in the window after the bot collapsed. "Shot. Target down."

"Assault, assault, assault."

Kel shifted to watch the corners of the house as the door charge exploded and the team entered behind a flash of purple stunner tossed into the room. There would be another random number of bots in the house to pro-

vide problems for the team to solve, but no more targets outside for a sniper. There wasn't anything for him to do now except go through the motions of providing containment while the team did their thing inside.

"Endex," Captain Yost said after the end of the shooting. "Coming out."

"Good shots, Turner," Bigg said. "Come on down and we'll do an eval."

It was then that the trouble started. He stood and shouldered his pack and rifle. The tower swayed and he stepped to the edge. Butterflies flapped their wings in his chest as he had a thought.

What's to keep me from jumping right now?

He knew it was an irrational thought. He would never act on the compulsion. But standing at the edge—it was no different from the tailgate of the Talon. He ached to feel the rush of the fall. And for the first time since becoming a legionnaire, Kel doubted his sanity. He knelt and crawled down from the tower, gripping the handholds a little too tightly as he descended.

The next day they worked on the free climbing wall and at the top, Kel felt the same compulsion. To jump out and away, as though he could sprout wings and fly.

Later in his quarters he shared the confusing episodes with Tem. The leej who'd spotted his potential and brought him to Dark Ops would know what to do.

"It's like I have to restrain myself. I have to talk myself out of jumping anytime I'm up high. Am I crazy?"

Tem laughed. "Happens to everybody. To anyone who'll admit it, that is."

"What do you mean?" Kel asked.

"It's like this. Overcoming the natural fear of falling causes some confusion in your brain. Any sane person knows that stepping past the edge is certain death. So's running into a room full of gunmen just waiting to blast you down. So's most of what we do."

"So, what do I do? Other than not jump at the wrong time, that is?"

Tem handed him a beer. "Sometimes jumping is the right move. Sometimes it's the wrong move. Then there's the time you should, but don't. Let your natural instincts take control and don't jump, you let yourself down. So long as you know when the time is right, keep making that jump. The other times, just know you're a little crazy, but that's okay. Because you're not alone in that way."

"Well, that's clear as mud." Kel took a swig.

"Don't overthink it. Sometimes it's the jump you do make that saves your life."

Kel was with Tara on the sofa in Jim and Caroline's family quarters. Ochio was absent on watch so it was just the four of them. They'd just finished a game of tiles, the multicolored rectangles still lying on the table. Though he was looking forward to a long night of sleep, Kel sipped kaff, the only one to do so. When it was time for bed the drink never interfered. After two weeks of training watches in engineering and on the bridge, this was the first night he could spend without responsibilities.

"I've been considering our options," Jim said, pushing himself deeper into his chair, relaxation evident on his face. "We're on a course for Pegasus Station, but we've been discussing things." He nodded toward his wife.

Caroline was the ship's purser. She looked at her datapad. "We don't have a shipment lined up immediately, but we are definitely near time for a run to Meridian. That's a contracted run for us, and it's still one of our most profitable."

Kel perked up. He'd played a central role in the *Callie* becoming intimately involved in the trade from the edge world to the core. All goods destined for the capital world of Liberinthine had a lucrative market awaiting them, and the Yomiuris had become rich in the last two years as the first and favored contractors to be carrying those goods off Meridian.

"I was thinking of cutting our losses running with an empty hold and replotting for Orion Station," continued Jim. "We can pick up any competitive contracts to carry goods to Meridian, and we'll certainly leave there without a cubic centimeter of space. We might be on Meridian a week, but if so, we might get a chance to duplicate our family beach vacation."

Tara clapped her hands and threw her arms around Kel's neck, almost knocking the half-full cup out of his hands. He set the cup on the table and returned her hug.

"Oh, Dad, that would be incredible," she said and give her parents hugs, too.

"We had another idea," Caroline said once they'd sat down again. "After we deliver back to Orion, we're due to go home for an extended stay. It's been nine months. What do you think?"

Tara broke out into a squeal. "I can't believe it! Tell me you're serious and not joking!"

Jim smiled. "Yes, honey, we're serious."

Tara broke into tears. Kel was confused for a moment when he saw her distress, then understood her rapid change in polarity. She looked at him with tearful eyes.

"Oh Kel, it is so *perfect* for you to be here. You're coming *home* with us."

The night dwindled on a while longer and then Jim and Caroline excused themselves for bed. Kel remained with Tara as she talked about their upcoming itinerary leading up to their trip to Callie's World. He was energized by her electric excitement as she held his hand and told him stories of home in a rushed, rapid onslaught of recollections and descriptions.

"Oh Kel, I know you're going to love it. It's the most beautiful place in the galaxy. There's water and mountains and lush forests. The sky is so blue you can't take your eyes off it. There's nothing but nature everywhere you look. We could carve out a whole territory for ourselves and never see another soul unless we wanted to. It really is a dream."

Kel listened as she described every detail about their family settlement and its history. It sounded nice.

"Look!" she said as she produced her link to project holos over them. "Isn't it just like I said?" She swiped through dozens of pictures as rapidly as the emitter could transition to form the next captured moment. The timber-framed homes and outbuildings looked like something from a studio-produced drama. Snowcapped mountains lined the background, and Kel shifted to peer at the slopes hidden by the thick forests. Happy children played in ankle-deep water, holding up small armored amphibians with long necks. Breezes formed gentle patterns on endless crop fields. It really did look like a paradise.

"I want to take you everywhere. This is the greatest night I've had in a long time."

Kel didn't want to spoil the moment. He'd started doing some math as soon as the Yomiuris revealed their plan. A few days to Orion, a week on Meridian, a week back, then almost two weeks to Callie's World; Kel couldn't remain with them in their home for more than two weeks before he would have to return to reality and his responsibilities on Victrix. Tomorrow he would talk privately with Jim about the timing. For now, he kept his thoughts to himself.

Tara rested her head on Kel's chest. "We're going to be so happy back home."

The captain listened to Kel's concerns about the itinerary and assured him that he had taken into consideration Kel's temporary availability.

"The *Callie* will deliver you back on time," he said as they sat in the wardroom alone, Kel projecting the calendar from his link between them. "I may have been a little ambitious about taking extra downtime on Meridian. I know everyone feels the same about getting home. We can shave time off on Meridian and skip the beach. I'll have a hypercomm message out to the shipper as soon as we hit Orion Station. They'll have plenty of time to get the consignment ready to load once we land on Meridian. Or at worst, we'll cut our turnaround down to a couple of days. Anything you need to do while we're there? I know you spent a lot of time on Meridian."

Kel admitted there were a few friends he wanted to see. "It would be a nice opportunity to see some acquaintances. I honestly didn't know if I'd ever make my way back."

"Any reason you have to be… careful, if you know what I mean?"

Kel understood his friend's inquiry. "Not at all, but thanks for asking." He smiled easily.

Jim looked relieved. "Good. I remember not long after our first visit to Meridian there being some civil unrest and a coup not long after that. We're never on the ground for too long, and we've never had anything but good experiences getting in and out of Argolis. I guess I just always wondered, you know… I always wondered if any of that had anything to do with you."

Now Kel laughed. "I'm on very good terms with their government. In fact, you could say I'm an honorary citizen." He thought about his friends in the Hoplites and the enigmatic man who now ran the planet. "But just to be sure, I'll send a message ahead that I'm coming."

A small part of Kel wanted to show off for his family as he considered the reception he could anticipate. *For once, I'm not going to flinch from the limelight*, he thought. *After all, I am a Knight of the Order of Achilles.*

Kel would look back on that moment to wish he had remembered one of his favorite quotations. It was one he thought tempered his behavior, but would never apply to him. An irony he would feel the bitterness of later.

First pride, then the fall.

"It's a beauty all right, Kel," Eric said to him as they sat together on the command deck. Kel was starting his first independent watch on the *Callie*, and Eric had stayed to spend some time with Kel after giving him a formal sign-out. "I think you're going to love it there."

Kel was surprised to learn that Eric had an infant awaiting him that he'd not seen since the *Callie*'s last visit home. He hadn't even known that Eric was married.

"Yeah. That happened not long after you left us the first time," Eric said. The first officer produced a holo of his wedding day, the same comely homes and mountain peaks of Tara's holos behind the smiling families and the happy couple.

"I'm a lucky guy," Eric said as he brought up another image of his wife holding their child. "Santander is one in a million. We've known each other since we were kids. She's a real Ballantine, though. Beautiful but stubborn."

Kel knew the short version of the history of Callie's World. The Yomiuris and the Ballantines were two of a handful of families to settle the planet. Like the Yomiuris, they supported their extended family as merchant spacers, bringing income to the world by their efforts across the galaxy. Eric's wife was a flight deck officer herself, and after their courtship they'd made a tour with the *Callie* before she returned home to give birth.

"It's pretty much how we do things. Caroline and I are Sullivans. She married Jim, and it wasn't long before I joined my big sister on the crew of the *Callie*. If you and Tara go the distance," he paused to let that sink in for Kel, "it will bring in some fresh blood to our community."

Kel said nothing as he considered the enormity of the conversation and where it was leading.

"Have Jim and Caroline had *the talk* with you yet?"

A hollow pit bored into Kel's stomach. Like the time in basic phase one when he realized he hadn't polished his silver to perfection. Casting a motionless glance down only to realize it was too late as the inspecting officer made his way nearer. The time of judgment was upon him. Doom would surely follow. He was trapped.

"No. I think I'd remember if they had."

"Don't worry," Eric assured him. "We've had the talk already about you and Tara."

Is this how it happens in their family? Does the family arrange marriages? Is he about to tell me that it's time to step up or I'm no longer welcome? He knew leejes from worlds where that was exactly how it was done. *Time to marry my daughter or move on, buddy.*

"Everyone in the family thinks it's a good thing," Eric said to Kel's profound relief. "I know Jim and Caroline are trying to be respectful of your developing relationship, but it's bound to come up soon. Have you thought about it?"

Now Kel realized the true reason why Eric had hung around during his watch. "Well, of course I've *thought* about it. I just haven't, well, I just haven't..."

He struggled for the words.

"It's okay, man. Spit it out. Whatever you say goes no further. I promise. Just say what you're thinking," Eric encouraged.

Kel's head swam with conflicting thoughts. "I love Tara. I mean, I haven't told her that exactly in those words. We're still getting to know each other. I mean, I just want to know more and more about her. And I don't think about anyone else in the same way. Anyone."

Eric nodded with approval. Relief. "That's good to hear. Not just for my niece. We're all kind of fond of having you around, too."

Kel blushed. He couldn't hide it anymore and blurted out his deepest fear. "I'm just... I'm just afraid that I'm wrong for her."

Eric frowned. "Why is that?"

Kel looked up from where he'd been staring at his own lap to meet Eric's eyes. "Because of who I am, because of what I do."

There. I said it out loud.

"It wouldn't be fair to her to be with me while I'm still in the Legion."

Eric leaned back in his couch. With a quizzical half-smile, he asked the question Kel knew was coming.

"So, what do you think you're going to do about that?"

Kel gulped down what felt like a smooth stone stuck in his throat and choking him. "I don't know yet."

After his shift, Kel lay in his bunk alone with his thoughts, unable to sleep as his mind raced with possibilities. It had been difficult for him to concentrate on the ship's systems the rest of his watch, but he ran through his checklist of stations every hour as he forced himself to do his duty to the ship and its crew. His family.

But what about his other family? His kill team?

He turned his attention to something more concrete than his conflicted emotions. There'd been many times since his mission on the planet Qulingat't almost eighteen months ago that he'd considered the problem of Callie's World. The Yomiuris' home was a rich world, but like many in the galaxy, its biome was not entirely compatible with human life, particularly to human agriculture. He knew that the residents struggled to make what few modified crops they had to thrive there. It was an enormously expensive undertaking to bring in specialists to consult on the problem. On Q, he had seen a huge corporation partnered with the Republic government work together to solve just such an issue. It was a colossal undertaking.

Kel had become friends with one of the scientists working on that endeavor. He'd been fascinated with the work she was doing to modify the local environment to accept human agriculture, all the while wondering if there were similar things that could be done to aid Callie's World. Perhaps now was a good time to take action.

When they arrived at Orion Station, he would visit the Republic consulate and use his credentials to make a search for his friend Tatiana, the xenobiologist and horticulturist who worked on the same problem back on Q. Maybe she was still there. If he could contact her and explain the situation, perhaps she could give him suggestions about how to solve their particular problem, or even consult for them herself.

Kel relaxed as he thought about it. If he could find her and get some advice, he would share the results of his investigation with the family. If he came up with nothing, he would keep his efforts to himself. Better not get anyone's hopes up just yet.

But what about his hopes? What was it he wanted?

He'd been pensive, daydreaming these last weeks, lost in the past and thinking about the lessons he'd learned from the many guides in his life.

His father. "You have to trust yourself. You're stronger than you know."

The legion survival instructor. "Know when it's time to move on, got me?"

Tem. "Sometimes it's the jump you *do* make that saves your life."

Had his subconscious been feeding him the ammunition he needed to fight this battle for his soul?

Kel drifted off thinking about seas of grass swaying in the breeze.

The uniformed traffic controller's face filled the viewscreen. "*Callie's Dream*, you are cleared for berth two-seven. A tug will meet you on station at ten thousand kilometers, and a pilot will transfer to your ship for docking maneuvers. Welcome to Orion Station."

"Roger, Control. Good to be here. Out," Jim replied as the viewer closed.

"Wow, that's fortunate," Eric said. "To get a berth immediately on arrival never happens. You're bringing us nothing but good luck, Kel."

Kel sat in the jump seat as he saw the enlargement of the sprawling station on the viewer over the pilot's console. He was anxious to get to the consulate and contact his friend. When he'd awoken this morning, he'd felt refreshed and sure. He'd made his decision.

The Orion Station Commission pilot completed the docking maneuver, and after Jim placed his bio-signature on the man's pad, the pilot left the deck with a tip of his hat to them all.

"Shutdown complete," Jim said. "Tan and Ochio are getting the gangway locked. Let's go see."

Kel followed the two men out of the command deck and down the companionway to the waist deck where the main passenger lock sat. Caroline and Tara waited for them as Tan appeared through the doors. "All secure, Captain."

"Let's get to it."

Caroline offered her pad to Jim. "I'm on the station net. There're a few possible hauls. I've already got a reply from a consigner who has cargo for Meridian."

Eric turned to Kel. "See what I mean? You're a good luck charm, man."

Kel let the others start down the covered gangway as he fell in next to Tara, reaching out to take her hand. Bigg's voice came to him from a time when he needed his mentor's guidance most. After his best friend had been killed, Kel doubted his ability to continue on as a foot soldier of galactic policy for the House of Reason. The words had given him the courage to know that no matter what he chose to do, he wouldn't be less of a man in Bigg's eyes.

"Whatever you decide, you have my support."

I've made my decision, Kel thought. *It's time to start a new life. I don't feel like a legionnaire anymore. I feel... free.*

Kel would always remember the warmth of Tara's hand in his, the lightness of his heart, the lack of doubt as he bounced down the ramp, certain he was to begin a life unexpected.

That was the moment. The moment where if he'd had a time machine, he would've returned to tell his younger self that legionnaires shouldn't dream.

As they reached the bottom, Kel's sense of danger ignited. Armed troops in station security uniform waited for them. A wide man and a taller woman in dark suits stood at the head of the group, the woman holding out an identiholo like a zealot brandishing a religious symbol.

"Which of you is Captain Yomiuri?"

Jim stepped forward. "I am."

Kel repressed his instinct to reach for his pistol.

"I am Special Agent McKee from the Republic Justice Enforcement Bureau; this is Special Agent Comerford of the Securities and Exchange Commission. We have arrest warrants for yourself, Caroline Yomiuri, Eric Sullivan, and a warrant to impound and search your vessel. Please come with us."

"What are the charges?" Kel yelled to be heard above the exclamations from his friends.

The male agent stepped forward presenting en-er-chains. "The three of you are under arrest for violations of the non-aligned worlds immurement and technology transfer act. Specifically, illegal transfer of Republic technology to proscribed planets, insider trading, and violations of galactic securities laws."

09

The Spacers' Guild sent a representative from the relief society to meet them at the port receiving station as Kel, Tara, and the other adults comforted the children. The agents were sympathetic to Tara's pleas, and supervised the gathering of essential belongings to sustain them until they could figure out their next move.

Kel collected his gear from around the stateroom, returning items to their places in his grav container as the female agent looked over his shoulder. There had been a short argument when Special Agent McKee had balked seeing his armor and weapons. "You can't be in possession of those items!"

Kel shut her down instantly as he flashed his credentials. He tried to remain as cool and nonconfrontational as possible, but his voice betrayed his tension. "You have zero authority over me or my equipment. Zero. If you have any doubt about that, one bounce will see that misconception evaporate."

The agent tried to mount a counterargument, but on examining his holo, realized it was a futile effort. She begrudgingly harrumphed as she stepped out of his way to allow him to pack. "What is a special operative doing on this commercial ship?" she asked as he finished sealing the container.

Kel was cooler now and answered stoically. "Not in your need-to-know, Special Agent." Kel was the last off the *Callie* as a security officer placed a seal against the hull, identifying the ship as impounded and off-limits.

The tall woman stood with her arms folded as she watched the process.

Kel in turn watched her and his temper burned again. "Special Agent McKee. What's going to happen to the people you've detained?"

He fumed at the sight of Jim, Caroline, and Eric being placed in ener-chains and escorted out of the berthing area, Tara crying as her parents were perp-walked away.

"They're being taken to the station detention facility. Once processed, they'll be allowed to see counsel. In the next few days, a judge will hold a preliminary hearing to review the charges and determine a bond," she replied icily. "But I can tell you, that's unlikely to happen. They're too great a flight risk. At least, that'll be the recommendation I make to the Republic prosecutor."

Kel's temper rose higher still. He took a cleansing breath before asking, "How long until we can see them?"

The woman shrugged, checking her chrono. "Difficult to say. I doubt any sooner than tomorrow."

Kel knew it would be pointless to protest the Yomiuris' innocence. He moved back to the receiving center to rejoin Tara and the rest of the family, his grav case in tow. He ached to put his armor on and KTF, but knew it was a counterproductive thought. Not every problem could be solved with violence. Just most of them.

Yoshi and Meiko stood with Tara, speaking to an older woman whom Kel thought was most likely the representative from the Spacers' Relief Society. Kel had studied the Spacers' Guild Guide and the services afforded its members. The relief society had a representative at every major station and port.

The woman spoke to them with great empathy. "First we need to get quarters for you all. The Repubs have probably already frozen the *Callie*'s credits. Your premiums are paid and your dues are up-to-date. The Guild will cover all living expenses until your insurance coverage kicks in. Let's get everyone settled at the hotel and the children fed. The Guild lawyers will already be at the Republic Justice Center to examine the warrants and will work to get a bond hearing set as soon as possible."

"It sounds as though you've done this before," Kel said as he walked up.

"This is Kel Turner. He's a member of the crew," Yoshi said, introducing him to the woman. "Kel, this is Ms..."

"I'm Amber Pickering, Mister Turner. I'm the Guild aid coordinator for stranded spacers. And yes, I've done this before."

Tara wrapped both arms around him as Meiko explained through gritted teeth, "It's not uncommon for rogue police or corrupt local governments to pull stunts like this, trying to extort bribes from spacers. I never expected the Republic to pull such a cocked-up maneuver, though."

Yoshi placed a calming hand on Meiko's shoulder. "It's going to be all right, my love. There's just been some sort of mistake."

Ms. Pickering nodded. "First we have to get you and your crew sheltered. I'm sure it's going to be resolved soon." She smiled weakly. "We never abandon our own."

Kel appreciated the sentiment. It was very much what a legionnaire would say.

"Oh Kel," Tara sobbed into his chest. "This is a nightmare. What could be going on? My parents have never broken the law. Never."

Kel couldn't think of anything to say. He held Tara tightly as she continued to sob into this chest.

What is going on? He was just as confused. *I'm going to tear this whole station down if that's what it takes to find out.* Kel's mind raced with possibilities as their gathering of refugees followed Ms. Pickering out of the commercial port and into the bustle of the concourse.

What do I really know about them?

He watched Tara hold a toddler in each arm. Had the Yomiuris taken their good fortune and tainted it with some illegal activity? Kel had known at least one leej to betray his honor by crime. He and his squadmates had been shocked to find that one of their own had robbed a merchant like a cheap thug. When it came to credits, people could be unpredictable. He fought to balance as many of the children's belongings as he could on his grav container, his doubts about the family consuming him until a new thought intruded.

Is there some chance I'm responsible for this? He couldn't construct a scenario where that was possible.

The new concern stayed with him as they wove through the crowds, hanging over him like a broken branch, ready to fall when the wind picked up. He could feel the force of a storm building.

Their coordinator remained with them long enough to get them checked in to the hotel. The accommodations were not luxurious. Tara and Meiko worked with the women to get the children settled while Yoshi and Kel huddled with the other men in the common area to discuss their plan of action.

Ochio's strain broke. "Why would they do this? My folks are the most law-abiding people in the galaxy. This is criminal! Who do they think they are?"

Tan balled his fists. "This is crazy, just crazy."

The other men broke into similar exclamations.

Yoshi raised his hands to silence them. "All right. All right. We all feel the same way. None of this is going to help right now. We just have to wait until the attorney contacts us to let us know what's happening."

Kel knew everyone's protests were genuine. Now, he reproached himself for doubting his friend's innocence. The whole family was as outraged and shocked as he was.

"What about it, Kel?" Gilbert, one of the deck crew, asked him. "Can't you do something?"

Everyone nodded as Kel found himself the center of hope. But for the life of him, he couldn't think of a single thing he could do to help. For the first time he could remember in his adult life, he was without a wiser leej to turn to.

What would Bigg do?

Always return to the basics, he heard Bigg say. *Whenever the situation seems chaotic, security comes first.*

"Our first responsibility is to the women and children," Kel said. "This is especially rough on them. I suggest everyone go be with your families and help get them settled. Concentrate on their needs first. Yoshi and I will go to the detention facility. We'll report back as soon as we know something."

Yoshi nodded. "That's right. As soon as we know what's happening, we're going to the Guild, and I'm going to fire off a hypercomm home and find out where the *Callie Supreme* is. If we need the Sullivans to come retrieve us in the *Supreme*, they need to know as soon as possible."

"Leave without the *Callie*?" one of the men asked.

Yoshi shrugged. "I'm no cop, but I've been around long enough to know that if the Repubs have impounded the ship, we're not going to be getting her back anytime soon."

This brought a wave of angry protest. Yoshi looked to Kel, imploring him for help.

"Family, please!" Kel pleaded.

Everyone silenced to listen.

"Yoshi's right. We must start planning for the worst. Be patient. Let's let the attorneys work. We'll go find out what we can and let everyone know, ASAP. Go be with your families. Let them know it's going to be all right."

Yoshi shooed everyone away, repeating the same assurances. Once alone with Kel, Yoshi shook his head in disgust.

"This is unbelievable. What could the Repubs have on us?" he sighed. "Wait for me. I'm going to tell Meiko we'll be gone awhile. Tara and Ochio are rooming next to us. I'll tell Tara not to worry about you. Be right back."

Alone with his thoughts, Kel kept replaying the shock of seeing his family arrested. *My family.* Kel thought about his elation only a few minutes before. He had been fantasizing about how he was going to ask Tara to marry him. Bigg was going to be his best man. His eyes watered as he felt his helplessness return.

Snap out of it! he thought, steeling himself. *What do you do when ambushed? Counter assault! Get off the X. Regain fire superiority! Use your violence of action and momentum to overwhelm your opponent. It's time to act!* He'd go to the military side of Orion station and call one of the Navy JAGs. They might be able to help. It was a start.

His link buzzed in his pocket. What he saw on the screen confused and disoriented him. He hadn't answered it, but there a man's face appeared. *Who could force a comm through on my link?* Dread filled his chest as he recognized the oddity for what it was.

An omen.

"Don't close the link," the man said. "I'll just force through again."

Kel blinked. "What do you want? Who are you?"

"You'll want to meet me. I'll send you a grid. I'm here to help."

Kel had been to this pub before. He took the directions and sat at the corner booth, his back to the wall, watching the entrance. With one hand he carefully moved his pistol between his legs and placed it on suppressed mode, the other hand concealed it with his tunic. A man appeared at the table from out of his peripheral vision and sat.

"Relax, Lieutenant Turner. And don't do anything rash. I told you I'm here to help." The man kept his hands on top of the table to indicate his lack of hostile intent.

Kel met the man's eyes with daggers. He slowed his breathing and remained silent.

The man pursed his lips. "Good. That's a good start. Let's stay calm. Just so you know, I'm not alone here. Killing me would be a bad reaction on your part."

A threat.

Kel was not in the mood for threats. "Your men might get me, but not before I turn your head into a neutron crater."

The man smiled. "True. But that would be murder, and you have a great future ahead of you. Prison would be a waste of your talents."

Kel didn't shift his eyes to look for the man's cover. Maybe his guest was alone, maybe he wasn't. Most likely it was a distraction, the plain man trying to get the drop on him.

"I told you I'm here to help, and I meant it," the man reiterated, lifting his open palms. Now Kel noticed the stubble on the man's chin and the heavy jacket worn over cheap clothing. No question the man concealed at least a hand blaster. His appearance was natural, not affected. But it was the appearance of someone *trying* to be unremarkable. Too plain. Too pedestrian. He recognized tradecraft when he saw it. The man might as well have worn a sign saying, "I'm an undercover agent."

"Enough preamble. Tell me who you are and what you want."

The man relaxed back against the cushion. "Fair enough. There's someone who would like to talk to you. Do you love your Republic?"

Kel walked with the man, Jack, through the busiest part of the concourse to a crowded block of low-end apartments. A locked stairway led to a sublevel where, through a maze of access tunnels, a locked utility room halted them. Jack entered first, gesturing Kel in behind him. Once the door sealed, he told Kel, "We'll wait a minute for some friends before we go on. I know you understand the sequence of things."

Kel upped his rating of Jack's tradecraft, based on the surveillance detection route they took. If Jack truly had people providing rear security to prevent any unwanted followers, or to take Kel out if he decided to get leejy, they were good. He picked up no one.

I'll give him that, at least. His skills are better than the earlier marks I gave him for his right-out-of-the-textbook intelligence operative costume.

Kel felt sure about the who and what of Jack.

The why... that he still couldn't figure.

The door slid aside again and two men as nondescript as Jack walked in. The older of the two, a thin blond man in his fifties, nodded to Jack, then told Kel, "We wait before we go farther."

The other man, much closer to Kel's age and size, stared at a datalink. Kel remained silent as he continued to evaluate the three. None of the men impressed Kel as legionnaires or even military. *Nope. They're RI clowns. Republic Intel. All the way.* His prejudice against RI not-withstanding, they moved with a calm assuredness that betrayed a high level of training.

Since Jack's initial plea to remain calm, he had. He didn't feel threatened. *They haven't tried to disarm me. I've been brought this far without cuffs or a blindfold. They don't care that I've seen them; they don't care that I know where we are.* Kel was still far from trusting them. *Jack says he's here to help me. I'll believe it when it's materialized. Still...*

Kel assessed which of the three he would kill first. The man his own age would be the most likely to represent a challenge. It would be him.

The younger man put the link away and nodded to Jack before sliding the door far enough to peer through the crack.

"Okay, we can go," Jack reassured him. "A little farther and we'll be at the meeting place. You'll get your answers there, okay, Lieutenant?"

"I don't suppose you can tell me anything right now about why I'm here, could you?" Kel knew before he asked that his question was futile.

Jack shook his head; his eyes held a tinge of sadness. "I know how you feel. Trust me, I do. A little farther and we can talk."

Something about Jack's manner made Kel relax another degree. *It's almost as if he's regretful about his role in this.*

They exited, the younger man tilting his head in the direction of travel, allowing Kel to follow behind.

They're sure not treating me as a prisoner, Kel noted. *They're almost treating me like a colleague.*

After walking few bends more through the corridor of the underground utility access, the older man unlocked a door revealing a service lift, and held it open while Kel trailed Jack and the younger man in. None of the men looked at Kel; all seemed absorbed in their own thoughts. After rising several floors, the elevator doors opened, and Kel again followed the strangers down a windowless hallway to pause in front of an unmarked door.

"We're here," Jack said in low tones. "We never meet in the same place twice. Inside will be two men. Only the director will be speaking. You won't see his face. You'll, well... you'll understand soon enough. Ready?"

Kel nodded. It was past time he learned what the mystery was all about.

The room was bare save for two chairs facing each other. A lone individual sat in one. A thick goon—his frown made more pronounced by his unibrow—stood just behind the person seated. Was it a man? A monster? The goon watched Kel with a hand resting inside his jacket, obviously on a blaster. The seated individual wore a loose fitting gray suit with a high collar.

Bipedal. Human-looking hands, Kel assessed as he forced himself into calm, choosing to focus on something basic. Something recognizable. Something that didn't inspire revulsion. In place of a head, a pale holo floated above the shoulders, an undulating pattern of white and gray static, a cruel mock of a disguise.

"Sit, Lieutenant Turner. You have nothing to fear."

The voice came from the datapad atop its lap. The case on the floor next to them made a pulsing hum Kel didn't hear but instead felt in his bones. A disruptor field. Disabling any electronic intrusion to surveil their meeting.

"I know you're wondering why I've asked you to join us."

The voice was genderless and without human quality, unrecognizable as even biologic. It was more than a cheap theatric. If the intention was to intimidate Kel, it worked. The hair on the back of his neck stood. The ghastly apparition floating where the head should have sat flickered and bathed them all in a sickly glow. Kel thought of his friends and let the fire of his anger warm the last chill of his creeps away. His first response to the intimidation faded as he imagined smashing the face behind the macabre holo into pulp.

"Got that right. I'm curious why I am here, Mister Director. Do I have to ask, or will you simply tell me what it is you want from me?"

The static pattern of the mask vibrated and changed course to oscillate in waves running toward the top of its head, the glow now bright enough to cause Kel to squint.

The questioner hammered him rapidly. "How concerned are you for your friends? Do you think of them as family? Are they sacred to you? Would you do anything to save them from their predicament?"

Kel's fury grew. "What is that to you?" he demanded, unsure whether to look at the desolate shifting patterns of the mask or the creature's lap from where the inhuman utterances emerged.

A single finger pointed accusingly at Kel. "First, answer my question, Lieutenant. What happens next hinges on your *truthful* answer."

"Yes!" Kel bellowed. "Yes. I would do anything to save them. Why am I here?"

The pattern on the mask changed again, now running in horizontal ripples. The intensity of the light dimmed. "Because I can make it all go away. For a price. Now answer me another question. Do you love the Republic?"

The more Kel listened, the more his head swam. He was dizzy. Nauseated. Not even his anger could burn away the feeling of weakness that overwhelmed him. The masked creature told Kel what he wanted of him.

"What I need to hear now is that you agree," the voice said.

Kel stared into the blank face. "What if I say no?"

The shoulders raised in a shrug. "You return to the life you knew. Back to Dark Ops. But for your friends, the life they knew is over. They'll be convicted of their crimes. They'll lose everything. You'll have to live with the knowledge that you could have prevented their demise. If that's something you *can* live with."

"This is preposterous!" Kel scoffed. "Your theatrics notwithstanding, I have no reason to believe that you can get the charges against my friends dropped."

"Oh, but I can. I can prove it to you."

Kel seethed. "I'm listening."

"If you agree, when you leave here, you'll find your friends have been released from detention. The charges will not have been dropped. Instead, they will be released on bond pending further investigation. Their ship will be returned to them, and they'll be free to go. Provisionally. Once you complete your assignment, they will receive notice that all charges have been dropped with apologies for the inconvenience, even thanked for their cooperation with the Republic. Until then, they'll live with the threat of reincarceration looming, all the time unaware that their chance at exoneration rests in your capable hands."

Blackmail was as hateful a crime as Kel could imagine. He felt violated in every way. "My friends did nothing wrong. What if they take their chances in court?"

A mocking laugh came from the datapad. "Not even a white knight as yourself could be so naïve. They will be convicted without appeal. I promise you that."

For some reason, Kel knew that if these people could arrange the false charges against the Yomiuris, they could also arrange a false conviction.

Before he could answer, the disembodied voice came at him again. "You're aware that you still haven't answered the question. Do you love the Republic?"

Kel shook his head. "I... I don't understand." The question was as grotesque as the creature's appearance.

"Of course you do!" the voice yelled. "It's a simple question. Do you love the Republic?"

Kel stammered. "I... I love the Legion. I try to live a life of honor and always do what's right. I... believe in the Republic. Yes... yes. I love the Republic." Kel was unsure if his answer was the right one.

The neutered creature stood. "What you do now for your friends, you also do for the good of the Republic. Do you agree to the terms?"

Kel gulped. "Yes. I agree."

The man beside the creature lifted the grav container as Kel's tormentor moved to another door. It was a dismissal. "Jack will be your guide."

Kel didn't verbalize the threat. He knew it would fall on deaf ears. These people felt infinitely powerful and rightly so. Kel realized the apparition's title as director was much more than it implied. He was not a director in the sense that he controlled or supervised. He was the director of their lives. A god.

God or no, it didn't keep him from making a silent oath.

Someday the throat under that mask will be in my hands. Someday soon, I will kill you, Scarecrow.

"Let me have the room, guys," Jack said as he took the seat vacated by the Scarecrow. The two men left Kel and Jack alone. "I said I was here to help, and I meant it. You're not alone in this. We've all been through what you're going through now."

Kel rested his face in his hands. He felt dirty. Used. "I can't believe this." He snapped his head up. "Why me? Why the blackmail? The threats?"

Jack looked at him with pity. "Because. No man can serve two masters. The director insists he have your loyalty. Not the kind of loyalty sealed by an oath or whose source is some abstract sense of moral commitment. *That* kind of loyalty can always be corrupted. The kind of loyalty he demands is from your soul. Whatever you hold most dear, he controls it to ensure your fealty."

The perversity made his bile rise again. "But why me?"

Jack grunted. "You're not going to believe me, but in a weird way, you should feel flattered. You've come to the attention of the most powerful people in the galaxy, and they want you to serve them."

"Who in the karking seven hells *are* you people?"

The sadness in Jack's eyes was replaced by fire. "We don't have a name, but we're the Republic's saviors."

That was as far as the conversation went. Kel walked alone out of the building and back into the crowded concourse. As he joined the wave of bodies pushing him along toward the center of Orion Station, his link buzzed. It was Tara. He swiped the crystal hurriedly to see her smiling face.

"Oh Kel! It's wonderful! They've been released! We're free to go! Where are you? Dad can explain it better than me. They're free, but there still has to be an investigation. Kel, did you hear me?"

The blood drained from his face. "Yes, Tara. I heard you. That's wonderful."

"Get back as soon as you can. We're returning to the ship and leaving as quickly as they'll let us. Oh Kel, we're going home, home to Callie's World. Dad said we won't stop until we get there. Where are you, Kel? Yoshi said you disappeared. We've been worried about you, too."

A fist squeezed his heart. "I'll be right there," he managed. "Tara..." he faltered.

"Yes, Kel?

Words failed him. He had so much he wanted to tell her. He thought of Eric's wedding holos, and how he'd pictured Tara and him in the same scenes, surrounded by family, the sun shining on Tara's perfect face. "I'll be right there."

Dread filled him. After today, he would never see her again.

"But why, Kel? Why do you have to leave now?" Caroline implored. They stood at the gangway leading up to the ship. Kel's grav container and kit bag lay at his feet. "Don't you believe we're innocent?" Caroline asked, hurt in her voice.

"I know you're innocent! This has nothing to do with that," Kel tried to explain, badly.

"Kel," Tara sobbed. "This makes no sense! I... I thought..."

Kel melted as he felt his own tears start to form. "I can't explain." He looked at the ground. He hadn't thought of a way to excuse his sudden departure from the family. "Captain," Kel turned to Jim Yomiuri who looked as perplexed as his wife and daughter. "Sir, I have to leave. If I go, you'll be free."

"I don't understand, Kel." The pain on his face made Kel wish he'd never reentered their lives.

He closed his eyes and swallowed. "Please, I have to go."

Tara wailed as her mother held her. "Kel, I thought you loved us!"

Kel sobbed out, "I'm doing this *because* I love you."

Tara's tears flowed harder.

"Captain, take them home. This will all be okay for you. I promise."

Kel's tears fell on the deck as he bent to retrieve his bag, droplets of rain where there should be none. He broke into a run, dodging between grav carts for the port entrance, running so fast that bystanders questioned whether they should call security.

Only a guilty man fled so swiftly.

10

Kel returned to the meeting room where he'd ruined his life. He told himself it was enough to be removed from the incredible pain of leaving Tara and her family. But the place made him feel dark and violent. A bad spot. He gazed at the grainy pattern of the encrypted link scrambling the holo image floating above a datapad. The encryption made the static concealing the face appear even more chaotic and disorienting than before.

"I'm in," Kel began looking to the man called Jack, who stood at his side. "I believe you. You did what you promised. But I need something else."

The mutilated image betrayed nothing in his face and Kel had no idea how this would be received.

"It is already done," the soulless voice said. "Jack?"

Jack stepped up to place his own datapad in front of Kel. On the screen were the orders from the Legion confirming Kel's temporary assignment to "Office 319." Colonel Hartenstein's signature sat at the bottom. They'd already anticipated that Kel could not be AWOL without becoming the subject of a massive investigation by Dark Ops.

"We don't want you burned out of Dark Ops, Lieutenant," the voice cackled. "Once you've successfully completed this assignment, you'll return to your normal duties and your life, though there's nothing particularly *normal* about the life you lead."

There was no face to see, but Kel imagined the smirk behind the mask.

"We don't need normal people with normal abilities. You are a valuable man with rare talents. And the Republic will continue to need those talents. As long as you remain useful, that is."

The link closed and the Scarecrow's haunting image disappeared.

Kel felt the hollow in his gut deepen. *They mean to use me... forever.* He turned to Jack. "What's Office 319?"

Jack shook his head. "It's deception. Nonsense. There is no 'Office 319.' Anyone who tries to follow up on that will retrieve nothing. It doesn't even need to be denied."

Kel frowned. "That's the best kind of cover. My team. They think I've been seconded to some black project?"

Jack nodded. "Well, you have, haven't you? Your work with RI and your many covert assignments won't make any of this seem extraordinary to your people."

Kel knew that was true. *When the rest of the team gets back to Victrix to find me gone on another solo assignment, they'll think I'm out doing something great. They'll be jealous, even.* Kel saw Poul's face at the news. Still, he wondered. *Who are these people that they can perform such fantastic manipulations?*

Jack noticed Kel's disbelief. "You come from the nether world, buddy. Now, you're even deeper."

Kel didn't see a way out of the well he'd been thrown down. "My friends are never going to be fully in the clear, are they?"

Jack shook his head slowly. "No. They'll always be used as leverage against you." His guide must have correctly interpreted Kel's murderous thoughts at this admission. He attempted to steer Kel in a new direction. "It's not always going to sting so badly. The work... the work is important. The director is placing great trust in you. No one is going to be threatening you after you finish this. You'll see. The director always rewards loyalty. You're going to be brought in. Part of the team. I remember feeling trapped. Extorted. Now... I understand. It has to be this way."

Kel spoke in a cold anger. He pointed at the other two men in the room—the older blond man, Lothar, and the younger man, Zev. "What do they hold over your head? Over yours, or yours?"

Lothar was the one to answer. "Believe me, how they've captured us is no less painful than what they've done to you."

Zev's lips parted to say something, but closed again.

"There's no sense in worrying about that now," Jack concluded. "There's only what remains to be done. It's time to get yourself ready."

"For a third-class spacer, you're handier than most," the bearded bosun said. "But I wouldn't be too handy, know what I mean? The regular crew will think you're trying for their billet. Watch yourself, Teets."

Kel's cover was good. Mark Teets was a Plenaxian refugee with a third-class spacer's ticket and a minor criminal record. Assault, strong arm robbery, and many other charges without convictions. Any search would reveal the picture of a small-time criminal with a penchant for violence and sympathy for radical political movements.

Plenax had been a world of haves and have-nots, with the have-nots resorting to violent revolution every generation or two. It became a moot point when the nanovirus engineered by the government to identify and kill those with certain ideologic traits backfired and exterminated most of the planet.

Once cleared by medscan and years of isolation in an internment camp on a barren moon, the few surviving Plenaxians became galactic refugees. Kel had known at least one legionnaire who claimed ancestry from the planet. What he told of his family's experience was a chilling, almost incomprehensible example of a totalitarian attempt at population control. Plenax was placed under complete quarantine, perhaps never to be opened again for settlement. It had been determined that it may never be possible to guarantee the world was once again safe to inhabit. Bioweapons were universally forbidden for just such a reason. For Kel's purposes, the silver lining to it all was it had created a class of displaced persons whose backgrounds were particularly difficult to verify.

Jack, Lothar, and Zev had gone ahead to lay the groundwork for his unceremonious arrival on Sonestra. He'd been on the junk freighter for two weeks, working as a deckhand. The work was easy, but frustrating. The deckhands Kel shipped with were very much the type of criminal he posed as. The *Calderon* was the kind of ship that filled every desolate spacefield around the edge. When able, such ships carried goods of whatever type to any destination that paid. When unable to find cargo to haul or down for repairs, the crew turned to other means of finance. Some of the crew had bragged about a colony they had terrorized for weeks, hanging around to rob—

and worse—even after the repairs to the ship had been extorted from the locals.

Kel joined the crew as an unpaid deckhand in exchange for transport off Orion Station. If he worked out, the first mate had assured him there would be a chance to become crew and receive shares if he chose to stay on. He'd been with them for one haul, out to the edge and back, now headed for the mid-core and his destination, Sonestra. The planet of his assignment.

No doubt the shadow organization he now worked for had interceded to supply the cargo that brought the freighter to the mid-core, and Kel with it. The shifts were long—sixteen hours. Every shift after his duties in the hold were completed, he was rotated into a hazard suit to clean up the toxic coolant leaking from the plasma convertors. In his downtime he trained his body and studied, no differently than he would for any mission, half-sleeping as he anticipated attack from his crewmates.

During their first meeting, Scarecrow told him he had to accept a task worthy of his skills in order to win freedom for the Yomiuris. At their last meeting before his infiltration, the mysterious visage had made his instructions clear. Kel was expected to perform an assassination. How he would accomplish the task was not so clear. As he lay in his bunk, back against the bulkhead, he listened to the other deckhands snore. The specs let him read while still maintaining situational awareness. He hadn't had to answer any attacks. Yet.

He thought about his final meeting with his handler. The director.

"We interfere when it is to our benefit. The edge is the edge," the Scarecrow lectured him. "We're not the galaxy's policemen. The mid-core, on the other hand... you understand that's different."

The words contained as much static as the face that mesmerized him. Kel understood, though. The Republic's sphere of influence had been expanding since the ebb of the Savage Wars. He and his brothers had been the foot soldiers of the Senate's ex-planetary policy across the galaxy. Most of that effort had been out on the edge. The mid-core had been largely calm.

"The man you need to kill is upsetting the balance of the mid-core worlds. Sonestra has been a stable and productive partner of the Republic. The popular revolution against the oligarchy has waxed and waned for generations. It's an old story, as I'm sure you have witnessed."

Kel didn't want to participate in a discussion of planetary geo-politics with his extortionist.

"This time it appears the subversive forces may actually be close to toppling the government, an achievement we've been able to thwart in the past, or more precisely, a threat kept minimal due to the subversive's persistent incompetence."

Kel could appreciate that much of what his tormentor was telling him. Often, subversive groups were too inept to succeed, even with a just cause.

"Part of their recent success has been a strategy of not just demonizing the inequities in their own system but implicating the Republic. Tying the Republic to the oppression of the world's underclass would be worthy of ignoring except that it has been successful in uniting the different factions of social justice seekers."

Before this moment, Kel wanted to succeed only to secure his family's safety. But now, a small part of him became interested in the mission itself. Preparation was everything. If accepting the situation as just another mission would aid his success, it would help his family. It was time to stop sulking.

"Elsewhere in the galaxy," he asked the apparition, "RI would be running a covert program to undermine the revolutionaries. If there were openly combative factions, DO would be infiltrated to work with one side against the other. Why not on Sonestra?"

The static pattern changed on the holo. Expanding concentric circles spread the same as a pebble dropped on a pond's smooth surface, turning the chaos into a calm and orderly projection.

"So, I have your interest?" the ghoul said softly, the voice reconstruction betraying approval. "That's better. The reason why we don't use more traditional means of interference is partly a matter of optics, partly a matter of exigency.

"The Republic's attempts at heading off this instability have faltered. Evidence suggests that the revolutionaries are receiving support from sympathetic worlds elsewhere in the mid-core, that some worlds may even be waiting to form a larger revolution. Revolutions must have someone to revolt against. The Republic would surely be the target. Such a revolution exported throughout the mid-core would be disastrous."

"The optics," Kel repeated. "Any intervention plausibly attributed to the Republic would coalesce any fomenting rebellion. No matter how covert, if RI or DO's footprint was discovered, it would be as bad or worse than if the revolution succeeded on its own."

The apparition glowed blue for the first time, a soft calming blue. The message was clear. Kel had pleased his master. He felt ashamed that his pride and intellect had driven him to seem cooperative and subservient, and that his analysis agreed with the Scarecrow's own.

More so, he was ashamed because he was hooked. It was a mission. His life was about the mission.

"You know, you were chosen, yes? Chosen from many potential candidates. Tell me you haven't always fantasized about being so special, so unique, that you would be recognized for just such a distinction? Don't try denying it; it's a part of your psychometric profile. Oh, not just yours, all of your class of action seekers and ideologic thrill-boys. Such a strange combination."

While the dissection irked him, Kel supposed it was true. Didn't every boy have fantasies about being a secret agent like in the holo-dramas? His fantasies had become reality, though, once he'd gone to Dark Ops. He said nothing, vowing to hold his tongue. His intellectual hubris might drive him to share his examination of the mission data, but he'd be damned if he would reveal anything personal to the demon before him.

"So yes, it is a mission not for a small group of men, but for one man."

Again, much to his chagrin, Kel agreed. If he'd had to plan it, he would have done it the same way. One man with a good cover could be disposed of, denied, forgotten. If he failed, there would be no trace leading back to the Republic.

"The leader of this rebellion is the glue that holds it all together. And for the rebellion to fall apart, that man must be killed. But it must be in a way that is not obvious. It can't be a political assassination. He must die, though. It must be done in a way that doesn't martyr the man with the Republic his persecutor."

It was unbelievably simple for Kel to kill. If he could see the man through the optic of his N-22, he could kill him at any distance. But the Scarecrow was right. That would do nothing to dissemble the revolution. It might even bolster it.

"We don't have enough time to allow more covert programs to insinuate themselves and build into a slow success against these malcontents. We have months, but not years."

That was the exigency.

Kel looked at the dossier and the picture of the man he was sent to kill. Gerald Grenada would die. The question he still did not know the answer to: could he kill the man without sacrificing his own life in the process?

Kel looked at himself in the reflection. The biomods had darkened his skin to a deep brown. His hair was now jet black and fell off his head in an untidy mop. His eye color had been altered to a dark brown as well. His facial features were unchanged, but the helmet of hair hid them. There would be no way to alter his body further with the time they had available. Clothing and posture would have to do the rest.

"Think you're pretty smart, huh?" a voice came from behind him.

The communal fresher was crowded after shift. Kel had taken a quick sonic shower and had been attending the scraggly beard he was growing. The Sonestrans did not have thick facial hair and it was an effort to trim his to look naturally thin.

"You ain't no engineer, mate. Fixing coils ain't your job. Trying to make the rest of us look bad to the first mate?"

The deckhand Dharo was an ignoramus, but a dangerous one. He'd bragged about how he wanted to find more colonists' daughters to "squally with."

Kel knew exactly what that meant.

Dharo looked at Kel expectantly. He was not alone.

"We say what you do or don't do around here," the derelict next to Dharo said. His name was some guttural sound like Gank, or Gark. A dialect Kel didn't recognize from his travels. A sound one made when choking on sour vomit. Both were covered in body mods, raised patterns carved into their skins depicting acts of violence. Dharo's chest was covered with an explicit pictograph of a man strangling a woman.

"Easy, men," Kel said as he turned to face them. "The engineer needed help. I helped him. If that coil ruptured, we'd all be dead."

The ship was in a constant state of disrepair. Kel had no doubt his life expectancy in combat was better than the odds these spacers faced on an average day on the dilapidated *Calderon*. The universe would see to it that their luck ran out before justice came to them some other way.

"Maybe so," another thug said. "But you still need a lesson in how things are done around here."

Kel raised his hands, seemingly in surrender. "Let's talk about this, Dharo."

The man laughed. "What do you say, boys..."

Dharo exposed his neck as he turned to look at Gark as he taunted. Kel struck at this moment. The man was relaxed, confident in his superior numbers. Kel's knife

153

hand drew power in a small circle as he drove with his hips to chop into the neck, the thug exposing his carotid artery perfectly for Kel.

As the large man buckled, Kel was already moving. The thug to his right had stepped forward to attack, merely multiplying the force of collision as Kel's left hand shot out to stab the man's eye. Kel did not stop until the soft resistance halted at bone. The shriek told of his strike's effectiveness.

Gark couldn't easily close, his advance temporarily halted by the two bodies at his feet as he extended his arms attempting to grapple with Kel. Already off balance, it was natural to continue with the flow of his attacker's momentum. Kel caught the offered arm and turned as he pulled the man forward. As he felt the man's body against his side, he swept rearward with his leg, bending deep from own waist. Kel was now united with the man. Gravity would do the rest. As he knew the man's feet would be pointed skyward, Kel allowed himself to fall, driving the man's head to the hard deck. He felt and heard the snap.

Kel quickly recovered to his feet. Dharo was regaining composure and now sat up. Kel planted a kick squarely on the man's face, rewarded with the man's head snapping backward to send him to the floor once again.

"I'm going to kill you!" the man whose eye Kel had gouged out shrieked. He rose to sit on the sink ledge, one hand still jammed against the hole where his eye had been.

Kel leaped, one foot finding purchase on the man's offered knee, vaulting up as he grasped the man's head and drove his knee into the face, blood now exploding from the flattened nose. More gurgling shrieks spilled out as the man fell.

Gark was rising from the floor. Kel drove a punch over the man's kidney, driving him back to the floor with a hollow suck of air issuing from a wide mouth, proving good effect. Kel turned quickly, looking for the next attack. The man with the destroyed eye and broken nose might be out of the fight. The other two were still capable.

Leaving the three men only partly disabled would not work. Kel looked about for a weapon. In the entry was an emergency response locker, a panel that held equipment for damage control. Inside he found several old atmosphere masks in bad repair and what he had hoped would be there. An autospanner. It was rusted and frozen and incapable of undogging a frozen hatch. It did not matter.

If Kel killed the three men, he would probably get spaced by the bosun and his crew, self-defense or not. Dharo was the first. Laid out on his back, blood bubbling from his lips. Kel aimed a blow at the man's wrist. The bones gave way and Dharo screamed. Kel moved to the man's leg and did the same to one of his ankles. The man whimpered as he curled into a ball.

Kel moved to the next two and repeated the same grizzly act, taking one wrist and one ankle. He stood over the three, evaluating his work.

"What in the bloody hell is going on here?" The bosun stood in the corridor, two spacers behind him carrying sections of pressure tubing as bludgeons.

"You all right, Teets?" the bosun asked.

"I'm fine. These three jumped me."

The bosun pointed at Kel, the two spacers looking unsure as they approached him warily. "Take him to the brig. The captain's going to have to make the call on this. I hope you don't get spaced, Teets."

Kel sat naked in the brig for two days before the bosun appeared with a set of coveralls in hand. He tossed them to Kel through the bars.

"Didn't I tell you not to be too handy?" the older man said wryly. "Time to see the captain."

The man opened the cage and let Kel out. He followed the bosun forward through the narrow passages to stand outside the captain's quarters.

"What's going to happen to me?" Kel asked, genuinely concerned.

"That's up to the captain. But don't worry, if we were going to space you, it would have happened already."

The man knocked and received a loud, "Come," in reply.

"Spacer Teets as you ordered, Captain."

"Get in here and stand to, Spacer," said the voice.

Kel proceeded in and stood at attention, unable to conceal his military bearing.

"Look at me."

Kel dropped his head to see the captain sitting at his desk. Beside him stood the ship's engineer.

"Mister Crawford, join us," the man said to the bosun, who slid in behind Kel. "The only reason you're not trying to breathe vacuum right now is these two men have made statements in your defense. Seems you've made a good showing of yourself while on the *Calderon*. You crewed much before? You only have a third-class ticket, Teets."

"Sir, yes, sir," Kel replied. This part of his cover had been worked out. "I grew up in a spacer family. After we got out of the exile camps, I made my way up to engineer's mate but could never test for a ticket."

"Plenaxian, huh?" the captain asked. "And a criminal record. Pretty much two strikes against you."

"Yes, sir."

The captain squinted. "Maybe a Plenaxian should get a break. What happened to your people..." The man shook his head. "The only reason you're not spaced is 'cause that idiot Dharo has been trouble from day one. The other mongoloids with him are only slightly less problematic. Discipline must be maintained. No one told them to bring you into line. They got what they deserved."

Kel relaxed a little.

"You've crewed before. You know it would have been easier to take a beating and fall in line if you'd wanted to fit in."

Kel knew nothing of the sort but remained silent.

"We're putting you off on Sonestra. We don't need the trouble. I doubt anyone would try to retaliate against you—Dharo didn't have that many friends. But you'll stay in the brig 'til then. Dismissed."

Kel resisted saluting, turned, and waited for the bosun to lead him back to the brig.

"Thank you for keeping me alive, Mister Crawford," Kel told the man as they snaked back to the belly of the ship.

The man harrumphed. "It was Dharo who hung himself. He lied to us. Told us it was a dozen men who'd jumped him. It took two days to get the story straight, until Poshall got out of the medcomp. You did a number on him." That must have been the man Kel blinded. "He's too stupid to lie. Here you are," the bosun said, directing Kel back into the cell.

Kel hesitated. "Mister Crawford, they can get me in here maybe easier than anywhere. Dharo comes after me again, I'm defenseless in there."

The bosun laughed. "Dharo's been spaced. Everyone knows they touch you without permission, they got the same thing coming to them."

The port was shabby and dilapidated. For a mid-core world, Sonestra so far displayed all the decay but none of the development of an older core society. Gone, too, was the vibrancy Kel felt on edge worlds. Crowds swarmed the customs booth, no order to their queuing, people stepping in front of each other if even a millimeter of space opened up. Disinterested officials collected fees and dismissed travelers with a wave. At the exit, two gray uniformed police with blaster rifles stood watch. The weapons were export-type N-16s, not the full power model the Legion used, and without the grenade launcher of his K-17. Still, a capable weapon.

Kel followed the throngs into the sunlight outside, pausing to take in the capital, Potenza. It reminded him of so many urban agglomerations of sparse glistening towers rising above the mundane collections of the stone-colored buildings they dwarfed, a gray haze sitting just above it all. He followed the map in his specs, grateful that what little gear he had brought was returned to him at his departure from the *Calderon*.

He gathered information as he walked, his hood pulled up around his head, pausing in doorways to peer at the motion around him wherever the cityscape showed a transition. He'd moved out of the busy industrial section adjacent the spaceport to an upscale borough where expensive speeders wove through roundabouts and hurtled away. Here the architecture mimicked with plasticrete what skilled hands had once done with stone. The buildings appeared worn, not from neglect but from well-earned age. Kel was dressed in secondhand, nondescript clothing. Around him, pedestrians wore fashionable suits and colorful tunics. This was where the wealthy and mobile lived and worked.

Deeper he went into the city, where the differences in wealth became stark. Buildings crowded each other, some separated by the occasional filthy alley. The crowds on the pedestrian thoroughfares grew dense, packed with people dressed like Kel. Finally, he arrived at his destination.

Mission of the People's Justice, said the sign. The doors were open. People walked in empty-handed and came out holding plates of food and pouches of water. Kel ducked in to see a communal area filled with crowded tables.

"Come to us for help, Compeer? I haven't seen you before." A woman of middle age and stern features addressed him. She looked Kel up and down. "If you seek justice, you're welcome here."

"Yes, Compeer," Kel said, copying the style of address. "I have come asking for help, but I am also looking to help. I wish to serve the cause."

The woman nodded with sad eyes. "Justice needs servitors, and we are all equal in the struggle. Come. First you need nourishment. Then we'll see Compeer Jacinto. You look like a brother who knows how to work."

The food was simple but nutritious. The men and women ladling the food onto his plate all smiled at him warmly and told him, "Stay strong, Compeer," as they did to everyone they served. Kel ate appreciatively as he studied those around him. They were thin and desperate-looking. Few laughed or smiled. No one met his eyes.

"Compeer Daniella says you've volunteered to serve the cause." The man sat beside Kel, leaning his elbows backward onto the table, his face intruding into Kel's space. "You don't look like you're from Sonestra."

Kel kept his eyes on his plate as he continued eating. "Do Sonestrans have a particular appearance, Compeer?"

The man snickered. "Most. But outward appearance is not the most important thing. What drives a man's conscience is. From where do you hail?"

Kel shielded his tray with his forearm, playing the downtrodden. "I just walked from the spaceport. I was a deckhand on the *Calderon*. Before that, I was on—"

"I can see you're a spacer. Where do you hail from originally?"

Kel heaved a sigh. "I'm Plenaxian, okay?"

The man's haughty manner dissipated. "Forgive me, Compeer," he apologized. "I did not mean to offend. What happened to your people is an *infamnia*, a disgrace. Few people have ever been as oppressed as was yours. I am sorry."

"It's okay. I just prefer not to talk about it." Kel picked at his food.

The man perked up. "Is this what brings you to us? You seek justice for all oppressed peoples?"

Kel waited to answer, knowing he had the man's attention and read from his script. "Compeer, I know injustice when I see it. Injustice anywhere means we are all oppressed. The history of Sonestra, what happens here now, well... I'd be lying if I said it hadn't inspired me."

The man placed a hand on Kel's shoulder, an electric excitement sparking in his eyes. "Yes! It inspires us all! Gerald is leading the way. The whole galaxy is paying attention now! The Republic quakes at the thought of us shrugging off our masters. It has brought you to us!"

"Yes, Compeer. That is why I am here."

The man beamed. "I am Compeer Jacinto. I am the district organizer here at the mission, and you are very welcome. Come. You have a place to stay? No? Do not worry. For a man who is willing to serve justice, nothing we have is denied."

11

Kel wore the red shirt and mask of the Dignity Cohort. He held a small wooden pole with nails driven through it, clipped short so as to leave punctures in the skin but not long enough to damage deeply.

A stout man with a gray stubble beard faced them from his perch on top of the driver's cab. Compeer Xavier. "All right, get on the sleds. The crowds of our compeer are forming, and it won't be long before the police send reinforcements. We have to bolster their resolve to resist dispersing until we have disrupted as much of the city as we can. If we must fight the oppressors today, so be it. On to justice, Compeer!"

A cheer went up that Kel joined in as he loaded onto the sled.

Compeer Xavier led the Dignity Cohort. Kel was presented to Xavier the day after his arrival, in order that he might "aid the struggle."

"You look like you can handle yourself," Xavier had said. "Not afraid to scuffle to show the oppressor we mean business, no? Good. The Dignity Cohort is the public face of rectitude for the movement. We are the protector of the compeer. When the police try to break up our peaceful protests, we encourage them to think twice. Many of the compeer are well meaning, but physically, not so much, you know? All are equal, everyone has a rightful place in the struggle, but some are more able than others at the task, yes?"

Compeer Xavier went on to explain how the Dignity Cohort used the tactics of the police against them. "In the old days, if a protest turned violent, the police or the military would crack down, and this would be done hard. It was the Republic we have to thank for squelching that. Yes, I know, they are our oppressors as much as any, but the media attention helped shame and constrain the oligarchs into restraining the police.

"Now the media represent the people and not the oligarchy. The crimes of our oppressors are broadcast for all to see. If a riot cop retaliates against one of us, it is the state who is vilified. We've come a long way, and the victory is within our grasp."

Kel plastered an amenable smile on his face as he took instruction.

"Compeer Teets, stick with Compeer Nacinto," Xavier told him, gesturing to a short, stocky man. "He'll show you the ropes."

Kel took the offered bench next to his new guide and listened as they hovered along the gray streets.

"The idea is to taunt the cops into retaliation," Nacinto lectured. "They're pretty disciplined, but every so often, one will break ranks and run after one of the protestors, trying to discipline them. We look for those opportunities to use these." He hefted his own club. "We don't want to kill one of them; that'd look bad. Instead, we show the people that the cops aren't invincible. The compeer know that we will protect them. There's safety in numbers."

"What about the media?" Kel asked. "Do we want them to holo us, even with our masks to protect us?"

Xavier grinned. "Oh, we absolutely want the broadcasts to be full of the Dignity Cohort meting justice on the oppressor."

Kel thought he understood. He'd studied subversive tactics for years, but had never been this close to their application and the psychology of the radical.

"Believe me, no matter what the antecedent was, the holos will show things favorably toward us. It used to be different on this planet, you know. The media tried to paint us as violent anarchists, but when we started protesting the media, calling them the tool of our oppressors, things changed. Now, they've collectively seen the error of their counterrevolutionary thinking. They support the people now."

The night before, Kel had gone on patrols with the Dignity Cohort to observe. They'd wandered through one of the nicer neighborhoods Kel had passed through on his arrival walking tour of the city. They visited merchants to put up posters advertising rallies, extorting contributions "for the people," and shouted intimidating slogans at pedestrians as they passed. The most common chant was, "Gerald frees the people!" as they raised their left fist high in the air in unison. Police watched them from a distance, never approaching, but also never ignoring their presence. He had been assured that as long as they committed no violence, the police would not interfere.

Kel knew that what he was seeing was a prelude to escalating violence on both sides. The radicals were trying to provoke a truly oppressive response by the oligarchy, and given enough time it would come. If the oligarchs felt genuinely threatened, eventually the secret police would retaliate and kidnap members of the movement, "disappearing them" after they had revealed as much to interrogation as possible. It was probably already happening. This would justify even greater revolutionary violence in response, especially against the innocents they accused as being part of the system. Terror would of course cause the police's tactics to escalate. Freedoms would be lost. People would die.

There was nothing new for Kel to see here. The only question in his mind was which side would prevail. If he had to bet, he'd bet on the oligarchs. They'd suppressed many revolutions in the past. At some point the attenuating influence of the Republic on the ruling party would fail, and their embarrassment by the Spiral News Network and others would cease to restrain their actions to restore order.

"What's this rally trying to accomplish, Compeer Nacinto?" Kel asked his companion.

"I forget you are so new to Sonestra and our cause," Nacinto condescendingly said.

Kel was quick to retort with the language of the revolutionaries. "I fight for justice for all in the galaxy. I may be new to Sonestra's cause, but the cause of justice isn't constrained by location."

Nacinto's eyes widened in surprise. "Yes, Compeer. Xavier has told me of your history. We are lucky to have you. We protest in preparation for the elections this serotinal—our high summer. We have to keep up pressure on the oligarchy to allow the vote to go forward. Gerald stands a good chance of winning. He has the vote of the worker, and we are swaying the middle class. They are the key. The more we can demonstrate the selfishness and the inequities of the system against us all, the better chance we have of victory in the ballot chamber. And if we lose, well, then we can claim the election must have been rigged from the start, eh?" he said to Kel with a grin. "Then the *real* revolution will start, no? Either way, we will win."

It was a riot, not a protest. Kel stood with a group of twenty of the Dignity Cohort. A pulsing mass of protestors taunted the formed up riot police. People shouted curses and hurled packets of foul excrement at the columns of shield-toting cops. The police selected only giants for the riot squad. They stood behind a barricade—helmet visors down, batons humming blue electricity, repulsor shields forming an impenetrable wall at the front rank. From somewhere in the crowd a homemade plasma cocktail flew end over end to land on the steps behind the riot squad, dispersing harmlessly as the purple arcs faded away.

"It won't be long now, Compeer," the man next to him, Tocaro, presaged.

"Been to many of these, Compeer?" Kel asked.

Solemn, Tocaro nodded. "All of them. I've been with the movement seven years, ever since Gerald was released from prison. Well, except the six months I did behind bars myself. I was never even sentenced. It took that long to have a hearing before the magistrate freed me. Don't worry, Compeer. If you are arrested, you'll never be convicted. Even the courts are sympathetic to the cause of justice. There goes another," the man said as they both watched a second plasma cocktail sail out from the crowd, this time landing at the feet of the front rank of the formation, causing some of the cops to let the line waver momentarily. The thickly shielded jumpsuits the police wore diverted most of the energy. The one man receiving the brunt of the charge staggered slightly before making his way out of the formation to be replaced by another from the second rank.

"Get ready for the gas," Tocaro told him as he placed the emergency atmo-mask over his face. The mask would give the wearer about thirty minutes of oxygen, and was the same commercial mask stocked in spacecraft emergency supply lockers. Kel slipped his rebreather from his pocket under his facemask and inserted it. His ocular implants would protect his eyes against anything noxious. He felt the rebreather move uncomfortably posterior to block his nasopharynx, then settle into a tolerable position, muting his voice only slightly.

Tocaro saw this and puzzled. "Don't you want a full mask?"

Kel shook his head. "This will last indefinitely. Core tech. We'll have to see about getting some of these for the cohort."

Tocaro nudged him and pointed. "It's started. Let's go."

The riot police moved past the barricades and into the crowd as drones dropped narc gas cannisters over the swirling mass of protestors. Voices from the drones commanded overhead. "Disperse. Disperse. Clear the streets. Return to your homes." The riot squad marched at a steady pace, repulsor shields interlocked and pushing the crowd back. When a protestor tried to flank them, stun batons appeared between shields to shock them away as the formation advanced intact. The narc gas was having some effect; protestors swooned and were scooped up by less affected compeer.

"Stunners coming now," Tocaro said to him.

They reached an open spot near a large duracrete planter, where several protestors perched, throwing bags of offal at the police. Their poor aim pelted as many of their compatriots as enemies.

"Too late for that," Tocaro yelled at them. "Get down and help recover your compeer who've been gassed."

The youths had donned promasks of their own and were slow to respond to Tocaro's command. He prodded the closest one with his baton to get his attention. It worked. The youth howled, looked down at the red-masked compeer to nod and pull his friend down with him to run into the surging crowd.

Drones dropped purple plasma balls onto the remaining clusters of rioters with good effect. As bodies fell, the police advanced. A female youth produce a baton from her backpack as she weaved toward the front rank of the advancing riot police. From where he was, Kel could see the long, protruding barbs at its tip. This tool had been made for one purpose: to cause grave injury. She waited for the right moment, hunched over to hide between two taller compeer, then sprinted the few meters to the front rank. Leading with her baton, she found a gap between shields where she made her lunge. The short spear connected with the neck of a cop above the shoulder and blood shot out as did a howl of rage.

The thin woman raised her fist in triumph before fleeing back into the crowd. If the police were disciplined, they would let the lone assailant go. Instead, it had broken the last straw of the riot police's restraint. Nerves frayed and tempers held in check for too long, the call went out.

"Charge!"

In pairs, police pushed into the crowds, prodding and stunning with their electric riot batons, repulsor shields buffeting away anyone they encountered. As rioters fell, the shields were used on edge to bludgeon the heads and chests of the rioters.

"Time to get busy. Keep those cops from hurting anyone," Tocaro said, moving toward a lone shield bearing policeman punishing a fallen rioter.

Two policemen pursued the female rioter into an alley. Kel took off after them, dodging and hitting both police and rioter alike in his path. At the end of the blind alley, the two pursuing policemen unleashed their fury, rained blows down on the woman until she fell, cowering under raised arms. Kel didn't pause to think. He flew at the two police, his first blow landing under the nearest man's floating ribs, angling upward as he drove through with his whole body. The man crumpled.

The huge cop next to him turned, his arm still raised with the baton. Kel cross-stepped in a hop, cocking his front leg as he closed, and side kicked the man squarely, knocking him several meters to collide with a wall.

Kel sensed a rush behind him and turned. Someone flew toward him. He stepped aside as he redirected the hurtling cop, driving him headfirst into the opposite wall. He continued turning to face around as a newly arrived cop drew his sidearm. Kel doubted surrender would save him now. His roundhouse kick caught the man's upper arm, halting the gun mid-draw. Then he grasped the wrist holding the gun with both of his hands, turned as he stretched the man out, then turned again, folding the man's arm back on itself, and drove his whole body to the ground to land on top of the man. He felt the shoulder dislocate.

Immediately he threw the gun away and picked up a riot baton. The first two men he'd fought were trying to stand. Kel gave each a brief stun to the unprotected neck, their limbs splaying uncontrollably as they fell again.

The gangly girl knelt, gasping for breath.

"Come on, we've got to get you out of here." He lifted her to her feet. "Can you walk?"

The girl smiled weakly before collapsing again.

Kel dropped to a knee and hoisted her over his shoulders. He ran, keeping her folded around his neck as he pumped his other arm and built up speed. The crowd was dispersed, gas floating in wafts.

Compeer Nacinto waved from within a circle of the re-formed cohort. "This way. This way!" He circled his arm above his head.

Kel ran toward them, fewer bodies blocking his way now, as the crowd of red-masked compeer parted to allow him entry.

"Time to go," Nacinto yelled. "We've done what we can."

Many of the cohort aided injured rioters, supporting them as they limped away with their protectors.

What have I done? Kel wondered. He hadn't really thought about it. He'd simply reacted. *They were going full-bore on this kid, but I didn't want to hurt them. Oba, I pray I didn't kill anyone.*

"Hey, let me down," the voice came from his right ear. "It hurts to breathe."

Halting, Kel dropped to a knee, unwrapping his rider and returning her to her feet. "Can you walk?" Kel asked as he steadied her by her shoulders.

The girl nodded. "I think so. Thank you for saving me," she said weakly.

"What the hell were you thinking?" Kel blurted. "You stabbed one of those cops in the neck. You had to know they were going to come after you. You tried to kill him."

The girl looked puzzled. "That kelhorn? He's not even human. All the oppressors need to die."

They gathered in the main hall. Kel sipped kaff as he listened to the multitude around him relive the events of their perceived success. He closed his eyes and tried to forget seeing the bright red blood issue from the wound in the cop's neck, caused by the girl's spear thrust. His distress was interrupted.

"Come look, come look!" a voice yelled above the horde.

Kel snapped around, expecting to see police bursting through the doors. Instead, a holo was enlarged to play over the end of the hall.

Kel watched himself from above, fighting the four cops as he rescued the collapsed protestor at his feet. The SNN drone had captured the event, starting with the two cops raining blows onto the balled figure of the girl beneath them, and ended with Kel hoisting her onto his shoulders to flee.

"It's Compeer Teets!" a voice shouted in recognition.

"Look at him go!" another said.

"Amazing." The man next to him slapped his back in congratulation. "Our Compeer Teets could win the revolution all by himself."

Kel shrank, trying to avoid notice. It was impossible. Men pulled him upright and thrust him onto their shoulders as they paraded and danced around the hall, putting him down at the front where the leaders stood. The holo played over and over above them.

The stern older woman who had greeted him on his arrival at the mission was the first to reach him. She put a kindly hand to his cheek and her features softened. "I knew there was something special about you, Compeer."

More hands slapped his back and shoulders as Compeers Jacinto and Xavier positioned him between them.

Xavier raised his hands to quiet the crowd. "This has been a great day, made even greater by the useful truths recorded for all to see. The oppressed fight back against overwhelming odds to bring justice to all. A single warrior of ours is purer than a hundred of theirs. Anyone can see that Gerald will bring the same justice to the oppressed, just as our own Compeer Teets has done. This is the kind of compeer Gerald draws to him to join the fight for justice."

A cheer went up as howls and trills filled the hall. Music broke out, tinny horns and deep bass blaring and thumping, festive dancing breaking out in every open space.

Jacinto leaned around Kel to hold his link up for Xavier to see. "He's coming! He's seen."

Xavier smiled and turned to Kel. "Gerald will want to meet you."

By Kel's estimation, Gerald Grenada was not a handsome man. He had a bushy black mustache that matched his slicked back hair and a large mouth full of equally large white teeth. But it was obvious that his charisma made up for his medium stature and round physique. The compeer cheered and crowded to touch the man as his retinue broke the waves of bodies to steer their leader ahead toward the platform. The mission leaders beside Kel all grinned widely, even Compeer Daniella, as Gerald propelled himself onto the riser. After more cheers, the smiling man raised both hands to beg for quiet.

"Justice will not be denied the people!" he boisterously said. The crowd responded appropriately and cheered for minutes before he could calm them again.

Kel's eyes were glued to the man, witnessing his effect on the crowd.

Gerald talked in the same catch phrases and programmed political slogans all the revolutionaries did. The crowd was energized, even fervent, as he mouthed the same rhetoric Kel had already heard dozens of times. The morose, introverted people he had first dined with were practically foaming at the mouth as Gerald praised their commitment and talked about the blow they had again dealt the oligarchy.

Meanwhile, Kel considered when and how he would eliminate his assigned target, his purpose here playing in his head in an endless loop of simple truths.

He dies; my family is free.

I can go home.

He dies.

"Compeer Teets's actions demonstrate our resolve better than a thousand speeches or banners," Gerald said, pointing at the replay of the holo above them—Kel's first blow knocking the armored policemen off the cowering protestor. "Our cruel oppressors use every tool of violence to demean and control the people, beating a defenseless woman simply using her speech to protest the inequity of the oligarchy. Do we answer them with the same? No! We answer injustice with honor and strength, as shown by Compeer Teets!"

Xavier and Jacinto, still flanking Kel, now grasped his hands in theirs and raised his arms overhead to receive the worship of the crowd.

Gerald now stood before Kel and took his hands. He faced the roaring crowd. The demagogue leaned toward Kel. "We will talk. The movement has need of you elsewhere."

Kel sat in the back of the sedan, the shaved head of Gerald's security chief uncomfortably close to his own as they faced rearward at Gerald, who lounged across the seat.

"Compeer," Gerald began. "I have spoken to Compeer Xavier and Jacinto about you. They have many good things to say. You are a man of action, no?"

Kel didn't know what to say. He was playing a part, but it was always best to stick close to the truth. "Yes, Compeer, when it is right to take action."

Gerald nodded approvingly. "See, Castoro? Not just strong, but wise."

The security chief's smooth head bobbed, but the man remained silent.

"Anyone can fight, but knowing *when* to make the fight, that takes brains. Do you have those?"

Kel tried to look deferential. "I do not have much formal education, but I've learned a lot in my travels. My people have had great opportunity to learn from experience."

At this, Gerald looked solemn. "You are Plenaxian? What happened to your people is... criminal does not begin to describe it. It was an act of devastation. The ultimate oppression by the oligarchs. Only, their bioweapon backfired. It might have destroyed a hundred worlds."

In that Kel agreed. Had the Republic not acted swiftly to intervene, the weapon might have been a greater threat to human survival than all the Savage civilizations combined.

"How many of you survived?" Gerald asked.

Kel played his part. "Maybe ten thousand. Some died in the quarantine. I was a child when we were exiled. I grew up inside the isolation moon. It was a prison, though we'd committed no crime."

"Your crime was you dared live," Gerald stated. "And the ruling class knew no other way to control you. Where did you learn to fight?"

Kel used some of the story his Legion acquaintance from Plenax had shared with him. It didn't take too much additional imagination to weave the story together.

"It was a fight for survival every day. Older members of my faction helped me, taught me. Even though we were all exiles, factions formed and tore into each other constantly. Many died not from the plague, but from warfare between the different refugee districts. There was never enough food or necessities. I think they simply locked us up and waited for us to die. When I turned sixteen, we were declared clear of any sign of the infection and turned out to fend for ourselves. But we had no home to return to. Lucky for me, my family had been spacers—skilled workers. I was trained, and after I reached the age, I made my own way and tried to leave the factions behind."

Gerald shook his head. "A victim of a government that should have protected you. I have heard of the plight of your people but never met a soul from your world until now. Thank you for sharing your tale with me." The man did not seem false in his manner. "But now, you come to us, and already you prove you hate injustice as much as any of the compeer, perhaps more. Why does our plight matter to you?"

Kel knew this was the moment. He recited, "To toil and tear my skin so the blood of my body may feed a generation that will someday know freedom, that is all that matters today. For tomorrow, justice will come." Kel produced his link and pushed a holo showing Gerald Grenada behind bars, and the cover of the opus the man had written while imprisoned for labor organizing.

"How did you come to read this?" Gerald asked, surprise on his face as Kel recited the passage from memory.

Kel shrugged and put his link away. "I guess I've always paid attention to injustice. Your words... they meant a lot to me as I was trying to choose the course of my life."

"A man of political conscience as well as action," Gerald said. "The movement has need of you, my friend. The Dignity Cohort is useful, but there are other ways to serve the movement. I think you must go where you can serve justice best."

They drove on to a palatial, walled compound in the hills above the city. The sled came to a halt and they exited, Gerald taking the stairs to the main house where staff competed for his attention. The security retinue from the other vehicles gathered around their leader, Castoro, and Kel.

"Compeer Teets," the smooth headed man began, "Gerald likes you. Gerald sees the best in men. I do not know you. But I know that others have tried to get close to Gerald."

The man snapped his fingers, and rough arms grabbed Kel. He remained calm as Castoro took his bag from him, tossing it on the floating sedan. One man took his specs and link away and handed them to Castoro. The man poured the contents of his bag onto the vehicle and sorted through them, removing the datapad and feeling the clothing for weapons.

Kel spoke up. "I have a vibro-blade in my boot."

Castoro nodded and one of the men patted him down, finding only the knife Kel reported. Castoro nodded to the men and he felt their hands drop away. "We will return your items to you after they have been examined."

The taciturn man directed one of his underlings to get Kel settled. "Be on your best behavior. Rest well, Compeer," the man said behind his back. "Tomorrow, you may be asked to die for the cause of justice."

Days passed. Though Castoro never addressed the subject, Kel knew he had been investigated and found to be trustworthy. Kel had been provided clothing that matched the uniforms of the security detail. The clothes came close to fitting him for length, but the shirt and jacket were much too narrow for his back and chest. He caught a rare glimpse of Gerald, but always fleeting. It was clear that what the revolutionary had in mind for Kel was to fold his talents into his personal security team.

It was evening, and Kel waited for Gerald with the other guards in the courtyard. Soon the revolutionary descended the stairs, followed by Castoro and a young woman carrying a datapad.

"Ah, young compeer, I see that you are getting acclimated," Gerald said, smiling at Kel as he walked to his sedan. "We have a public appearance to make tonight, and it is important that we look strong. The opposition will be in attendance, you understand. Appearance is everything. You will stand as a bodyguard in my private box. See you there."

Gerald followed the young lady into the sedan, Castoro behind them as the door slid closed and the repulsors came to life.

Kel and the other guards found seats in one of the utilitarian sleds waiting to lead the convoy. Some of the guards concealed the bulge of weapons beneath their jackets.

"Are we expecting trouble?" he asked the man next to him.

The man sneered. "Aren't we always, bigshot?"

While Kel hadn't spoken much with the rest of the guards during their communal meals, he hadn't sensed any outright hostility. Until now.

"I saw the holo of your little fight. Your job is to stand around and flex those muscles. If there's any trouble, just put yourself between any blaster bolt and Gerald. We'll do the real work. Got it?"

Apparently among the guards, the comradeship of the compeer did not extend to him.

"Where are we going? What's the event?" Kel pressed.

The man frowned in annoyance. "It's the start of the rest day, dummy. We're headed to the null arena. Gerald has to make an appearance. Don't you know anything?"

Kel didn't argue. He didn't know much. His preparation had been rushed. He'd read the psychometric analysis of the Sonestran culture. It emphasized the overabundance of virility and the culture admiration for exaggerated displays of masculinity and power. He had missed any specific references as to how that was exemplified by sporting events, which made him curious about their destination. An arena.

The vehicle stopped, and Kel rolled out with the other guards to form a perimeter. They made a clear space around the trailing sedan, pushing back crowds of celebrity seekers anxious to touch the hero of the working class, Gerald. Kel followed the others' lead. It was natural work to him, providing security, and he intuitively kept himself between the crowd and Gerald and his closest companions—Castoro and the young lady. Without much effort, the crowds parted to allow their progress.

The marquis holo above the entrance answered Kel's earlier question. Two men floated in micro gravity as they pummeled each other, fighting to break a grip that would allow the other to strike with force as the gravity suddenly resumed, the pair falling to the floor only to commence their combat until unexpectedly, they again floated into the midst of the cube.

Null combat was not familiar to Kel as a sport. It was familiar to him as a vital skill.

"You're going to get your brains bashed in!" Kel's companion yelled to him above the noise of the crowd as they were channeled down into the sunken entrance. "Castoro is going to find out if you're really as tough as everyone thinks."

12

The private box had a commanding view of the arena. The ring of suites around them held parties similar to theirs, the rich surrounded by their protective details. Violence was obviously a concern in Potenza. Protection was a growth industry here. Kel stood behind Gerald seated with his two confidantes and listened as Gerald made commentary for Kel's benefit.

"Castoro does not approve. He thinks it is illiberal to enjoy the same distractions as the oppressors. But shouldn't we enjoy the sweet grapes that make our wine? Or the perfection of the combative struggle? These things burn in the heart of every true Sonestran. They are a part of us."

"Here he comes," Castoro said, ignoring Gerald's critique of his distaste for sport.

Horns blared and the crowds quieted as the musical notes became a dirge. Directly across the arena was the largest of all the private boxes. It was filled with men in military-style uniforms, all surrounding a single figure. The man in the green suit waved to the crowd before snapping to attention before the holo of the Sonestran seal that fluttered above the arena.

Standing, the crowd sang their anthem as the funeral march played. Kel was accustomed to standing at attention for military ceremonies, some of which were excruciatingly long. Kel darted his eyes to see that everyone, revolutionary and wealthy alike, stood respectfully as they sang. The Sonestran identity was strong, regardless of political persuasion. After the song began yet another chorus, he found himself wondering how long the hymn would continue. He'd lost count of the stanzas already sung as his mind wandered. Kel resisted the urge to look at his chrono. After what felt like an eternity, the song ended with a dramatic conclusion of drawn out brass notes. It had to have been the longest anthem he'd ever heard.

No sooner had the party in front of him taken seats than Gerald spoke loud enough for those around to hear him. "That bastard is going to fall, and fall hard. This time, there is no way out for him. We use their own system against them." Gerald's gaze was fixed on the green-suited figure across from them. He waved, catching the dignified man's attention, who responded with a pursed lip nod.

Kel recognized the figure. It was President Viktor Allhambra, the leader of the Liberty Party. Gerald Grenada had risen through the political ranks after being freed from prison for his labor-organizing activities, and was the party leader of the Worker's Union, the largest party in the Popular Unity Coalition which now challenged the traditional order.

Allhambra had been a de facto dictator for over a decade. Five years ago, a token election had been held in which the Liberty Party again took a majority. Now, with the growth of the many opposition parties and their successful coalition under Gerald's leadership, the senator was poised to win the next popular election.

Kel spotted a face of interest. A distinguished man in military dress sat next to Allhambra. The silver-haired man scanned the crowds, alert and purposeful, unconcerned with the activities organizing in the arena below.

The man seemed to sense Kel's prolonged attention and met his eyes across the chasm. He recognized the face.

A member of Sonestra's aristocracy, General Jeremiah Flores had proven himself a capable soldier. As a young officer, he'd served off-world in the Republic Army before returning home. His biography had made mention of a campaign against the Savages where he distinguished himself in combat. Kel did not look away, and neither did the general until the president spoke to divert him. The man was older but not elderly. He had the bearing of a hunter, and his attention to his surroundings told Kel he was a professional.

"Ah, the first bout," Gerald said, breaking Kel's train of thought. "Compeer Teets, have you ever seen our famous null combat before?"

"No, Compeer Senator." Kel wondered when the boom was going to fall. His fellow guard had spoiled the surprise that Kel would be expected to fight tonight.

"Watch carefully. Many times, the fight is over before the end of the first segment."

Two fighters clad only in tight trunks made their way into the arena. The orchestra pit blasted brassy horn notes up into the auditorium, adding to the deafening cheers of the crowds. The fighting arena itself was a transparent cube ten meters in dimension. The cube's floor was sprung, the fighters and their tenders bouncing slightly as they entered from opposite corners.

"Sonestra is well known for its love of combat," Gerald said, his gaze fixed on the assembling duelists. "It is said there are no rules, but of course, all games have rules. It would be more accurate to say there are no penalties. A fighter who hopes to have a long career does not try to maim or kill an opponent because surely, his day will come in turn. Nevertheless, some do not bother with long careers."

As the tone sounded, the two men advanced toward each other. What Kel saw was not unlike any unarmed combat he had seen or practiced. Even alien forms of unarmed combat, unique to their own body morphology, had elements common to all martial arts. The fighters closed after trying to land strikes with hands and feet, the fighter in the red trying to clinch before being broken apart by the blue fighter's successful knee to the midsection.

Suddenly, the fighters stopped their attacks, floating upward into the center of the cube as the grav plating energized to create a microgravity environment. The floating red fighter flailed as he ineffectively tried to right himself. Relaxed, the blue fighter waited for his vector to carry him to a wall. That done, he grasped a handhold, checked his flight path, then launched at the red fighter, tackling the floating man as they both slammed into the opposite wall. With two legs wrapped around the red fighter, the blue gladiator drove elbows into his opponent's head. As they neared the wall, the blue fighter grasped a protruding hold. Now he used a fist to rain hammer blows on the red fighter's head and neck, holding the man against the wall as best he could.

The red fighter tolerated this for a second before his feet found the wall and kicked away, sending them both hurtling toward the ceiling to collide and split apart, tumbling in different directions. The gravity slowly returned as the men descended toward the floor, the blue fighter arriving first, landing softly on his side before righting himself, just in time for the red fighter to ease to the deck. The red fighter flailed to right himself midair, only sending himself in an uncontrollable end-over-end spin to land on his head as gravity reached normal acceleration.

The blue fighter was prepared. He was already stepping into a side kick as the red fighter landed, contacting the man in the chest and sending him crashing into the clear wall beyond. The blue fighter continued his assault, landed on the man's shoulders, pummeling his face with fists and elbows until blood spattered the wall. The red fighter waved his hands in compliance, signaling his surrender. The blue-trunked man danced away as the tenders flooded into the arena to recover the defeated fighter who now stood and bowed curtly to the crowd.

Kel found the bout interesting, but not as dramatic as the picture Gerald had tried to paint. This was no free-for-all. It was almost impossible to generate striking force in microgravity. What blows had been landed in midair were unlikely to cause serious harm to an opponent. The most effective strikes during the floating melee occurred when the red fighter had been tackled midair by the blue fighter's launch to collide against the confines of the cube. The final clash had favored the blue fighter, the first to prepare for attack once the gravity had increased sufficiently. He was unimpressed with the spectacle.

Gerald rose and turned as Castoro and the guards matched him, essentially boxing Kel in place. "Compeer. There will be two more bouts of lower ranked fighters. The fourth bout of the night will be a fighter who has represented the Liberty Party for three seasons. Last month, he defeated our compeer, Lucado."

"We checked you out. The bosun of the *Calderon* gave an interesting account of your time there." Castoro's dark eyes glittered. "What do you think? Are you up to the challenge? Will you fight for the honor of the Worker's Union?"

"You came to us at an opportune time, Compeer," Gerald added. "The president is watching. If you defeat his fighter in front of him and all of Sonestra, you can imagine how it will be perceived. We have great momentum. Now, Compeer, help propel us faster toward justice!"

Kel smiled. "It would be a pleasure to serve, Compeer Senator."

Kel warmed up as the two bodyguards with him respect-fully observed, giving him space in the small locker room. He wore white trunks, contrasting harshly with his dark bio-modded skin, still odd to him as he watched him-self in the mirror throw strike after strike. He'd learned a lot about the Sonestran character in the last few days. Boisterous drama appealed to them, as did displays of purposeless daring. Goading him into the fight—appeal-ing to his sense of revolutionary pride—was a cheap ma-nipulation. Kel knew it was not a spur-of-the-moment act. This was a test. Had he refused the fight, he didn't doubt he would've found himself back in the Dignity Cohort by morning.

That wouldn't serve his purpose.

Still, he had yet to decide how to kill Gerald. He'd been close enough to do it a dozen times, but it would've been an act of suicide. That wouldn't serve his purposes, either.

He noticed, but did not focus on, the subsequent bouts as he worked to get his core temperature up and joints limbered. Using techniques no different from what he had witnessed in the first fight, the fighters that followed were either not particularly advanced in skill... or the null combat was more a spectacle than a display of combative art.

Castoro appeared. "Almost time. Are you ready?"

Kel continued his routine, springing from a deep crouch to bring his knees to his chest, then landing to assume a prone position before springing to the crouch again. After a few more repetitions, he stood. Castoro stared.

"Yes."

"They're ready," a costumed man said from the threshold. As Kel took the cue and moved out, Castoro leaned into his ear. "Gerald would like a show. Not too quick, eh?"

Kel strode by as though he had not heard the man. *Gerald gets what Gerald gets. It'll happen how it's going to happen*, he thought, unconcerned with anyone else's wishes as he strode forward, eyes fixed on the giant cube ahead, ignoring the spectacle around it as he focused. *Concentrate. I believe in my skill and my will to win.* There was too much he didn't know about the sport that could harm him.

The crowd cheered for the fighter already entering from the other side of the arena, as Kel wound a narrow path between the masses on the floor level. He ducked through the portal only to see a retinue of scarlet attendants preceding the man he would soon be pitted against. Above them, the suspended holo of his own face, the Worker's Union flag floating behind him, and the face of his opponent, the state seal behind his. *It's pretty clear who the players represent*, Kel thought, amused at the blatant recognition of the political rivalry.

He had no time to muse on it further as his opponent drew close. The first thing that struck Kel about the man was the thick brow and deep scars above the eyes. The man had earned the mild disfigurement from many blows. He was only slightly shorter than Kel, maybe not at all, but he was wider than Kel by half a body width. The man had no neck, merely a helmet for a head perched on massive trapezius muscles. He was unlike the previous fighters Kel had discounted. *Figures. I get the ringer.* Kel cleared his mind. Regardless of the intimidating appearance, he would fight him no differently from any man. Kel knew his own strengths and weaknesses. Soon, he would know the other man's.

The scarlet-clad staff left the cube. Gerald's bodyguards leaned on the transparent wall just outside his corner, raising fists in support. The cube became eerily still as the portals closed, the thunder of the crowds around their fishbowl all but silenced to a dull hum.

"Die well, you malcontent puppet," the man growled.

Apparently, this guy wants to make it personal, Kel quipped to himself as he took a few deep breaths. He didn't reply. Instead, he watched the man lower his center and place his weight forward, ready to charge at him. The tone exploded from above.

As he'd predicted, the man rushed with full force, not slowing as he closed the distance, indicating he was not going to strike but rather tackle him. Kel had expected something more refined. Kel stepped backward as the man closed, matching the momentum as he grasped the thick, outstretched arms, dropped to the floor, and threw the man over him. Kel melded with the mass and rolled up on top. He still had the man's one arm and threw a series of sharp, vicious open-hand blows to the side of the man's head. Kel sprung off and rolled away, releasing the man to stand.

Kel had felt a fleeting doubt when he first saw his opponent, intimidated by his mass and evidence of previous battle. That evaporated as soon as he acted. Now Kel saw an unskilled fighter who relied on his size.

Okay, Gerald, you wanted a show. I'll give you one.

"That's the only easy one I'll give you, agitator," the man said. He moved to close with Kel more cautiously this time.

The fighter telegraphed a kick, badly. Kel stepped inside and caught the leg, then entered to slam his open hand into the large nose, sweeping the planted leg from inside and behind the knee with his own, following the man down, driving his great, bovine head into the ground. They both bounced. The man drew his elbows in to protect his face, Kel following the return bounce down to hammer his fist into the man's midsection. It was like stone.

Kel broke his mount to roll away, reaching a crouch as the thick man started to rise, when he felt it. He had been awaiting the shift to weightlessness but had not been thoughtful of it, aware that in the previous bouts it had occurred randomly. As he strategized earlier, he considered the opportunity weightlessness would provide him and now acted. He spotted a protruding handhold nearby and launched himself up. It lay five meters above. It was a jump he could never make against full gravity, but in the descending shift to null, he had just enough velocity to reach it with his left hand. Now the micro-G environment was at full effect.

No matter how adept the other fighter might have been, he would never equal Kel in his mastery of maneuver and combat in weightlessness. Kel tucked his legs to place his feet against the cube and craned his neck around to see where his opponent had flown. The man floated upward into the center of the space. At a time when other fighters might've flailed, this brute remained still to avoid an unwanted spin or roll. Kel launched. He intercepted the fighter lower than he had hoped, contacting the man's waist, and wrapped both hands around him as they hurtled to the opposite wall. Kel felt blows rain onto his back. There was little force to them as they floated. Whoever could first grasp one of the small handholds or crevices could use it for leverage to generate striking force. As they hit the wall, his opponent's wide back colliding first, Kel brought his feet around to push off again, trying to drive them both to a higher trajectory. More blows rained onto Kel's back, and now he released his grip and pushed the man away, tucking as he continued in a new trajectory toward another section of the clear ceiling.

Kel spread-eagled as he reached the ceiling. His hand found a crevice which arrested his motion enough to allow him to tuck. As his feet found the ceiling, he pushed off straight down at the floor. *If I timed this correctly... Yes!* He felt the gravity rise as he pitched forward to orient upright, and reached the floor with enough momentum lost to keep him there as the null gradually abated. His opponent rolled in midair as he sank slowly downward. When he was two meters above the deck, Kel cross-stepped and hurled a side kick into the suspended figure with enough force to send the massive body across the cube. Gravity's pull reached full effect as he moved to close again, just as the harsh tone resumed.

It had been the first bout of the night to complete one segment.

The second segment was more of the same. It was frustrating to Kel. It was virtually impossible to strike with enough force to cause damage to his opponent during the shifts to null. The wild, careening paths and elastic collisions of the bodies may have entertained the spectators, but annoyed Kel. He continued his strategy of closing and using hard strikes against soft parts of his opponent's body, and soft strikes against his opponent's thick head to wear him down. He'd come close to getting a rear choke hold on the giant, only to find there was no neck to attack. As the gravity disappeared, what power he'd been able to derive from the ground evaporated, and all he could do was ride the man until gravity resumed and another segment ended.

Kel leaned against the cube as he awaited the next tone. In the last exchange the fighter had clawed at Kel's thighs, hoping to break his hold. Small rivulets of blood formed in the nail tracks. The man had also tried to gouge Kel's groin as they grappled in midair. He'd defeated the cheap blow by rolling his thigh inward and maintaining his tight mount, but it aggravated him. It was a move of desperation. Kel dominated every engagement. He did not know how long the fight would be allowed to continue and decided this segment would be the last. The tone pierced the cube.

As he closed, Kel spoke his first words to his opponent. "I'm through being gentle. Now, I've got to mess you up."

The fighter lunged at Kel with a grunt. Kel evaded and traded blows, keeping the man at a distance. The heavier man landed a few ineffectual blows on him, Kel getting the better of him as his constant assault of strikes and kicks drove the man to retreat each time. His opponent tried the same lunging tactic several more times before Kel let him close. The large man tried to bowl Kel over and simultaneously strike his head. Kel slid his head inside a long jab and retreated, encouraging the man to strike again. He had his opening. His own arm shot out and around the extended arm as he dropped onto his back. The man fell with him. Kel let his breath leave as he crunched his abdominals and rotated to one side.

The fighter tried to break away and rose to a knee. Kel continued to trap the man's arm underneath his own armpit. His leg snaked out over the man's shoulder to tuck his foot behind his own opposite knee, the man's arm and neck now trapped between Kel's scissored legs. A moment of panic overtook the man as he attempted to strike Kel's face with his free arm. Kel easily blocked the blows with his arm and gave another series of open strikes to the man's face and ear. Now Kel felt it again, the ease of strain on his body as the weight of the man on top of him diminished. The man gave a push with his legs as their bodies lifted, sending the entwined pair into an erratic spin as they left the floor.

Kel readjusted his position to allow his left arm to wrap deeper around the thick corded arm he trapped and leaned back, leveraging his weight against the elbow. The man tried to flex his arm to prevent the lock. He squeezed his knees together around the massive neck, felt the arm slowly straighten, fatigue and oxygen deprivation finally overcoming the large man. The elbow's elastic resistance failed, and Kel felt the slack leave completely. It would have been easier to apply the choke had they been allowed to wear clothing, but with no collar to grasp, Kel took his free arm and wedged his knife hand in between the man's neck and shoulder and rotated his forearm until his ulna pressed against the neck sharply.

The man's last attempt to flex his elbow ended. Kel arched his body harder, leveraging the joint in the direction it was not intended to bend. The man flailed and grunted. As they contacted the ceiling, Kel knew he too was fatiguing, and forced himself to breathe deeply as he continued his effort. He couldn't tell if the man was tapping against his side in surrender, or was merely continuing to launch ever weakening attacks.

He didn't care at this point. Kel would be the one to say when the fight was over. He didn't enjoy cruelty, but at the moment, his anger and frustration boiled over as the intimidating giant flailed weakly. "You'll get no tap out from me. I'll tell you when you've had enough, buddy." He wished it were the Scarecrow entwined in his death grip right now. He felt the fighter's resistance fade as he continued his strangle, increasing his efforts with all his strength as the man's body softened.

The familiar feeling of weight returned and Kel felt himself slowly sink to the ground, the giant still wrapped in his embrace. As Kel's back touched the floor, the cube unsealed and people rushed in. Kel released the man and rose to his feet, breathing deeply and feeling the fatigue from holding the tonic contractions so long, but ready to fight if anyone attacked. Roars filled the cube from outside. Kel was lifted off his feet as Gerald's guards hoisted him aloft.

The noise was deafening as he fought a new battle, one to return oxygen to his tissues. He sucked air deeply, his heart pounding in his ears. He had to stand, desperate to contract his quadriceps and send blood back up into his chest and on to his brain. "Let me down, let me down!" he pleaded in a gasp.

"Let him down, Compeer!" Gerald yelled above them all, and he felt himself lowered onto his feet. Gerald was there, raising Kel's arm into the air as he turned Kel with him around the cube for all to see.

"You've done it," the toothy smile returned. "Compeer Teets, you've done it! Never did I doubt. A man of advanced political conscience will always win over the hereditary oligarchs. You've proven we are the superior men once again. Nothing can stop us now." Gerald dropped Kel's arm to raise both of his own as he cheered and faced the crowd, pumping his fists overhead and shouting.

Far above them, in his private box, President Allhambra grimaced. He leaned over to speak to the uniformed man beside him. The silver-haired general, Flores, rose and stepped forward to the edge of the box. He formed a crisp hand salute, holding it at his brow as he dipped his chin to meet Kel's gaze.

Hours of food and music followed. Attractive young women took turns sitting on Kel's lap as he winced, the nano-dressings on his legs and the medicines not taking away the deep ache that remained. Finally, they returned to the compound, Kel riding with Gerald and his close entourage, the young female assistant snuggled beside Gerald, his arm draped across her shoulders.

"Arinka was quite worried about you, young Mark," Gerald said. The young lady smiled at Kel. Gerald drank much during the revelry and was now quite inebriated. "I told her it was for nothing."

This would be the perfect time to kill Gerald. Him and his entourage. Kel couldn't. He was exhausted. Instead, he vowed to force the epiphany that would make a suitable plan clear to him.

"Thank you for your faith in me, Compeer Senator," Kel instead said with an exhale of fatigue.

Gerald laughed. "I told you, when we are alone, you must call me Gerald. Just as I call you Mark. You are part of the inner circle now. Isn't that right, Castoro?"

The very sober man next to Kel agreed. "It is so. It was a great victory tonight, Mark. You avenged our compeer, Lucado, though his sacrifice for the struggle will be remembered."

Kel took the meaning. "Lucado, was he... ?"

Gerald preempted the rest of the question. "He didn't have your luck. Or skill, I suppose. Still, he was a valuable compeer and will be missed."

Information I could have used earlier, Kel fumed. *I wouldn't have entertained the request to draw out the fight had I known the null boxer killed Lucado.* He still didn't know the fighter's name, not that it mattered now. Kel thought about the prostrated form as it was dragged out of the cube and placed on a repulsor gurney. Perhaps with regen the fighter would regain some of the brain cells Kel had killed with his prolonged strangle. He really didn't care, though. It was becoming a true effort to conceal, but Kel had taken a dislike to what he'd experienced of this part of Sonestran culture. The posturing. The boisterousness. The bullying. The fighter had been the epitome of the local character at its worst. He'd seen much kindness and beauty here as well, but the more time he spent with the revolutionaries, the harder it was to recognize. *At the end of it all, what will I remember about his place?* he wondered. *When I look back, I just want to remember that I freed my friends.*

As they departed the sedan, Kel turned toward the dorms where the guards quartered, anxious to see the tiny room he had bedded in.

Gerald laughed in his irritating manner, made even more irritating as the man slurred, "Not so fast, Mark. Arinka, get our valued compeer settled before you come to bed. You don't belong there anymore. You deserve much more. 'From each according to his abilities,' and I say your need is a reward from the people. Tomorrow, the struggle continues. Sleep well, warrior for justice." Gerald staggered up the rear stairs, singing in some foreign language Kel could not identify.

Arinka placed a hand on Kel's elbow. "Come, Compeer. We have a room prepared for you."

Too tired to protest, Kel followed the young lady up the stairs and through the grand foyer, descending to a lower floor where a luxurious entertaining area overlooked a lighted pool on a terrace. She led Kel down a pleasantly dim hall to a set of double doors. She grandly opened the entrance and turned to Kel for his approval. Every comfort he had lacked for months lay before him. He would trade it for a small berth on the *Callie* right now.

"If you need anything, there is a servant on duty in the kitchen and guards, well, you know them. Sleep well, Mark." She closed the doors behind her as she left.

Kel removed his jacket and inspected the room. He stripped and stepped into the shower, real jets of water soothing his muscles as opposed to the dry sonic waves he was accustomed to. On the dresser lay his travel bag with the items that had been taken from him on arrival. He sat on the edge of the bed and examined the datapad, smaller link, and specs. Even his vibro-blade had been returned. He put on the specs and opened appliance programs on both devices. After several minutes both reported a green status. The devices given to him by his handlers could not be penetrated and the programs contained within could not be deciphered. To any attempt at evaluation, they were nothing more than basic commercial models of information tech.

Kel activated the appliance programs in sequence, scrolled the new menu, and activated the innocuous icon. After a moment, another green indicator appeared. No form of intrusive surveillance was detected. He blinked at the menu and waited. In a moment, a screen opened and Jack appeared, alert and dressed as though he'd been expecting the bounce. Kel knew his handlers had been observing tonight's events.

"I'm in."

13

"It's more important that it be done right than done quick- ly," Jack reminded him. Kel had risked a single clandes- tine meet with Jack and the operatives Lothar and Zev, hoping for clues as to how to advance the mission.

"Your instructions on that are absolute," Lothar, the oldest among them, said. It was the first time he'd given Kel advice. "The manner and timing can't be forced. Have you discovered any health issues you could exploit? A medication to switch or overdose? A local opponent who can be goaded into killing him? A jealous husband is al- ways good."

Kel had agonized over just these possibilities for weeks. "Nothing helpful's appeared. Otherwise, I'd have done it already."

He was frustrated. The method and the act itself had to avoid causing any suspicion linking the death to the Republic; that had been made abundantly clear. Poisoning could always be detected. An accident like a fall or drown- ing or a death by misadventure is what he was hoping to orchestrate to meet the terms of his instructions.

Zev, the man nearest Kel's age, scolded, "I know you legionnaires are action hounds. Don't get frustrated and just kill him. But if there's no other way and you must, then don't get taken alive afterward. If you don't suicide, we'll have to end things for you. Even then, disappearing your body into a mass converter will raise suspicion and promote conspiracy theories. A murder without a murderer to hold accountable is no good. Our orders are to assist, not set you up as a patsy."

Kel was glad to hear the previously hostile young man verbalize their reluctance to kill him, even for pragmatic reasons like orders. Still, he wasn't deeply comforted. "Assist me? What are you guys doing to help me while I'm playing revolutionary?"

Jack frowned at him. "We're working as hard as you are, you can be assured of that. If we find an answer to your dilemma, we'll be in contact."

Lothar gave Kel a conciliatory, almost fatherly smile. "I know it seems impossible. But a man like Grenada will have a weakness you can exploit. Just keep looking. When you've accomplished your task, then we can get you out."

Even the taciturn Zev agreed. "The first one is always the hardest. The director makes it that way for a reason. When you're done, you'll understand."

Kel doubted that.

He learned more about Gerald's Workers Union and the strategy to topple the Liberty Party in the next election. His days were spent close at Gerald's side—as close as Security Chief Castoro—acting the part of celebrity and conferring the appearance of strength wherever Gerald appeared. The thought of how to kill the man and meet the terms of his ransom never left him. He fought the anxiety and stress by reminding himself that his only purpose in life was to save his family from ruin. But the longer he remained on Sonestra, the further away the attainment of his goal seemed.

They rode to another rally, Gerald's obsessive commentary dominating the conversation as usual. *This isn't a mission.* Kel tried to silence the voice in his head. *It's an incarceration. It's torture.* The impulse to end his limbo by snapping Gerald's neck nearly overcame him while Gerald continued an endless diatribe about justice. There were times when what Gerald said seemed reasonable, but then his logic took a twisted course to invalidate whatever he'd just said.

"The state is a criminal organization. It has mobilized its military, police, and intelligence apparatus against the people and our fight for a just society. The Liberty Party and Allhambra have delegitimized themselves." Kel sat next to Castoro in his usual place in the sedan, facing Gerald and Arinka as she worked on her datapad, seemingly oblivious to her lover's evangelizing.

"The Liberty Party is in bed with the largest crime syndicates on Sonestra, the ones who prey on the worker. In areas of lawlessness where illicit activities, human trafficking, and the drug trade reign, the Liberty Party and the state apparatus do nothing.

"You see," Gerald pointed to Kel, making sure he was receiving his transmission fully. Castoro and Arinka both stared at their datapads. Not the new audience for his sermon, they were exempt from his personal attention for the moment. "It all serves their goal of suppressing internal opposition by the worker class."

Kel played the strong, silent disciple, absorbing the wisdom Gerald dispensed. In truth, it was not a different persona than the one he assumed in any setting outside of the comfort of his kill team. It was easy to play. Had he been forced to pose as a gregarious socialite, his skills would have failed him without more training. Quiet, coiled, deadly; that was easy. That was him on most days of his life. The Yomiuris had been the only ones to bring out the part of Kel that let him display the peaceful, happy man he had discovered.

No matter the outcome of this task, sadly he knew that part of his life was over.

His attention had briefly faltered and Gerald sensed it, having not received the near constant nod Kel gave after every major proclamation. "I see you are now lost and I must explain further, Compeer." He continued without pause. Gerald was on a roll.

"The state delegates authority to criminal organizations wherever it does not want to expend necessary resources. The workers and the poor do not interest them. So, by allowing criminal enterprises to rule in unsavory places, opposition is squelched, the state saves resources, and the partnership between the criminals and the state grows. It is a win-win situation for them both. For the people, it is misery."

Kel thought about Gerald's view of the state as a criminal enterprise, then contrasted that with what he had witnessed of the Workers Union since becoming part of the inner circle. One night he'd taken part in a shakedown operation as the Dignity Cohort collected "taxes" from several factory owners and small businesses that employed members of the Workers Union. It was as criminal an operation as any he could imagine. At the first visit, they collected a large payment from a distressed factory owner at his plant that printed plasticrete molds for construction. The middle-aged man was bullied by their crew of thugs in his simple office, no indication of wealth or comfort on display.

"I work the same as any man." The owner shook with frustration as he counted out the credits. "What I have, I earned. The people I employ I pay for their labor. If I lose this factory, who will they work for? Who will feed them?"

The chief thug for tonight's shakedown, Tocaro, laughed at the man's pain. "When is what is required to live ever enough for the likes of you? Why do you deserve more than the worker on the floor? This is a small tax to make up for your greed. When the Workers Union is in power, you'll be grateful that we'll remember who cooperated and who didn't."

The rest of the night's visits went smoothly, and Kel was not forced to suffer the sight of violence against any of the extorted.

"What happens if they don't pay up?" Kel asked one of the thugs with him.

"Oh, the workers interfere with productivity by sabotaging equipment, ruining goods, stuff like that. The next step is a strike. Then we threaten the owner and his family. Last step is burning down the place. We've only had to do that once. They get the message—if you're a parasite who exploits the work of the people, at least you're going to support the party of the people."

On another occasion, he witnessed a similar tactic used against a gang called the Kurks dealing in narcotics and other criminal activities in one of Potenza's worker districts. What Kel thought was an act of vigilantism to remove a criminal element preying on the poor turned out to be yet another act of extortion to secure credits for the Workers Union. Castoro himself oversaw the operation. When the security chief recruited Kel for the mission, he was able to answer the serious man's question with honesty. "Yes, Compeer Castoro. I am very competent with a blaster."

Kel stood next to Castoro brandishing a civilian knockoff of the N-16 along with a dozen of Gerald's guards, the Dignity Cohort armed with powerful but old slug throwers and cheap blasters as they stood in the gang's central offices.

"This is a courtesy," Castoro shared with Kel on the way to their destination. "A friendly visit to make sure they understand the way things are going to be. Whatever bribes they've been funneling to the police and any local politicians they're going to have to match to the Workers Union. That is, if they want to stay in business."

The meeting was tense, but they outclassed the Kurks by double the numbers and triple the guns. The message was received. They departed; a figure agreed upon for regular payment.

The head Kurk asked the obvious. "We pay protection. What's keeping us from sending the cops after you?"

"When the Workers Union wins the elections, who do you think will be running the cops?" Castoro answered mirthlessly. "Everyone now in a position of authority will be replaced with our people. There will be only us to deal with soon."

On the ride back to the compound, Castoro confided in him. "When Gerald wins, one of the first things we'll be doing is sending the police in to break up that gang. They all need to be dead or in prison."

For a moment, Kel saw a glimmer of hope. It was a genius of a plan; extort money from criminals to further the aims of the Union, then when in power, destroy the criminals for the betterment of society. Kel's head swam momentarily with the deviousness of it until Castoro said, "Our own people need to be running those activities."

That night, Kel made his first crucial error. Castoro briefed Gerald on the outcome of the meeting to extort the leaders of the drug den as the three sipped kaff alone after a late meal. Instead of acting as the sycophant Mark Teets, he slipped and spoke up as Kel. Adding insult to injury, his timing couldn't have been worse, as Gerald was just about to launch into another of his homilies.

"This seems wrong. Drugs destroy communities and lives." Kel immediately regretted the outburst.

The silence that followed was his first indication he'd made a fatal error in judgment. The scowl on Castoro's face was the second. The bald security chief took in a deep breath from which to power the coming rebuke when Gerald raised a restraining palm toward him. "It's okay, Castoro. The compeer is speaking from his heart."

What did I just do? Kel's brain screamed. *I'm breaking under the stress. I know better.* The next moments would be critical. If he was about to be removed from the inner circle for his outburst, he'd have no choice but to kill both men here and now.

These might be the last moments of his life.

Gerald looked to Kel with compassion. "It's okay, Mark. You are new to the ways of our warfare against the state." Gerald put a hand on his shoulder, a parent explaining to a wayward child. "How things must be *now* is not how things will be *after* the revolution. We are artists shaping a new society. What we have to work with is not gold or some pure mineral, but men. Flawed, selfish, weak men. To build the new man, we must first use the tools at hand to destroy the status quo. Our first task is tearing down the old. If we do not first succeed in that, there can never be a rebuilding."

Acting cowed, Kel nodded vigorously to demonstrate both agreement and a new enlightenment on his part. Of course, that alone would not be enough to satisfy. He must humble himself.

"I apologize, Gerald. Sometimes I am impatient for the new society. I will redouble my efforts to be a fighter for the people."

That did it. Gerald beamed his toothy smile. "I never doubted you would, Mark. You need prove nothing, though you take every opportunity to prepare yourself for the next challenge. I see how hard you work. Don't act surprised—we all do."

Kel tried not to betray his new fear; there was a warning hidden in the man's praise.

I'm being watched. How closely, though?

It was a question he asked himself constantly. Kel had taken to frequent workouts. He'd made it known that to maintain his abilities as an elite fighter, he had to train vigorously. For the first time in his career, Kel's unarmed combat skills were the difference in his survival. He enjoyed martial arts. Mostly, they were a way of training the body and mind, of building combat aggressiveness. A legionnaire's skill with any number of complex weapon systems won fights. Not using fists and feet to injure an enemy. Now, his survival and success in getting close to his target had been due solely to his hand-to-hand talents. He intensified his training not only for his cover but for his very survival. It also gave him a perfect excuse to be alone.

Castoro encouraged him to take time whenever possible to work out and had instructed the other guards to leave Kel the space to do so. Kel's minor celebrity as a symbol of the Workers Union was valued. When Gerald was on the compound, Kel would remove himself for solitary training. When at his senatorial offices, Kel could leave Gerald's security to the guard detail and disappear into the city for long runs.

This is when he was able to make his one rendezvous with Jack. He took long, circuitous routes through the city, dodging through traffic and making untelegraphed jogs down narrow alleys as his specs guided the way. He made the same bizarre, random patterned run daily. Did they suspect he had been clandestinely meeting a contact? He could not have been followed on foot. By drone? The anti-intrusion shield they spoke under would defeat any electronic means of detection. But had the act of being solitary itself raised suspicion? Now as he met Gerald's eyes, his toothy smile fading, he wondered if he was under suspicion.

"To serve the people sometimes we must do what is unpleasant," Gerald said with a frown, his tone changing as the sermon became a lecture, the harshness of the words an order. "And to serve the people, you must serve those who lead the revolution. Are we clear, Mark?"

Kel gulped. "I serve without question."

Gerald leaned back and smiled. "I think that's all for tonight. Rest well, Compeer. The debates are tomorrow. We need a show of strength. I'm depending on you."

Kel stood and bowed. "I won't let you down, Senator. Good night." He then bowed to Castoro and departed, feeling the eyes of both men on him as he left the room.

They're on to me. He hurried to his room. *I'm going to be caught. I'm going to fail. It has to be soon. Gerald must die.* Kel sat in his room, his back against the wall, waiting for the guards to burst in.

To forsake paranoia was suicide.

The debates were more a carnival than a metered exchange of viewpoints. Kel stood in the wings as Gerald and President Allhambra shouted over each other, the audience jeering and cheering along. Fights broke out in the house, mirroring the discord on stage.

It was crowded backstage. Kel played his role of thug, surrounding Gerald with the rest of the train escorting the candidate into the stadium, and now with little else to do, watched the spectacle. The rage boiling over on the floor was contrasted by the quiet heat of tempers held in check behind the stage. The two opposing bands of followers had tried to stay segregated, but soon everyone was divided into smaller groups intermingled with the opposition as they strained to get a vantage point to observe their own leader. In both factions, people scowled and frowned, expanded their chests and threw back shoulders, all signaling intent to their enemies—predators forced into a common territory, posturing to show their deadly capacity. Kel felt a presence in his personal space, pressing and intrusive.

A mild, understated voice aimed itself in his ear. "It's an entirely different kind of warfare, isn't it?"

General Jeremiah Flores stood next to him, tan skin contrasted by his smooth silver hair. He wore a tailored suit rather than his uniform. Kel was momentarily at a loss for words. "Warfare takes many forms," the general continued, looking past the intended recipient of his musings toward the two men ranting at each other on stage. "This is perhaps the most treacherous combat of them all."

Kel was intrigued. "Yes, General Flores. Perhaps. At least, it's the most dishonest."

Now the general met Kel's eyes, approval on his face. "I've wanted to compliment you on your victory in the null ring. It was most impressive. It reminded me of fighting skill I have seen in few places and among only a select group of soldiers."

Kel's blood froze. "I'm not a soldier, though, General."

The older man looked back to the orators as he nodded in acceptance. "Pity. But nonetheless, you've learned the skills of a warrior. I suppose to survive the incarceration of the Plenaxians, it was necessary."

It didn't surprise Kel that the Sonestran intelligence service had targeted him for investigation.

"Still, I recognize in you something special."

Kel looked around cautiously. The attention was on Gerald and Allhambra. Castoro stood in the wings nearest the stage, his back to Kel. No one seemed to notice their conversation. He decided to risk further entertaining his curiosity.

"I'm not special, General. But I'm curious. One warrior to another. What makes an aristocrat leave his mansion to serve in the Savage Wars?"

Now it was the general's turn for surprise. The man's composure broken for a microsecond. Kel plunged deeper.

"You see, General. I know about you, too."

Flores gave a curt smile.

"I think you know the answer already. For a warrior, sometimes the challenge is as much without as it is within. We go where the fight is, yes? Certainly, the Savages were a threat to us all. It would have been... cowardly to not rise to the occasion."

Kel nodded knowingly and looked away, conscious to not let his attention to the general be noticed.

"This isn't going to go the way your boss thinks. You know this, yes?" Now the general's tone was urgent, his voice lowered. He stepped closer.

Kel fought to remain aloof and betray no response, his attention fixed on the stage.

"I would see a pure warrior as yourself spared the dark path that awaits Gerald Grenada. If he wins, and if he does what he says he will do... it will not end well for him. He thinks he has enchanted the planet with his spell. He will never control the loyalty of the army or the police. He is deluded to think he can transform Sonestra into his vision for utopia overnight."

Kel remained silent. *Why does the general risk telling all this to me?*

"You are new here, Mark Teets. Listen to me. Flee this man. He is insane."

An overwhelming ache filled him. Suddenly, he felt defenseless against the older man. Flores reminded him of men he respected, admired, even emulated. Colonel Hartenstein, Nail, Bigg... for a moment, he longed to unburden himself and tell the general everything. For a moment.

Duty called him back.

"Thanks for your words, General. I must go. There's work to do against the oppressor. See that you stay out of our way if you don't want the same fate that awaits Allhambra." Kel pressed between the bodies to make his retreat, leaving the general behind.

EXIGENCY

As he moved, he saw Castoro's attention turn upon him. He met the man's eyes briefly and gestured toward the exit. The debate was winding down. "I'll check the path to the sedan," he mouthed. He received a scowl, then a nod.

Did he see me with Flores? Damnit! I'm a fool. He cursed his stupidity. *I was already under suspicion. This isn't going to help.*

Back in the sedan, Gerald beamed and frenetically recounted his victory. "We've won, I tell you, we've already won! We have the dogs panting in fear. Did you see how the crowd frothed to tear into the elite! Allhambra is a fool if he doesn't abdicate and flee while he still can. Surely, the dolt must know what is awaiting him after the elections!"

"What did that old fool Flores want with you?" Castoro blurted.

Kel had been distracted, thinking about the general's warning to him, still wondering why the man had sought him out for the candid talk. He didn't hesitate.

"He complimented me on the fight. I had to restrain myself from pummeling the arrogant elitist. But I knew the time wasn't right. I did tell him he'd be getting the same treatment as his boss if he didn't get with us on the right side of history."

Gerald laughed in approval. "See, Castoro? I keep telling you how smart the young compeer is." Gerald leaned forward and slapped Kel's knee. "You'll get your chance, Mark. We'll let you know when it is right to unleash your talents. Don't worry, my friend, it won't be long now."

This seemed to satisfy Castoro who turned his attention to Gerald as they continued to strategize. Kel relaxed, his deception successful.

Gerald, however, did not relax.

"The more I think about how we will punish those pigs, the more I look forward to their suffering, just as they've made us suffer. Every day I sat in that cell, I thought of this." Gerald's self-proclaimed victory did nothing to placate him. Instead, the ever present mania increased as they rode, a fury overtaking him, a madness possessing him. Gesturing violently as he had done during the debate, he pounded the armrests and roof of the compartment. Wincing, Arinka retreated from his side, while Gerald continued to physically punctuate his frenzied speech.

"I tell you all—I tell the world—no man has done what I am about to do!"

His energy could not be contained by the small space. Gerald opened the roof hatch and stood, screaming into the night air as they rode. Arinka's eyes pleaded with Castoro and Kel to help the agitated man, who was so clearly losing control.

Gerald screamed into the darkness, "Without me, the revolution is nothing! It is *I* who lead the people to a better future. It is *I* who will overthrow the oppressor. *Me!* Do not stand against me, or you will be crushed under the righteous weight of my army. Without me, the people are blind. The fire of my soul explodes as a burning star, ending the very galaxy itself!"

Arinka pleaded with him as she tried to pull Gerald down into his seat.

Kel frowned at Castoro, who seemed at a loss. "What do we do?"

Face drawn, the demagogue's right-hand man looked feeble. Kel had not seen him helpless before. All the while Gerald continued his howling proclamations, no indication that he would stop.

"We've seen him like this before," said Castoro quietly to Kel. "We've got to get him home. It will be all right."

Arinka sobbed as she surrendered her struggle to calm the raving man, collapsing into her seat.

"I *am* the nation! I *am* the people! I will crush the tyrants and break their hold forever! And when I do, you will all worship me as your god!"

And suddenly, Kel knew how to kill Gerald Grenada.

14

The Worker's Party won the election by a slim majority. What followed wasn't pretty. Rather than a smooth transition of power from one party to another, almost immediately rioting began. Not by the losing side, but by the Worker's Party. Even the media had difficulty spinning the violence as justified. Gangs of revolutionaries pulled "enemies of the people" from their homes and businesses and committed heinous acts against the losers. Everywhere cities burned.

Gerald pleaded for peace publicly, calling for understanding and unity, while in private expressing sympathy. "We must let the compeer have their revenge," he explained to Kel. "As soon as we have the reins of government secured, wanton lawlessness will not be tolerated. They must learn to obey. It may be a tough lesson for some. But, there will still be elitists to scourge. Of that I will assure them."

Calm returned and Gerald was inaugurated. With the Worker's Party in the majority and Gerald as their leader, their plan exploded during the first legislative week. Government control was made absolute. Freedoms were abolished. Fear spread.

There was no second legislative week.

Flores's warning to Kel had been correct. The police and military remained loyal to the Liberty Party and now surrounded the palace. Former president Allhambra was firmly in control.

Lights pierced the windows of the presidential office, undimmed by the protective energy screen surrounding them. Shrill sirens and loudspeakers with their garbled words filled the air outside like a storm. Kel knew their purpose was to confuse and distract. It was working. Gerald Grenada sat in the ornate chair, the holo floating in front of him casting a pale glow on his catatonic face.

"It's over, Gerald, come out," Allhambra's voice spilled from the link. Gerald was in crisis, his uncharacteristic silence betraying his desperation. His unfocused gaze came to rest on Arinka's sobbing form on the couch. For a moment, Gerald seemed to regain his wits. "Don't worry," he said to her in consolation. "Castoro will come. This is not over."

Kel peered down at the combat sleds and heavy armored vehicles crowding the grounds, their blaster cannons aimed upward at the office of the president. Kel had pulled the new president and his lover from their bed and into the office as the raid commenced. The presidential protective and security details followed the army's orders to surrender and marched out of the palace grounds with arms raised, leaving only a few members of the Dignity Cohort below to exchange fire with the troops storming the building.

The president's office was the most secure place Kel could move the pair, their egress to the escape tunnels already blocked by the army. The duranium blast doors were deployed, concealing the elaborate artistry of the entrance to the presidential chamber.

"Castoro will be bringing our forces," Gerald said to himself. "The blood of the elite will spill today. I promise. Justice will prevail." He rocked back and forth as he chanted his mantra.

The voice from the center of the room returned. "Your revolution is over, Gerald." The declarations from the floating holo of Allhambra remained unanswered by the unhinged revolutionary. "Surrender before we come in and get you. No one else has to die."

Gerald closed the link again.

Kel's opportunity approached.

Another bounce forced its way through Gerald's link.

"Gerald," Allhambra coaxed. "I want you to hear this from someone you know."

On the link, Allhambra's face disappeared. Someone else came into view. Castoro.

"It's over, Gerald. You must come out. President Allhambra has assured me you will be fairly treated. There will be a trial. You will surely be found guilty of violating the Covenant Supreme. Someday, you may have the opportunity to try again. There's always hope where there is life."

Gerald's fury unleashed itself as he stood. "Traitor! Enemy of the people! How could you?" The cowed man at the end of his rope was gone, the manic Gerald restored. "What deal did you make with them? How long have you been their puppet?"

Castoro remained impassive. "It doesn't matter. Come out, Gerald. It's time. No one else need die. Is Arinka there with you? Don't put her in a position to be hurt. For once in your life, don't be selfish."

Allhambra's face returned. "Gerald, we won't draw this out. The nation needs to recover. This ends tonight. Come out before the army comes in to arrest you. The people need to see justice done."

The link closed from the other end. Gerald collapsed into the chair. Arinka rushed to kneel at his feet. "Please, my love. We can try again someday. The time was not right. The people will love you even more if you are unjustly imprisoned again. Everyone will see your persecution is for them. You can build a new movement. It will be even more powerful. The world sees the tyranny of our oppressor now more than ever before. Gerald..."

Kel's opportunity came.

"Gerald."

It was the first he had spoken since leading the two to the safety of the office and sealing them inside. The power of his voice shocked Gerald and Arinka. He had their attention.

"The oppressor does not mean to bring you to justice." Kel had thought carefully about how he would launch his attack on Gerald. After months of studying the man's philosophy and logic, he had mastered the language of deception used by the revolutionary to justify his worldview. "The oppressor is incapable of justice."

Gerald's eyes seemed clear. "Yes, my friend, that is true." The basic tenet of Gerald's philosophy was undeniable to him. "You've learned much from my teaching in so short a period of time."

Even now, the man self-aggrandizes, Kel thought.

"Gerald, listen to me. This is a hard truth, but you know it to be correct. If the oppressor gets hold of you, they will use every means at their disposal to defile the revolution, to destroy its essence, to mutilate it. They will use *you* to do so."

For the first time in their association together, Gerald remained silent.

"They can coerce you with drugs and psych manipulation. They can torture you. In the end, they can make you say anything they want you to say. They can make you renounce the revolution."

Gerald nodded weakly, his eyes transfixed on Kel.

Kel moved closer and spoke softly. "If that happens, the damage to the revolution will be incalculable." Now, Kel waited for Gerald's logic to come up with the solution. Seeing the realization on his face, Kel cemented the thought with the words he had longed to say.

"Gerald, for the good of the people, you must kill yourself." He laid his pistol on the desk and stepped back.

"Gerald! No!" Arinka screamed as she stood and reached for the gun.

Kel pulled her away. He spoke calmly but forcefully. Commanding, not pleading. "To be the great revolutionary that will break the bonds of tyranny, he cannot allow himself to be captured, Arinka. Gerald knows this is the only way. Gerald," he repeated in hypnotic tones, "for the good of the people, you must kill yourself."

Gerald stood, chin on chest, mesmerized by the gun in front of him. A step. A reach. The gun was now in the hand of the man he had been sent to kill. Kel threw Arinka aside. If the man hesitated, he could still intervene. It wouldn't be as clean, but...

"Tell the story, my friends. Let the revolution burn in the heart of all." Gerald rose to his full stature. "For the good of the people."

"No!" the woman cried as Gerald placed the gun to his head and pulled the trigger.

Kel moved to the desk and activated the controls. The duranium blast doors parted.

The woman sobbed on the floor.

"Arinka, listen to me. We aren't out of danger. Lay on the floor with your hands outstretched. They'll be here soon. Don't move." Kel knelt and pushed her prone to the floor, spreading her arms as her body shook with lament. Vibrations and the sound of approaching boots quickened his heart as he assumed the same pose.

He had no time to issue his surrender as those boots surrounded him. Arinka yelled out as the blows from the buttstocks landed on him from all sides. He feared the same treatment for the woman. "No! Don't hurt her!" A blow struck the back of his head.

The world went black.

He came to groggily, still on the ground. The copper taste of blood in his mouth, the ringing in his ears, the shade to his vision familiar from many times being choked, concussed, injured. Rough hands grabbed his arms. He struggled to his side to look for Arinka when pain escaped his lips, his shoulders and elbows reaching their limit before dislocating.

"Stop resisting," the voice yelled. Then, a new voice.

"Do this man no harm!"

The twisting stopped. "Sir, he is one of the bodyguards," a different voice answered.

"Get him out of here. And the girl. Restrain them but do not harm them. Put the man in my car. Now."

"Yes, sir."

Kel passed out again.

He came to. *Sitting. Soft. Car?* He tried to move. Enerchains buzzed his arms and legs.

"A medic will check you, but I think you'll be all right. This isn't the worst beating you've ever taken, am I correct?"

Kel focused on the face across from him.

"General Flores?"

The general looked as dignified and perfect as always in his blue fatigues and black leather coat, the field uniform of the Sonestran army.

"Is the girl safe, sir?"

The general chuckled. "Very chivalrous of you. Yes. We have her. She's safe. Tell me, if Grenada had not killed himself so cleanly, would you have killed her to leave no witness to the contrary?"

Even in his daze, Kel was afraid of the answer. "Can we just say I'm glad I didn't have to face that possibility, sir?"

The general's face and uniform were in better focus now. "So, I was right all along. Only a soldier can carry the burden of such a duty. We must get you out of here. Your people are waiting."

The sedan floated smoothly and though he couldn't see out the tinted security screens, the hum of the repulsors told him they were moving at a high speed.

"Where are we heading?"

The general leaned forward and removed Kel's ener-chains. "To the spaceport. Your coercion was perfect. I enjoyed listening to you manipulate Gerald with his own twisted logic."

Kel knew that the room would be monitored.

"I have the only holo of the event," the general said, an amused smile on his face. "Your presence will be unknown to fulfill the terms of my agreement. It serves both our purposes. The scene of Grenada's suicide is sealed. It will pass any investigation; of that I am certain. Tell your people."

Kel's confusion was from more than his head injury. *He's said it twice now*, Kel realized. *My people. Jack's work?* *He assured me they'd been working as hard as I was.* Before he could formulate a question, the general answered.

"I will remove Allhambra from power as agreed and assume title of Protector Supreme until the covenant can be restored. With Allhambra gone, I can bring forward reforms and defuse most of this revolutionary sentiment. It should satisfy the House of Reason that I can return order and stability not only to Sonestra but the mid-core. Tell them that, and give them my thanks for their aid."

The grogginess was all but gone. "Won't his suicide inspire the revolutionaries? Won't it actually work in the way I sold it to him?"

The general shook his head. "You've learned much, but have much yet to learn about us. Suicide in our society is a weakness. A real man would never do such a thing. He let his political delusions cloud his Sonestran heritage. That is why your manipulation was so brilliant. There will always be some who see Grenada as a heroic figure. Most will see his weakness as an admission of failure."

The sedan slowed and descended a slope before halting. "We're here."

The general stepped out. Kel followed. They were in a maintenance garage. "You're safe in this place," the general said as he turned to board again. "Your people will retrieve you presently."

Kel looked around at the grounded vehicles and mechanic benches. "What will happen to the girl?"

The general halted and looked back. "It depends. She will be treated gently. Can we ever free her, though? I think it's safe to say she'll be somewhere safe and in our care for a long time to come." He moved again to depart but stopped and turned to face Kel. "You have the mark of the Legion on your soul. Tell me I'm wrong?"

Kel gave a single, sharp bob of the head in reply.

"Hah!" the general said with a laugh. "I knew it when I saw you fight. I came close to turning my back on my family obligations when I saw how the Legion fought. To serve the Republic was an honor, but the Legion... well, that's something else entirely, isn't it? It is maybe the only regret of my life. But I have my duty, just as you do, and we both can do no less. Goodbye, Legionnaire."

Before Kel could return the farewell, the vehicle pulled away, up the ramp, and was gone.

Is this the beginning of the end to this nightmare?

He didn't have long to contemplate his situation when Jack appeared from a hidden door. "Ready to go home?"

Lothar and Zev had gone ahead to prepare for their arrival at Canopus Station. A new identity and clothes, a brief visit to a medcomp, and Jack and Kel boarded their flight as businessmen, Sonestra behind them. Under the security field in their cabin, Kel could hold back his questions no longer.

"Did I do it? Did I meet Scarecrow's expectations? Am I done?"

Jack puzzled. "Scarecrow? Oh... I see. Yes. Your solution was what the director hoped for. He's aware. We'll meet on Canopus and get our next instructions. You proved you're everything he told us you could be. That was very well done."

"'Next instructions?'" Kel spat. "If I've accomplished the mission, he has to hold up his end of the agreement before anything else happens."

"Calm down, Kel. He keeps his word. Your family is going to be fine. He doesn't want you unhappy. He wants you to know that he holds you in high regard. I know it's seemed like you're being extorted. That's going to change. You've passed the test. He's going to show you how valued you are to the group. It all starts now."

Kel still fumed. "'Seemed like extortion?' There's a better word for it? And *what's* going to start now?"

"Easy, man. It's going to be good. Better than you can understand right now. More will be explained when we meet with him next. You'll see. It won't be like the last time. You're with *us* now."

Kel wasn't so sure. "*Us?* There's no 'us' until my family is cleared. He promised that *and* my return to Dark Ops."

Placating him, Jack threw up his hands. "Then that's what's going to happen."

Similar to his first meeting, Lothar and Zev were waiting out of sight, having prepped the scene for their arrival on Canopus Station. Kel had never been to the hub before, but there was nothing to distinguish it from any of the other major stations. It was not as clean as Orion, but was likewise packed with commerce, shipping, and trade, along with diplomatic missions from nonaligned worlds. The station was home to thousands of souls. There was a Republic Navy port as well. When he got his identity back, he considered the possibility that the base might be his next stop, the surest route back to Victrix and Dark Ops. Home. The safety of a Navy transport held great appeal for him.

After a complex routing through the hidden accesses of the station, Kel found himself once again in a meeting location. Jack pointed to a door. "He's waiting for you."

Inside, the grotesque figure sat in front of him, the inhuman voice broadcast from the pad in his lap. "We were right to be impressed by you. You succeeded brilliantly. Do you see how what you've done has maintained the peace? Saved countless lives?" The holo glowed the same white static where the head should be. "You are a valuable man. Truly special."

Kel didn't feel valuable. He didn't feel special. He felt drained.

"Please. The Yomiuris. Can you..."

A hand raised. "It's already done. The people you care for are restored and prosperous again. We keep our word. When you are loyal to us, the reward is always great." The apparition's voice though inhuman, was not domineering or commanding as it had been in their first encounter. Jack had told him things would be different now. "It is ugly, to hold a threat over you. We know this. It has to be this way. Has Jack explained the situation to you?"

A man cannot serve two masters. The kind of loyalty they demand is over your soul.

"Yes, sir. Jack explained it."

The white static transformed into the light blue glow that Kel had come to think of as a reward. *Sir.* Kel almost choked as he said the word. *I must swallow my pride. I must hide my anger. They've got to think they own me. That I've surrendered.*

"Good." The Scarecrow seemed placated by his act.

"What now, sir?"

The blue deepened, like the soothing waters of a shallow sea. "As promised, it's time for you to return to Dark

Ops and your life. We'll be in touch when we have need of you." The Scarecrow stood and turned to leave, his body-guard entering from the other portal. The bulging man glowered at Kel. The white glow returned as Scarecrow spoke. "You have a good memory, so I don't need to re-mind you that we demand fealty. Your family is restored to their fortunes... for now. If you were to jeopardize our relationship, however..."

Kel understood their relationship. And the threat.

"I understand, sir. I truly do."

The intensity of the white glow diminished slightly. "You are part of the most select group in the galaxy. One of the true elite. Ever vigilant, Lieutenant. Stay ready."

The Scarecrow departed, leaving Kel alone.

Special, the Scarecrow had called him. *Select. Elite.*

What compliments would the Scarecrow gurgle when Kel choked the life from him?

15

It was late when Kel arrived at the spaceport. It was good to be home. Mount Fronius hid the sinking moon. Kel could pick out the faint lights of the Dark Ops compound from the plateau of the spacefield. Before they parted ways, Jack returned his grav container to him, his armor and weapon, possessions he had thought defined him, returned at last. He'd inspected his gear closely during the voyage home. He had survived without any of it. *Despite. Not because*, he thought as he held his bucket in both hands, staring at the visor, wondering about the man that lived behind the mask. *Is it still me? Am I the same? Who was the man out of this armor?* It all seemed like a bad dream. Most of it.

He loaded his gear into the autonomous sled, but before he stepped inside, he pulled his bucket from where it had sat dormant for many months nestled in its molded niche. Kel had already decided what he would do. Not knowing if Bigg was even on Victrix, he tried L-comm.

Nothing.

He's probably home asleep, if he's here at all.

He pushed a bounce through by datalink and in a moment was greeted by Bigg's squinting eyes.

"Kel! Hey kid, we got your message. Glad you're home. Been waiting to hear all about—"

"Bigg. Don't talk. We need to meet in the QSZ. Now."

Bigg's voice lost its grogginess. "Understood. Should Braley be there?"

"Yes. We may need to wake up more people before I'm through."

The Quantum Stasis Zone was the most secure facility yet devised by man. When sealed in the QSZ, no form of electromagnetic wave could penetrate or escape its confines. Other espionage methods like protein-encoded sequences could be sorted out by the scans when entering or leaving the facility. The field would dissociate any molecular spy-tech, breaking the bonds of the DNA in an instant death sentence. If there were a malfunction of the system, a human melting into unconnected amino acids would be the result. The only way classified information could leave the facility was by the human brain. Without speaking, the three of them entered the corridor and paused on a mark to be scanned before stepping into the QSZ chamber. The interior looked much like any conference room. No sooner had the door sealed than Kel found himself the recipient of bear hugs from the two operators.

"What have you been up to, Lieutenant?" Bigg stepped back and hammer fisted Kel's chest.

Braley rocked him side to side, his arm still around Kel's shoulders. "No rest for the wicked? What's so urgent we have to meet in the zone?"

No explanation required, in the middle of the night, Bigg and Braley came just because I asked. Who would ever leave Dark Ops? Kel gulped back his emotions. *What was I even thinking? Me, a spacer? A husband?* It all seemed a lifetime ago. Then he was slammed by a wave of anger, remembering why he was here.

"I've got to tell you what I've been doing. Dark Ops is compromised. It's my fault."

Bigg and Braley listened, asking few questions. An hour passed. Kel's throat was so dry he croaked as he finished the last of his tale. "They had my armor, specs, weapons—everything. Who knows if they've penetrated any of it?" Until recently Bigg had been his team sergeant. He was still his most important role model. The older man grunted. "We'll get the tech section working on it immediately. As far as anyone knows, it's impossible to break the L-comm encryption. But they could have added a parasite to copy your comms, sliced into your armor and left other nano trackers."

"First," said Braley, "I'm stepping out. The colonel needs to know. Kel, have something to drink." He passed Kel a hydration fluid pouch. "You're going to be talking for a long time."

He started at the very beginning for Colonel Hartenstein. Bigg and Braley now got the full story. His relationship with the Yomiuris, how that had been used against him by the unnamed organization, his mission to assassinate the revolutionary on Sonestra. He described his debrief by the Scarecrow. As he recalled the images, the daze of the experience cleared.

Colonel Hartenstein was a giant, intimidating in every way. His sharp intellect and competence inspired loyalty from everyone he had contact with. Kel appreciated the colonel must know that about himself; that he was a man who if he chose could inspire by fear rather than respect. Instead he seemed to go out of his way to assure his subordinates with small gestures and a calm demeanor that he was approachable. At first glance, it would be easy to dismiss him as an ogre. To the men of Dark Ops, he was the demi-god of intelligence, reason, and courage.

The Dark Ops commander shifted in his chair, removing his blaster from under his shirt to place beside him on the table before settling back, apparently more comfortable now. Kel had been talking for over an hour again. He finished his tale, waiting to be raked over the coals by his personal gods. His three confessors looked at each other but remained silent. Kel could hold himself still no longer.

"I'm sorry, sir. This is all my fault."

Thoughtful, the colonel shook his head. "No, Lieutenant. It is not."

Kel felt a glimmer of hope that he was not about to be ousted from the life he so desperately wanted to regain. The colonel looked at the old-fashioned stylus notes he had taken.

"You repelled a Macrobian pirate attack. Foiled an Ootari agent. Maintained cover against RI and diplomatic probing. Those activities I was aware of before your... posting away.

"Then you went off the grid. Now, I understand you went on to discover a conspiratorial organization operating in the Republic sphere. You infiltrated a subversive movement destabilizing the mid-core and with patience and perseverance, orchestrated a clean removal of its leader. I have to do some checking... but I have no reason to doubt the veracity of your version of events, Lieutenant."

"Thank you, sir," Kel said, relieved the colonel understood his explanation. He was afraid that the lack of interruptions during his tale was an indication of impending doom.

"In each case, it seems you acted on orders, in a manner consistent with what Dark Ops expects of an operator, and what I expect of my officers."

A lump formed in his throat. Kel's relief was like micro-G for his soul, a lightness returning to it for the first time in months. This was quickly replaced by concern. Not for himself, but for Dark Ops. The significance of the transpired events hung in the room. He remained silent, knowing that another weight was about to crush them all.

"What has yet to be determined, is who has the power to abscond with one of my operators and what that means for Dark Ops. Captain Yost," the colonel directed, "please get Lieutenant Turner settled and make sure he has what he needs."

Braley stood, understanding he was being dismissed as well.

"Sergeant Biggetti, stay behind."

Kel followed Braley out of the QSZ, both waiting to speak until they were well out of the facility.

"Come crash at my place, Kel. Your quarters are security sealed. We'll get it sorted in the morning."

"Thanks, Braley. But what happens in the morning? Am I still on Three?"

Kel's promotion to first lieutenant had occurred immediately before his departing for leave. He'd not moved to officers' billets, and the question of what kill team he would be on afterward had not been answered.

"As far as I'm concerned, you are," Braley assured him. "Your name's still on your gear cage."

They hopped into Braley's speeder, a Weldon Transatmospheric, capable of orbital ascent. Braley was single, and they all knew that their team leader spent a fantastic amount on the luxury vehicle.

"We'll get it sorted out tomorrow. You can look forward to a new set of armor, too. Tech is going to be tearing all your gear apart looking for tampering. Don't count on it ever coming back."

Kel shrugged. "I suppose you're right." That set of armor was as familiar to him as his own skin. He didn't relish losing it.

"What do you suppose the colonel and Bigg are working out together?" It had surprised Kel that their commander had dismissed Braley in favor of Bigg to discuss the situation further.

Braley grunted. "There's a lot about Bigg we forget. It's easy to overlook what a legend he is. He and the colonel go way back. But you know Bigg. When he can tell us, he will."

When the QSZ sealed and the green light returned, Bigg huddled with the colonel. What had to be discussed was best done in hushed tones. It was human instinct, impossible to override, a primal need despite their surroundings.

"This cannot be ignored."

"No. Agreed. We're not going to lay down." Somehow, the colonel's words seemed even deadlier spoken so softly.

Bigg had an inspiration. "Of course, these people may think they have a man inside Dark Ops when really, Dark Ops has a man inside their conspiracy."

The colonel considered this. "But waiting to let their cabal develop further until they need Turner next... I've already considered that. We'll make that the last option. My preference is to act sooner rather than later." The colonel leaned back. "Tell me, Matthew, anything troubling you about how Dark Ops is being utilized?"

Bigg didn't hesitate. "Do you mean the Proteus Four mission?" The mission to investigate the Savage civilization on the isolated moon had raised many questions for them before, during, and afterward. Why they had been saddled with the many layers of obfuscation about the moon, its history, and even the true purpose of Three's mission had not been settled to Bigg's or the colonel's satisfaction. Whoever had authorized the mission and insisted on the participation of two civilian "experts" had never been made clear to them, either.

The colonel raised his eyebrows. "That. And the secret arrest warrant we were tasked with serving on Lorrian." The Lorrian mission had also troubled Bigg. Apparently, the colonel had similar reservations.

"You think there's some common thread, sir?"

"I'm asking you what you think."

"All right, sir. We're a covert action force. By nature, what we do is directed by political considerations, meaning the House of Reason or Senate. The Proteus mission, serving the arrest warrant, some of the surveillance missions we've fulfilled, now this press gang recruitment of Kel into some black organization..."

"What do you think about that?" the colonel interrupted. "How did Turner come under their scanner? How was he compromised?"

"To the politicians, one legionnaire is the same as another. Interchangeable. Replaceable. Faceless and nameless. But Kel is extraordinary."

The colonel grunted. "Turner's name has been bandied about by the diplomats, RI, and anyone who's been around him who has a pipeline to Liberinthine. He's gained the attention of someone powerful. My gut tells me it's the same machine that's using Dark Ops."

"What does Legion Commander Steiner think?" During the Proteus mission, Colonel Hartenstein had gone around the civilian authority, straight to General Steiner to get them the support they needed after it had initially been denied.

The colonel paused to choose his words with an unconscious grimace as he did, revealing to Bigg what he feared was going to confirm his lack of faith in Legion command. "General Steiner has stepped back since Proteus. Orders and directives still come directly from his command, but for the last year, they come to me without comment or the commander's intent included. There's no more personal input from him. It's... odd."

Bigg processed that. "The Legion commander is rubber-stamping orders to Dark Ops?"

"For the most sensitive missions, yes."

"Is that abnormal, sir?"

The colonel shrugged. "To be in Dark Ops, even as the commander, is to live in a world where you don't ask questions. It's part of having deniability. You accept that what you are ordered to do is from a legitimate authority, and move out."

Bigg agreed with the colonel's synopsis. He'd been in the dark world for decades. There was simply a way things *were*. A way things were *done*. He questioned now whether he'd been guilty of suppressing appropriate questions from his own team when there had been doubt about what they had been ordered to do.

"I aired my concerns to you and the team after Proteus," the colonel reminded him. Bigg remembered too well what he had shared with them.

"What we experienced was a flaw in our system of oversight for covert activities. The command authority that governs Dark Ops is at times nebulous.

"We know there are other black activities run by the Republic. We don't know who they are or what their function is, but this seems to be evidence that they may be operating outside of legal oversight. Of course, the House of Reason has almost unlimited power to determine what's legal and what constitutes an authorized activity, so..."

Bigg's anger rose from deep in his chest like slowly streaming lava. "So now we know our concerns are more than conjecture. It's a reality. It's slapped Kel and Dark Ops in the face. It means none of us have any protection from however they choose to wield us." He thought about the empty threat the little man from Liberinthine had levied at them before the Savage mission. "It's got to be a politician. What about that weasel from Grand Senator VanderLoot's office who tried to control the Proteus mission?"

The colonel smiled. "Interesting that you mention that, Matthew. After Proteus, I tried to investigate the chain of authority for that mission. I was shut down almost immediately by Steiner."

"So. Seems like positive confirmation you hit the mark, eh?"

"Our mission tempo has kept me from spending more time on the investigation. We've been busy, wouldn't you agree?"

It was true. Not only Three but all of DO had been working nonstop.

"Sir. I know you've considered this, but we do have another option. Is it time to call on the Primus Pilus Society?"

Colonel Hartenstein leaned forward again. "I came to the same conclusion. If I can't get support from within the Legion, we have no choice but to call on the society. That's why you're here, Matthew. At least three members have to agree."

"Nail will be our third, of course. For what I think we're about to recommend, though, I wish Rex were alive. He would make things clear for everyone."

The colonel murmured something so incredible, Bigg thought he misheard him.

"Did you say, 'maybe he is?'"

The colonel shrugged. "Sorry, Matthew. My personal theories aren't helpful right now. I've had suspicions about the general for a long time. As incredible as Rex is—was—there's a lot about the general we don't know."

Bigg sighed. "A topic for another time. Either way, Rex is gone. Dark Ops is on its own."

The Primus Pilus Society went back to the earliest days of the Legion. A secret elite within an elite, founded by General Marks himself to guarantee the Legion would always be steered by the most loyal, the truest, the purest.

Bigg had been inducted the same time as Colonel Hartenstein. Both had been in Dark Ops for more than a decade at that point. Both had proven that the sanctity of the Legion mattered to them above all.

Rex himself had been there that night, the head of their order. In their decades as members, the society had acted but a few times. Only once had they directly intervened when a member questioned the rectitude of the Legion on behalf of one of their own. Bigg had voted unanimously with the society to act in that case. An unjustly convicted legionnaire was rescued from his prison by the society and set free, with a new identity and credentials provided. Bigg had been chosen to lead the operation.

The society had access to funds, investments growing for decades from contributions made by its members. Precious minerals, treasures, even technologies were returned by members to the society and managed, waiting to finance the will of the society to support and aid the Legion and her warriors. Bigg wondered if the source of some of the early investments wasn't in reality the result of looting by their select membership. Who knew what really happened during the worst of the Savage Wars? Bigg learned not to judge after his own opportunity to contribute.

He had come across a cache of Panthellian diamonds when destroying a gene weapons lab. He hadn't hesitated to bring the gems to the society. The day he set the wrongly convicted legionnaire on his way to an edge colony carrying a chip crammed with credits, he knew he'd done the right thing. It was a weak gesture to offset the wrong that had been done the man. Taking the valuable minerals instead of letting them be destroyed with the lab was an act he never regretted.

"Have you told Nail?" The Dark Ops sergeant major was the only other living member of the society in DO beside the colonel and Bigg. Nail had been selected by Rex himself as one of the first operators when he formed

Dark Ops. He was the only original member of the unit still serving. Bigg thought Kel would surely be the next nominee to their order.

"I wanted to talk to you first to make sure I had your agreement." Nail had been inducted before either of them, and in the world of the society, was senior to them. "If you think we're justified, then having Nail's approval would give me what I need to take the next steps."

"What will that be?" Bigg was unsure how far the colonel was willing to go.

"Destroying whatever cabal is trying to corrupt Dark Ops."

16

Maybe the colonel had absolved Kel of his guilt, but didn't quell the anger that bubbled up in him anew as he stepped out of the fresher. He was cleaner, but not cooler. He paced around Braley's guest room unable to take respite from his predicament by retreating into sleep. Perhaps the colonel and Bigg were coming up with a plan that would facilitate his murdering the Scarecrow. He could only hope. Anger or no, exhaustion was interfering with his clarity.

He was at a loss for how to start the journey toward his reckoning with the man that hid behind the holo. If only there were a nav program to guide him through life like the one in his bucket, a cursor pointing the direction to the next way point for him to follow. Or an interpreter program that could take his scattered thoughts and translate them into something orderly, like the gibberish of so many alien species.

He lost his train of thought as he pondered the pitfall of his wish for a tech to order his jumbled thoughts for him. Not even translator programs were infallible. Once when working with the split-lipped Shareen, the first attempts at deciphering the speech of the furries produced sing-song sentences of grammatically correct gibberish. They all took turns assembling nonsensical sentences like, "dried grass for silage Poul, overtake the molten dressing." The first to correctly translate the effort into the true meaning, "hey Poul, pass me the hot sauce," received high accolades from the rest of the team. The translator program adapted, but by then the novelty had worn thin. Kel knew of other situations where mistakes by the translator software—as opposed to the use of a dedicated bot—turned violent.

He surrendered to the invitation of the turned down bed and crawled in. The memory of the mistranslation episode sparked another recollection.

Kel drifted to sleep in the memories of his introduction to Dark Ops...

"Anyone armed, drop 'em where they stand," his new mentor had said in his thick accent. Papa Bear had taken him along to find the best observation point from which they could spot the gathering of dead-enders, the resistance fighters trying desperately to repel the invasion of Antione.

Kel liked the N-22 above any weapon he'd ever held. Everything about it made intuitive sense, as though he'd held one since birth. He excelled during the Legion Target Interdiction Course, but this would be his first opportunity to become a sniper in more than just name. He'd yet to engage an actual target in his brief Legion career.

"I'll start the party," Papa Bear said as Kel squeezed shut and opened both eyes rapidly to clear them. They'd been observing from the hide for hours, waiting for as many of the killers as possible to show up to the rendezvous. Finally, it appeared they were about to split up. Food and water had been distributed from one of the sleds. Munitions came out of another and were being divided and loaded.

"I'm taking right, you start left. Meet in the middle."

Two thousand meters away a dozen of Lady Shah Khan's guard huddled in the dark, believing themselves unobserved.

"Rog," Kel whispered into L-comm, settling the reticle over the squat bearded man leftmost in the pack. This one carried a short sword in addition to his slug launcher. Was he the one who'd been cutting off the heads of civilians suspected of cooperating with the Republic invaders? He hoped so. The old man who told them about the guards who'd stolen the provisions at gunpoint deserved to be protected. He took in more deep breaths as he settled deeper into the stillness and calm, sinking beneath the smooth surface of the bottomless black pool of water he imagined.

"Three, two, one," Papa Bear counted. Kel didn't wait to hear his new boss shoot when he reached "one." He pressed the trigger and paused just long enough to spot his impact before he shifted to the next body, and the next. By the time they finished, not a one remained standing. The scene was as tranquil as the place in Kel's mind.

"Nicely done, Turner. It seems you've already learned one of the greatest lessons I could've taught you."

"What's that, Papa Bear?"

"When the local language is violence, be fluent."

A final thought occurred to Kel before he succumbed to sleep.

He had mastered the language of the radicals on Sonestra and it helped him to kill Gerald. What language would he have to master to kill the Scarecrow?

The QSZ was crowded. Their sometime teammate Meadows and longtime friend Joe Crane joined the rest of Three and filled the last chairs. The colonel and Nail asked Kel who he trusted most among the other operators. He hadn't hesitated in his recommendations. Braley and Bigg made no dissent.

"Gentlemen." It was Nail who addressed them. "What we are about to discuss will not leave this room. Your inclusion in this matter is because you have demonstrated not only the highest level of commitment and excellence as operators, but also for your loyalty to the Legion and the principles it was founded on."

Comforted by his friends' presence Kel had almost shed the weight of it all. Their blind commitment to come just because called. Now the anticipation of what Nail was about to tell them returned, the pounding of his heart, the burning in his throat.

He was surrounded by the most powerful force in the galaxy—their own cell of righteous warriors. The light of Dark Ops. His brothers. Together to fight the darkness of the Scarecrow. He felt comforted, but also saddened. Now they were about to be burdened with the knowledge he carried. There was rot trying to eat at the Legion.

The colonel took over. "A rogue entity is trying to infiltrate Dark Ops. They're using Lieutenant Turner's loyalty against him to carry out their objective." The colonel looked to Kel who in turn looked around the table.

"While on leave after the Proteus mission, I was with friends when we were attacked by pirates..." Kel told his entire tale as best he could.

When he finished, the room exploded.

Meadows was first. "So, we need to find this Jack and his crew and interrogate them. That's how I'd start it."

"I'll slice into everything from the datastream. The closer Kel can give me date time groups matching which locations he was with these characters, the better my chances of finding them in the stream," Sims said. "Not to worry. No one can conceal their movements by erasing public data. There's too much of it. They'll show up on surveillance feeds wherever they poked their noses out of their caves. I'll find them."

Joe Crane raised a finger. "How do we know we aren't working against a lawful agency of the Republic?"

Poul jumped to answer. "Destabilizing a revolutionary movement is a legit covert activity, Joe, but framing that family with drummed up crimes to extort Kel? There's nothing legal about that."

Sims was quick to add. "That's right. These people are running a blackmail cult. They need to be smashed. Think they can frell with one of us?"

Joe sent back a thumbs-up. "I'm with you. I just didn't want to be the only one not asking the question. Colonel Hartenstein, do we have any read on who these people represent?"

The colonel, sitting at the head of the table nodded. "That is one of the primary things we need to root out about them, but as we've discussed, Lieutenant Turner's episode makes us suspicious that it's part of a much larger pattern."

"Proteus," Poul said. "Things got odd starting then. What happened to that creep, Mister Patrick? And what about that other geek from the Senate, that VanderBlanc guy who tried to intimidate us? What became of them?"

Braley grunted. "I think you're on the nose. Sarah and the alien tech boondoggle, the political interference with that mission, but even before that—the earlier missions like snatching Xenon Boothe. Whatever happened to him? He was another one talking alien tech absurdness. Famous guy like that goes off the stream, and there's no news about it? Maybe it's not nonsense."

"I say we get some one-on-one time with the head-man," Meadows said. "We get the mask off this Scarecrow guy and we'll have the whole organization."

Bigg sighed. "First, we gotta find them."

"Gentlemen." It was Sergeant Major Nail who halted the free-for-all. The silence was like the quiet that follows the report of a neutronium detonation, the echoes of their energy bouncing around the QSZ. Kel's heart raced. It was the same feeling he had when stepping off the tail-gate of a Talon in orbit. His teammates were planning the operation to take down the Scarecrow. Without even being asked.

"While we appreciate everyone's insight, let's not get ahead of ourselves. The colonel has asked you all here to invite your voluntary participation in the mission to penetrate this rogue actor. By your enthusiasm," Nail paused to look at Poul who had a wide grin on his face, "I'm thinking you're in. But we need to hear it from you first."

"Participation in this mission may have unforeseen consequences," the colonel said. "Not just for you personally, but for Dark Ops, the Legion, maybe even the Republic. This operation will be run by me, without the knowledge or support of higher echelons. There's a possibility that you may be subject to criminal penalties, even by expressly following my orders. That's why you have the choice to participate or not." The colonel wasn't through.

"Many of you know that I have regrets concerning my inaction after my own mission on Proteus." The colonel had been on the moon as a young sergeant and when ordered to remain silent about the Savage planet, had done so. His platoon leader had used the chain of command to voice his concerns about what they'd witnessed on the Savage world, and subsequently disappeared.

"I will not let inaction endanger Dark Ops or one of my operators."

No one spoke as everyone considered the colonel's warning, and his inspiration.

"Sorry, sir." Joe was the first. "I meant to make it clear earlier. I'm absolutely in. All the way."

"That's right," said Meadows next to him. "And we're the only ones who can do it."

"I'm with you, sir." Sims grinned. "None of this is right. If we don't do this, no one will."

Poul still had a smile plastered across his face. "Of course, I'm with you all. This whole thing stinks of pols who think the laws don't apply to them. It was a very sophisticated piece of work to get to Kel." Poul looked to his friend. "It took a lot of support to pull off. This goes to the highest levels in the Republic. It must. That means they could manipulate any of us to be their puppets. Kel can't be the first one they've done this to."

Kel thought about Jack and his two compatriots, Lothar and Zev. *What they've done to us is no less painful*, Lothar had told him.

The colonel quirked a smile. "Very well, gentlemen. We're agreed."

"It has to be done." Poul shrugged. "Kel's my brother. He'd do the same for me. And besides, who but Kel Turner takes a break from his day job only to assault a bunch of Macrobian pirates, join a secret project, and assassinate a subversive? He's too entertaining to lose to some secret cabal."

Colonel Hartenstein was the mission commander with Braley the tactical commander, Kel his second. The group moved to the isolation facility under Mount Fronius to begin work. Nail made himself their isolation support team, the one person who would be their link to the outside world as they planned and trained in secrecy.

Before getting locked down, Kel made a trip to his quarters and retrieved a few comfort items to see him through the next phase. A phase of his life he didn't know how long would last. A phase that might end with him on the run, or an inmate on a prison world—the ultimate end they all half-joked about as they flew around the galaxy performing mayhem. The colonel made it clear that it could be more than an idle threat this time. As he looked around the small set of rooms, he realized that he owned almost nothing. He gathered some clothing and left, not sure if he would ever see the apartment again.

In the ISOFAC, he joined the rest of the team in the hab module, the same one Three occupied before the jump onto the Proteus moon. It seemed appropriate to begin the mission here. With Meadows and Crane joining them, the space was a little crowded. After dropping his few items into one of the sleep chambers, a double where he found Poul's items on the other bunk, he returned to the common room where Bigg was already at work. Stylus in hand, Bigg jotted a rough course of action on the wall slate. The colonel and Braley sat near, the three of them engaged as Bigg erased notes, moved others, and continued to refine the elements of their plan.

Planning any operation, from the smallest patrol to the most complex joint-force planetary invasion, had common elements. There was a process for organizing. At this stage, they knew the purpose of their mission and what they wanted to accomplish. Determining how they would do so was the next hurdle. It was like standing on the shore, pondering the depth of the ocean. The unknowns could be daunting, almost paralyzing. Not for them. They were legionnaires. The unknown was their domain.

"Lieutenant," Kel heard behind him. Nail had just walked in. "I talked to tech. They confirm someone has tried to slice into the systems in your bucket and armor, but they don't think it was successful. Nevertheless, they can't give us a one hundred percent assurance that it's uncorrupted and bug-free."

Braley grunted. "Then the decision is made. It's a whole new suit for you, Kel."

He'd been afraid of that.

Nail gestured out the door. "Sustainment is waiting for you now. I'll take you myself."

Kel looked to Braley. He didn't want to leave during the early stage of planning. He had very specific ideas about how they should proceed.

"I already know what you're thinking, Kel," Braley said. "You have to get kitted out first. That's a priority. You'll be back by dinnertime."

"Don't worry," Bigg assured him as he looked back from the slate, the wall-sized board no longer blank but half filled with incomplete ideas and his own abbreviations. "We won't have it all worked out today. Go get some new duds and we'll see you back later."

"You're right. I won't be long." He followed Nail out of the hab, dreading the day he would lose in the sustainment cell, being poked and prodded as a new set of armor was fitted around him. More than that, he knew what happened when you were the only one on the team not present.

"Don't hurry, smart guy," Poul said before the portal slid closed. "We gotta talk about you while you're gone. Plus, give you the worst job."

Kel returned to find the team sitting down around the common table, data pads and papers cleared into heaps to make room for plates of steaming food, cold beverages dribbling pools of sweat onto the smooth surface. The colonel was absent.

"Told you he wouldn't miss chow," Poul said as he cleared a spot in front of an empty chair. "Get a plate."

Kel helped himself to the trays on the kitchen counter and grabbed a pouch of ice-cold juice before joining the team. His eyes strayed to the slate behind them. It was filled with Bigg's unmistakable script, but what caught his eye was the columns of tasks with names underneath them. Under "Collection Analysis" he saw his own name.

"Hey!" Kel protested. "You weren't kidding about the worst job."

The same section of the slate had a decision tree drawn, with multiple headings at branches. "Office 319," the name Jack assured him was nonsense, was at the first fork leading from "Dark Ops" and Kel's name. The left branch read "Jack, Lothar, Zev." Underneath was a column, "LKL," meaning last known location. Both Orion and Canopus station were listed with the dates Kel had supplied, as well as the dates of Kel's time on Sonestra. Underneath the stations were Sims's and Meadows's names. Beneath Sonestra were Crane's and Braley's.

Another heading branched from Orion. "Justice Directorate." Poul's and Bigg's names sat below.

The branch jutting to the right said, "Scarecrow." A question mark sat below it.

The last heading was "Boothe, VanderBlanc, Patrick." Underneath all three were the initials AH.

"The colonel's already gone," Bigg said. "He's off to have a personal chat with someone he hopes will shed light on the whereabouts of the three missing persons we've named."

"The rest of us will be gone by the end of the week, too," Braley told Kel. "You'll be staying here."

"Staying here? Why? I'm the only one who can positively identify my handlers."

"Which is one of the reasons you'll be staying here," Braley answered.

Sims took a swallow to clear his throat. "Everyone will be sending holo packets to the intel cell annex here in the ISOFAC, which you in turn will be poring over. There's going to be hundreds of hours from the different surveillance feeds. With your input, and some parameters we feed to the search AI, we'll narrow down when, where, and who to look for. It will speed things up, but you've got to be the one to make the positive."

"When you've got a positive," said Bigg, "getting that back to us in the field will let us pursue a physical trace. It's the best chance we've got."

"Everyone will have a week outbound and days on site to splice into those feeds before you send it here. That'll take days to reach me. Very little of my time is going to be spoken for then. I could go with one of the Orion teams," Kel pleaded. "It'll speed things up."

"Oh, you have something to occupy your time here, Lieutenant," Braley said with a hint of tease in his voice. "Did you think being bumped to officer came with only perks?" Braley picked up a datapad and bounced something to Kel. Kel glanced at his link. There was a packet with dozens of titles within. *Courts and Boards Manual. Law of Battlesphere Warfare. Joint Operations Doctrine.* There were more. "That's from the colonel. As a direct commission, you still have to pass the Legion officers course curriculum. It's a year-long program. Because most attendees are also being trained in Legion basic, it's more like a six-month didactic package of classes you have to get through. Still, it's a lot of material."

"Think of this as the next step in your progression, Lieutenant," Bigg added, mockingly. "Being an officer isn't all about leading from the front. Somebody has to do the paperwork."

The look on Kel's face must have betrayed his dread as he perused more of the titles. *Logistical Sustainment Matrices for the Legion Company* was the largest of the documents. *I've never even heard of some of these manuals or the subjects.*

"Don't worry," Braley tried to comfort him. "The colonel assigned Captain Mahalik in ops cell to act as your tutor. He's going to check in with you later this week."

Captain Mahalik? Kel thought. *He got assigned to the planning cell from the Legion. He's not even an operator. He's some minor staff officer who sits at a desk all day.* Kel couldn't conceive of how he would generate enough fake enthusiasm to placate the standoffish Captain Mahalik. The man always showed clear disdain for him or any of the operators whenever in the planning cell.

Braley laughed. "First, Sims will get you working on the search algorithm. Then, you can start your reading."

"Hey, look on the bright side," Meadows offered. "If we get a trace, you'll be on the first thing slipping space to meet the rest of us for the takedown."

Kel only hoped it would be that easy.

They turned in early. Kel lay in his bunk as Poul got into his above him and commanded the lights out. Kel sighed, unable to sleep again. This had become too common an occurrence. Before his current troubles, hitting the sack was like flipping a switch into sleep mode. He considered pulling out his link to start reading one of the tomes the colonel had assigned him, when Poul spoke.

"Kel, I haven't had a chance to tell you, but I'm really sorry about what happened to you."

"Thanks."

"Wanna talk about it?"

Kel thought about the Yomiuris. About Tara. He sighed. "Not so much." He could feel Poul's nodding head above him.

"S'okay. I understand." Poul's nodding head lightly rocked the bunks. "You know, we were all really curious when Bigg told us why you weren't back from leave when the rest of us hit the team room. We all figured you got chosen for one of your special little jaunts again." Kel had the reputation of being selected for many solo missions away from his kill team. "Instead, you were out there fighting for your life. Alone. Sorry I was secretly wishing you a hard time."

Kel laughed. Some of his solo missions had put him in the lap of luxury, working with the diplomats and pols of the Republic. "It's okay, Poul. No hard feelings." Kel wanted to change the subject. "What about you? Where'd you spend your leave?"

In the dark, Poul's voice broadcast the grin Kel knew he wore. "I went home. My folks are still there. So's my sister and her family. I got to play uncle, and catch up with everyone. It's been years since I was back. My folks are getting older. I guess it didn't really strike me until this trip just how old. It was good to be in their lives for a while. Who knows when that chance might come again, or if they'll even be around the next time."

Kel had never been to Greenhome, but knew enough about Poul's world to know it was almost mythical in its reputation for beauty.

"I made the most of it. I spent every day with my family. Took my niece and nephew with me everywhere I went. Whenever Sharla let me, that is."

Kel thought about sitting in the galley of the *Callie*, bouncing children on his lap. Auntie Meiko putting a cup of kaff in his hand as she paused to pat his back. The holos of Callie's World. And Tara's smile. Always, Tara's smile.

"You know," Poul continued, "I guess I hadn't really considered the possibility, but I was pretty brittle by the time I got home. It took me a few weeks to relax, even around my family. I was jumpy, irritable... I don't know how they put up with me. I guess, well, Three has been hitting it pretty hard this past couple of years. I think maybe I..." Poul let himself trail off.

"You're right," Kel filled in the empty space. "I wouldn't have thought I'd been affected either. I felt the same the first few weeks on the ship. Remember watching that Mark Four go off?" he said, referring to the mission where they'd aimed a tactical nuclear weapon at an occupied airfield.

"I'll forget my first morning in Legion basic before I forget that."

"I thought about it constantly." Kel stumbled to find his words. "Watching the Q ambush Seven on the ground. Meadows's face when we retrieved him. Those kids we lost on Mercia. Coming into the team room to find out Tem had been..."

"I know, man. I know," Poul said before he could continue with more examples of their shared trauma.

They remained quiet.

"Kel," Poul broke the silence. "Did you ever think about leaving the Legion?"

Poul's question surprised him. "Have you?"

"There were a few times back home when I suppose I considered it. Maybe more than a few times. I saw how happy my sis was with her family. I even met a nice girl. Seeing that there's a different world, it makes you think about the possibilities, you know?"

Kel couldn't keep it in any longer. "I know. I met someone who made me want to change my life. I was ready to stop it all, just to be with her. Then..." He had almost started to tear up, when the anger replaced his melancholy. The Scarecrow's glowing apparition filled his thoughts.

"Kel, you know I was raised a Cosmic Universalist, right?" He knew that about Poul. Greenhome had been colonized by the Church. Kel didn't think their beliefs were so very different from many other religions he was aware of. "I may not be the believers my family are, but I think there's some real truth to some of their philosophy." Poul looked down over the edge of his bunk. "Oba gave each of us a cosmic spark. Other sparks are sent into our lives that make ours grow even brighter, until someday, we're as bright as a star. Because the spark from Oba crosses

time and space, no continuity is ever closed off completely. There's always a connection, a string binding them. Us
to Oba, and to each other. You know what I think?"

Kel truly did want to know. "What?"

"When the cosmic flux is right, your continuities will
cross again. If your spark was made brighter by your new
family and the girl you love, the link can't be severed by
time or space."

Kel tried to process what Poul said. *I don't understand
the way he's talking about it, but if he means there's a
destiny where Tara and I could be together, maybe just
this once, I can pretend such a thing exists.*

He felt Poul turn onto his side above him, his last
words of the night muffled. "You're a good man, my brother. And whether you know it or not, the universe is looking
out for you."

Ten days later, Kel pored over stream after stream of the
feeds sent to him by the teams from their different locations. Each had sliced into the security surveillance of the
two stations and of the spaceport on Sonestra. Even with
the feeds narrowed by the time frames when Kel knew
the presence of their targets was guaranteed, there were
hundreds of hours of footage.

It took the better part of a day in the intel cell to orga-
nize the material, even with help from the AI program. It
was all raw data. One sample came from a camera on the
commercial receiving docks. The next would be from a
completely different part of the station, like the adminis-

trative offices of the port authority. After learning how to sort the feeds based on the different locations in the station, he found the locations and time period he wanted to search first.

He remembered the meeting in the pub when Jack surprised him at his booth, and the long walk across the concourse that followed. It was late afternoon station time when he became their pawn. He found a feed that showed the entrance to the restaurant. He skimmed it, the AI pausing at each face that met the basic description parameters he'd given for the three suspects. Finally, he saw himself, walking into the pub. *Got it.* For the first time in a week he was excited about something. Providing Captain Mahalik with an oral summary of "the law of land warfare as it pertains to disposition of non-sentient alien species used to implement operations against opposing forces" was less than enthralling.

He skimmed forward and froze the image. Jack leading him out of the pub onto the concourse. He touched the image of Jack.

"Isolate image. Capture facial features. Can you reconstruct?"

The dull voice responded, "More samples will increase accuracy. Do you wish to continue without?"

Kel sighed. "Give me a preliminary and continue search."

"More samples will increase accuracy," the machine persisted.

Kel grunted. Working with dumb AIs was not his strong point. He missed Phillip and Bertie, the two advanced AI autonomous combat multipliers they'd had assigned to the team.

Those two you could just talk to, like real people, he lamented.

"Never mind. We'll find some more angles of the suspect's face. Label it as 'Jack' and save it." It took time, but he was able to locate camera feeds from other spots along their route through the concourse and after he had a few more examples, the AI was satisfied.

"Highest probability of accurate reconstruction achieved," it said as a holo appeared.

Kel gave the floating image a light spin. It was Jack. He opened his link to see the sergeant major's face. "I've got something. Care to meet me in the intel cell annex?"

Nail smiled. "We'll be there. The colonel's back."

The Sergeant major brought the colonel almost immediately.

"So that's your handler?" Colonel Hartenstein asked.

"That's him, sir. I'm working on the other two. I'll find them. They ran counter-detection for that first meet with the Scarecrow. They're in there somewhere, too."

Nail picked up a chip. "Best to get this off to the other teams. It might take a very long time for the intel cell crew to get a match from the image. If he doesn't have any criminal history or if they wiped his records, there may be nothing to find."

"Agreed." The colonel stood. "But with at least this much, he won't be able to hide forever. Keep at it, Lieutenant. When you get more, bounce us."

"Sir, did anything come from your investigation?"

The colonel's face betrayed nothing. "Keep working. We'll meet in the QSZ tonight and talk more."

By that evening Kel had images of Lothar and Zev. He remembered their nondescript dress and unhurried movements. They were more difficult to find than Jack had been, but after the first hits, the AI was able to locate them in subsequent feeds until there was enough to satisfy its need to produce only "the highest probability of accurate reconstruction."

In the QSZ, Kel had the images of the three conspirators floating in a row over the conference table when the colonel and Nail walked in.

"I've already transmitted the images to the teams and have the intel cell working on ID searches," he told them. "With this much, the team can start searching the local archives for any other appearances." Kel knew what a boring time his friends would be having now, guiding the program to evaluate all the feeds they'd sliced into. "Crane and Captain Yost have the location of the meet I had with the three on Sonestra. If they get any useable bioquantum traces from the rendezvous site that reconstruct to match the phenotypes of the suspect's physical descriptions, we can use the DNA for a better ID trace."

The database of genetic identity was immense. It was also not controlled exclusively by the Republic. Beyond the Republic's need to keep track of its citizens' identities, commercial medical research, non-Republic governments and their intelligence services, galactic banking conglomerates, even the plethora of corporate retailers, had duplicated, sliced, or generally collected the same information. And Dark Ops had access to all of it. Even if Jack, Lothar, and Zev had been scrubbed out of most every official government record, a genetic match could be located from one of these other repositories. A person's genes and bioquantum signature could not be suppressed unless they retreated to a black hole and never purchased another thing again.

The colonel looked grim. "There's a change of plans. You and the sergeant major are going to sterilize the ISOFAC then make a heavy loadout destined for the *Shinshu Maru*. She's sitting at the Navy end of the space-field." The craft was a profoundly disguised assault ship, outfitted and manned by the Navy. Kel had only been on the ship once. It had a different name then. Its registry changed frequently to disguise its true nature as a covert platform. It was rarely on Victrix.

"By heavy, I mean heavy. Pull anything out of the team lockers you think any member of the team may need. An MSP is on its way over to the ship now." A mission support package was a densely packed container module that provided sustainment, repair, and replacement of every essential item they used. It contained duplicates of all their small and heavy arms, and many other items, all stocked, ready for delivery to keep any kill team outfitted for whatever mission contingency might arise. Supposedly, there were MSPs cached around the galaxy, ready for Dark Ops emergency use.

The colonel's intent was clear. They were headed out.

"Sir, where are we going?"

"First, to Orion Station. I'm recalling the rest of the teams and having them link up with us there."

Kel's brow furrowed.

"We initially thought we would spend weeks collecting and analyzing, then reassemble in the ISOFAC to plan. That's not going to be necessary. We have actionable intelligence right now."

"What is it, sir?"

"When we're assembled, we're headed to Abaddon. I know what became of Mister Patrick."

17

Mister Patrick, Kel mused as he did another handstand push up. It would be three days until they reached Orion, a familiar destination to Kel. The hub station had been the gateway to many of his best missions, as well as the site of his greatest moment of shame: his abandonment of the Yomiuris. He was certain he would never think of Orion Station without feeling the same crushing helplessness he felt as he ran like a coward from his predicament.

Patrick, or so he called himself, had been assigned to Three for their incursion last year onto the Savage moon. They never learned what government agency he represented, only that he had the authority to interfere with almost every aspect of the dangerous mission. The man had been uncooperative, abrasive, and irrational. He'd hindered the safe conduct of their mission so much that Kel had poisoned the man to keep him from endangering the team further.

What they were able to piece together with the help of their other civilian straphanger—a scientist from some off-the-books research lab—was that someone in the government had been exploiting and studying Savage tech for years. The Savages they were to observe on Proteus were being allowed to incubate new tech, and some unknown authority, represented by Patrick, had sent Three to harvest that tech. He remembered seeing

Patrick hauled away in chains by agents of the Justice Directorate, unable to feel pity for the caustic man.

A bizarre episode, they rarely talked about it on the team. Their role in it all was still incomprehensible. That they had been used, probably unlawfully, had made the colonel question the sometimes nebulous chain of command above Dark Ops. Since then, their concerns had only been deepened and reinforced. Now, they were headed to answer the who and why that had sent them to ferret out the secrets of the Savages, and were also attempting to exert their influence over Dark Ops.

The *Shinshu Maru* was empty, save the three of them and the Navy crew. Kel assumed they were Navy. They could have been civilian contractors, but it made the most sense to Kel that they were military space jockeys, assigned to their own covert unit. At least, one of the crew was. On boarding he'd gotten a vigorous handshake from the chief engineer's mate. Joseph Lopez had been on the *Black Cat*, the stealthed fast attack ship that delivered them for the covert mission to the Proteus moon. Kel had liked the crusty spacer almost immediately. It was more than just coincidence that Lopez was on board now.

"Good to see you," Chief Lopez said as he pumped Kel's arm. The man had a droopy mustache and a growth of salt and pepper stubble everywhere else. His unmarked flight coveralls were stained with different fluids and greases, light scorches apparent in other areas. "What brings a fine gentleman such as yourself to slum with the likes of us?"

This made Kel laugh out loud. "Oh, you know. This and that."

Of course, the chief had been joking. The question of what had brought them aboard the disguised ship was a secret in and of itself.

"So, the usual? Destruction and mayhem?" They both laughed.

"Chief, how are the drivers on this boat?"

The chief grinned. "First class. Only the best for the best."

Kel promised to catch up with him later. He wouldn't ask, and the man wouldn't tell, but it seemed that his abilities to support covert ops had been noticed and rewarded by someone in the Navy hierarchy. Kel had been impressed by the man's competence as well as his ability to adapt to fluid situations. After Kel had disabled Patrick from joining them on the drop, Lopez let Kel know that if there were any trouble while the team was waiting for retrieval, Patrick would end up sucking vacuum. Kel was sure he'd meant it, too.

The colonel entered the common room where Kel was working out, bringing him out of the floating state of mind he was in while he trained. "Trade a few with me, Lieutenant? If you're not afraid of an old man?" Kel did a controlled forward roll and stood. The colonel was already stripping off his shirt, leaving him in his green, silky protective skins. Kel wasn't sure how to proceed. "We don't have to take any falls on this deck. Don't want to bruise each other up too badly. Tap outs respected, too. Agreed?"

Kel feared fighting no man he'd ever met, at least, not once the first strikes were exchanged. After contact started, he wouldn't stop until he was the only man standing. Still, the colonel was a behemoth. The age on his face was not matched by his physique. There was no sign of softness on the commander. The corded muscles of his back and arms tensed like steel cables as Kel watched him warm up.

"Agreed, sir."

The colonel wasted no time and sprung at Kel, halting just out of reach, trying to intimidate Kel by his greater size. Kel didn't react but simply faded to the side, continuing his motion to circle the older man. He ignored the colonel's feints with hands and feet until the colonel exploded into an attack, shooting for Kel's legs. Kel threw a hard fist into the man's advancing arm and effortlessly danced out of reach. The colonel wordlessly withdrew and shook out his numb arm before closing to throw another series of fast strikes, this time with intent, but unable to connect with Kel and his evasive movements. He'd seen the colonel train many times before. He was unnaturally strong but also unbelievably quick for his size.

The colonel again committed to another rushing attack, attempting to grapple. Kel didn't evade this time, but shot in under his reach and scissored his waist, turning just enough to begin the throw before breaking his hold, allowing the colonel to regain his balance. The colonel's eyes widened. The message was received. A little follow-through on Kel's part and he would have ended up with his face on the deck.

Kel rose and stepped back. His opponent gave a grudging grin. "Pretty good, Lieutenant. Don't hold back. Give me your best. That's an order." He didn't have to be told twice. Kel took a few blows to his body to get inside the colonel's reach as he protected his head with raised forearms. The taller man took the bait and when he went for the grapple, Kel collapsed and turned under him, beginning a hip throw. Kel halted and let the colonel recover his balance, the message again received. As he let the colonel rock back onto his feet, he sensed a moment of relaxation. Kel attacked again. He swept the colonel's forward leg from inside, sending the man to a gentle fall to the deck. The colonel responded to the hopelessness of his situation by receiving the fall to ease gracefully down onto his side. Kel remained standing, but would normally have followed his opponent to the ground and mounted to then throw his most incapacitating strikes, strangle, or stab with his vibro-blade.

"Ha! I haven't been suckered like that in a long time," the colonel laughed. "Grappling with a smaller man is usually a losing proposition. All you guys with lower centers of gravity. You think I'd have learned that lesson by now."

"Isn't that everyone compared to you, sir?"

The colonel shrugged. "You'd be surprised. There're some pretty big boys out there." He stood. "All right, I can't fight your game. Let's trade random attacks and counters and try to get a workout that way."

"You first, sir."

About an hour later, Nail entered the room to find the colonel and Kel both resting on the floor in pools of sweat. Kel was still a little dizzy. One of the colonel's giant fists found the side of his head at the end of a short, circular hook. It staggered him momentarily, the colonel halting to steady Kel before he nodded that he was ready to continue again.

"Oh, no, sir! You're not breaking the lieutenants again, are you?"

Hartenstein laughed. "No, Dave, not by a long shot."

"You gotta look out for the colonel, Lieutenant Turner. I've been on the receiving end of one of his supposedly reserved practice strikes more than once. He gets a little competitive sometimes."

"At ease that noise, Sergeant Major. Kel, that's the man that broke my elbow. Twice. Wore a regen sleeve for a week both times."

"Some people it takes twice to teach them, sir."

Kel. Since he had been given the promotion, he had not been addressed by his first name by anyone off the team. It was always a sign to Kel that he was in good stead with the colonel and the sergeant major when they spoke to him familiarly. He missed it.

"Sir," Kel said, thinking the time was right, "how did you find Patrick?"

The colonel shook his massive head. "I can't tell you that."

Kark. It had been worth a try. There was so much that always went unsaid, unasked, and unanswered in their black world. There were times that rather than enlightenment, being on the inside meant more mysteries.

"It's because there are other entities that have an absolute trust placed in me," the colonel said in a conciliatory manner. "What I can tell you is that the Legion is small. And we have deep, deep connections. You know how loyalty works for the elite in our government?" Kel admitted he did. "It is even deeper for us. And it's not because of some superficial connection from ascribed status. It's from blood." Kel knew these things. He knew he didn't need to tell the men in the room that he did.

"We aren't entirely on our own," Nail said. "Not all the way." Kel knew there was no point in asking more. Within the cryptic response was a subtle invitation to another unknown world, knowledge that would be revealed to him when the time was right.

The colonel stood and offered Kel a hand. He didn't need it, but would never reject an act of respect from his superior. "Go get cleaned up, Lieutenant. Hit the books. I have a few questions for you later about logistics and sustainment theory. And you better impress me."

Kel was about to take his leave.

"Oh, Lieutenant. I saw some container padding in the hold. Tomorrow, we'll get a real session in with some groundwork."

"Yes, sir," he said, smiling as he departed for his berth. Escaping the colonel's holds from on the ground would be a challenge.

The hatch closed before the sergeant major spoke.

"It won't be long before they open the books," Nail said to his friend and commander. "He might be young, but I think he's ready."

The colonel grunted. "Biggetti will stand with us for the nomination. If we're not all under a death sentence for treason by then."

Bigg had everyone's attention. "While we wait for Captain Yost and Sergeant Crane to arrive, we have options to consider." Everyone but the two members of the team detailed to Sonestra were with them on the *Shinshu Maru*, floating a few hundred kilometers off Orion Station. "If we're trying to find out who has enough influence to drum up charges against the Yomiuri family, then have them summarily dismissed, I suggest we work the problem here and now before the primary players disperse. Or… we put all our eggs in one basket and make Patrick our priority."

Everyone looked to the colonel, who betrayed nothing with his usual expressionless demeanor. "What have you found out?"

Poul swiped his datapad. Kel recognized the figure in the holo. It was the agent who'd served the warrants on the Yomiuris. Poul narrated as he bounced the results of his and Bigg's surveillance to them all. "The records of the warrant, the booking records for the Yomiuris, the preliminary criminal hearing, even a release order—all gone. I can't find anything that shows they were even on Orion. Someone has wiped the system."

"That's proof of a conspiracy," Bigg added. "Or, it will be when we have more evidence of what else they've done."

"We're not gathering evidence for prosecution," the colonel said. "We're gathering intelligence for a strike at their cell."

Poul continued. "There are two magistrates assigned to Orion. I can't find the clues to indicate which of them had a hand in the Yomiuris' case. Unless you tell me differently, sir." He nodded to the colonel. "I don't think it's ideal to snatch both of them for interrogation."

Nail looked pensive, as though considering the option.

"Agreed, Sergeant Radd. You have another idea?" The colonel pointed at the floating face of the Justice Directorate agent. "Continue."

"She's dirty."

Kel skimmed the document Poul bounced them. It was a review of credits transfers. "Agent McKee is getting rich during her time at the Justice Directorate field office." Large but not outrageous sums that Poul had highlighted, conspicuous not just for their amount, but for their regularity and unusual source code. The code traced to a holding company registered in the mid-core. "I think she's the weak link in their chain."

Bigg took up again. "We've already set up a site for interrogation. We know her routine. We can snatch her, brace her, and maybe get some answers. It's our best chance at getting higher up the chain quickly."

Kel liked it. The agent was not innocent. Confronted with the evidence of her financial irregularities, it would be unlikely she would try to officially retaliate in any way.

The colonel grunted. "Make it happen."

Kel waited in the interrogation room. It was not far from where he'd met the Scarecrow for the first time, a location the team had already scouted from Kel's description.

"Two-minute warning," Bigg said. He stood peering through the cracked door, then opened it rapidly as Meadows and Sims pushed the sled through, the coffin-sized tool container unremarkable.

"Trouble?" Bigg asked Poul who was last into the room.

"None. Smooth. She never knew what hit her. I tranqed her and searched her as soon as we got her in the container."

"Good. Let's get her prepped." In a few minutes, with their faces covered and voders in place, Kel administered the reversal agent to Agent Tasha McKee's neck. The results were near instantaneous. She startled awake to find herself secured to the reclined chair, surrounded by her large, masked abductors. The look of terror in her eyes as she found her head restrained to the cushion, her mouth gagged, told him they were achieving the desired effect. Kel felt no pity.

"Agent McKee," Bigg spoke through his mask, his voice fuzzed and even deeper than normal. "You are here to answer questions about the payoffs you've been receiving and the violations of your oath of office as a justice agent." The records of her finances were projected above her head. Her eyes darted across the lines of code.

"Financial records are encrypted," Bigg continued after seeing the recognition on her face. "Especially Neu-Suisse banking records. So, you have some idea of who we are? We're not concerned with bringing you to justice and embarrassing the Republic. We want answers."

The woman's eyes darted about wildly. Kel removed the gag, ready to replace it if needed. The agent gasped, but remained silent.

"Good." Bigg sat close to her head, looking down at her like a med tech ready to investigate a tooth. It was a position of dominance, one that made the subject feel at the mercy of the powerful, one that Kel had experienced when undergoing training to resist just such an interrogation. It was dreadful. He would have felt empathy for the dread the agent felt now, save for his hate. The agent was panicking, her respiratory rate increasing. From behind, Kel applied the hypo to her neck and administered the depressant. She made a startled noise, then relaxed.

"You have a choice, Agent McKee. Answer our questions truthfully, or face prison."

"I didn't do it for myself. My family... needed credits. It was too much to pass up. They said I was helping the Republic."

Bigg ran the interrogation masterfully. In thirty minutes, they had all they needed. Bigg gave her the final instructions. "We believe you've been truthful. So, we'll allow you to leave. Your restraints will dissolve in an hour. From that time, you must be off the station in twelve hours. After that... you don't want to find out. Your bank accounts are intact. Use the credits they bribed you with. Contact no one. No. One. Once you're outbound, tender your badge and find another line of work. Because if you don't, we will come for you. Do you understand?"

Tears flowed from the agent's eyes. "I understand. But there was no harm done, those people were released—"

"You don't want to see us again, do you, Agent McKee? Or want us to visit your magistrate friend and her family?"

Even with her head still restrained, the shaking indicated agreement.

"If we have to come find you, you'll never see us coming." He let the implied threat hang. Bigg nodded and Kel gave her another dose. Her eyelids dropped, and Kel followed the rest of the team out of the room silently, down the hall, and into the lift before removing their masks.

"Is it worth going after the magistrate?" Poul asked.

"Doubtful. She identified Lothar as their contact. She didn't even know why the Yomiuris were being charged. It's unlikely that magistrate will know anything more. Besides, kidnapping a Republic judge might have repercussions that threatening a crooked cop won't."

"Bigg, what does this tell us?" Kel asked as the lift came to a halt.

"Her ID'ing one of our three knowns as her contact tells me that their organization is small, even if they do have a lot of power."

"What's the play if she doesn't follow instructions and squawks?" Sims asked.

"Nothing," Bigg said as they weaved through the access tunnels beneath the station concourse and back to the shuttle. "She's dirty and she knows we have her dead to rights. Any hint of trouble, Poul'll send a bounce with all the evidence to justice directorate HQ on Liberinthine, including info on the magistrate. They don't treat criminals gently, especially ones in their midst."

Meadows spoke. "Yost and Crane are on board the ship. We can go."

"On to Abaddon?" Sims asked.

Kel gritted his teeth as he remembered the smirking face that made him see red. "On to Patrick."

Underway on the *Shinshu Maru,* their immediate task turned to analyzing the data they'd collected so far. While Bigg and Poul worked the intrusion into the justice directorate and the surveillance of Agent McKee, Sims and Meadows had continued their collection of data from around Orion, focused now thanks to the reconstructed images of Jack, Lothar, and Zev. They would've moved on to Canopus to do the same had the colonel not changed their orders. Braley and Joe Crane brought with them physical specimens collected from the rendezvous on Sonestra, and more holo feeds, narrowed by the same parameters thanks to the facial recognition AI.

It was on their second day underway that Sims stopped them all in their tracks.

"What. Is. This?" Sims exclaimed, loudly enough that everyone looked to where he sat cross-legged on the deck in their makeshift team room, holos hanging over him in a wide arc like fruit hanging from a tree. "No way. Is that... ?"

Kel rose from his chair to slide behind Sims who moved a holo into the center and enlarged it. He recognized the face immediately. VanderBlanc. It was the staff member from Grand Senator VanderLoot's office who had come to the ISOFAC to threaten them all before their departure for the Savage mission. He stood at the base of the gangway leading from a luxury yacht, the sheen of his iridescent green suit drawing attention like the bounce of a beautiful woman. In his case, the fashion made him ugly and foul to Kel's eye, the putrid nature of the man not disguised by his wealth. A step behind was the thug that had stood by... the Scarecrow. The epiphany made Kel roar.

"VanderBlanc's the Scarecrow!"

Kel quickly ran through his logic. "Why else would VanderBlanc be on Orion the day before I arrived with the Yomiuris? I bet if we get the Canopus Station feed, we'll find him there, too."

"And that's the muscle who stood behind the masked man on your first meeting?" Bigg said, pointing at the enlarged head.

"I'm certain."

"That means it's VanderLoot at the top," Braley said. "The grand senator is running a black cell to... to..." He strained to find words to describe what the connection implied.

The colonel leaned forward to pick up where Braley left off.

"To rule."

A new sense of motivation energized them all. As with many ventures, success breeds success, the thrill of winning inspiring the discipline to continue, to bring the next infusion of satisfaction. They were all hunters. Naming their quarry made the anticipation of the pursuit even more exciting. As powerful as the pols were on their own playing field, they had wandered into the dominion of the warriors. The place where threats were answered with action.

Kel knew everyone felt the same as he did as they poured over holos, a dull, tedious activity, as removed from the romanticism of being an operator as a fish was from a bicycle. But the reality was, being an operator was more about brains than brawn. Developing and analyzing intelligence was why the operators were more than just sharp instruments, more than arrows aimed at a target not of their choosing.

They all took short breaks, exercising in place, doing repetitions of body weighted exercises to failure, then sitting behind a holo again to recommence the search for more appearances, more clues, more connections to... to anything that might let them fill the voids in their knowledge about their enemy. Which is what the Scarecrow and his cronies were. An enemy.

"Kel, come take a look at this," Braley beckoned. Joe and Bigg sat almost touching, each manipulating several holos in front of them. "We got a hit from some of the material we collected on Sonestra, and the sequencer made a pretty close prediction for the youngest of the three of your handlers, Zev."

He leaned forward, hands on the backs of the seats, to stare over their shoulders. Side by side, the facial morphologic reconstructions from the collected DNA came quite close to the features of their man, Zev.

"So, we ran with it, and look what came up," Joe said as he swiped a larger screen in front of the rest. Zev's image appeared. Some kind official image, like an ID. "Ranack Oswell. Thirty-four. Born and raised in the core. Degrees in accounting and trade law." Joe swiped more holos in front. "He disappears from the excise roles about four years ago."

Braley spoke. "I found a record of his application to the Ex-Planetary service a year before that. My guess... he is or was Repub Intel."

Bigg chuckled. "Here's what nails it for me." Bigg pulled over another image, one of Zev in a suit, exiting a commercial credit bank on Lorrian, a financial center known to them all. More interesting, Zev was crowded by uniformed and plain-clothed police. The next image accompanied a news article with the headline, "Nether Credit Scam Brings Down Speculators at Center of Scheme." He skimmed the article. It seemed like one out of a thousand similar incidents.

"I think the indicators are all there that he was a Republic asset working under nonofficial cover. Whether he committed an actual crime or was set up for leverage, just like they did to you, either way, afterward he disappeared right off the map."

Lothar's words came to him again. *What they've done to us is no less painful than what's being done to you.*

He grunted. "Any traces on the other two?"

If they found Zev among the billions in the galaxy, Jack and Lothar could be outed as well. It was impossible to exist without a trace. They'd just proven it.

Joe harrumphed. "What, not impressed on what we got here? No 'amazing work, thanks, guys'?"

Kel laughed in reply. "Amazing work, guys. Good job."

Braley rolled his eyes. "We all stopped to follow this trail as it's the first successful hit from the reconstructions we pulled together. We'll get back to work on the other two ASAP."

Kel prodded for more. "Sims, anything else come out of the VanderBlanc sighting on Orion?"

Sims yawned. "He was a little evasive in his conveyance pattern, but not overly so. I have a path traced under the cover name he's using, Lexall. Looks like several origins with repeat visits. None of them too far out, all core and mid-core. Nothing from the edge."

The Scarecrow had made his appearance at two major stations. It didn't seem like he was the sort of character to be too far removed from the seat of galactic power.

"I'm betting he's running his operation from somewhere central," Kel intuited. "He likes to be the one in control, and that means having a personal presence."

Nail's voice from overhead interrupted their conference. "We drop out of hyperdrive in the Abaddon system in twenty-two hours. The colonel and I will be there in an hour to start planning."

"The colonel really hasn't told us what his plan is for Patrick's repatriation," Sims said. "I'm not really sure if we're getting ready for a prison break, a social visit, or something in between."

"No matter," said Bigg. "It'll be another case of show-ing up to the ball with flowers and a blaster, and we pres-ent accordingly. Same as we always do."

18

"We have clearance to land. Prepare for atmospheric entry," the pilot boomed over ship comms.

Volcanic planets naturally broadcast hostility, the scorching heat and incendiary colors communicating threat against trespass in the most primal way. Abaddon telegraphed despair. The planet was a gray ball wrapped in uniform clouds, hazy and grim, casting a sleepy pall on Kel as he watched the featureless orb fill the viewer.

Habitable atmospheres made any telluric planet worthy of settlement. Those which had sources of wealth—dug from its mantle, grown in its soil, or created by innovation—became prosperous and crowded over generations during the different phases of mankind's galactic diaspora. Abaddon offered only a surface on which to cling. Among the first worlds discovered, water and oxygen made it a paradise. As worlds more accommodating were discovered, Abaddon became an almost forgotten rocky dot among the stars.

The population centers were small and condensed. It was home to many races, none of them native, who lived and worked in the industrial and scientific research communities that surrounded the equatorial belt. Shallow seas of polar ice melt were hidden by the only significant native life form. Sprawling beds of algae floated across the pools, producing the thin oxygen atmosphere that made the planet barely habitable. To those not accustomed to

Abaddon, supplemental oxygen had to be worn until visitors acclimated to the thin, low pressure atmosphere. The drab rocky surface was contrasted by the mats of floating brown weeds, occasionally stirred up by strong winds into a bobbing, undulating mass, the only source of change in the landscape.

"I hope the colonel's right about his source being reliable," Meadows said. "Even a reliable source can lead you to a dry hole, though." Meadows was just saying what they all knew to be true as the atmosphere buffeted their descent. "But if I had to choose a place to rendition someone, I guess this would be it."

The colonel seemed resolute that Patrick was held on Abaddon after disappearing from Republic custody. Whether the sentence of some secret tribunal or on the order of someone powerful, like the grand senator, no matter what Patrick's role in things, his current address lent to their suspicion that there was an extra-legal component to the irregular imprisonment.

"The whole place reminds me of a prison cell," Poul said. "Cold, drab, depressing."

They descended through the last layer of clouds to see jagged mountains surrounding the settlement's central plain. Through the haze, dingy snow filled the crags along the sharp mountain ridges.

Kel shook off the listlessness and gloom that seemed to penetrate the hull and his armor, draping him in a veil of melancholy as grim as the scenery below the clouds. "If he's here, we'll find him." There was something about the energy of this world that vibrated hopelessness.

"Let's nab him and get off this rock," Joe said. "I haven't even set foot down and I want to go skids up already."

Poul chuckled. "I'm sure we can find you some vacation property on the cheap."

"Thanks for thinking of me, but no thanks," Joe replied. "I doubt there's a strong enough hypnomodulator to shake the depression that would set in on this place."

"I feel it too," Meadows said, normally not one to share feelings. "The haze, the gray... it's more barren than some of the asteroids we've been on."

Bigg broke up their collective pondering. "All right. It's a tomb. I get it. The colonel and Nail will be back on board once we touch down. Let's be ready to roll immediately if we have to."

Their L-comms interrupted. The colonel's voice. "Three, I'll board and give you a brief. Be ready to move out and to do so heavy. We have the target site."

"Good copy, sir. We're ready to roll," Bigg replied. "You heard the colonel. Get it on."

The *Shinshu Maru* barely settled before Chief Lopez had the pax lock open and the colonel's form dominated the portal, his long brown coat dripping gray snow melting off his shoulders. Nail, Braley, and Sims had accompanied the colonel in the shuttle two days before to scout and observe while the rest of them waited in orbit.

"We've got the facility located," Colonel Hartenstein told the team. "It's in a decently isolated canyon. Sergeant Sims can shut everything down so they can't call for outside assistance. They have a security force. Too well armed and large of one to be consistent with a research facility. Plus, they're Gomarii."

Gomarii? Puzzled, Kel tried to recall what he knew about the alien race.

"Gomarii wouldn't be here unless there were credits and suffering," Bigg said. "They're empathic, even telepathic by touch. They thrive on the pain of their victims as much as they do the money. Probably some of the last real slavers around. I've seen them used for jailers and guards. The zhee are fanatics. The Gomarii... they're sadists."

Meadows nodded knowingly. "Wherever those jumbo squid faces can be found, there's something frelled up going on, you can be sure."

The colonel shed the overcoat and pulled his bucket from his pack as he continued. "It'll be dark in an hour. When the sun drops here, it goes dark fast. I've got two sleds outside. We move to the staging area, and when Sergeant Sims kills all their access to the stream, we take the whole facility."

"Do we know where our target's held inside the facility, sir?" Poul asked.

Kel hoped they had something solid besides a suspicious location.

"No. But I know he's in there somewhere."

What is he not telling us? Kel thought. It irritated him, being subjected to the same kind of vagueness the pols so frequently treated them to.

"What are our rules of engagement, Colonel?" Bigg asked.

The colonel seated his bucket, everyone taking the cue to do the same. Their words sealed within L-comm, their commander continued. "Anyone unarmed, restrain. Any threat, eliminate. We take the facility, we find our target, and we leave. Then, we do a rendition of our own on Patrick."

They stayed buttoned up in the sleds as Braley and Sims took turns narrating the simulation Kel watched in his bucket. They were parked in an industrial area, where a few plasticrete-block cast buildings formed a loose compound. Speeder and sled traffic zipped in and out, making their presence innocuous. A rough highway sat nearby, the rocky ground treated to form a road, not as purposeful or clean as duracrete, but just as permanent. It curved around the ridge to where, in the adjacent valley, their target waited.

The windowless complex was covered by a transparent dome, shielding it from weather as well as information. "What works for them to keep the stream from entering or leaving, works against them when I take control of it. I've penetrated their system and can lock it down at will," Sims said with confidence.

"Sims will pop the entrances for us," said Braley, "so we won't have to breach through the dome or the main entrance. Once they realize we control their systems, they can of course mechanically seal any section. So don't worry, Bigg, you'll still get to wreck a few barriers."

No one could see his face, but Kel knew Bigg was smiling.

Sims's voice returned. "I was able to infiltrate nano drones with pedestrian traffic and we've got a good reconstruction of all but one part of the facility."

The image animated. The floor plan appeared in three dimensions through invisible walls. The layout of the main section was unmistakable.

"This is a housing block."

The image enhanced. Cells. A surveillance holo, two-dimensional to indicate it was obtained from one of the limited nanos, showed a grainy view of a two-story chamber. A perimeter of repeating closed doors ringed each level, singular in its designed purpose: incarceration. One of the roving Gomarii snapped its head toward the drone, the tendrils that hung from its upper lip and covering its mouth swaying from the sudden motion. It detected a presence, and the transmission halted. The blue tendril-faced giant had reacted to something when the drone shut off its capture.

"It's unlikely the nano was spotted," Sims commented without being asked. "The nanos will stop any collection at the hint of attention." He brought up a still of the Gomarii jailer. A whip hung coiled from his belt, a stun baton on the other hip. "At least within the cell block area, it doesn't appear the guards have blasters."

Meadows spoke up. "Don't let that keep you from using deadly force against them would be my recommendation."

"Sergeant Meadows is correct," the colonel said. "I'm authorizing the use of deadly physical force against any Gomarii on the installation. Not that they'll surrender, even if given the choice."

The words hung in their ears, the silence that followed the colonel's proclamation an emphasis heavier than anything that could have followed, like the echoes of thunder rolling in the distance. They were going to kill the jailers. All of them.

Braley broke the stillness. "This is the only section we couldn't penetrate."

The reconstruction highlighted a section of the complex past the open cell block.

"Don't know what's in here. It's high security, though. Administrative and support areas seem to be accounted for," Braley explained. "There's been only one movement in or out of this section in the last day. The nanos didn't bring back anything from inside. I don't think it's worth losing our momentum to wait further and try for a penetration."

"Agreed," the colonel said. "We're here to find out what's trying to control Dark Ops. Unless there is a reasoned objection, I think it's time to get some answers."

The plan was simple. Sims would hijack the complex's network. A rolling vehicular assault would end with their entrance. Sims, Nail, and Crane would remain outside on containment, controlling access in and out. If a relief force responded to their assault, the heavy blasters would make quick work of them. The rest of the force would work the interior, restraining, or disabling anyone in their way. Except the Gomarii. The colonel had already given them a death sentence. Once they recovered the target, they would lock the facility down, the *Shinshu Maru* would make an expedient landing nearby on the improved plain, and they'd be off. The shuttle had already been recovered aboard, the crew awaiting their retrieval order. Then the answers they sought would be at hand. They hoped.

As they eased from their assembly area, Kel wondered if they would find Patrick a more cooperative soul than he had been during their time together. Freeing the pompous ass from captivity should render him grateful, were Patrick a normal personality. Kel pushed the speculation from his mind as they came to the turnoff.

"They're blocked," Sims announced. "We own their system net. Punch it."

Kel was in the front sled, driven by Nail. The repulsors whined as the acceleration pushed him rearward into Poul on the bench next to him. Joe knelt by the access and pulled the panel back, the ground speeding by outside as they readied.

"Thirty seconds," Nail warned.

"Gate's open," Sims confirmed. "Good hunting, boys."

The sled reversed thrust and slid sideways as the dome and semi cylindrical passageway of the entrance came into view. Kel was in the air, leaping out of the sled before it stopped. The entrance was open, Sims's mastery of slicing continuing to impress. Poul was on his right as they trotted through the tunnel and broke through into the open space before the building, which sat like a plant in a greenhouse. Sims followed their progress. Somewhere above, nano drones swarmed the interior of the dome, their unblinking eyes looking where they could not. The portal to the main entrance slid open as Sims anticipated their arrival.

"Launch," Kel said and halted. Poul did the same, their rifles presenting together. Two grenades issued forth, leaving wispy trails behind them. Then came the hollow sound of explosions.

"On me." Kel reinitiated their momentum.

He knew the rest of the team was with him, though he never turned to look, or heard a word. Independently but together, extensions of a single organism, moving, probing, killing.

Kel and Poul entered first. The visual denial grenades had discharged their payload, the reflecting sparkles of the metallic dust glinting sporadically through the thick black haze. Their buckets cut through the mask of smoke, rendering everything shades of black and gray. Poul was the first to fire. A nearly three-meter tall outline appeared to their front. It was not the outline of the Gomarii that attracted Poul's fire. It was the blaster he held.

Several smaller humanoid outlines stood paralyzed behind a receiving area. Kel tossed a stunner into their midst; figures collapsed. The rest of the team pushed through as Kel and Poul threw ener-chains around the bodies, the restraints wrapping themselves over torsos and limbs.

"They're not going anywhere," Kel said as he kicked the blaster out of the dead Gomarii's hands.

Poul tossed a chain pack over the body. "If there's more, they ain't coming out to play yet. Let's go."

The two trotted down a twisting corridor to catch up with the rest of the team, passing the evidence of how busy they'd been. Portals to rooms were frozen open. Bodies lay across thresholds, stunned or dead. They slowed. Up ahead, the rest of their formation was halted.

"Sims, what's the holdup?" Bigg asked. The security door was sealed; two Gomarii lay dead beside it.

"Their systems are totally disabled. Only mech-locks can be in place."

"Rog," Bigg replied.

Kel posted in the opposite direction. His teammates would be doing likewise as Bigg worked. The thick haze from the VD grenades still filled the air. He heard Bigg and Meadows make few exchanges as the two placed their charges.

"This one's going to be hot. Back it up."

Kel knew he was far enough away to be safe. He'd continue to keep his back to the breaching charge, ready to move with the rest of the team after Bigg worked his magic.

The air grew intense with light; plasma burned. When the charge faded, the thick security door stood pivoted, its borders glowing. Braley aimed his K-17 through the triangular opening and launched a VD. As he faded to a side and broke the action open to load another grenade, the colonel fired a stunner, bouncing it off the long line of cell doors to travel deep inside as it discharged. Like the unerring turn of a gear tooth, Braley returned to launch another stunner on its heels.

Meadows tackled the stuck door; the impervisteel panel fell with a ringing clang. Two stunned Gomarii lay ahead on the main floor. Kel flowed in with the team and found himself on the left side of the rectangular dormitory.

"Movement on the catwalks," Kel said to the team. The second-story catwalks on both sides held dark figures moving through the murk. Already the colonel was bolting up the left-hand access. Kel jumped to follow, close behind as the colonel sprinted up the stairs.

"We've entered the cell block," Braley informed the team outside. "Give me a sitrep."

"All quiet. No sign of detection," Sims said.

Kel kept his running ascent, chasing the colonel. Without pause he brought his rifle up and fired a snap burst at a massive Gomarii outline down the catwalk. The DO commander hit the landing and charged at the figure, stopped by Kel's blast but not down. Kel double-timed to catch him.

I know the colonel likes to KTF, but he's acting like he's a one-man kill team.

On the right, someone was on the opposite catwalk, firing down at figures on the ground floor.

They've got it handled over there, he knew.

He sprinted all out until he was on the colonel's heels. On Hartenstein's back was a single-handed blade. Too long to be called a knife, not long enough to be a sword. He'd wanted to ask the colonel about the weapon, but the time had not been right.

The strip of walk was not wide enough for Kel to move on line with the armored giant, and it was impossible for Kel to see past him. Above the colonel a hulking Gomarii appeared out of the mist, drooping tendrils writhing about its misshapen mouth, its raised arm holding a glowing whip.

The colonel drew his blade from over his shoulder and met the Gomarii midair, severing its arm. Whip and muscular arm flopped to the ground. As he landed the blade turned in another circular arc, severing the beast's remaining arm raised in defense. Shouldering the giant chest, the guard fell. The colonel launched over the armless opponent and continued his drive down the catwalk, short sword in hand.

The Gomarii struggled to rise but Kel butt-stroked his head. Tendrils splayed as liquid sprayed from the hidden mouth to join the pool of blood forming from the severed limbs. He paused for only a second to grab one of the chain pouches from his waist and throw it onto the thing's legs. The enerchains snaked around the jailer as the colonel exploded to catch the berserker ahead of him.

Kel stopped in place at the sight of Hartenstein. The colonel was a cyclone of blade and body. The hideous beasts dwarfed even the giant colonel. Yet the two Gomarii fought crudely, ineffectively, pointlessly. Their motions seemed stunted as the colonel's blade drew across torso and limbs, long cuts and short stabs interspersed with kicks and blows from empty fist and the butt of his short sword before neither stood.

"Behind you," Kel said as stepped close, not wanting to crowd or surprise the one doing the killing. The colonel grunted in recognition, then kicked the kneeling guard in the chest, sending him to the deck next to his partner. Kel likewise chained the two as Bigg called them all.

"We have the ground floor locked down. Splash four."

So, four guards eliminated.

Braley spoke from the opposite catwalk, "We've cleared the right catwalk. Splash two."

"We've got three wounded Gomarii chained," Kel said. "They'll bleed out without attention."

"Doubtful, Lieutenant," the colonel countered. "I've seen them survive worse. Continue on to the next breach point. We're secure up here."

"Assemble on me," Bigg said. "We're setting charges on the last section now."

The colonel left the moaning captives and moved to the descending access. Kel followed.

"Oba's beard, Kel," Poul's voice came over a sub-channel. "That was mad! I saw it all. The colonel went through them like nothing I've ever seen."

"The Gomarii are undeserving of mercy," the colonel said over the team channel. Whether he had heard Poul on the private channel or was simply lecturing, it was eerie. "If we need information from the guards, this is the only way. To dominate them completely and humiliate them... it's the only thing that comes close to a negotiation. Those three won't be feeding on anyone's fear. They'll be ready to answer questions after they've been helpless awhile."

Kel paused at the bottom of the landing. He caught Poul's visage from the opposite stairs, his bucket tilted in surprise. The colonel's words were spoken with weight. The heaviness of hard experience. It made Kel wonder. If he got the chance to ask the colonel about the Gomarii, he would. He sensed a story there. Something personal, etched deep into their commander's ethos of combat. Like a scar on a tree made deeper with time and growth.

"Sims, we're getting ready to breach the last room," Braley said, updating the team outside. "Anyone attempt to leave? We drawing any attention?"

"Negative, boss," Sims returned. "You're nine minutes on the clock."

Has it only been nine minutes we've been at this? Kel mused. Time really was subjective.

"All quiet. If we lose comms, I'll send someone to retrieve you if we need to get moving, SOP."

That was their standard contingency if they were separated and lost comms between groups on an op; person-to-person communication as delivered by the oldest form of travel, the foot.

"Rog, Sims." Braley broke to look at their team sergeant. "Bigg, we up?"

"Ready to burn," Bigg acknowledged. Meadows again stood on the opposite side of the portal from Bigg, eyeing the plasma strip charges they'd placed around the door. The way in looked nowhere near as resistant as the entrance to the cell block. A biometric pad was inset into the wall beside it. Kel's weapon unconsciously raised with everyone else's in response when without warning, the portal slid aside.

"There's no need for that. I will not resist you," a soft voice said from within. The alien voice was feminine in timbre, her Standard smooth, perfect, and haunting like a dream.

"On me." Bigg was first to move, Meadows next.

They poured into the space, where a lone figure perched on a float in the middle of the white, sterile environment. Four thin arms, curved and flexible like a sea creature's tentacles, were half raised to the height of the smooth, green head. Her clothing matched the environment. White, unblemished, unnatural. Kel looked around the room from above the optic on his K-17. Five other weapons pointed at the central figure.

The alien was a type Kel had never seen before. It's watery black eyes quizzically studied them one by one. "I'm sure I can be of assistance. There's no need for violence."

Kel lowered his rifle farther. Dim colored lights pulsed from out of the alcoves lining the white room. His curiosity drew him to the nearest. Revulsion filled him.

"Get chains on her," Kel ordered. Harshly. Hatefully. Cruelly. "Now."

The calm voice, cool and detached, said, "I am incapable of harming a soul."

But Kel couldn't look away from the horror before him to evaluate if her manner matched her disarming words.

"Maybe so, lady," Poul said. "But let's just say this is for your safety as well as ours."

"What is it?" Braley stared over Kel's shoulder.

"Oba!" Meadows blurted.

It took no training in medicine as advanced as Kel's to understand what lay before them. A very human brain floated upright in a thin tank filled with viscous fluid. The spinal cord and its lattice of nerves splayed out as if awaiting a new set of flesh and bones. The rainbow of colors spilling out of the dark recess were from fibers pulsing around the thousands of nerve endings, interacting in some way with the disembodied person.

"It's looking at us," Braley gasped.

Indeed, two eyestalks floated in the colloidal murk, each framed by a thin silver rim. The eyes went from bucket to bucket, regarding each dark operator.

The chained prisoner spoke in a sympathetic tone, as if eager to please. "If there's someone you're looking for, I'm certain I can be of assistance."

The colonel broke their stunned silence. "I never suspected it could be something like this."

Meadows's voice held a quality he'd never before heard from the fearless man. What he said chilled Kel. Because he knew Meadows was right.

"We've found hell."

19

"I'm the custodian of all those consigned," the sickly smooth voice continued. "How did you find us? Others have tried. We would be most grateful to know how you discovered our location. Our integrity and client protection are our most valuable assets. Your cooperation in this matter would be greatly appreciated and rewarded."

"Kel," Braley said. "Are those things... alive?"

"I can assure you," the custodian answered for him, "the discorporate are quite alive. They have merely been freed from their physical constraints."

The floating eyes darted around the alcove at the legionnaires. Kel fought his revulsion to retreat, and instead concentrated on the readouts on the panel next to the tank. Most of the figures meant nothing to him. He settled on what appeared to be the electrical trace from neurologic activity of the organ floating beside him.

"This is most irregular. While I am authorized to offer incentives for your cooperation, I must warn you that there will be consequences if you display any more of the violence you have already shown in gaining access to our—"

"Enough!" the colonel shouted.

The custodian recoiled. Her thin lips split like the skin of an overripe fruit.

The colonel stalked over to her. "I have questions. You will answer them. Otherwise, it is I who must warn *you* of the consequences."

The custodian remained still, membranes shuttering over her inky black eyes.

"What is this facility? Who are the beings entrapped here?"

The custodian swelled out of her shrunken state. "No one is entrapped. They have been freed." There was pride in her voice.

"Why are they here? I will not tolerate any more evasions."

The custodian gestured using her trefoil lips, puckered, and pointed toward the tank beside Kel. "Senior Barcalan found us as a last resort to his Mendenhall's dystrophy. No medical treatment remained that could stave off the death of his human body. His mind remained without blemish. Now, he lives on." Kel recognized the surname. It was an old-money name from the core.

"Others placed themselves in our care for simpler reasons. They tired of their bodily existence. Khal Tropa is a heteronistic philosopher and artist who spends his new life in the simulacra, creating and—"

"So, this is a medical facility?" Kel interrupted. "No one is here against their will?"

The custodian hesitated, a slight noise, a gurgle, then sealed her lips.

"Pfft. That's a tell," Kel said over L-comm. "These aren't all wealthy people avoiding death or geniuses exercising their brains."

"We're looking for someone," the colonel growled. "I don't know if he's in this madhouse or in a cell next door."

He touched his forearm and a holo of Patrick appeared. "Take a good look."

The custodian barely looked at the holo. "The retreat is a separate entity. Please understand, we are located here solely because of the extreme need for protection of the discorporate. The retreat facility's security benefits us."

Retreat, Kel marveled. *Euphemisms!* It reminded him of how politicians misnamed things to hide their true purpose. *A cell is a cell.*

"Look," the colonel ordered, sticking the holo in front of her. The custodian's teardrop face swiveled back to the colonel. She took in the picture. The membranes closed over both orbs as she froze.

Silence.

"So. He's here," the colonel interpreted. He hefted the custodian off her float and held her suspended. "Where?" Just as gently, he lowered her to the floor. "Show me. Now."

Head sunken, the pointed tips of her four arms flaccid beneath the ener-chains, she glided deeper into the room, passing recessed chamber after chamber, each with its own horror suspended in gel. Some brains had eyes tracking their travel, while others seemed frozen in place.

"It's like they're looking at us," Poul said. "What is this place?"

"I don't know. But maybe the colonel does," Kel said.

The custodian paused at the last alcove. "I believe this is the discorporate you seek."

This alcove was darker than the others. Another ghastly dissection floated before them. Somehow Kel knew it was Patrick. No microscopic lights vibrated color onto the neural tissues. Instead, a yellow pulsing light haloed the brain. Its eyestalks hung limp, as if in resignation.

"This one is not like the others," Kel said. "This one is being denied stimulus. That's correct, isn't it? The others are linked into some kind of virtual construct. This one is being... punished?"

Stiffening, the custodian said, "It is as the client requested."

"How do we know this is Patrick?" Braley said.

"You may speak with the discorporate," the green alien replied. "But you may not receive answers. The discorporate is... not attuned to the expanded plane of reality without the body."

"What could anyone have done to deserve this?" Meadows said. "It's a, it's a..."

"It's a transgression against humanity," the colonel said. "They're as bad as the Savages."

Kel asked aloud what they were all thinking. "But who are they? Who did this?"

The custodian convinced them to unchain her so that she could manipulate the controls allowing them to speak to the floating gray blob. The ends of her pointed arms elongated to form fine tips as she danced them across the panel. "He can hear you now." She folded her arms across herself and stepped back from the panel. "You may speak to him."

Braley nudged Kel. "You try."

Kel looked to the colonel, who nodded. Kel's mind was blank. Where should he begin? *Think of him as a patient. Someone who needs help. Disregard the blood; don't empathize. Treat the problem. You can't help someone unless you can detach yourself from their pain.*

Because without being told, Kel knew for a fact that the surreal visage before him was in pain.

"Patrick, can you hear me?" he said softly.

"It may take some time for him to connect to the outside stimulus," the custodian encouraged, a hint of excitement in her voice. "It has been over a week since the discorporate has been contacted outside of his simulacra. This will be a welcome disruption of his routine, I'm certain."

"I doubt you'd swap places with him, lady." Kel ignored her and tried again. "Patrick, is that you? Do you remember me? It's Kel Turner."

This time the eyes raised, the silver rims of their frames glistened in the dim yellow light. Words appeared in holo, projected onto the tank, as a dull, lifeless voice intoned, "Who is that? Is there someone there?"

"Oba!" Poul said. "It's alive. It's actually a person in there."

Kel felt encouraged. "Yes, we're here. Patrick, is that you in there?"

"I am here. I am... Patrick. Yes. That is my name. I know it. It has been so long."

In the same cheerful voice, the custodian said, "His simulacra is primitive. When the client approves, he will be given greater latitude, and can even create his own environment. For now... would you like to see what the discorporate perceives as his environment?"

The arms unfolded and began rabidly tapping across the black panel of lights until a tiny holo appeared next to them.

"It is always projected from the discorporate's view." In mincing motions, she wrapped her arms around herself and stepped back.

A bright white room. Even more sterile than the facility they stood in. A table. A chair. Walls.

The eyes in the tank raised. The holo showed a window in the white wall, and the group of armored legionnaires staring back at themselves.

Kel removed his bucket. "Patrick, it's Kel Turner. Do you remember me? The mission to the Savage moon? Your friend Sarah was with us? Do you recognize me?"

There was a pause. "Yes. It seems so long ago, yet... there's so little to remember since. You're a... hero. A strong man..." the voice mumbled. The projected symbols of words became squiggles. "Are you here to save me this time? Is it my turn?"

"Sometimes the discorporate become confused," the custodian interjected. "This one has not been acclimated yet."

"Where am I?" Patrick continued. "I can't feel anything. I can't see my body. I'm just... floating."

"Ask him what happened after he was arrested," Bigg said aloud. "We need to know how this happened and who did this to him."

"I remember," Patrick continued. "I remember. I could feel. I could see my body. I was... Oh no!" the voice stuttered.

"Patrick," Kel coaxed. "What do you remember?"

"This interrogation is disturbing to the discorporate." The custodian stepped forward in protest. "I cannot allow this."

Poul placed himself in front of her. "And maybe I need to put you back in chains." He pulled them out and guided them around her waist and arms.

"This is interference," she said. "Interference in things you know nothing about."

"Pipe down, lady," Poul said. "I'll gag you if you don't."

She pursed her lips in response.

"Grandmother told me about the lower world," Patrick continued, the weariness gone. "I never believed her. Is that where I am? I was so wrong. I'm so sorry." His words became leaden and pained again.

Kel tried to console him. "Patrick, we're going to help you. We need to know what happened and who did this to you. Can you tell us?"

The colonel stepped forward. "Patrick. Who controlled your mission to the Savage moon? Who did you work for?"

After a long silence, the dull voice said, "Accius. Accius promised we would be together in the senate. He promised we would control the Republic. That we could finally bring order to it all. There's so much to be done, he said, and we have the power to do it."

"VanderBlanc? Accius VanderBlanc?" the colonel pressed. "Is that who controlled you?"

Again silence, as if there were a delay in the transmission across the single meter to the tank in front of them. "We all answer to someone. He... he knows everything about us. He controls our families, our fortune, our future. He promised that if we obeyed, we would have a place in that future. We would share in the power he would control. We would be rewarded. Oh, what have I done? This can't be happening. I can't get out. I've been here forever. Am I dead? Is this because I've been a bad boy? Oh, Grandmother, you were right, you were right..."

"Patrick," Kel said. "Are you saying that you were forced to do these things? Were you blackmailed by VanderBlanc? Did they threaten your family?"

"Help me. Please. Help me."

Cold horror rose in Kel's chest. "Patrick, we need to know where they are. Where are the people who did this? Where is VanderBlanc?"

Again, the long pause, as if Patrick's mind searched for the answer.

"I remember the colors. I remember being scared I would fall. Accius told me not to worry. We were safe. It was such a long descent. The elevator. The colors were so beautiful. It was the only place I ever felt safe, above the clouds."

The colonel spoke. "Patrick, was it Plenathon? Were you on Plenathon?"

Kel recognized the name from the list of waypoints Sims sliced from VanderBlanc's flight plans logged in Orion Station.

"Plenathon. It was so peaceful. It was our safe place. I only want to go back. I don't want to be powerful. I am so sorry. I was wrong. Everything I did, Grandmother's voice was always there, telling me to be good. I am so ashamed. Can anyone help me? Forgive me."

The heaviness of pity filled Kel's chest. Patrick had been a subject of his contempt. He'd resented the weak man and the damage he'd caused. Kel had found himself wishing ill on the man, hoping to be the one to punish the contemptible wretch. To make him pay.

Now, it was Kel who felt shame. His hatred burned a hole inside of him.

He turned. "Custodian. He's suffering. It's not right. Help him. Can't you please help him?" Kel couldn't bear the pain he felt. The dread of Patrick's hell squeezed his soul. No man deserved such suffering.

The green face looked contemplative. "He can be introduced to the full simulacra. He may yet be accommodated to an existence of the mind. It can be... most fulfilling. It is not what the client has approved for him as of now, though."

"Kel," Patrick intoned. "Kel. I remember you and your friends. I was so jealous. You were all so strong. Everything I knew I wasn't. I wanted to hurt you all. Please, forgive me."

Kel swallowed the lump in his throat. "Patrick, it's all right. We know it wasn't your fault. They used you like they tried to use me. We know. Why did they do this to you?"

Pause.

"I failed. I didn't want to hide. They were going to send me away. I told them I was tired of their games. They jailed me. It was like this, only, real. I decided I was going to resist. I wasn't going to be their tool. Then... I don't remember. All I know is..." Patrick's reconstructed voice took on a lucid tone for the first time. "Please tell me. This isn't a dream. Where am I? I'm not dead. I know that much. What's happened to me?"

Kel hesitated. He brought his bucket up to the glass. He moved it closer to the floating eyes and held it still.

"He sees it, I think," the colonel said.

The holo showed the window through the wall of Patrick's white, featureless cell. Through the window stood Kel holding his bucket, surrounded by his armored companions. The reflection in the visor, Patrick seeing himself for the first time as he now was.

The voice was calm. "Kill me, please. Release me to the void."

"There's nothing more he can give us," the colonel said.

Kel knew it was up to him. "I have to end this. Step back." He raised his rifle at the tank. The rest of the team moved back as he'd commanded.

"Hey!" Poul exclaimed.

Kel snapped around to see Poul and Bigg struggle with the custodian, dragging her backward as she fought. Her ener-chains glowed as she resisted, green limbs stretched abnormally beneath their constraints. Elongating. Thinning. Writhing. The pointed, smooth terminus of each limb was now covered in long black spines, stretching toward Kel's uncovered head.

"You must not!" the alien shrieked. She twisted and bucked, her outstretched tentacles directed at her captors, bouncing harmlessly off their armor. "You have no right!"

"Whoa!" Poul said. "So, all that 'no harm' stuff you said was bogus!"

Meadows slapped another set of chains and guided them around her hips, lashing the pointed tentacles to her side as she cried in pain. The chains tightened under Meadows command until they dug into her flesh.

Kel felt a hand on his shoulder. "Do it, son." It was the colonel. "End his suffering."

He looked at Patrick a last time. "There's another light beyond, Patrick. A warm light that will receive you. You'll never be alone again. You're forgiven."

Kel fired.

Before the glass shattered and its contents disappeared, disintegrating in the bright glow of his full particle beam, Kel glimpsed the words broadcast on the glass.

Thank you, friend.

"What the... Kel, our squid friend isn't doing so well!" Poul said.

"Ease her down, ease her down," Bigg said. The custodian writhed and convulsed as Poul and Bigg laid her on the floor. Kel knelt beside her just as the seizure stopped. She went limp. Kel got a thin panel out of his med kit and placed it on the still chest.

"She's dead." Kel stared at the flexible panel. "What happened?"

"She just started shaking and dropped," Braley said. "It's like she overloaded or something."

"Neurotoxin," the colonel said. "If she'd reached you, Lieutenant, you'd be dead." He pointed at her arms, the black-tipped barbs at the ends of the limbs slowly retracting as she expired. "Some Agnathans can purposefully suicide. For some, it happens unintentionally. An endocrine release. That's why most of them are very docile; stress induces the death response. I'd say we stressed her."

Agnathan, Kell thought. He'd heard of that species but had never seen one—not even a holo.

Meadows stared down at her. "I was looking forward to interrogating her further. I still want to know who runs this place, and who her clients are."

"Sims, how're we doing outside?" Braley asked.

"All quiet."

"Meadows and Poul will meet you at the entrance to lead you in. We've got some data for you to slice. Then we're outta here." Braley knife-handed the two. "Get Sims here and let's make quick work of getting what we can, and fast."

"Colonel, what do we do about this place?" Braley asked.

Kel had the same question.

The colonel looked around at the many chambers. Without answering, he turned on his heels. "Lieutenant, with me."

Kel pulled the K-17 from his chest and moved to the colonel's left as they departed the cold, clinical space for the jail block. Kel had not forgotten about the wounded Gomarii, and knew the colonel had not, either.

The closest two of the subdued Gomarii remained on the catwalk a few meters away from the top of the stair access, still but not lifeless. One had moved to prop against the wall into a hunched position. Wet air hissed from a wound in its chest as it struggled to breathe. The other lay on its side, its abdomen heaving. The smoke grenade mist was clearing. Farther down the catwalk, the other guard so decisively conquered by the colonel lay on its back.

"What can they tell us about this place?" Kel asked the colonel.

"They can't tell us anything I don't already know. I have a message to deliver." The colonel looked down on the Gomarii propped against the wall between two cell doors. The jet-black eyes stood out from the blue skin stretched over its clean skull, the mouth tendrils pulsing. "What clan are you, dishonored one?"

The creature tried to answer, but only wheezed. Kel knelt and produced a chest seal, applying it to the long flat puncture over its hard thorax. As the chest heaved with struggled breaths, Kel felt the ribs. They were wide and flat, much broader than a human's. How the colonel had found the entrance to the cavity behind... Kel suspected it was not luck.

"Who wants to know?" the alien gargled.

"Dying bound and defeated is a death for a weakling, Gomarii. But there's no shame in it. I want you to live, and feel the shame my clan brings to yours. What clan does a runt like you come from?"

"Gomandii. Gomandii soo Parka. That is my clan."

The colonel laughed. "Then someday, in shame, you can tell the Gomandii soo Parka that the Chara of Subeda Four do not forget. They live and thrive while your clan will see the last of its days. Tell them." Without waiting for a reply, the colonel strode away. "Let's go, Lieutenant. Time to leave."

"We're getting some activity outside," Nail said. "Nothing big. A sled pulled into the canyon, saw us, and hightailed it out of here. Someone recognizes that there's a party going on here, and didn't want any part of it."

"Copy," Braley said. "Everyone get that? We're compromised. Time to go. I'm calling for our ride. Let's get out of here."

Kel stayed on the colonel's back as they halted at the entrance to the white room, the rest of the team assembled.

"I pulled everything." Sims lifted his datapad to show them. "Won't know if I can break into the files until later. Looks very encrypted, even some DNA coded barriers. Got everything from the prison data stream, too. I may be able to crack that; it's not so shielded."

"Sir, what do we do about the facility?" Braley asked. "There must be live prisoners in all these cells. And this..." He gestured back into the white room. "I don't even know what to recommend."

"Sir, what is this place?" Kel asked out of turn. He was not going to be held off. "We can't make a decision without knowing more."

"I've made the decision," the colonel calmly said. "Captain, get everyone out. Lieutenant, Sergeant Meadows, remain with me. We won't be long. Move out."

Wordlessly, Bigg, Braley, Poul, and Sims departed. Sub-channel talk between them was muted in Kel's bucket as the colonel directed them.

"Help me get this door into place. We're going to tack it in into the frame."

The three hefted the door up and walked it onto place. Just before the steel door was refit into its frame, the colonel removed a grenade and tossed it into the white room. The octagonal body had a red stripe encircling it. "Torches. Spot-weld where you can." Kel and Meadows followed directions and began to work. Some of the edges aligned and allowed rejoining as the white-hot metal cooled red and then black. The colonel stepped back as he extinguished his own torch. "That'll be sufficient. Let's go. We've been here too long already." He broke into a trot.

"Bird inbound. Let's go," Bigg said over L-comm. They'd cleared the exterior and were running down the tunnel to see Crane gesturing to them from the open sled.

Kel was the last in. "Last man. Go, go, go!"

"There she is," Nail said from ahead, driving the lead sled. Kel peered ahead from the rear compartment, ducking to see above the horizon of the front windscreen. The *Shinshu Maru* banked as it descended onto the rough, rocky plain at the base of the valley mouth, just the other side of the roadbed.

"Sergeant Sims," the colonel said, "do you have your link active with the facility still?"

"Yes, sir."

"Isolate the fire suppression to the white room and shut it off. Let me know when you've done so."

A moment passed.

"Colonel, I have that part of the system shut down. I can't promise it hasn't shut off in other parts of the facility as well, though."

"Thank you, Sergeant."

Meadows knelt by the open door. He held up a fist, then opened his fingers in a flourish, mimicking an explosion.

"Un-ass, gentlemen," Nail said from ahead, just as Crane flared their sled to a quivering halt.

Kel leaped out. Meadows took off for the ship, leading the way as a line of armored bodies met him from their flank. Kel checked the sled. He almost always took the role of last man, ensuring no one and nothing was ever left behind. Satisfied, he trotted to the front of the sled to see Bigg bringing up the rear from his side.

"Last man our sled, Bigg."

His mentor returned a thumbs-up. "Last man here. Let's go."

They ran together to see Chief Lopez at the forward port pax door, waving them on. The grizzled man slapped each on the shoulder as they ascended, counting out loud. "Eight. And nine. I got nine heads."

"Count's good, Captain Yost," Bigg said.

The colonel moved to the open hatch and gently nudged past Chief Lopez. "One moment." He brought his forearm up and swiped. "All right. We can make for orbit."

As the chief sealed the hatch and made his way into the ship, Bigg thumped Kel on his chest and pointed to his ear with a single finger. Kel shook his head, "No." It was paradoxical. Sealed from the rest of the world, they communicated with each other in complete silence and privacy by L-comm. If the colonel utilized his command privilege, the only way to answer Bigg privately would be with their buckets off. Kel wanted to answer Bigg's question about the colonel's actions, but when he could be assured privacy. He needed Bigg as his sounding board for what he'd witnessed. And for what he'd done.

They steadied themselves, pushing against the narrow walls of the passageway to reach the open pax area. The rest of the team had settled into cushions. Poul had his bucket off already, vigorously scratching his head. After plopping down in the seat beside him, Kel followed suit. The chief inspected them from the hatch, as natural as a juggler, tossing nine balls in the air, unconcerned as he swayed. The colonel beckoned the chief with a single finger, who bent over to offer his ear. Words were exchanged. A nudge from the colonel and Nail joined them to depart forward, leaning into the climb of the ship as it carried them higher.

Buckets off, Bigg and Meadows leaned forward to conference, the hum of the engines pulsing through the hull and the seats underneath them.

Bigg started. "All right. We'll after-action with the captain and the rest once we're out of the atmosphere and settled. What happened back there with the colonel?"

Meadows answered. "He had us close the white room back up and he tossed a command thermoplex grenade in."

"He bounced the det signal before we sealed up. Torched the place. Everyone in there is cooked now." Kel hesitated to use the word "everyone."

"Were they people?" Poul asked. "I don't even know how to think about what those... things were. What about that swordplay with the Gomarii? I wish I had that on a chip. If I hadn't seen it, I wouldn't have believed it. What'd the colonel do to those Gomarii?"

The three men's eyes were locked on Kel.

"He didn't interrogate them. He said he already knew what the place was. It was something personal. He said he had a message to deliver. Asked the one Gomarii who his people were, then gave them warning." Kel told them as best he remembered what the colonel said.

Bigg nodded knowingly. "It was a long time ago. I wasn't there, but the colonel's had a grudge against the Gomarii for decades. There was a time when they were a real menace. They raided and slaved on many worlds. The colonel was a young lieutenant," he nodded toward Kel, "when he led missions against them. As much as any man, he and his legionnaires are why the Gomarii are so rare. This is while I was still in the First Guards. Before Dark Ops was stood up..."

The ship leveled off.

"Attention," the voice came overhead. "High polar orbit achieved. It will be about an hour before we leave system. I'll issue a warning before we jump."

Crowded around them stood the rest of the team. Braley coughed to get their attention. "Everyone okay?" Nods went all around. "I think we need to move back to the bay and have a little AAR time."

The colonel's voice boomed behind them. "It's time for me to tell you all what I know." It startled Kel, as it did the others. The colonel stood in the passageway from the command deck. "I know you all have questions. You deserve answers."

The image of the dissected Patrick hung in Kel's mind.

Poul leaned in to whisper, "I'm not sure I want to know."

20

Kill Team Three shed their armor and sat on floats and cushions in the confines of the bay they used as their work area, ration and liquid pouches in hand. The colonel eased onto a pull-down desk. Even with thighs fully seated on top, his feet still touched the deck.

"I'm impressed with your outstanding work, men. I've never asked anything more difficult of you, and you delivered with perfection. All of you."

Kel remembered the colonel slicing through the giant Gomarii like a surgeon with a laser scalpel and wanted to voice his admiration for their commander, but knew it was not the time to do so.

The colonel continued. "In answer to your questions... yes, I knew about the existence of the extra-lawful prison, and its purpose. No, I had no inkling about the nature of the abomination we found deeper within the white room."

Sims sat behind their group, listening, but with a data-pad on his lap. He had specs on and pushed holos around, his eyes following text as he swiped images aside in quick succession like batting away bothersome insects.

"The prison is run by a concern that provides a private service." The colonel clenched his jaw. "Many governments, including our own, have contracted with this group to keep custody of its enemies. It is an extra-legal function. In some cases, in my opinion, even necessary.

Housed within those cells are some of the worst criminals in the galaxy."

Kel frowned. *If they're criminals, why aren't they in a real prison?*

The colonel seemed to sense Kel's skepticism. "There exist cases where an accused cannot be brought to open trial, where evidence cannot be presented in an open courtroom. Either the confidential nature of the crime or how the evidence was obtained makes a public trial impossible. Revealing government secrets and all. In that case, a secret tribunal is held, and the guilty are renditioned to a site such as the one on Abaddon for incarceration, with complete plausible deniability."

The colonel was telling them in a matter-of-fact way that there existed a justice system that did not follow the laws of the Republic. Kel glanced at Poul, who shrugged, as if he understood. Kel did not. "Sir, what's to keep a privileged group from sending a political opponent to such a place, or even an innocent person who's simply gained the wrong enemies?"

"Nothing. The same concern that accepts these prisoners from the Republic accepts them from clients of non-Republic worlds of all races. They're not in the business of confirming right or wrong. They're in the business of incarcerating who they're paid to incarcerate. It's a very ugly, very dark part of the galaxy, Lieutenant."

On that, Kel agreed.

"Of all the sites for rendition we knew of," the colonel nodded toward Nail, "this was the one our sources traced Patrick's path to after his disappearance from custody by the Justice Directorate."

Sites? Kel noticed the colonel used the plural. *There are more black sites like this one? Do any others have the nightmarish white rooms, dissections hung like trophies on the walls?*

"Sir, did we know that Patrick was held in the... other place?" Braley asked.

The colonel remained stone-faced. "No. It was simply my suspicion that, being the most secure and compartmentalized place in the facility, it likely held the most valuable treasure."

Treasure! Kel thought. It was a word they used to denote valuable intelligence, or a high-value target. What they found had not been a treasure.

"Colonel, how did we leave things on Abaddon?" said Bigg.

The colonel nodded. "I'm glad you asked. First off, the decision was mine alone. Second, I'm not looking for anyone's approval. It had to be done this way, understood?"

No one spoke.

"Good. We could not leave the white room intact. Besides my personal objection to the inhumanity we found there, it was necessary to disguise our tracks. I believe relieving Patrick's suffering," the colonel looked at Kel, "was an act of true mercy.

"Now we know the nature of our foe. Anyone who would do that to a human soul is not deserving of mercy or understanding. They must be brought to justice. If they can do that to him, imagine what else they're capable of in their quest to hold power.

"Whether the other entities in that place could be said to be alive... I'm not a philosopher or ethicist. It was my decision to render that site inoperable. If I killed innocent beings, I'll be judged for it, and I'll accept that judgment. It won't be the only thing I'll be held accountable for someday. You all are relieved of that burden.

"But if our enemies are alerted to the destruction of the white room—which they will be, and soon—we've left no evidence of motive, or who, or why."

That's wise, Kel thought. They were probably not the only entity motivated against the institution and the secrets imprisoned there. If their goal was to stop the rot that was attempting to infiltrate Dark Ops, leaving the rest of the facility untouched would surely alert their antagonists by having only destroyed Patrick's... soul? He still didn't have a handle on what the disembodied nervous system had been. Was it really the intellect and being that had been Patrick?

"Regarding the rest of the facility, there simply wasn't time to play judge and determine if any of the occupants were unjustly incarcerated and should be freed or not. I know for a fact that there are many there who deserve imprisonment, or worse. At least one, I've had a hand in bringing to justice. I couldn't justify freeing them, no matter how distasteful I find their captivity at the hands of the Gomarii mercenaries."

Nail interjected. "But we also couldn't leave the occupants jailed there to die, much less the staff we left chained. Not even the Gomarii." The sergeant major looked at the colonel as he said the last.

Is Nail scolding the colonel? Kel wondered. He detected a tone of reproach for the colonel. Everyone knew Nail was a plank holder in Dark Ops, one of the first, selected by Rex himself. There were many times they all got the feeling it was the sergeant major who really helmed the course of the operators in their unit. It was Nail who sat in judgment of what was right and wrong. The man at the head of their tribe.

The colonel picked back up, showing no sign of agitation at Nail's words. "We contacted the constabulary before we left. Someone right now is poring over that facility. What happens to the staff and the prisoners is out of our hands."

Nail grinned. "But that's not all. I bounced an edited slice of our surveillance feed to a contact at the Spiral News Network."

Sims sputtered a liquid cough, choking on the pouch he sucked from. Even Meadows, usually silent and grim, wasn't the only one to gasp.

"SNN?" Poul asked. "Dark Ops fed SNN?"

The colonel raised his palms. "It's another way to throw anyone off our trail and give us more time to work the problem."

Kel had a thought. "Remember Xenon Boothe?"

Kel and Team Three had been sent to snatch a trillionaire industrialist from his mansion two years before. They did so under a secret arrest warrant from the House of Reason. Their possibly delusional prisoner told Kel that he'd been a man who knew too much. Boothe had never been heard from again. A famous man whose arrest and trial should have been on the Spiral News Network daily simply disappeared after Team Three abducted him. Had they participated in just such an extra-legal rendition? Had the unfortunate Xenon been one of the men locked in the cells they had failed to liberate?

"Ahead of you," Sims said. "I wondered the same thing. Boothe's dead." He pushed a holo overhead for them all to see. "He was here, though. There's a record of his registration a few months after we arrested him. There's not much else until this notation."

The simple entry next to the date read, "Deceased." It was from a few months ago.

"So," Bigg said. "He died in their custody." His voice reflected the same guilt Kel felt. "He wasn't in great shape when we saw him. I doubt he could have fared well."

Sims shook his head, as if tasting a bitter pill. "No. There's more." He flung a new holo over them. Kel felt a flutter in his chest as he read. A similar entry. *Patrick Rosen.* The registration date was six months prior. A link beside it held more files. Kel wanted to read through them. What stopped him from asking Sims to open them now was what he saw next. *Deceased.* A date from six weeks before sat beside it.

"If Patrick was in their custody until he was pronounced deceased six weeks ago..." Sims began.

Poul finished the thought. "Is the prison just a waypoint for the white room next door? If they can't get what they want from them there, do they send them for... what did she call it? Discorporation? Could Boothe have been in the white room? Who else was in there?"

Kel felt the weight on him. Were there two men he'd had a role in consigning to oblivion?

After more silence, the colonel continued. "So, we all know the magnitude of what we face. Is there anyone who thinks we should turn back?"

"No!" Kel found himself shouting before he could restrain himself. He looked about the room. All eyes were on him. He stood. "No, sir. I want to bring a justice to these monsters equal to the injustice they've brought on their victims. I want to stop them from doing the same to anyone else. We have to stop them from using me or Dark Ops to do their work for them. We need to go all the way."

"All the way, sir," Poul said next to him.

"Never leave a leej on the drop zone. All the way, sir," said Meadows.

The rest joined in.

"Opposed?" the colonel asked. The room was still.

"Where to next, sir?" Braley asked.

"Plenathon."

As with the respite after any op, the anxiety of what await-ed next hounded them. Would they be found unprepared for the next call to action? Guilt and shame were the soil where their vigilance grew. Gear was cleaned and inspect-ed, weapons made ready, pouches topped with charge packs and grenades. Kel ran his vibro-blade across the tuner, making sure the harmonics were aligned to per-fection before returning it to the sheath sitting high on the chest of his armor.

Plenathon. His curiosity was subdued only by his ex-haustion. The colonel had connected the tortured Patrick's description to match Plenathon. After a few hours' sleep, there would time to ponder and prepare. It would begin there. Did Plenathon hold the answers that would end his quest for justice?

Meadows and Poul were the only ones still in the bay with him, the last to be working on their gear. Poul grum-bled as he removed the spherical mini-stunners from the pouch and stuffed them back again, one at a time, trying for the noiseless configuration of a perfect fit. The mission support package sat at the rear of the bay, drawers and cabinets open, barely a dent made in its inventory after they'd topped off their tanks.

"Kel." The quiet voice startled him. It was Meadows. "I wanted to ask you something." The big man paused as if waiting permission, his salt and pepper stubble making him look older than Kel remembered his friend.

"Sure, Meadows." Kel was curious. When Meadows spoke, he usually vacillated between boisterous and taciturn. This was neither. "What is it?"

Meadows hesitated. "That stuff you told Patrick at the end."

Kel remembered. "Yeah?"

"Patrick was the guy who was going to get you all killed trying to recover that Savage tech on Proteus, right?"

"He sure was, man," Poul said. "Guy was bad news. I thought about killing him to keep him from making things worse for us. Kel's solution was kinder. Maybe. I guess, seeing as what happened to him... now, I don't know."

Meadows shook his head. "No. What I mean is, he was the guy that wronged you so badly. The guy who you think may have brought the Scarecrow down on you."

Kel shrugged. "I don't know. It's my suspicion. Probably wasn't just him. I think Patrick was little more than a pawn."

The big man sighed. "It's what you said to him, Kel. About there being a warm light waiting for him. That he wouldn't be alone again."

Kel waited.

Meadows looked down at the weapon in his lap. "Do you think it's true, Kel?" A mist gathered at the corners of his eyes. "We've lost a lot of fine brothers. I'd like to think it's all true, like we say at the memorials. That someday we'll all be together again."

Kel knew Meadows was thinking of his lost teammates.

"It's true." Poul stood, his face glowing with a bright smile, his fatigue and frustration gone. "Our buddy Kel is a know-it-all and a show-off but, sometimes, he gets things right. Occasionally I'm even jealous of him."

Meadows was looking up at Poul too, who still smiled down like a kindly teacher.

"We don't go to some void," Poul continued. "I don't know what happens. Maybe it's not exactly like my folks believe, but I know something happens. No matter what bad things Patrick did, Mister Kel Turner forgiving him and easing his suffering is one of the reasons I know there's a place for us all together somewhere after we're done."

With that, Poul headed into the passageway toward the cabins.

Meadows's heavy countenance was replaced with a smile, his gloom evaporated, struck just as Kel was by Poul's declarations.

The *Shinshu Maru* settled over Plenathon's celestial pole, letting the team admire the view as they floated stealthed in the torus of the magnetosphere. Bigg multiplied the viewer magnification as Kel, like the rest of the team, gawked at the image. Live, it looked every bit as stunning and surreal as the holos had. The planet's swirling colors moved in concentric bands of varied widths. Occasionally, red, gold, and purple vortices arose, growing in size to disrupt the flowing bands. Linear streams of color crashed into the rotating pools before the whirlpool dissipated, and the rivers of revolving colors resumed their orderly carousel.

Kel watched one that continued to grow until the clockwise eddy dominated the daylight side of the hemisphere. Just as Kel wondered if the rotating cloud would engulf the entire surface, it reached its critical mass and faded, the orderly racetracks of color beneath displacing the rising plumes and returning the surface to order. The spectacle started anew, new vortices appearing in a mesmerizing randomness.

The dreamlike quality of the gas giant was disrupted by the linear column of the elevator, like a price tag pinned to the center of a beautiful painting. The thin black column rose from below the clouds, swelling at its midpoint before narrowing where it extended to tether the rocky satellite, Freyja, above. More correctly, the elevator descended from the moon to penetrate the dense interior of the gas giant. Terraces sprouted like fungus growing from the bark of a tree, the habitats for manufacturing and tourism protruded from the stalk. The habs were attached in an irregular helix around the elevator, the last of them floating on the edges of the gaseous atmosphere itself.

"Cadex and the stairway of stars, am I right?" Poul said, breaking Kel's introspection. "It's like watching a ship take off. Doesn't matter how much I know about the physics behind it, it seems so frelling unnatural."

Kel had never visited a world with a functioning lift. Before the efficiency of repulsors, space elevators had been one of the most economical ways to lift material into orbit.

"There's nothing natural about something weighing tons levitating off the ground," said Joe. "Even something as small as a Talon... how it does what it does to defy gravity... guess I'll never really understand it. Same here." He pointed at the elevator and the spokes of communities wrapped around it. "Why the whole thing doesn't collapse like a stack of tiles is beyond me."

"Planetary lifts were common at one time," Bigg said. "After it was determined they were almost impossible to defend from Savage attack, most lifts were disassembled. Always wanted to bring one down..." he mused, the wheels in his head turning. If Bigg was in charge of such an endeavor, even a marvel of engineering like a planetary lift would collapse like a house of cards.

Sims and Braley appeared in the bay. Sims looked frazzled. He'd been burning the candle at both ends, slicing into every feed from the data stream emanating from all sources below. Though they'd all taken a share of the material to evaluate, Sims had been obsessed with managing the effort as he continued to collect and analyze ever more material.

Braley watched the viewer with them as Sims glued himself to his workstation, pushing and sorting a dozen holos into position.

"The colonel and Nail will be with us in a few," Braley said. "We need to divide and conquer again."

The team had sat in limbo for almost two days, essentially paralyzed from ignorance as they waited for orders. Every piece of gear was prepped and ready.

Collecting and analyzing their own intelligence was a major task. It had the benefit of removing the middleman; every bit of information came without the filter of someone else's analysis. Of course, collecting their own data had the drawback of hampering their momentum when all they wanted was to dive into action. But there was no choice. Without a specific location to raid, any attempt to plan or conduct the final assault to recover VanderBlanc would have been as useless as trying to find Luthian diamonds in the desert without a shovel.

While Kel had developed a healthy mistrust of the intelligence gathering apparatus, having to dedicate the time and effort into doing so independently made him wistful for the days of having it provided to him. It was laborious work. Dull, eye-straining, and often fruitless work. *And I have a personal stake in this*, he mused. *How boring would it be to sort through all this data and never get the chance to blast a bad guy at the end of the trail?* Those poor signal slicers.

Since Abaddon, Kel had turned even more inward than usual, rethinking his personal animus toward the conspirators. Somehow Patrick had gone from enemy to coconspirator to victim. Like an injured child or wounded pet, Patrick had been a discarded pawn, not afforded any decent human treatment.

After the horror of the white room passed, Kel found reassurance in knowing he'd done the right thing. The team's approval bolstered his confidence. Now, he vowed to leave the images. Not forgotten, but filed for future reference, to be retrieved like a trusted weapon at the right time. Professional detachment would serve him better than vengeance ever could. Killing demanded a calm mindfulness. Otherwise, mistakes happened. Mistakes that could be fatal to himself or his teammates.

Kel had forgiven Patrick for his excesses and abuse of Team Three. But what about VanderBlanc? Was there anything Kel would learn that would make him reevaluate his judgment about the political vermin? What if he could prove the man was the Scarecrow?

When I find VanderBlanc, he will meet the calmest killer in history.

Bigg was speaking. The colonel and Nail stepped into the bay, and Kel snapped out of his reverie.

"Gentlemen," Bigg welcomed the two, "we were just discussing how to divide up tasks for target exploitation. Meadows was never under VanderBlanc's magnifying glass. Sergeant Crane was also not in VanderBlanc's presence during his visit to Victrix and the isolation facility. They're the best candidates to infiltrate under cover and act as our advance force."

Braley picked up. "Extraction engineers have the best access. From Freyja down the elevator to Plenathon, there are maintenance sites and stations for the workers. Gives them free run of all the habs."

Most of the products siphoned from Plenathon's atmosphere ended up in the processing plant on Freyja. Gases like ammonia—used as a plasma coolant—to the abundant and simpler elemental inert gases like argon, all traveled up the elevator and were collected and refined on the moon. Some of the habitation terraces sprouting along the shaft were industrial; many more were the communities and stations where daily life and commerce were carried out. One terrace stood out, the largest and lowest along the chain of floating stations.

Kel wasn't really listening. Bigg and Braley discussed organizational assignments for them all, the familiar table drawn out on the holo. Sims would serve as chief of collections, the rest of them divided to analyze the intercepted data streams, guided by the AI, but still requiring the human brain to assign significance to the information. From the elevator Meadows and Crane would be able to insinuate slices into closed systems, provide surveillance on the ground, and when their target was located, bring the rest of the team to a secure support site from which to launch the mission.

Bigg was in mid-sentence when Kel rose and spoke. "VanderBlanc is going to be in one place," he said to a now silent audience. "We could spend the next two weeks doing a full target exploitation profile. It's a waste of time. He's going to be there." Kel pointed to the domed monstrosity that sat lowest on the totem pole of the elevator, balanced by the smaller chains of branching habs above it.

Rather than be annoyed at the interruption, Bigg responded with genuine interest. "What makes you say that?"

"Our target isn't going to be in some lunar cave," Kel said. "He's a perfumed prince. Look at his bio."

Sims took the cue and enlarged the smaller window with VanderBlanc's face, the pol's CV next to it.

Kel had spent many hours concentrating on the smug man's history. From what he knew of the Liberinthine elite, he felt assured of his psychologic profile of their quarry. "He's never lived in discomfort a day of his life. From the fanciest schools on Liberinthine, to his time in the Ex-Planetary Diplomatic Service, then lifted up to the highest levels of the government to serve as personal assistant to Grand Senator VanderLoot.

"He's never missed a meal or had a night's sleep on anything but synth-silk sheets. He's not in hiding. He's living in comfort. He feels in charge, in the mistaken belief that he's the predator, not the prey."

Sims followed where Kel was leading them, and now the holo of Kalos took center view. The domed station sat tilted toward Plenathon, forsaking the convention of the other habs which took orthogonal positions along the elevator stalk. The skewed orientation offered residents the broadest possible view of the gas giant below. Luxury tourism was the mainstay of the station's economy, but a resident population of the super-rich from around the galaxy called Kalos home—or at least, one of their many.

"If that's the case," Sims said. "This might be even easier than our last effort. We already have his image. If he feels safe here and isn't trying to avoid detection, my bet is we slice into everything out of Kalos and we'll find our man."

Braley nodded. "It certainly fits with what we know about him."

"Fine," the colonel said. "But let's get Sergeants Meadows's and Crane's identities and credentials hardened. If we have nothing by tomorrow, they go in."

Could it be we're finally there, Kel wondered. *Our final step on the long way to closing this link for good.* He wasn't superstitious but didn't say it aloud. He'd learned his lesson.

The galaxy always punished a legionnaire with a nasty bite when their pet animal hope got out of its cage.

21

"I'll say he's not hiding," Poul exclaimed. "VanderBlanc's set up like Xenon Boothe. Biggest mansion in the dome."

Kalos was easily accessed. They docked the *Shinshu Maru* at the receiving port and prepared as Meadows and Crane departed for their evaluation of the target area, dropping drones along the way. The port was filled with luxury craft and merchant vessels, the *Shin* comfortably lost among the many space vessels either docked in the bay or, like the *Shin*, attached to the hab by umbilicals and gangways.

Their reception at Kalos was smooth. The elevator was a corporate venture, and Kalos a subsidiary venture of the refinery. Tourists and merchants came and went liberally. The port master's questions were undemanding, requiring only payment in advance for the berth.

Security around the station was minimal. A small private police force enforced laws designed to maintain civility among workers, residents, and tourists. The company could remove the welcome mat for any undesirable unwilling to follow what few courtesies were demanded to remain on the elevator.

They got hits off the station security feeds within minutes of initiating their search. He truly was not in hiding. Dressing as flashy as a Parminthian poke-jack star, VanderBlanc frequented many of the restaurants and entertainment spots on Kalos. A protective detail escorted him, low-key and unobtrusive, but not invisible. The men were clearly not friends or associates, as they didn't join him at the lounges. Though the moving sidewalks carried most of the foot traffic around Kalos, VanderBlanc moved around the station by cart, a rare sight in the small city. Tracing the vehicle and VanderBlanc to his home was effortless.

"This whole section of homes title to an entity that in turn is a subsidiary of a holding company registered on Lorrian," Braley said. "I can't find any direct connection between any of the dozens of corporations listed under the holding company and the refinery, or any obvious connection to anyone in the House of Reason or Senate."

"It's there, somewhere," Kel assured him. "It might take a team of lawyers from the justice directorate to find, but it's in there. Somewhere deep."

"We'll table that for later," Colonel Hartenstein said. "First things first. We get VanderBlanc."

Kel grunted. He wanted VanderBlanc more than anything, but bringing down the whole conspiracy mattered. VanderBlanc could not be the end of it, and their chance to make those connections was finally here.

"We've got eyes on the target house," Sims said.

Drones gave them all sides of the luxury complex. It was not unlike a terrestrial city block. These multi-story homes were built with an eye to architectural beauty as well as to minimizing the crowded apartments' footprint. Narrow walks separated the properties. The ultra-luxury section sat at one edge of the clear dome, farthest from the hub of the elevator stalk, the most select piece of real estate in the most select terrace of stations on the elevator. Patrick's disconnected description of the cloud colors came to mind. Kel tried to project from which of the rooftops Patrick formed his indelible memory of Plenathon, recalled during the last moments of his inhuman existence.

Balconies sprouted off most of the rooms above the second level, and all had rooftop gardens. Within the luxury homes beckoned the uninterrupted vista of the kaleidoscopic planet beyond. From the rooftops, horizon to horizon, a viewer would be literally surrounded by the spectacle. The tallest and most opulent residence sat at the center of the apartments. VanderBlanc's.

"Entry's not going to be a problem," Bigg said. "We hit from high and low. Majority of us breach from the ground floor; another team works from top-down. We pile on whoever finds the brass ring first. Piece of cake."

"What's the subterranean access?" Braley asked.

Sims flung a schematic up. "Very limited. In that section it is truly just conduits and cables in crawl spaces. Not much substructure at all."

"So, we go in pre-BMNT," Braley said, using terminology for when the first usable light of day appeared on a terrestrial world, the time when most humans were in their deepest sleep. "Station time 0400." He checked his chrono. "About six hours from now."

"Meadows and Crane have located some maintenance vehicles," Bigg interjected. "They're small, but with three of them, we can get everyone from here to the target with decent concealment."

"Someone still needs to be available for route clearance off the target," Braley said. "Colonel, it would be helpful to have you and the sergeant major available for that. If there's a reaction from station security that could interfere with our way off the objective..."

"Any compromise or alert once you've started your egress, I can probably deescalate it without violence, but if need be," the colonel looked at Nail, "there'd be no problem we couldn't solve between the two of us."

"I can force a system blackout and monitor all emissions from the objective," Sims offered. "I don't need to stay back here to do that. We're going to need every one of us on the target to make quick work of it."

"I'll go with Kel," Poul said. "We'll take the top-down job."

Kel winced. He'd hoped to go in on the ground floor rather than making another climb. But he'd pigeonholed himself as the team's second-story man by volunteering to climb so many times before. Now it was just assumed he would do so again.

"I mean, you are going to take the lead, right?" Poul prodded after Kel's prolonged silence.

"Yeah. Wouldn't have it any other way."

Of course, maybe this time, we don't have to climb to get to the top...

The hour of arrival was a deceptively still time on Kalos, there never being a true dark period on a domed station. Human circadian rhythm required a regular period for sleep, preferably during dark. The pedestrian level remained illuminated, the light intensity the same as prime hours despite station custom of activity during third cycle mimicking the period of deepest night. The view of the planet was unaffected by the ground level lighting, all of it projected down rather than up to avoid reflection against the dome interior. The higher elevations were bathed in the natural light from the ether outside. The bright albedo of the merry-go-round planet and the dimmer stars around it penetrated the artificial envelope of the dome.

Three maintenance sleds convoyed silently through the concourses and successively narrower streets as they came to the residential section. A few drunk revelers stumbled out of the casino that marked the edge of the commercial area, oblivious to the carts and their passengers. Bigg led, the route of their transit barely wider than the vehicles themselves. They slowed to a halt between two buildings, concealed by the balconies jutting above them.

Braley hailed them all over L-comm. "Kel, Poul, give us a 'set' and we roll."

"Rog," they both said as Kel slid out of the compartment, Poul beside him. He hugged the wall, his route planned per the bird's-eye view of the drones, using the rising apartments and balconies to conceal their approach to any elevated observer.

When stationary, the mimetic camouflage of their armor disguised them against their background almost flawlessly. When crossing the open spaces between the narrow domiciles, the armor maintained the texture of the plasticrete walls, but couldn't match the variety of decorative colors coated on the homes. Anyone looking directly at them would see their motion, the oddity of shapeless, fuzzy distortions shifting across their horizon.

The tallest apartment was ringed with the same balconies as the other buildings. Transparent panels and railings framed the overlooks. Perhaps he could simply scale the exterior, Kel thought. A pair of self-deploying creepers would find the jutting platforms and grasp them with ease to form a trellis as sure as any ladder. The real problem was maintaining surprise. A panorama of windows and decorative lights made concealment during a climb impossible. Given the lower gravity rating of the Kalos station, he had a better plan to preserve surprise.

"You ready?" he asked Poul.

"As I'll ever be," Poul half-laughed. "Hope I don't break my fool neck."

"Don't volunteer us next time if you're worried. And don't overshoot the rooftop."

"Great advice. Thanks," Poul intoned unenthu- siastically.

"Almost set. Stand by," Kel said over the team channel.

Braley returned immediately. "Rog. We're in posi- tion. On you."

Kel and Poul both stepped around the corner of the closest building and looked up at the rooftop five sto- ries above.

"Set. One, two, thr—"

Kel froze at the sight of movement above.

Three dark clad figures appeared. One looked directly at Kel, then smoothly turned and joined the other two as they jetted off the rooftop. They bounded to the next low- er rooftop, made another power-assisted spring, then he lost sight of them.

"Poul, let's go!" He triggered the jump jet and sprang. The EVA assist pack wouldn't give much of a vertical boost against full planetary gravity, but as the Kalos en- vironment maintained things at a very comfortable one- third G, at full power, it would work. As he rose, he alert- ed the team.

"I got three bodies just jetted off the rooftop. Sims, get us drones tracking." He guided the HUD icon to the center of the rooftop as he came to the height of his arc, and let the EVA package do the rest. He cast an eye toward where he'd last seen the trio headed. He landed. "Bouncing an azimuth to you of their egress direction."

Poul landed a few meters beside him.

"Go after them," Braley ordered. Kel could hear the motion of the team behind Braley's voice, already breached and working the building below his feet.

"I've got drones locked on them," Sims said.

"They're headed for the elevator," the colonel said. Moving to the edge of the roof, he hadn't yet had time to check the projected course of the fugitives. "They're not headed directly to us at the spaceport. We can't head them off before they get to the elevator. We're moving to block from above. They have to be headed up the shaft."

"Ready?" Kel asked. Poul stood on the parapet, aimed at the next building's rooftop, just a story shorter. "Moving."

"Move," Poul replied as they both jumped. The jet assist was unnecessary, and Kel took note of the cell level on the EVA package, knowing they would need whatever was left to make the most rapid descent from the last rooftop, a few buildings ahead. Each was successively shorter, but at the end of the residential complex it would still be a several-story drop to the pedestrian level. They ran full out, hurtling across each of the four-meter gaps between roofs until they reached the last building. It was not unlike taking the stairs.

"Boost down, man," Kel said as he led, the ground rushing up faster than he would've liked. The jet assist fired and he hit the pavement at a full run.

Poul landed a step behind. "Kel, forget the vans. Let's run for it."

Kel had a window open in his bucket and involuntarily halted to orient to the drone feed. He clicked his teeth as he looked at the trotting figures. The three moved well, but there was something telling about what he saw. Two larger, armored figures with jump packs ran outbound.

Between them, they carried a smaller figure, his feet barely touching the ground.

"Let's go," Poul said as he passed him. Kel sprinted after him.

"You see that?" Kel asked. "It's gotta be our man. His PSD's getting him out of here."

"That's what I'm betting," Poul agreed.

"I have the sidewalk and the trams halted," Sims said. He'd activated the slices he'd put in place in advance, ready to paralyze the transport systems. "I have the lifts frozen, too."

"Good man," the colonel said. "We've taken a tender from the shipyard and are headed out. We're going up the elevator. The first major access point is a dish array deck. We'll enter there and work down."

Solid response, Kel thought approvingly. With the colonel and Nail racing up the elevator to block from above, they would have VanderBlanc trapped between them.

If VanderBlanc's personal security detail were professionals, they'd planned for multiple means of egress. As soon as they discovered the lifts were frozen, they'd make for another means of transport. If it were Kel, he would have manned maneuvering units and vac suits cached somewhere. It would be a viable means of evading route detection and making it to a waiting ship. He felt certain that was what the trio were doing.

Nail echoed Kel's thoughts. "If they're trying for a stashed MMU on that deck, they'll never make it."

"They're in the lift station," Sims narrated.

Kel glanced at the window in his bucket. He and the team were masters of multitasking, but maintaining a dead run in low-G, one that let him cover meters with each stride, wasn't forgiving of tripping. A wipeout wouldn't produce an injury, but would be epic just the same.

"One of the goons just tossed a pursuit deterrence. Sorry. Drones are dead." The last Kel had seen, one nano was essentially on the trio's back as they paused to program a pulse lift. "I'll have more on site in a minute to pick up the feed again."

"Okay," Poul said. "But I'll make a toss when we get there. Look to pick them up." Poul placing drones to swarm would be faster than waiting for them to travel from Sims's location.

"The domicile is empty," Braley said. "Crane and Meadows are joining pursuit. We'll stay here long enough to SSE and move out." Braley, Bigg, and Sims would expeditiously gather whatever they could from VanderBlanc's domicile as rapidly as possible and join them.

No doubt between Bigg and Sims they can slice anything in a few minutes and be out of there, Kel thought as he sped through the concourse, past closed restaurants and commercial venues and on toward the elevator hub.

How did we blow it? How did they see us coming? Kel wondered as they slowed to a rolling walk, the terminal entrance finally in front of them. "We're hitting the elevator terminal now."

"Be there in three minutes," Meadows said. Kel heard the whine of repulsors in the transmission. They were bringing a van.

Probably not as fast as what we ran the distance in, he thought. The vehicles all had governors for safety, making their top speeds on the domed station barely faster than a brisk walk.

The terminal was one of the public access points to the elevator. The high-speed pulse lifts took passengers in comfort between the different stations along the elevator. If time were essential, direct transit by spacecraft between Kalos and the moon was much faster than the high velocity speeds of the lifts. Traveling between adjacent stations, the efficiency of the high speed lifts was preferable. Most commercial and residential habs occupied the lower stations along the elevator, separated by industrial habs. The suburbs alternated all the way to the moon, where most of the industrial processing, refining, and product shipment took place.

Poul brought up his hand for Kel to see, a stunner in his grasp, indicating that he would be the one to toss. The double doors sensed their approach and irised open. Kel brought his carbine up as Poul pitched. They held in place as the purple arcs spread out, then pushed into a spacious reception area, empty couches and datapad docks along the walls.

"Hold," Poul told his partner as he reached behind him and produced a cube that he pitched behind the information desk. "Sims, take over," he alerted their teammate. With just the two of them, it wasn't possible to monitor the drone outputs and still be aware of the potential dangers around them as they searched for their evading targets.

"On it," Sims acknowledged. "Wait one for them to disperse." The drones would coordinate with each other to search and map any potential paths, Sims also prioritizing their function to look for hoppers, the term they used to describe fleeing enemies. It was slang they adopted long ago, co-opted from their native troops who used it to describe the short leaping bounds of fleeing zhee—especially when attempting to escape a raid on their high-walled compounds. Hoppers never got far.

"Boom. Got 'em. They're making their way up the maintenance shaft."

Now Kel blinked to accept the pulsing request icon. A window appeared. A spectral enhanced drone view showed the three figures ascending by their EVA assist packs. Within the elevator, micro-G was the norm. The trio rocketed upward.

"See this, Colonel?" Kel queried.

"Yes, Lieutenant. We're through the deck level access and moving to the maintenance shaft. We'll block from above. Make sure those lifts stay shut down, Sergeant Sims."

"Affirmative, sir," Sims replied. If they had to go kinetic, with lifts traveling around them... killing bystanders was a bad thing.

Kel and Poul found the lift tunnel maintenance access. Working in the shaft required a vac suit. A lock gave way to a short tunnel that opened into the maintenance shaft, running between the two lift tunnels.

"Nothing," Poul said, looking straight up. "How far ahead of us are they?"

Kel stepped into the shaft and looked up as well, about to answer when blaster fire dispersed from the darkness above, skirting down the walls around them. He blindly returned fire before he stepped back into the access tunnel, making room for Poul to follow.

"Not that far."

"It's a bad idea to shoot in here," Poul said. "Somewhere on the other side of this shaft and the lifts are the gas extraction pipelines. I'd hate to rupture one." Even though the siphoned gases were primarily inert, some were not, and were boosted up the elevator column at high pressure.

"Good point," Kel admitted. "Colonel, do you have a location for our hoppers?" He hoped that from somewhere above, the colonel and Nail had a handle on where their subjects were temporarily stopped.

"Wait one," Nail said. Then, "Sending."

Kel accepted the new feed. A simple schematic showed the elevator in profile, a red dot almost equidistant between the maintenance portal where the colonel and Nail were a thousand meters above, and where Kel and Poul stood at the level of Kalos. The drones had pinpointed the trio.

"Stay clear of the bottom of the well in case one of these makes it all the way down to you," the colonel said. "Stunners out."

"Whoa, back it up!" Poul nudged Kel a few steps back to the entrance of the maintenance tunnel. They knew what the colonel was doing. It was inventive, but suboptimal. Using the launcher on his K-17 to bounce stun grenades down the shaft in hopes of one landing in proximity to the trio might work. But there wasn't a way to precisely deliver and command the stunners to detonate. If they had one of the larger drones, they could drive it right to their three miscreants and command det a large stunner right on them. He was about to tell Meadows or Crane when they rolled up to bring one of the large drones from the van when Bigg interrupted.

"Hey, listen up," the team sergeant said to them.

"... got them covered, unless I'm looking at one of you." It took Kel a second to recognize the new voice.

Kel entered the open channel. "Say again, Chief Lopez? We didn't get your last transmission."

"Roger. I'm in a boat patrolling just outside the elevator. I've got guns on an open portal, about escape pod—

sized. If that's not someone from your team, I think it's your bad guys trying to exit. Looks like they're maneuvering a runabout into place for an exit... Yup. They just took a shot at me. Want me to light them up?"

"Nice work, Chief Lopez," Colonel Hartenstein replied. "Don't fire on them, but don't get yourself shot, either."

"Roger, sir. Not to worry. These little boats are beasts, just like the *Shin*. They can take a lot of damage. I'll do my best to keep them in place for you."

"How'd the chief get into the fight?" Poul asked.

"I tagged him for the duty," the colonel said. "Turns out we don't have enough crew to snatch a perfumed political prince."

Kel winced as the colonel quoted him practically verbatim.

"He is turning out to be a little wilier than I would've thought," Poul quipped, not bothering to go to a private channel, knowing the colonel was probably using command privilege to listen to everyone, anyway.

"More likely he's hired competent help," Nail said from above.

"All right, let's work the problem," the colonel returned them to the current situation.

"Meadows and Crane coming in," Kel heard, and the two legionnaires came through the small oval lock window. He told them his idea to run a drone up the shaft with a stunner. Crane departed wordlessly to retrieve one while Kel asked the team if anyone had a better idea.

When no one offered any, the colonel said, "Let us know when you're in place."

Kel and Poul glided along the surface of the elevator. The dome beneath was bright, as bright as the planet that dwarfed it. He returned his attention ahead to the corrugated nano-tubule surface of the elevator as they continued their flight, skimming along just above the skin. He and Poul were the only ones equipped for EVA, still wearing jump packs. The boat from the *Shin* hovered just ahead. Somewhere inside, their three targets were trapped. Another flurry of blaster bolts left trails of lightning behind as some contacted and scorched the nose of the craft, while the chief maintained an oscillating path in front of the exit.

"Colonel, we're set outside," Kel said as he and his partner stopped short of the opening and locked themselves to the surface.

"Rog. We're in place above and below," their commander relayed.

Meadows took his turn. "They're holed up in some kind of workstation. Left over from the construction, I bet. Must have unsealed a section of the skin. Pretty slick place to cache a runabout for an emergency egress." Kel had to agree.

"Okay. I'm forcing an all-channel comm," Kel said as he looked at the icon and blinked. "VanderBlanc. You're surrounded. Come out before we come in after you." He said the last with purposeful annoyance in his voice, as if speaking to a child, which is what the man was in Kel's book. A petulant, spoiled child. It was time for his spanking. "You're coming with us. It's over. Surrender and no one gets hurt." Kel had the program repeat the phrase on loop as the message transmitted several times over all common waves. The program halted automatically when a response returned.

"Whoever you are, halt your activity. Your pursuit is illegal." The voice was somewhat distorted but recognizable. VanderBlanc.

"VanderBlanc. This is Colonel Adolphus Hartenstein of the Legion. You are being apprehended and remanded to custody for treason against the Republic. Comply and present yourself with hands empty. Our goal is to bring you to justice. I'd prefer to do so with you alive. Resist us, and the other option is viable."

The pause grew. Kel was beginning to wonder if a return response was coming when, "You don't know what you're interfering with here, Hartenstein. You and your Legion apes need to back off now..."

Meanwhile, Kel was giving the commands. "Ready, ready, now!"

Kel and Poul raised their K-17s above their heads, aimed their carbines by HUD into the gaping portal, and launched. From the other side, Crane drove the drone from the shaft and into the trio's midst. Fading electric arcs poured out of the hole as Kel and Poul loped into the room. Kel went headfirst as Poul halted to cover from outside, then followed Kel in, swimming and propelled forward by a small burst from the jets.

"They're down. They're down!" Kel activated his locks and let his feet find a surface. Three bodies stood swaying, arms splayed, held in place only by their grav boots. The impotent runabout hovered near the exit, the skeletonized frame and empty seats tethered by a single cable to the deck. Without Chief Lopez's blockade, they'd still be in a pursuit, trying to predict the trio's destination.

Bad luck for you three we have more friends than you do, Kel thought.

Three bodies swayed like kelp anchored to the ocean bed, unconscious and limp. Kel chained the one nearest him as armored bodies swam from behind into the cold space to help.

"Hey, this one's got a suit tear. Big one," Poul said as he chained one of the figures. Now Kel saw the jet of gas leaving the melted rent at the elbow joint of the smallest figure. VanderBlanc. The two men on either side looked massive. With gear and tactics like that, Kel knew without a doubt who they were. Legionnaires.

"Seal that," he said, pointing at the leak.

"No can do," Meadows said, trying to close the gaping hole with his hands.

They didn't carry soft seals. Their armor sealed internally or, in the case of an amputation, sealed the breach by tourniquet. The trio wore soft vac suits with semi-rigid helmets, the modular armor placed over the suits for protection.

Kel removed an auto-tourniquet from his side and placed it high on the injured arm. It turned green as the escaping jet below stopped. "Hey, we have to get this one in atmo and out of that suit." A flashing red indicator on the forearm pad blinked faster. "There's not enough oxygen to purge his vac suit back to a breathable level."

"Chief," the colonel said. "We're coming out. Piggyback us to the *Shin*. Time is critical."

"Take an arm," Kel said to Meadows as they each grabbed an arm and the safety belt around VanderBlanc's waist and moved to the exit. The boat was now just a few meters off the elevator skin. A short burst and they maneuvered together to find boarding rails along the hull, normally used to ride externally on just such a craft when making an assault to seize another ship. Now they held onto the extensions.

"Last man on," Nail said.

"The *Shin*'s ready to leave." Chief Lopez's voice was like velvety cream. Cool and smooth. "Rest of the team is on board and waiting to receive us in the rear hold. Thrusting now."

Kel looked into the visor of the limp body between him and Poul. There was no movement.

"You think one of his PSD had a blaster discharge and scorched his vac suit when we stunned them?" Poul asked, looking back from his spot in front.

Kel was worried about the man's color. It was always hard tell by vacuum starlight, but he looked blue. "I think three stunners was probably a little much in such a small space. Hard to say what caused it."

"Well, that's why we call them less lethal rather than nonlethal. Anything can happen."

Kel looked at the thin man's face again, urging their ride to go faster. *He can't die like this.* Kel admitted the ugliness of his thoughts. The face behind the visor was peaceful.

This was not the death he wanted for VanderBlanc.

22

The bay cycled and as the atmo indicator turned green, Kel removed the vac suit helmet and forced an airway past VanderBlanc's loose jaw. Poul helped him race the man to the medcomp.

As they got VanderBlanc supine, Kel attached the ventilator and pulled his vibro-blade off his chest. He swiped across the spine, waited for the blade to glow safety blue, and ran it across the vac suit. Poul helped by pulling the panels apart until they had him stripped. They worked together to attach sensors, then stepped back to let the gantry ease sideways as the door closed. Pulsing bands of light now penetrated the invisible functions of the millions of cells that made up the man.

"It's all on the AI now," Poul said.

Braley stuck his head in, bucket off. "What's the word?"

Kel stripped his own bucket off. "Just got him in." He looked at the readouts. "He's alive. Barely. Early anoxia."

"Well, we're getting ready to pull out," Braley gestured with a hitch-hiking thumb. "Kalos is waking up. There's a lot of comm traffic. The security force is aware something went down. Pilots are itching to go, afraid they're going to shut down spaceport traffic. Colonel is holding us until he's certain there's nothing we need to go back for. Leave him and come look at this."

Back in the bay, the team had the two unconscious PSD stripped down to skivvies, chained again, hoods on. He saw it immediately.

"Competent help, huh?" Poul said in disbelief.

Over the heart of the pink-skinned one was the unmistakable body mod of a raised Legion crest in black and silver.

Kel stepped around to examine the other one. It was faint, but there was a slight difference in the color of the skin between the thigh and leg. "This one's had a limb regen," Kel pronounced. "He got amped at the knee. What do you think, Joe?"

Crane stepped over to look. He'd had his forearm regenerated. "I'd say that's a big rog."

"Leejes?" Meadows's voice crept up an octave. "You think?"

Kel straightened up. "Let's get them warmed and revived."

"That's right," Braley added. "We can talk to them later."

Meadows reappeared with two skids, the rest joining Kel to package the two prisoners and move them off the deck.

"I'll stay and guard the prisoners," Meadows offered. "I want to be on hand when they wake up. Leejes... sket," he trailed off, shaking his head.

Kel joined the rest back in their op center where Sims and Bigg set out items on a hastily cleared table as the colonel and Nail watched, everyone's buckets off.

"We grabbed everything that looked like anything," Sims said. "If it gave off any kind of a signature when I interrogated it, we grabbed it. Might've even grabbed the kaff maker by accident."

"We were moving pretty fast," Bigg admitted. "But I doubt we could've left anything important behind."

"How'd we get compromised?" Nail asked. "You get spotted from your LCC?"

Kel shook his head. "Doubtful." His last cover and concealment had been a building out of the target's the line of sight.

"Oh, no. It wasn't that," Sims said. "Check this out." He sent up a holo captured from his bucket. "They had surveillance and detection algorithms feeding them from everywhere."

The room Sims recorded showed holos running that covered not just the exterior of VanderBlanc's residence, but vantages from all over Kalos, including the spaceport.

"We were spotted early. I bet we only got as close as we did because there wasn't a human awake and monitoring. These programs alert based on parameters, activities like movement detected at odd hours. By the time it alerted the security detail and they processed what was happening, we were practically on them. They just barely got their charge geared up and onto the roof in time. A minute earlier, and we'd have had them dead to rights." Sims's professional admiration showed. "It was a decent security plan for a small force, using tech to augment their numbers. If they'd had more staff and someone monitoring full time, they probably would've gotten away."

"We're going to need some time to evaluate the haul," Bigg said, gesturing to the many pads, devices, and containers. "We have to go slow. Don't want to trigger any wipe programs. The good news is, if any of these are bio-coded, we have the master key laid out in the medcomp."

Kel thought about his patient. "I need to get back to the medcomp to check on—"

"We've got a situation here." The tinny quality of the voice broadcast from the panel didn't disguise Chief Lopez's gravelly voice. "Your guest is on the move."

"On the move?" Braley tried to clarify.

"As in, he's loose on the ship. He attacked one of my crewmen. We found Jacobi in the hall outside medlab and the coffin's empty."

How could VanderBlanc be out of the medcomp? Kel put his lid on.

"Where's he headed?"

"I haven't had eyes on him," Lopez continued. "My man's head's been cracked and he's bleeding badly. You need to find this guy before I do if you want him alive, because after Nguyen and I get Jacobi into the medcomp, he's burnt bacon. We don't have boarders on my ship."

"Moving," was all Braley said in return. "Meadows, stay on the prisoners. Sims, stay here. Two-man teams. Go. Chief, can you lock down everything?"

"He can't get into the flight deck or engineering without a bio scan." The chief addressed a new listener. "Flight ops, do you copy this? Legion wants a full lockdown."

"Roger." Kel recognized the co-pilot's voice. "Done. Except for Jacobi, all crew have reported in."

"Thank you, sir. Legion—"

Another voice broke in.

"Chief, he's in the port-two scrub locker. He's suiting up like he's trying to lock out."

"On my way," Chief Lopez said. "Legion, meet me there."

"Legion, we haven't released the umbilical to push back yet," the pilot said. "What do you want me to do?"

Braley and the colonel had a quick L-comm conference. "Getting us away from the elevator would give the boarder fewer options, Commander," the colonel answered.

"Roger." The pilot sounded relieved. "We'll be pushing back momentarily."

Kel followed Poul through the narrow corridor, moving aft and into unfamiliar territory on the ship. The rest of the team followed behind.

"Crane, with me," Bigg said. "We're going to the boat launch bay. If we need to go outside, we'll do it from there."

"Do it," Braley said.

They trotted until a sharp turn halted them. Chief Lopez and another spacer held up in a corridor near a set of locks.

"Hey, great job securing your prisoner," Lopez said as a hail. "He's in there."

He pointed at the sealed doors.

"What's that?" Poul asked as the rest of the team pushed into the crowded antechamber.

"Scrub locker. It's another lock chamber for hull access. It's the only lock rated for decontamination, so it's used for dirty work," he said, meaning handling any material or crew exposed to radioactive, chemical, or biological material.

"So, it's got vac suit lockers?" Kel asked.

"And EVA rigs," the chief added.

"But the command deck has everything locked down, yes?" Braley said.

The chief shrugged. "Yes, but if he knows how to activate the escape bolts, he could blow the outer doors."

"We've underestimated this guy too much," Kel admitted. "He may know more than we thought."

"Great," Poul let slip.

"Enough of this," the colonel said as he pushed between them and stood in front of the lock. Peering through the viewport, he punched the panel at the side. "Going somewhere, Mister VanderBlanc? What is it you think you're going to accomplish?"

The colonel slaved his view to the rest of them. Through the colonel's bucket, they saw VanderBlanc dressed in a vac suit, hard bucket in hand, examining the outer lock controls.

Without turning around, VanderBlanc said, "I've no time to answer your questions, Colonel, not that I'd be inclined to do so even if there were adequate opportunity. You've interfered with things you don't understand, one time too many."

"Feel that?" the colonel taunted, the motion of the ship evident. "We're off the station. Where're you going to go?" The colonel took his hand off the panel. "Chief, get ready to open these doors." Kel and Poul stood beside the colonel and brought up their carbines as they took a slight step back. The colonel had a stunner in hand.

VanderBlanc screamed as he flailed his arms in frustration. "You ignorant Cyclaxes! This is going to end with all of you in limbo, praying for my forgiveness! You'll—" He gagged and retched. "No. No, I didn't fail... Nooo."

The thin man froze. He choked and sputtered as though unable to breathe. A hissing exhale escaped his lips as the skin on his face tightened and shrunk.

"Chief, is the lock under pressure?" Kel asked aloud.

Chief Lopez moved to a panel. "Yes. Why, what's happening?"

"VanderBlanc's choking. We need to open the—"

"Look!" Poul exclaimed.

Kel's attention returned to the view inside the lock. He nudged the colonel over to look through the portal. He didn't understand what was happening. The lock was not depressurizing. VanderBlanc's choking had stopped. The skin over his face turned from pale white to blue, now darkening to black, as the vac suit collapsed to the deck, the body inside it limp.

"What the frell is happening?" Braley said behind him. "Look at him now." It was unnatural. The head collapsed like a rotten melon.

"I don't know," Kel said. "This is something I can't explain." He stepped back to let the others take their turn peering into the portal to confirm what they'd seen through their HUDs. It always seemed more real looking at something yourself. This was something that needed to be witnessed with the naked eye to accept.

"I don't understand it," Kel said aloud. "What could cause him to... melt?"

Chief Lopez took his turn at the portal. "Turner, do you think it's some kind of pathogen? A bioweapon of some kind? Because I tell you this, it's time to scrub that off the ship." The chief moved to the panel as he spoke on his own link to inform the command deck of the situation.

"Kel, what do you think?" Braley asked.

He sighed. "Chief's right. We don't know what happened. We can't risk contamination by getting a closer examination. Purge it."

"Colonel?" Braley queried.

"Do it, Chief," Colonel Hartenstein ordered, shaking his head. "We've been outmaneuvered." The colonel walked past them, neither asking nor telling who he thought outsmarted them.

The outer lock doors opened. Warm, expanding light from Plenathon bathed the pale blue chamber. The ship was close enough to the planet that it filled the chasm of the now open lock, the even edges framing it like a portrait.

"Purge and decon cycle starting," the chief recited. Kel tarried another moment to watch the remains as they were pushed out of the chamber, propelled like a sneeze by the force of the purging gasses. The body tumbled. Liquified chunks of tissue spiraled from the neck collar of the vac suit, forming another kind of a vortex, turning against the whirling dervishes rising from the planet's surface. Everything about the man and his end was contrary.

Kel didn't stay to watch the rest of the cycle. "Poul, come with me. I need another set of eyes."

"Where're we going, Kel?" his friend asked.

"The medlab. We need answers."

Chief Lopez came into the room, anger spilling out of him. "Is my man in danger in there?" he asked, pointing to the spacer lying in the medcomp coffin. "I'd have never put him in there after your prisoner if I'd had any inkling he was carrying some kind of disease. Did you know?"

"It wasn't a plague," Kel said, not stopping his activity on the holoboard. "Your man..."

"Jacobi."

"Jacobi looks fine. The coffin decon'd between uses, too. I checked. AI says he's got a fractured skull. Hit by something blunt and heavy. Maybe a spanner. No irreversible damage. Swelling is halted. He just needs repair time. But what I came to find is this." Kel enlarged a screen. "This was VanderBlanc's cellular scan."

"What are those?" Poul said, his nose wrinkling in disgust at the tissue section scan. "Those aren't supposed to be there. Not that many of them anyway."

"Captain Yost," Kel said. "I think everyone will want to see this."

In a few minutes, everyone crowded in and around the medlab, Crane and Sims leaning around the doorway from the corridor.

"They look like nanos," Braley said. "But there's so many of them."

Kel continued. "So, I think I know how VanderBlanc recovered from his vacuum exposure so rapidly. He's loaded with some kind of nano. I checked the scans. He went from hypoxic and in severe metabolic acidosis with deep cellular damage to essentially normal within minutes of being in the medcomp. It should have taken him days to recover, much less be able to attack a crewmember."

"Lieutenant," Colonel Hartenstein leaned against the bulkhead. "Were those same foreign bodies responsible for what we witnessed in the lock?"

Kel shrugged. "He underwent cellular degradation. Nanos that accelerate cellular recovery could also impede it. I suppose. It's my best guess, sir. With these scans, maybe the scientists could figure it out. Other than that, without the remains..."

"Why, then?" Nail asked from just inside the doorway. "Why'd he die just then, not sooner? He wasn't talking like he suicided to avoid capture."

"Someone triggered the response," Bigg said.

Sims made a noise. "Uh, would some kind of EM pulse do it? A command signal?"

"Could be. Why not?" Kel said.

"Because the whole grid got bombarded by some kind of emission same time as VanderBlanc did his melting act. I was working on the SSE haul since you had him contained. Just figured it was some kind of astral emission. Glitched my pad for a second, but that was all."

"You know what this sounds like to me?" Poul asked. "Like somebody has some kind of advanced tech, say—"

"Not this again," Bigg groaned. "Don't say it."

"—Savage or alien."

"I knew you were going to say that." Bigg dropped his head to his chest. "Oh, for the love of Oba, not more of this stuff."

Meadows had been listening in from where he guarded the two prisoners. "Captain Yost, not to interrupt, but I've got two alert prisoners down here who'd like to talk to us. I'm inclined to give them the chance. They're leejes for sure."

Meadows had the prisoners hauled up from their skid stretchers and propped them on floats with hands chained to their waists. The team were buttoned up again in buckets and now stood around looking down at the two.

"Names," Meadows ordered with one word, then point at Braley. "Tell the captain."

The paler of the two, who sported the Legion crest raised on his chest, spoke first. "Tyler. Joshua Tyler. Formerly of Tyrannus Company, Guards Regiment."

The darker man spoke next. "Seller. Davis Seller. Formerly of Victory Company, Wolfhound Regiment."

"That's easy enough to check out," Braley said. "But if you're lying, it's going to go harder on you."

Both men looked insulted.

"On our honor. A legionnaire doesn't lie to an officer, sir," Tyler said without sign of fear.

"What were you doing on Kalos and who were you working for?"

"Sir," said Seller, "we know who you are. I saw you work. Once. On Korraster. We recognized who you were right away. We had to do our jobs, but we never mounted a kinetic counter against you. We put some blaster fire down the maintenance shaft as a deterrence, but knew that wouldn't be lethal."

"That's right, sir." Tyler went on, "At first, Seller and I thought maybe it was a gang assault. The security AI woke me up to check an activity alert. Our systems picked you up from the spaceport. Your beeline convoy to us triggered our escape plan. We knew we were in deep trouble when we spotted you from the rooftop that last moment. I looked at one of you dead on."

Kel laughed to himself. The man saw Kel's contraction and threw his chin to him. "It was you, wasn't it?"

Kel remained silent.

"Who is your charge?" Braley continued his questioning.

"Lexall. Plenifer Lexall," the former leej confirmed. "Why, did you have the wrong guy?"

Kel looked to Bigg. That was the alias they'd discovered for VanderBlanc.

"What's your relationship to him?"

Seller shook his head. "Employee to employer. We're from Lanthanum. Lanthanum Concepts."

Nail groaned. "They're contractors."

Bigg scoffed. "A lot of guys are going private. The pay's good. More than a few leejes are stepping out of the armor to earn a better paycheck."

Braley pressed. "Out with it. If you want to avoid a one-way trip to a prison planet, tell it all."

Their story was convincing in its simplicity. The pair didn't know VanderBlanc as anything but Lexall. Lanthanum had a contract to provide a personal security detail for the wealthy Lexall. Teams of two men rotated duty every six weeks, escorting VanderBlanc around Kalos and adjoining habs on the elevator, occasionally taking short trips with him, but primarily maintaining security at his home on Kalos.

"It's a kidnap deterrence package," Seller offered. "He was concerned about that. It's a common package that Concepts offers. He's rich enough to afford it."

"Have you ever seen this man?" Kel stepped forward. He used his wrist link to show them the image. The goon that had accompanied VanderBlanc at Kel's first meeting with the Scarecrow. It was a reconstruction from the many images they'd obtained in their investigation.

"That's Hallux. He's Lexall's right-hand man."

"Where is he?" Braley resumed. "Lexall's domicile was empty after you egressed with him."

Tyler nodded. "His home is next to Lexall's. One of the smaller residences."

"We didn't get everyone, Braley," Kel spurted over L-comm. "Do we go back?"

"No," the colonel said. "It will risk an overt intervention. That we can't do. No use crying over spilt milk. We move forward."

Kel felt frantic. They had so little. He couldn't restrain himself. "Did you ever see Lexall in a disguise? A mask?"

Both former leejes frowned as they looked at each other.

"No," Seller said. "He was a pretty dandy dresser around us. He liked to dine out. He liked to make acquaintances of the tourists on Kalos when he wasn't traveling. He didn't wear a disguise. We didn't accompany him on his long trips, though."

"That's one of the things that made this a good gig," Tyler said. "He'd sometimes be gone two or three weeks at a time. That leaves whoever was on rotation here with not a lot to do. Lexall is a fastidious kind of guy. Disagreeable. Hard to like."

Kel understood.

Braley took charge again. "We're going to check all this out. If it comes back clean, we'll drop you at a major hub with clothes and credits. If it comes out you've done anything to hurt the Legion, I'll space you myself."

Both men looked shaken. "Sir," Tyler said. "We've been absolutely honest with you. If there's anything else we can tell you about Lexall and what we did for him as contractors with Lanthanum, we won't hold back."

"It's like we told you, sir," Seller implored with his chest out and shoulders back, assuming the best position of attention he could, given the circumstances. "We recognized your team for Dar..." he stopped himself. "For our breed. No contract in the universe could make us fire on another leej."

"Take them away, Meadows," Braley said over L-comm. "We've got time to see if their story checks out."

"Come on, leejes." Meadows gestured them up. "We'll get you some clothes and chow, but the restraints stay until we're convinced."

"Hey, leej," Poul said, "what's your day rate on this gig?"

Tyler grinned. "Thousand a day."

Poul coughed. "Oba."

When they were out of the bay, Braley was first to speak. "Well, what do we think?"

The colonel gestured toward Nail as he leaned against the hull of the parked boat. "What's your read, Sergeant Major?"

Nail laughed. "It all fits. Before we go FTL, I'll bounce the nearest Legion outpost and check records. But I'm already inclined to turn them loose. They stuck to the letter of their contract without ever going kinetic, just like they said. Their actions speak true."

They left the bay, small talk continuing. It had been a perplexing, exhausting day.

"Hey, buddy, you all right?" Poul asked as they walked to their ops center.

Kel's head drooped as they walked. "We did all this, and we've got nothing to show for it. Nothing."

Poul put a hand on Kel's shoulder. "We've got way more than that. We know we busted up their little conspiracy. We've hurt them badly." The doors parted as they entered the small bay, strewn with all their gear, tables covered in datapads and flimsy. "And look on the bright side. I bet Lanthanum is hiring. Thousand a day. Can you believe that?"

Crane was already at the MSP container, swapping charge packs. Sims was focused on one of the containers on the SSE table and looked up as they entered.

"I don't want to mess with much of the SSE, sir," Sims addressed to the colonel. "Most all of it is bio-encrypted and will probably wipe if I tamper with it. If we had the owner to help us... Otherwise, best to let the tech section tackle it. Even they may need help."

The colonel popped his bucket. "Yes. Let's not lose anything by being hasty. It'll wait."

"I'm going to put it all in the signal blocker. In case there's a remote wipe sent."

"Is anything out of what you recovered accessible now?" Braley asked.

"Just this. Almost got it." Sims fiddled with his pad over the flat box he'd been concentrating on when they entered. A blue light pulsed briefly and the lid opened. Sims peered into the small box before pulling out a thin circular band with an emitter set into it like a jewel on a necklace. He placed it on the table and returned to his datapad to play. A swipe, and the ring projected a column of pale, ghastly light, static and sparks flickering in waves across its surface.

"Is that what you saw, Kel?" Poul said. "Is that..."

Kel felt the same revulsion he felt the first time he saw the apparition.

"That's the Scarecrow's mask. That. Is. It." He popped his bucket, his revulsion turning into something else as he thought about VanderBlanc's final moments. He grinned.

"We got our man."

23

Tiberius was one of the planetary homes to the Legion, therefore home to all legionnaires who'd ever trained or been stationed there. Kel had not been here for years. He'd sucked swamp water here. Baked his brain in its deserts. Bled on the sharp rocks of its peaks as he climbed, knowing that a slip and fall would be the legacy of his failure.

They wouldn't be visiting any of the dozens of subordinate bases on this trip. Even so, far from any Legion installation, wearing their dress silks they wouldn't be conspicuous. Never here, though the population of former and current legionnaires was minuscule in comparison to the total on the planet. It was one of the few places in the galaxy where a legionnaire would be nondescript in armor or dress uniform. Even without it, here legionnaires knew each other. Knew to give respect. Knew when to offer help. Knew when to give privacy.

The northern clime made the hairs on his arms stand up. Braley marched next to him from the speeder into the unmarked building. It had been a long hop from the spaceport to their destination, more of a village settlement than a city. The columns and arches of the structure looked like real stone to him, not molded plasticrete imitations.

"This is the place," Braley said as he put his link away. "Let's get out of this cold."

Kel was inclined to agree, brushing melting snow off his shoulders as they stepped into the foyer. The door closed behind them.

"Guess we wait here."

Kel looked around. The walls were lined with art. Real art. Paintings and carvings. The work of hands and human experience, mocked into reality by passion. Holos were vivid, yet also somehow cold and lacking. He walked closer to one of the pieces, a massive canvas. The chaos of battle. Braley moved beside him. Kel thought he recognized the scene. The story it told. The depth it contained, much deeper than the millimeter's thick cake of paints, striated by bristles and pushed with pallet knives into recognizable form.

"New Vega," Braley said.

"The Failure on New Vega," Kel corrected.True waves of Savage marines in their myriad of shapes avalanched and crashed into broken ranks of fleeing soldiers, Savage arms raised in triumph as they breached the lines of the Coalition organized by the United Worlds Alliance, riding them down like driven prey. Kel pondered the scene. He felt contempt for the defeated in their brown and blue uniforms, as much as he felt hatred for the misshapen beasts that shamed them."Here," Braley said from behind. Braley stood in front of another large canvas on the opposite wall. Whereas the lighting over the New Vega painting had been dim, itself casting a pall of despair over the tragedy portrayed, over this scene, the light was pure. Warm. Divine.It would have been impossible for Kel or any legionnaire to stumble at recognition of the depiction. "Resolute-Seven." The battle was one of the Legion's many victories against the Savages. Braley's voice held the reverence Kel felt but couldn't express. Legionnaires.

How had the artist captured the armor in such detail? The dark grays and greens seemed not drab like camouflage, but brilliant and sparkling. The tiny portrayals of their predecessors were brought to life in detail more vivid to Kel than seeing his own teammates beside him in battle. Those pictures were often locked into his memory as black and white. These exploded in colors. He found himself doing as Braley did, shifting centimeter by centimeter over the painting, marveling at the diversity of scenes within the battle—the detail—capturing the elements of action so perfectly, so accurately. A leej purged a plasma jet before changing charge packs on a heavy. The old packs for that weapon could explode if removed with any charge left, requiring the shooter to run dry before changing. Another vignette showed a leej firing a multi-barrel laser into a flanking counterattack by a platoon of Savages, now collapsing under his fire. Another leej stood behind, ruby rods in his hands, ready to swap crystals.

He knew what every legionnaire portrayed was doing. What they were thinking. How they felt. The Legion victory at Resolute-Seven happened a thousand years ago. Yet Kel knew all these men. Knew they were his brothers as sure as those who stood with him each day now.The Savages lay torn asunder. Breaking. Dying. There was fear in their faces, in their postures. Even the ones without faces, the cybernetic monstrosities, the ones without bodies, the artist captured their desperation to escape. To live another day. Did they know fear, or feel the shame of defeat as a human would? What did it matter? Behind the bucket of every one of the victorious warriors, Kel knew the artist had painted a legionnaire with a determined grin. Beneath the armor a chest that swelled with pride in a battle fought well. And won. Victorious. When others had failed.*My Legion*, Kel realized. *Eternal.*The tall doors at the head of the foyer opened outward. Kel reflexively pulled his high collar tunic lower as he stepped next to Braley to face their hosts. Colonel Hartenstein stood in the threshold next to Sergeant Major Nail, Bigg in front of them. "Come this way, gentlemen," Bigg said as he moved aside. Flanking a black and silver carpet stood two rows of legionnaires, shoulder to shoulder, and at the end of the long carpet floated a sword emblazoned on a shield, with silver wreaths framing it. As the colonel and Nail parted, they began their slow march. "The Society of the Primus Pilus welcomes you, Legionnaire."

Kalos had been the last stop on Kel's odyssey. A conclusion to his secret servitude. The months since passed quickly, but not uneventfully for Kel. Finally home, finally reunited with his team, finally free. The decision was made to leave the still newly minted Lieutenant Kel Turner with Team Three. That suited Kel fine. But it didn't sit well with everyone. "Mission command is the essential function of a Legion officer," Captain Mahalik scolded him during a tutor session back on Victrix. "Not performing the action, but being the one ensuring the action takes place—when, where, and how it is to be done—that's the function of an officer." "Of course, sir," Kel said. "But on a kill team, even the team leader is an operator first and foremost." "Ridiculous," the staff officer fumed. "This attitude is why I've always questioned Dark Ops' organization to begin with." Kel shared his frustration with his tutor to Braley.

"Hah. Kevin's not a bad guy, but he's certainly not operator material. I have a feeling the colonel assigned him to be your tutor so you'd both rub off on each other. Him getting a close exposure to a kill team operator, and you to a traditional Legion officer. Hmm." Braley scratched his head. "If he's anti-Dark Ops, maybe this isn't the place for him to get staff time. I'll talk to the colonel about that. Methinks Captain Mahalik needs to go back to the Legion."Kel thought that sounded about right."But," Braley continued, "even if he won't be your tutor anymore, you still need to finish the course material and prove to the colonel you can perform to standard as a Legion officer."Kel couldn't imagine standing before the colonel, explaining how he'd flunked out. "I've got about another month left of studies at this rate. I've passed every exam on my first try, and even have superior scores." He hesitated. "On some.""Not on Republic Armed Forces Personnel Law, you didn't. Seventy-point-one percent, mister."Kel grimaced. The Legion fell under the same legal regulations that governed all the armed forces, but in practice, the Legion had few punishments for infractions. "How well versed do I really need to be in it? In the Legion, it's only lashes, discharge, or death."Braley groaned. "You know there's a lot more to military law and how it applies to personnel than just punishment.""I know, I know," Kel said. "At least, I do after those modules." Dull didn't begin to describe them. The words turned to fuzz in his brain, sentence after sentence. "How'd you get through it all?"Braley smiled. "I was a lot younger. I didn't have a clue what I might be responsible for, what was going to be important or not. I was just motivated to not fail." He laughed at himself, picturing the young recruit he'd once been, then turned serious. "I didn't score as high as you on some of these, but that's not excusing you to bomb any of them. You're enough older and more mature in the ways of the Legion than I was as a young candidate. Heck, you were an NCO, for Oba's sake. *All* of your scores should be higher than any of mine were."*Mediocrity is never acceptable*, Kel knew, and rededicated himself to working harder. He kept his nose in the books anytime he wasn't training with the team. Life in garrison could be dull, his time on Victrix always a page marker between missions. If he had to finish the course work, it might as well be here on Victrix.

They didn't leave Victrix for two months, and all the while he counted down the modules remaining out of the long list he'd started with. They caught a short mission, a quick trip out to assess the security situation of a Republic ally on the edge.

Kel found himself triple hatted. As the junior officer on the team, he was responsible for major portions of the report, continuing his studies under Braley's guidance, and performing as an operator. He pulled his turn at watch every night and acted as team medic, sniper, assaulter, breacher, intelligence analyst... At the end of the mission, he looked forward to returning to Victrix to sit for the last of his examinations. It would be a load off, like dropping the huge stone they took turns carrying on team runs, the dead weight dragging his shoulders down, his elbows and wrists straining to hold the symbol of adversity. Passing the stone off or dropping it at the end of the run was like rebirth.

That was how he felt when he got the results back from the final challenge.

High Pass. 97%.

The extra time back in his life would be welcome. What had he done with his hours before? It was difficult to remember.

No more cracking the books every night. No more multiple-choice exams. No more essays. No more Captain Mahalik's disdain.

Every session, Kel had felt like he had to defend not only his understanding of the material he was responsible for, but himself as a legionnaire. He tried not to take it as an act of disrespect on the captain's part. Compared to what the captain had done in his Legion career, Kel could've shamed the man, had he chosen to. He'd never brag about himself. Not purposefully. But too many times he'd had to bite his tongue, a better man sparing a lesser man's pride as the captain made sidebars about the unruliness of Dark Ops, its officers and sergeants.

He presented to the captain's office for the final session, which was to end with the captain's evaluation and recommendation for his suitability for permanent commission. What he'd come to realize was that his tutor's antipathy was aimed not at Kel personally, but at something else entirely.

"Lieutenant Turner, I'm pleased to tell you that my recommendation to the colonel is a positive one."

Kel was surprised at the praise. *That almost sounded like approval. I wonder if it hurts him to say it?*

"Mine is only a portion of your evaluation, but I hope it means something to you to know I think you've done well, especially under the circumstances. I know you've probably taken umbrage at some of my remarks about this unit."

That the captain was self-aware enough to note Kel's discomfort whenever disparaging DO, despite his attempts at concealing it, was more shocking than the words of encouragement.

"You're an exemplary legionnaire. You would never be where you are or given a direct commission were that not the case." The captain eased back in his chair as he selected his next words for Kel.

"Someday you may find yourself out of Dark Ops and leading regular legionnaires. As you know, they are amazing people. But not the same as the people you've worked with for so long here. Those legionnaires need someone who is not only a competent warrior, but someone who will ensure that they are competent. That standards of discipline are maintained. Someone who will provide that mission command we've talked so much about. You owe them that.

"It can't be how you operate with your kill team. You're all individuals. Self-directed. You can work together to accomplish great things, but at the end of the day, operators are lone wolves. A Legion company can't be run like a kill team."

Kel had spent enough time in the regular Legion to know that. At least, he thought he still understood that. What would it be like if he had to serve outside of Dark Ops? Would he still fit with the Legion?

"Anyway," the captain said as he stood and offered his hand, "if we meet again, I'd be proud to have you as a junior officer in my command."

Kel returned the handshake with gusto. "You make it sound like you're leaving, sir."

The captain grinned. "I'm heading to Tiberius and hopefully on to take another company."

I sense the colonel's hand at work here. Apparently, Kel's judgment about the captain's suitability to be on

Victrix had produced results more significant than any the captain may have passed regarding Kel.

He relayed his gratitude before departing, and left feeling pleased with himself, glad this chapter of his life was over. As he made his way across the sunny quadrangle and back to the team rooms, he thought about his satisfaction passing this most recent hurdle.

He loved the Legion, but one aspect he especially liked was the distinct feeling of beginnings and ends. Training, schools, missions—they all had firm beginnings full of preparation, anxiety, promise. They all had firm conclusions, too, like the big finish to a holo-drama. At the end of it, he'd been somewhere and accomplished something. What was life like for civilians? Was there ever an end or beginning to anything? Wasn't it all school, then work and bills for them?

Ironic. He shook his head. *Just a short while ago, I was ready to leave the Legion to do just that—live a life of routine. Ordinary. Predictable.* Then he remembered why he had come so close to making his departure from the Legion. He caught a glimpse of himself in the reflection of a window as he mounted the stairs and paused. Time had passed since leaving the Yomiuris. Not just time, but parsecs and gravity. Lives. Wounds. He'd healed, too. But some marks couldn't be erased. The man who looked back at him didn't match how he felt about himself just then. *I'm a lost little boy, caught in the body of a giant.*

He felt the pulse and pulled his link from his pocket. It was an unusual sensation, a trill the device only made to alert him when he received a message packet by relay. He maintained a hypercomm address in the system, but seldom received anything on it. Someone had sent a message to the blind address, not knowing whether he would receive it or not.

He knew who it was from before he opened it. *Would Poul say the cosmic flux was permitting our continuities to join?*

It was from Tara. He gulped his heart back down into his chest as he swiped.

Kel, it hurts to think about you.

At least the message was just text and not a holo. He would weaken further if he saw her. *Since you left us, my parents thought it best—the whole family, really—that I not contact you. I've had a lot of time to think about what happened on Orion. I have many questions. Did you save my family? Were you responsible in some way for what almost happened to them? You live such an enigmatic life. There are so many mysteries no one can understand about you. Maybe it's for the best that you can't tell us. Mom tells me to forget about you. That no matter how much love there may be between us, some things just aren't meant to be. I guess that's us.*

So, I've moved on. In his heart, he wished she were writing to tell him of her undying love. *I'm writing because I don't know who to turn to for help. My parents were cleared of the charges against them. We thought everything was over. But it seems it's started again. Some men from the Republic are on Callie's World. My family's business is shut down. We're not allowed to ship or receive goods while they "investigate" us. We thought this was done. No one's been arrested. They showed us the warrants and have all our ships sealed, not just the Callie. They're making a lot of accusations and threats about the consequences for concealing fraud, saying that as a Republic contract holder, if there's evidence of even a* *conspiracy to defraud, whether committed or not, they can close us down permanently.I've sent you some stills I took of the agents.*Kel swiped at the flashing icon that followed. *Good girl, Tara!* She'd captured Jack, Lothar, and Zev from various angles around the Yomiuris' settlement. He recognized the homes, the gardens, the mountains in the background. He'd committed so many of the images to memory, hoping to see them himself, anticipating the taste of the air.*I don't know if there's anything you can do for us. I'm hoping that no matter what else, you're still our protector.Tara*

Kel was about to start a reply when he noticed that there was not one message, but two. The icon indicated a holo, not a text. He supposed it was Tara, making a more impassioned personal plea, and swiped."Kel, you have an obligation to the Republic."

It was Jack."I know your girlfriend has contacted you. Told you their situation," Jack continued grimly. "Going rogue wasn't a good idea."

Kel seethed to a boil.

"Your presence is requested. This is your only chance to make amends with him." He burst into the team room. Braley and Bigg startled at his entrance. The look on his face must have betrayed his desperation."It's not over."

He traveled alone to Espiritu. The directive was clear. If he involved anyone else, the consequences for the Yomiuris would be immediate and irreversible. He had no choice. The planet was distant from Victrix but in an arm close to the core. Some destinations were farther in distance but shorter in travel. This was the converse. Crossing the galactic center added complexity and time to the journey; the density of stars and worlds hindered rather than helped travel in jump space.

In a week Kel was once again going through the routine, the three operatives guiding Kel through a maze to reach yet another safe house in yet another part of the galaxy. Kel was alone now with Jack, the pad on the table projecting the grisly display, the crackle of static furiously racing up the white blob of a mask. The Scarecrow lived.

Grand Senator Lucius VanderLoot found himself in a position he had not expected. Calculating how to regain a lost advantage.

There would be time for tallying the mistakes, and whose they were. *Perhaps I'm getting senile.* But that wasn't possible. The nanos kept that possibility at bay, preserving health and preventing aging. *The same that I activated to end Accius's regrettable tenure as director.*

It had been a miscalculation to allow Accius to remain so close, even more so to give him a central role as director. *After the Proteus debacle, I ought to have sent him into exile.* The incident had been kept quiet, but enough rumors circulated about the existence of a new Savage threat that his chief of staff had to be dismissed. *Perhaps he should have ended up in limbo as well.* Had he been unreasonably soft, swayed by VanderBlanc's blood relation with him? Was he too forgiving, knowing he himself had failed to anticipate the potential of the legionnaires to mutilate his desire?

Legionnaires! he spat, the thought of them as exasperating as the bitter taste of a poison. Their uncanny ability to do the unexpected, to act without guidance—

their arrogance and pride annoyingly magnified by their smug silence—they were everything he hated about the great unwashed masses. Individuals who thought they had the right to chart an unguided course for themselves.

It was my sentimentality for my family, he decided. *That's what clouded my judgment.*

He'd also trusted Accius to bring Patrick into the fold. *My fault again.* Patrick had every indication of being a good fit. He was known to their closed ranks, as were all who hoped to be close to the center of power on Liberinthine. The same schools. A family separated from Lucius by only a degree or two. The man had come from within the intelligence apparatus. His loyalty was unquestioned. He would be useful. Accius strongly felt so.

Had that been his mistake? Failing to account for variables more important than those? The ties, the status. The necessity that Patrick was first and foremost one of them. *Men are not created equal and not all are suitable for all tasks, not even one who comes from the political class*, he reminded himself as he remained distracted, not yet able to calculate his next moves as he lingered on the causes.

Whatever the failing, the result was catastrophic. That bumbling Patrick. He'd been unable to disguise his contempt for the legionnaires. Instead of using guile and flattery, instead of playing the respectful collaborator with the operators, instead of using the tools he should have learned as part of the political class to manipulate others, instead he played the petulant child. In doing so, he'd alienated them. Oh, had he only played with them as he'd been taught! When it surrendered no power, compliments and cooperation reaped dividends when manipulating inferiors.

Patrick's blundering lost him control of the mission and resulted in the failure to recover yet another trove of mysteries. Like the other mysteries that had helped the grand senator secure and maintain his advantage.

The medical technologies had helped him and the few he deemed worthy to extend their lives, to live in excellent health beyond that of the even already long-lived citizen. That alone was significant. It took time to build an empire, and senescence was the enemy of power.

He smiled as he considered the vastly superior hypercomm system he alone controlled. Communication across the galaxy without relays rendered him able to make decisions and order actions that seemed preternatural to others. The ability to communicate across the galaxy more rapidly than his opponents thwarted his enemies and helped to make the Republic what it was. *When I choose to utilize it.*

There were many others. Technologies harnessed and unharnessed, understood and not yet grasped, ancient and alien, filling the halls of their labs. The Section answered only to him. As a younger member of the House of Reason, he had stumbled across the anomaly in the budget. It had taken years of exploiting connections and favors, time spent rising in power and influence, until he could insert himself into oversight of the activity known as The Section.

Hundreds of years of effort remained hidden under the umbrella of secrecy that surrounded the lab. There was no clear record of who had started the endeavor. Had it been an egalitarian, trying to regain superiority over the Savages, hoping to harness the dark innovations of their twisted experiments for the benefit of mankind? Perhaps it had been a pragmatist, someone as far thinking as himself, trying to gain advantage.

He wondered if the dull conformists of the Legion ever suspected that the knowledge that made their precious armor and the L-comm possible had come from such research into the Savages, perhaps even from the ancient aliens?

No matter. He had realized the potential of The Section. Forgotten once the war against the Savages accelerated in civilization's favor, walled off by layers of secrecy, protected by its attendants. The scientists were a predictable lot; their passion for curiosity fed their greatest need, and the covenants of confidentiality and punishments for betraying such meant banishment from the secrets held in The Section's vaults. Controlling them was effortless. As long as they had access to the knowledge within and a modest financial reward—just a tad beyond their accustomed compensation—their loyalty was bought.

The Section was his own personal fiefdom. Controlled by him, for him.

The Proteus moon was of special interest. The Section had been thrilled at the prospect of a yet unknown source of technology. Little had been discovered for generations. He had been the one to agree with the staff's assessment. He had been the one who accepted their recommendation to allow the work of the marooned Savages to incubate. He had been the one who made the Savage moon disappear from all the records after the inadvertent reconnaissance by the Legion.

The technology the Savages had cobbled together on the Proteus moon, whether inspired by the Ancients or newly discovered—it mattered not—would have given him yet another edge. The limited material brought back from the Savage moon by the scientist from The Section had not yet revealed the secrets of the gravitic generator. *The staff may never reproduce the knowledge*, he knew. *Ah, but what if they do?* There was hope they may yet. Still, had Patrick not bungled the technology collection...

Accius had argued on Patrick's behalf. Even had the moon not been destroyed, the knowledge might not have been retrievable, he'd reasoned. Now, they would never know.

But mistake compounded mistake.

Accius's role in supervising the mission. His placement in the chain of command. Then post-debacle, the failure to maintain secrecy after the moon's destruction. By that time, it had become too big a problem to conceal. Too many eyes had seen. Lucius knew that VanderBlanc had to leave public service in the office of the grand senator. Allowing Accius to assume the role of director—the anonymous, all-powerful apparition, the face so to speak, of their organization—seemed natural. Let him hide where he could do some good. *The boy has learned enough from me to fill the role*, Lucius had told himself. But he hadn't.

And his biggest mistake? Trying to control the uncontrollable. *Bringing the legionnaire to heel, that was my greatest error. How I wish I'd never considered that young man a threat, never tried to control him, never brought him close to us! Left to his own devices, he'd have gotten killed by his own heroics.* Lucius pondered on the actions Kel Turner had taken under their direction. Orchestrating the death of Gerald Grenada had been well done. Turner had lived up to Lucius's estimation of the unique man's abilities. Then, just as he felt confident he had gained a powerful agent engaged in the furtherance of his personal conquest, the unexpected occurred.

What audacity! Conspiring to expose us. To fight back. To not accept his role as a servant. The grand senator seethed. Had Turner bent, his rewards would have been numerous. As a plebeian, he could never have been brought into the true fold, of course, but as a useful drudge, he would have been kept comfortable. Given a modicum of power. Given special treatment and allowed to enrich those he cared for.

Lucius reached into a drawer and pulled out a small case. It had been some time since he had played the role himself. He opened the cover. Inside sat the silver collar. He placed it around his neck and luxuriated in the familiar glow around him. He moved from the desk in his private study to look in the mirror. The glowing apparition had been his creation, envisioned in this very room, where the rich and influential had sought his patronage for decades. Careful orchestration and maneuvering had made him the most powerful man in the Republic, and therefore the galaxy. He laughed, the returning reflection confirming the visual response of the mask to his emotions. He raged, and the mask boiled. He soothed, and the mask consoled with pale colors. He was ready. He moved to sit again and activated the hypercomm link. Jack would have Turner waiting. No doubt, the man would be outwardly defiant, but inwardly terrified. Who wouldn't be after learning they railed against an omnipotent force? He considered. *Destroy him or retain him?* He had thought much about this. His first impulse was to have Turner killed. As much as he hated to admit it, Turner was more important to his future plans than VanderBlanc had been. The way forward was in action. Whatever else Accius had been by virtue of his birth, he was not capable. Turner was capable.

Retain him, he chose.

Plus, there was pleasure in domination of the weaker.

Turner could still be useful, could still be brought to heel. The psychometric profile had been correct. The man was an idealist. He valued loyalty. He trusted. He thought himself a hero. With pressure brought to bear on his most critical weakness, the man could be brought in line.

"In the myth of Cortes, the explorer burned his ships when he reached the new world to ensure his men knew there was no turning back." The turbulent mirage of electrons crackled across the Scarecrow's face. The haunting robotic voice rang with that same, familiar static.

"Even the Savages, for all their insanity, understood how to ensure such loyalty, such devotion to cause. How is it that you do not? How is it that you could fail to understand the simple truth? You will never leave my service."

Lothar and Zev waited in the anteroom, as they had at each of Kel's previous encounters with the Scarecrow. Jack stood over his shoulder while Kel occupied a chair positioned in front of a projection in the otherwise bare room.

"I guess I'm just thickheaded, Grand Senator."

By the silence, he knew he'd struck well. A new projection gave the Scarecrow's countenance a complexion unlike any Kel had seen before. The apparition turned black.

"And though I've never heard of the myth of Cortes, I get your meaning."

The Scarecrow reacted to something. The speckled projection returned over the face, to be replaced by a purple sheen of electrical static, not coming from the contrivance of the mask, but from something outside the view of the holo. Jack gasped as the stunner paralyzed the Scarecrow, many light years away.

Kel allowed himself a chuckle. "Jack, you might want to invite Lothar and Zev in to see this."

Ener-chains glowed around the arms of the seated VanderLoot, his collar now extinguished. Kel stood with the three clandestine agents as they watched the events unfolding on the other side of the galaxy in the grand senator's home. The view was narrow, but the armored legionnaires flanking the chained man left no doubt as to what was occurring.

The three men with Kel stood mute.

The view expanded. A giant armored figure dominated the holo. The colonel. In the background, legionnaires moved about, creating a surreal contrast between the stately works of art, the plush furniture, and the deadly leejes as they assembled into view. The men who watched with him would not recognize what Kel could: the subtle differences in the legionnaires' armor. A tiny crimson crest on one shoulder. The silver highlight on another man's chest.

"We have control," Colonel Hartenstein's voice reached them from across the galaxy. He spoke to the men with Kel. "There should be no doubt in your minds that this conspiracy is finished." A leej knelt beside the restrained grand senator. The prisoner reviving at his ministrations, coughing as he awakened.

"Lieutenant, please make the offer to your friends," the colonel said. "We'll wait for you to return before proceeding."

"Step outside with me." Kel opened the door to the anteroom without waiting for a response.

Zev was first to follow. "Hey!" the young man exclaimed.

"Easy, Zev," Kel cautioned.

Poul and Meadows stood in the anteroom, dressed like Kel in civilian clothes, blasters in hand, not raised but ready.

Jack placed a restraining hand on Zev's shoulder. "If the Legion wanted us dead, we'd be dead already. Isn't that right, Kel?"

"That's right, Jack." Kel motioned the three into the center of the room. "I've been given the leeway to make you gentlemen an offer."

"What kind of an offer?" Lothar asked. The older man had always been the most circumspect of the three. His face held the only look of hope among them.

"We want to give you your freedom. If you'll take it."

24

Kel stood on the end of the ramp, looking down on the rotating planet. Its bright cloudless surface looked the same
as it did in his dreams. The night before a jump he usually
had the same dream. In it, he stood at the tailgate's edge
and stepped off, the rush in his gut quickening his heart
until it woke him. He wondered why he never dreamed
about the next sequence, why he never saw the opening
of the canopy or his landing. He always fell back asleep,
half smiling. Stepping off. It was like nothing else. Maybe
that's why his subconscious liked to replay the scene for
him? It was an obsession.

Hunting the Scarecrow had become an obsession,
too. So, why hadn't those scenes replayed for him nightly?

Sure, he had the same dreams he supposed everyone had. The ones you thought you'd left behind years
ago. The one where you forgot it was exam day. The one
where your legs were heavy and you couldn't outrun
the monster. The one where you were lost and alone.
Remembered from dreams long ago. Not replayed.

Where was the Scarecrow? Tucked somewhere deep
in his subconscious, hiding in wait? Ready to ambush
him like a patient enemy? To torture his nights as he had
tortured his days?

Knowing that it was truly over, the first weeks, he'd
dreaded sleep. Somehow, he knew he would be haunted by that face each night, betrayed by his dreams and

forced to relive the events of the past year like a never-ending holo playback. If imagined childhood fears of helplessness caused repetitive dreams, wouldn't a real trauma torture him more profoundly? More inescapably?

It hadn't happened. The Scarecrow had not haunted him. And if it hadn't happened yet, would it ever?

But there was a new dream. He awoke that first morning, the rising light of day signaling the end of the retreat into his mind, a lingering feeling of both fulfillment and longing, of both warmth and loneliness clouding his awakening. At first, he couldn't recall it. His ability to reconstruct the vision mocked him, evaded him like a ghost.

The sense there was a missing piece of the puzzle was there the next night, too. And the next. Finally, with determination, he coaxed himself into lucidity and realized it was not a dream. It was a memory. And since, he'd welcomed its return nightly.

Tara. At his side. Surrounded by her family. The smell of the galley. The feeling of belonging. Of being loved. Her tiny hand in his.

He checked the Talon's flight path against his visual checkpoints and the plot, then let the pilots know he approved. He was sad to leave Three, but excited and anxious to take his own team.

My own, he thought with a mix of pride and the weight of responsibility that went with saying such.

Carryalls stuffed to capacity and exposed weapons. All dangled and clung to the four men with him in the back of the Talon, waddling into position as if they carried painful tumors waiting to be excised. Meadows had already pin checked everyone, including Kel, and awkwardly took his seat again. His team sergeant gave him a thumbs-up and returned to sit. Kel would've preferred Poul taking the senior spot on his new team, but Meadows had seniority and was due his turn.

Kel confided to Bigg his choices for the new team. No matter what, Kel would always look to Bigg as the fount of all wisdom. And Bigg had been right. Poul and he were too close of friends. Someday, Bigg would retire. When that day came, it would be natural for Poul to take Three. Change was inevitable. Even in Dark Ops.

Besides, we're a good balance, Meadows and me. He's a cold-blooded murderer, and I'm... He wasn't sure how to describe himself in contrast to Meadows.

I'm more the fatherly type, I guess.

Looking at his chrono, he had a few minutes until the next checkpoint. He gave the twenty-minute warning, then surrendered to the silence as he observed the world below. The revolving planet was part of the universal constant, one that required no consent or comprehension on his part. Was he part of that constant? Driven by forces he couldn't control and spinning like the planet below?

The ending of his odyssey had been abrupt, like the sudden stop that occurred at the end of a parachute malfunction.

"There are some people waiting who want to debrief you," he told Jack, Lothar, and Zev. "This is not a forced interrogation. We want as much information as you can give us about VanderLoot's cabal."

Lothar was the first to speak. "Lieutenant Turner," he said formally, politely, yearningly. "Exposing the director just now was the first we knew of our master's identity."

Kel's intuition told him Lothar's denial was genuine. These guys had never been hostile or cruel to Kel, especially Lothar. From the start he'd sensed a regret, a sadness even, in their extortion of him. The source of their regret was that the same had been done to them.

Jack spoke in a manner similar to the older accomplice. Contrite. Relieved. "I can tell you I always suspected someone highly placed among the Liberinthine elite, just never someone *that* highly placed."

Zev was the one who'd given Kel the impression of a grenade waiting to be activated, a compressed spring ready to uncoil, a fire raging beneath a façade. This time, his words seemed naked and exposed. "I want to believe this is all over." He sighed, the last of his resistance trailing away with the breath. "It just seems impossible."

"I'm willing," Lothar volunteered. "I don't know how it will help, but I'll tell my part in everything. There's much I'm ashamed of, including what was done to you, Lieutenant. I want you to know that."

Kel decided it was time to tell them what he knew. "We know who you all are. The circumstances of your own extortions."

Lothar grimaced. "Then you know I was not an innocent like you. My crimes made me vulnerable to their corruption."

The younger Zev made his own act of contrition. "My recruitment wasn't like yours either, Turner. I was guilty, too. I betrayed my oath as an agent and swindled those credit speculators. I deserved punishment. I wish it had been prison instead of this."

Kel felt the pain that accompanied the confession. "I want you to know that I never forgot that, despite it all, you treated me like a comrade. That you sympathized with my servitude. Because what happened to me was so painful, I understand the pain you all experienced, being manipulated as you were." He shook Lothar's hand.

"Walter Davila." He did the same to Zev. "Ranack Oswell." And lastly, Jack. "Gregg Wiggins."

Jack shook his head. "I don't think those men exist anymore."

Kel ached to offer some consolation. But what consolation could there be in mere words for men whose lives were erased, whose wills had been bent, whose skills twisted for such works?

"It will be your choices whether those men return to life or not," Kel finally offered. "Once you've helped us, there won't be anyone to pull your strings."

The Zev Kel knew was back, his contrition replaced by the familiar rage. "You can't believe that, Turner. These people can't be brought down. We may get free of this, but they'll do it to someone else."

Kel shrugged as he nodded to his two teammates. "Maybe you're right. But not if we can help it. Time to go, gentlemen." He signaled to Poul as Meadows opened the portal.

Jack was last to leave as they followed Poul into the hall. "Thank you, Turner. But he's right, you know? You may have saved yourself and us, but it's not over."

Kel nodded, waiting for the portal to close again as they departed. He turned to look at the door behind him, and hesitated. On the other side waited the assurance he wanted to give to the three.

He'll never do this to anyone again.

He tried to swallow, but found no spit. *What's coming is justice, all right.* But Kel knew that after it was done, he'd feel a stain on his honor forever. He took one last breath before waving the portal open. The colonel still stood at the center of the holo.

"They're cooperating, sir. Radd and Meadows are escorting them to the debrief site now."

Behind Colonel Hartenstein, VanderLoot sat erect. Recovered and undiminished, he fought the chains as his voice fought the seal over his mouth. Kel knew what was coming next. The knowledge of it did nothing to quell the bile in his throat, easing upward like an eel squirming in his stomach.

The colonel's bucket nodded. "Then it's time for sentencing."

The two leejes guarding the senator lifted the chair, startling the older man into silence, and deposited him gently in the middle of the room. Now more armored brothers stepped into the picture. A semicircle formed around VanderLoot, armored pauldrons over shoulders touching to form a wall. The colonel moved into the open space in front of their prisoner and removed the gag.

Shrieking, Kel felt the gasp pull air from across the galaxy and into the man's lungs as VanderLoot launched into invectives.

"I'll crush you for this! Attacking a member of the Republic Senate! You'll never see a prison because my guards—"

"Are neutralized." The colonel's voice was full of pity rather than condescension, hurt rather than anger. "Your estate is well defended. But not well enough to prevent the Legion from bringing you to justice."

"Justice!" VanderLoot spat with incredulity. "Who are you to bring a grand senator to justice? This isn't Article Nineteen; this is the Legion conspiring to overthrow the Republic."

"Not to overthrow," the colonel interrupted. "To protect. From you."

Another legionnaire stepped forward, this one as familiar to Kel as any in his life. "The Society of the Primus Pilus has judged your actions treasonous and a threat to the order of the Republic which we are sworn to protect. The sentence is death." He produced a hypo and stepped closer.

"No." The colonel's calm word stayed the hand as it moved toward VanderLoot's neck. The older man's eyes widened. "You can't be serious. If this an elaborate scheme to bargain for power..."

"No." The colonel held up an open palm, requesting the hypo. "The vote was unanimous, but the task is mine alone."

The legionnaire stood at attention, then handed the device to the colonel before stepping back to join the ranks of the judgment theater.

Colonel Hartenstein knelt at VanderLoot's side. Now Kel saw the fear.

"I order you to release me! I am the grand senator!" The device touched the man's neck and he recoiled in a spasm of revulsion. "No! *I* am in control. *I* am the designer of destiny for the Republic. You obey *my* will!"

Kel's revulsion grew. He'd seen many die. Friends. Enemies. Some fast. Some slowly. But never like this. He knew the look of death. The senator's wasn't a violent death. That he was accustomed to. This was bland. Almost banal. His was a demise as contemptible as the man himself. Life simply slipped out of Lucius VanderLoot, Grand Senator of the Republic.

Another legionnaire stepped forward. He produced the device from his side and held it over the senator. Had Kel been in that room, he would have taken the same role. The legionnaire resumed his place in the ranks. "I confirm the sentence has been carried out."

The legionnaire who'd given the judgment spoke. "Time to complete our task, brothers." Arms caught the body as the chains were extinguished, the limp corpse carried out of view. The colonel moved to the front of the viewer.

"It's done. Time for us to stage the scene. Time for you to leave as well, Kel."

Kel and Braley had been there for the unanimous vote. And it was Braley who'd volunteered to administer the cardiostatic hypo. *My brother Braley volunteered to carry the burden of executioner,* he marveled. He did it for Kel. The colonel intervened, sparing them both the guilt.

"Are you sure he's dead?" Kel asked. "He's probably enhanced in some way by nanoimmuno, just like VanderBlanc was." He wished he were there to do the death check himself.

The colonel grunted. "We're sure. We know about the nano concentration he carries. The electrical activity of his heart is stopped. His brain is silent. Even if the tech in his bloodstream imparts longevity, dead is dead."

With all members of the society working together, their diverse and deep resources tapped, a clear picture had emerged confirming their own suspicion about who sat at the head of the serpent.

"Colonel, the guard we missed at Canopus? The one I recognized who helped me connect VanderBlanc? Did we miss him?"

"He was here. He's the only one we killed. The rest we stunned and gave memory wipes. In a few hours, the senator will be discovered in his bed, dead."

There wouldn't be any evidence, just missing time on security feeds and foggy memories of the staff to fuel any conspiracy theories. What Kel had come to appreciate was that the legionnaires of the Primus Pilus Society made what Dark Ops did seem puerile in comparison. Now he and Braley were among their ranks.

Once the Society voted, action was immediate. Staged around the senator's estate were the Legion's guardians of the Primus Pilus. They awaited the confirmation of the Scarecrow's identity during the comm between VanderLoot and Kel. His anticipation was a boiling cauldron, excruciating as if held by bare hands, mentally urging the legionnaires to storm into the private study. Now, the exciting prospect of seeing the Scarecrow unmasked and humiliated had been replaced by something else. Repugnance. His disgust at the execution dimmed the relief he wanted to feel. Hoped he would someday feel.

"So, it's done," Kel said.

"It's done," the colonel repeated. "Now. Get home. You're needed there, Lieutenant." The holo disappeared. Kel had wanted to tell the colonel more. Wanted to give his thanks. To find some way to express gratitude for standing by him through his crisis. But as always, the colonel knew best. It wasn't time for talking.

It was time to go home.

The last checkpoint before Area Doxy came into view, the white plains rolling toward him from the edge of the curved horizon.

"Six minutes."

Changes were coming. There had been a week-long news cycle that was only now trailing off after the death of Grand Senator VanderLoot. Images of the state funeral on the Spiral News Network were replaced by pundits and analysts opining on the qualities of his peers who stood poised to form the next major coalition of power within the House of Reason. Kel couldn't interest himself in the platitudes and self-aggrandizement by the petty power brokers. What he had seen appalled him. Most ran campaigns promising change, drawing distinctions between themselves and the long entrenched VanderLoot. There had apparently been a movement Kel was unaware of, a drive to signal an end to the Savage Wars and the dawn of a new age. To christen a new epoch in the galaxy by renaming Liberinthine.

Utopion.

The name made Kel choke. Utopia was always imaginary. Even with VanderLoot gone, a Republic of perfect law and order would be no closer. Not at the hands of politicians.

His bucket flashed the signal as the final checkpoint rolled into view. Black canyons bordered the white sands of the drop zone on one side, with a mountain range on the other, framing Area Doxy.

He'd seen her face in flashes and when he least expected. Sometimes in the face of another long-haired woman as she passed. Sometimes from the corner of his eye in the reflection of a door or window, disappearing when he turned to look. Below, what he saw now was Tara's face smiling back at him. Trusting. Welcoming. Loving.

"Move to the Ramp, Twelve, and stand by." He moved to the edge, ready to lead Team Twelve to fall through the void to the surface a hundred kilometers below.

If Tara were to remain a dream, well, there were worse dreams.

He could live with that.

"Follow me." He leaped.

And fell into a dream.

AVAILABLE
SOON!
DOC SPEARS
JASON ANSPACH
NICK COLE
ANGLES OF ATTACK
DARK OPERATOR
BOOK 5
GALAXY'S EDGE

ABOUT GALAXY'S EDGE

Galaxy's Edge is an expansive, interconnected military science fiction series. Galaxy's Edge Season One, which begins with *Legionnaire* by Jason Anspach and Nick Cole, has sold over one million copies.

For news about upcoming Galaxy's Edge audio books, merchandise, lore, and events, visit www.galaxysedge.us and sign up for the KTF newsletter.

To connect with other Galaxy's Edge readers as well as the authors, join one or all of the Galaxy's Edge Fan Clubs on Facebook, Reddit, or Discord.

ABOUT THE MAKERS

Doc Spears is a United States Army veteran.

Jason Anspach is the co-creator of Galaxy's Edge. He lives in the Pacific Northwest.

Nick Cole is the other co-creator of Galaxy's Edge. He lives in southern California with his wife, Nicole.

HISTORY OF THE GALAXY

Explore over 30+ Galaxy's Edge books and counting from the minds of Jason Anspach, Nick Cole, Doc Spears, Jonathan Yanez, Karen Traviss, and more.

HISTORY OF THE GALAXY

1ST ERA BOOKS

THE FALL OF EARTH

1ST ERA SUMMARY

The West has been devastated by epidemics, bio-terrorism, war, and famine. Asia has shut its borders to keep the threats at bay, and some with power and influence have already abandoned Earth. Now an escape route a century in the making – the Nomad mission – finally offers hope to a small town and a secret research centre hidden in a rural American backwater. Shrouded in lies and concealed even from the research centre's staff, Nomad is about to fulfil its long-dead founder's vision of preserving the best of humanity to forge a new future.

2ND ERA SUMMARY

They were the Savages. Raiders from our distant past. Elites who left Earth to create tailor-made utopias aboard the massive lighthuggers that crawled through the darkness between the stars. But the people they left behind on a dying planet didn't perish in the dystopian nightmare the Savages had themselves created: they thrived, discovering faster-than-light technology and using it to colonize the galaxy ahead of the Savages, forming fantastic new civilizations that surpassed the wildest dreams of Old Earth.

HISTORY OF THE GALAXY

3ᴿᴰ ERA BOOKS

RISE OF THE REPUBLIC

3ᴿᴰ ERA SUMMARY

The Savage Wars are over but the struggle for power continues. Backed by the might of the Legion, the Republic seeks to establish a dominion of peace and prosperity amid a galaxy still reeling from over a millennia of war. Brushfire conflicts erupt across the edge as vicious warlords and craven demagogues seek to carve out their own kingdoms in the vacuum left by the defeated Savages. But the greatest threat to peace may be those in the House of Reason and Republic Senate seeking to reshape the galaxy in their own image.

4ᵀᴴ ERA SUMMARY

As the Legion fights wars on several fronts, the Republic that dispatches them to the edge of the galaxy also actively seeks to undermine them as political ambitions prove more important than lives. Tired and jaded legionnaires suffer the consequences of government appointed officers and their ruinous leadership. The fighting is never enough and soon a rebellion breaks out among the Mid-Core planets, consuming more souls and treasure. A far greater threat to the Republic hegemony comes from the shadowy edges of the galaxy as a man determined to become an emperor emerges from a long and secretive absence. It will take the sacrifice of the Legion to maintain freedom in a galaxy gone mad.

HISTORY OF THE GALAXY

5TH ERA BOOKS
REBIRTH OF THE LEGION

5TH ERA SUMMARY

An empire defeated and with it the rot of corruption scoured from the Republic. Fighting a revolution to restore the order promised at the founding of the Republic was the easy part. Now the newly rebuilt Legion must deal with factions no less treacherous than the House of Reason while preparing itself for war against a foe no one could have imagined.

HONOR ROLL

We would like to give our most sincere thanks and recognition to those who supported the creation of *Galaxy's Edge: Exigency* by supporting us at GalacticOutlaws.com.

Artis Aboltins

Guido Abreu

Chancellor Adams

Myron Adams

Garion Adkins

Elias Aguilar

Bill Allen

Justin Altman

Jake Altman

Tony Alvarez

Galen Anderson

Jarad Anderson

Robert Anspach

Jonathan Auerbach

Fritz Ausman

Sean Averill

Nicholas Avila

Matthew Bagwell

Marvin Bailey

Joseph Bailey

Kevin Bangert

John Barber

Logan Barker

Brian Barrows

Robert Battles

Eric Batzdorfer

John Baudoin

Antonio Becerra

Mike Beeker

Randall Beem

Matt Beers

John Bell

Daniel Bendele

Edward Benson

David Bernatski	Kris (Joryl) Chambers
Justin Bielefeld	David Chor
Trevor Blasius	Tyrone Chow
WJ Blood	Jonathan Clews
Evan Boldt	Beau Clifton
Rodney Bonner	Robert Collins Sr.
Thomas Seth Bouchard	Alex Collins-Gauweiler
William Boucher	Jerry Conard
Brandon Bowles	Michael Conn
Alex Bowling	James Connolly
Jordan Brann	James Conyers
Ernest Brant	Robert Cosler
Geoff Brisco	Ryan Coulston
Raymond Brooks	Andrew Craig
James Brown	Adam Craig
Jeremy Bruzdzinski	Phil Culpepper
Marion Buehring	Ben Curcio
Matthew Buzek	Thomas Cutler
Daniel Cadwell	Tommy Cutler
Brian Callahan	David Danz
Van Cammack	Brendon Darling
Chris Campbell	Alister Davidson
Danny Cannon	Peter Davies
Zachary Cantwell	Walter Davila
Brian Cave	Ivy Davis
Shawn Cavitt	Nathan Davis

Ashton Davis	Mark Franceschini
Ron Deage	Elizabeth Gafford
Tod Delaricheliere	David Gaither
Anerio Deorma	Christopher Gallo
Isaac Diamond	Richard Gallo
Christopher DiNote	Kyle Gannon
Matthew Dippel	Michael Gardner
Ellis Dobbins	Nick Gerlach
Gerald Donovan	John Giorgis
Ray Duck	Johnny Glazebrooks
Christopher Durrant	Justin Godfrey
Cami Dutton	Luis Gomez
Virgil Dwyer	Justin Gottwaltz
William Ely	Gordon Green
Andrew English	Shawn Greene
Stephane Escrig	Preston Groogan
Steven Feily	Brandon Handy
Meagan Ference	Erik Hansen
Adolfo Fernandez	Greg Hanson
Ashley Finnigan	Ian Harper
Matthew Fiveson	Jason Harris
Kath Flohrs	Jordan Harris
Steve Forrester	Revan Harris
Skyla Forster	Matthew Hartmann
Timothy Foster	Adam Hartswick
Bryant Fox	Ronald Haulman

Joshua Hayes	James Jeffers
Adam Hazen	Tedman Jess
Richard Heard	Eric Jett
Colin Heavens	James Johnson
Brenton Held	Randolph Johnson
Jason Henderson	Scott Johnson
Jason Henderson	Josh Johnson
Jonathan Herbst	Tyler Jones
Kyle Hetzer	Paul Jones
Korrey Heyder	John Josendale
Aaron Holden	Wyatt Justice
Clint Holmes	Ron Karroll
Jacob Honeter	Timothy Keane
Charles Hood	Cody Keaton
Tyson Hopkins	Brian Keeter
Ian House	Noah Kelly
Ken Houseal	Jacob Kelly
Nathan Housley	Caleb Kenner
Jeff Howard	Daniel Kimm
Nicholas Howser	Zachary Kinsman
Kristie Hudson	Rhet Klaahsen
Mike Hull	Jesse Klein
Donald Humpal	Kyle Klincko
Bradley Huntoon	William Knapp
Wendy Jacobson	Marc Knapp
Paul Jarman	Travis Knight

Steven Konecni	Jacob Margheim
Ethan Koska	Deven Marincovich
Evan Kowalski	Cory Marko
Byl Kravetz	Lucas Martin
Brian Lambert	Pawel Martin
Clay Lambert	Trevor Martin
Jeremy Lambert	Phillip Martinez
Andrew Langler	Tao Mason
Dave Lawrence	Ashley Mateo
Alexander Le	Mark Maurice
Paul Lizer	Simon Mayeski
Gary Locken	Kyle McCarley
Richard Long	Quinn McCusker
Oliver Longchamps	Alan McDonald
Joseph Lopez	Caleb McDonald
Kyle Lorenzi	Hans McIlveen
David Losey	Rachel McIntosh
Ronnie Loven	Jason McMarrow
Steven Ludtke	Joshua McMaster
Brooke Lyons	Colin McPherson
John M	Christopher Menkhaus
Patrick Maclary	Jim Mern
Richard Maier	Robert Mertz
Chris Malone	Pete Micale
Brian Mansur	Mike Mieszcak
Robert Marchi	Ted Milker

Jacob Montagne	Eric Pastorek
Mitchell Moore	Zac Petersen
Matteo Morelli	Corey Pfleiger
William Morris	Dupres Pina
Alex Morstadt	Pete Plum
Nicholas Mukanos	Matthew Pommerening
Vinesh Narayan	Nathan Poplawski
James Needham	Jeremiah Popp
Travis Nichols	Chancey Porter
Bennett Nickels	Chris Pourteau
Trevor Nielsen	Chris Prats
Andrew Niesent	Aleksander Purcell
Sean Noble	Joshua Purvis
Otto Noda	Max Quezada
Brett Noll-Emmick	T.J. Recio
Greg Nugent	Jacob Reynolds
Christina Nymeyer	Eric Ritenour
Timothy O'Connor	Walt Robillard
Grant Odom	Joshua Robinson
Colin O'neill	Brian Robinson
Ryan O'neill	Daniel Robitaille
Max Oosten	Paul Roder
Tyler Ornelas	Chris Rollini
Jonathan Over	Thomas Roman
James Owens	Joyce Roth
David Parker	Andrew Ruiz

Sterling Rutherford

Lawrence Sanchez

David Sanford

Chris Sapero

Jaysn Schaener

Landon Schaule

Shayne Schettler

Brian Schmidt

Andrew Schmidt

Kurt Schneider

William Schweisthal

Anthony Scimeca

Preston Scott

Rylee Scott

Aaron Seaman

Phillip Seek

Christopher Shaw

Charles Sheehan

Wendell Shelton

Brett Shilton

Vernetta Shipley

Glenn Shotton

Joshua Sipin

Christopher Slater

Scott Sloan

Daniel Smith

Michael Smith

Tyler Smith

Sharroll Smith

Michael Smith

Alexander Snyder

John Spears

Thomas Spencer

Peter Spitzer

Dustin Sprick

Cooper Stafford

Graham Stanton

Paul Starck

Ethan Step

John Stephenson

Seaver Sterling

Maggie Stewart-Grant

John Stockley

Rob Strachan

William Strickler

Shayla Striffler

Kevin Summers

Ernest Sumner

Aaron Sweeney

Carol Szpara

Travis TadeWaldt

Daniel Tanner

Lawrence Tate	Josiah Velazquez
Tim Taylor	Anthony Wagnon
Robert Taylor	Humberto Waldheim
Justin Taylor	Christopher Walker
Daniel Thomas	David Wall
Steven Thompson	Justin Wang
Chris Thompson	Andrew Ward
William Joseph Thorpe	Scot Washam
Beverly Tierney	Tyler Washburn
Kayla Todd	John Watson
Matthew Townsend	Bill Webb
Jameson Trauger	Hiram Wells
Scott Tucker	Ben Wheeler
Eric Turnbull	Greg Wiggins
Brandon Turton	Jack Williams
Dylan Tuxhorn	Scott Winters
Jalen Underwood	Jason Wright
Barrett Utz	John Wurtz
Paul Van Dop	Ethan Yerigan
Paden VanBuskirk	Phillip Zaragoza
Patrick Varrassi	Brandt Zeeh
Daniel Vatamaniuck	Nathan Zoss
Jose Vazquez	

Made in the USA
Monee, IL
12 February 2021

60300287R00223